Between desire and surrender is the most dangerous place of all.

taming
the
FIRE

"Sydney Croft is a fabulous new talent!"
—*New York Times* bestselling author Cheyenne McCray

SYDNEY CROFT

Author of *Seduced by the Storm*

Riding the Storm

Taming
the
Fire

SYDNEY CROFT

DELTA TRADE PAPERBACKS

TAMING THE FIRE
A Delta Trade Paperback / May 2009

Published by Bantam Dell
A Division of Random House, Inc.
New York, New York

Delta is a registered trademark of Random House, Inc., and the colophon
is a trademark of Random House, Inc.

Library of Congress Cataloging-in-Publication Data
Croft, Sydney.
Taming the fire / Sydney Croft.
    p.   cm.
ISBN 978-0-385-34227-8 (trade pbk.) — ISBN 978-0-440-33849-9 (ebook)
1. Sexual dominance and submission—Fiction.   I. Title.
PS3603.R6356T36 2009
813'.6—dc22
2008048040

Printed in the United States of America
Published simultaneously in Canada

www.bantamdell.com

BVG 10 9 8 7 6 5 4 3 2 1

With thanks to our readers,
who have as much fun in our world as we do.

TAMING

the

FIRE

CHAPTER
One

"You look like you need a daddy."

Trance merely stared down the Bear who was dressed in all leather, and gave a shake of his head. Wrong sex and wrong preference, but he didn't mind the attention. He had an open mind when it came to anything concerning sex, but women did it for him and always had. That wasn't changing.

So no, he didn't need a daddy, but hell, if the right woman came along, he wouldn't mind playing the daddy and everything in between.

He didn't hold out much hope for the right woman, though, which made his whole wouldn't-mind speech easier to feed himself.

Besides, he wasn't here for a soul mate—he was on a mission from ACRO—the Agency for Covert Rare Operatives—to rescue a now free agent named Ulrika. She was on the run from Itor Corp, a powerful agency that also employed agents with special abilities. Her name meant "power of the wolf," and she'd originally belonged to a small, rare European tribe of therianthropes, people who believe they are animals in human flesh. According to

ACRO's cryptozoologists, therians claimed to shift, spiritually and psychologically but not physically—that could be proven—into their animal.

By all reports, Ulrika had lived in harmony with her animal soul until Itor got ahold of her, mutated her powers without her consent. Now she was a powerful shape-shifter who used sex to control the angry beast living inside of her, and if she had a chance in hell of staying alive, she was going to need his agency's help.

Which was why he was here, undercover and posing as a sub rather than his Dom preference.

This wasn't one of the worst clubs, but it wasn't one of the higher-end ones either. No, Ulrika would be hiding in a place where she could stand out without fear of being caught, and this underground London club was off the map.

He'd been watching her all night as he sat on the smooth leather stool in a stance that signaled available. Most of the Doms avoided him, as they should. Even tamping himself down, the wild streak practically throbbed from him.

But Ulrika was drawn to that. From what he'd gathered, she liked her men hard to handle. Probably because the tamer ones were unable to deal with what she had to offer during sex.

Suddenly, she appeared next to him, catching him off guard. He took a sip of his whiskey, as if he were the one who called her over, but she wasn't buying it. She put a strong arm on his, and he let her push his hand with the glass in it to the bar, where he opened his palm and surrendered it.

Kira, another ACRO operative, an animal whisperer, had been right about pegging tonight as the night. Ulrika was definitely on the prowl.

She slid a firm finger under his chin and forced it upward, as if appraising him.

No, this wasn't going to be easy.

He forced himself to stay still under her gaze. If she was a true, born Dom, she'd have known that he wasn't a submissive, not by a long shot. But from the files he'd briefed himself on before he left the ACRO offices, he knew Ulrika's need for sex overrode most of her other senses. Especially now, when she was scared and on the run.

He would be the one to bring her in, even if it meant posing as something that went against every one of his most basic survival instincts.

The wolf lady was beautiful—long, reddish-blond hair, piercing gold eyes. And yes, he purposefully didn't avert his gaze, because if he was going to pull off his role as a sub, it was going to be as one who was nearly untrainable.

"Eyes down, boy," she said, her voice sure and strong, with the barest hint of a German accent, and he shot her one final glance before doing her bidding. "You won't be an easy one, will you?"

"I'm not a boy," he said.

She chuckled lightly. "You'll be whatever I tell you to be tonight."

His cock jumped at her words.

"Are you worthy of that privilege . . . boy?"

He wanted to strap her to a spanking bench and make her ass a pretty shade of red and then they'd find out who was worthy.

He bit the inside of his cheek instead of telling her that.

"You may speak," she said, her hand caressing his ass.

"I'm worthy. *Mistress.*"

"Good boy."

He brought his eyes up to meet hers again, and she merely raised her eyebrows at him. "Unless you'd rather call me *Daddy,* I suggest you lower your eyes and learn to love *boy.*"

He hadn't expected the sense of humor. She'd been watching him for longer than he'd thought.

He lowered his eyes, but only so he could stare at her perfectly formed breasts under the low-cut, gauzy blouse she wore. Much different from most of the leather-clad Mamas in this place.

She brought her cleavage close to his face. "Like what you see?"

He breathed deeply—her sweet scent belied what she really was underneath—part woman, part wolf . . . and he was the perfect one to tame the beast he knew was inside that body.

"Yes. I like." His voice was husky with need, and if she hadn't been able to tell from that, all she needed to do was look down at the massive bulge between his legs, straining to be set free from the black pants he wore.

"Room three. Face the wall. And keep your clothes on. I want to have some fun taking them off myself."

He nodded, pushed off the stool and walked toward the room without the requisite *Yes, Mistress*.

He heard her low growl follow him down the darkened hallway all the way to room three, with its heavy cuffs and chains hanging from the far wall. Which was exactly where she wanted him and the last place he wanted to be. No, he should be the one cuffing her, arms above her head, her breasts and body open to him for his pleasure.

Instead, his body would be in Rik's hands.

She was part feral predator and all danger, to herself and to the outside world if she couldn't learn to control the change. In order to help her do that, he'd have to first rein her in. Slowly. Without her realizing it.

He'd have to hypnotize her into wanting him to be her sub, again and again, because word on the floor was that Mistress Rik didn't take the same sub twice. Ever. And since his skill as an excedo had, as far back as he could recall, included the ability to tame most people with one look into his eyes, he really was the perfect man for the job.

It had been three months since Ulrika surfaced on the scene following a botched assassination attempt on the head of ACRO's new sister agency, The Aquarius Group. Ulrika's failure to kill Faith Black had apparently led to her escape from Itor when her handler was captured. She was now on ACRO's radar, and hopefully Trance could get her off Itor's before they tracked her down.

Now he remained facing the wall, feeling her eyes on him. She'd picked one of the private rooms, which gave him hope that she wasn't into displaying him for the world to see.

He wasn't heavily into the BDSM scene—not anymore, but when he was in his late teens and early twenties, he was a frequent visitor to all the clubs, first in the Chicago area, where he grew up, and later wherever the Army stationed him. These days, he wasn't looking so much for controlled sex as he was a woman he could fall in love with. But there were very few women who would understand what he was or the job that utilized those special skills to the best of his ability.

It was kind of hard to explain to a date that you possessed the gifts of super-strength, better than average eyesight and the power to hypnotize most any human who looked you in the eye.

It was even harder for him to truly let go during sex—because Trance knew his own strength, and his worries about hurting a woman accidentally during lovemaking had stopped him from ever getting past the formal stage with any woman—sub or otherwise.

Rik's breath was warm on the back of his neck. He turned his head to let it graze his ear and she caught his lobe between her teeth, nipped just hard enough to make him turn his head back.

Her hands came around his chest—unbuttoned his shirt slowly. As she peeled it away from his shoulders, she brought her nose in to smell him, to nuzzle his neck and to nip the sensitive skin at the nape. His senses were on high alert, every touch of her fingers was like fire against his skin. His heart beat loudly, his mouth dried, and maybe this was all a mistake.

A hand caressed his balls and then his shaft through the fabric of his pants. He'd wanted to wear his usual leathers, but in them he was certainly not unassuming.

"You're nervous," she said.

He didn't answer, didn't have to. It was more nervous energy than actual fear, but it all worked in his favor. Enhanced his role.

She rubbed against his bare back since he still faced the wall, eyes down, as she hadn't given him the command otherwise.

"Your safe word?" she asked.

"*Daddy.*"

Again, the deep chuckle. "You're a funny boy. I have a feeling you won't be as funny by the time I'm through with you, though. Are there things you're not comfortable doing?"

Yes, this. All of this. "My tolerance is high," he told her instead.

He didn't know if that was actually the truth or not, but he had no way of knowing, having never subbed as many Doms did in order to learn how to better their role. He only knew that he preferred pleasure over pain, used restraints with his subs only to enhance pleasure...He wasn't into humiliation and, from what he'd heard, neither was Rik.

It would definitely be a learning experience.

"Tell me your name."

"It's Trance," he said.

"That's your real name?"

"It's the name I use when I'm out playing."

"Fair enough. Turn toward me. Arms over your head."

He did as she asked. She pulled at the chains above him, shortening them so his arms would be held at the highest possible tension, while his wrists were caught in the soft leather binding.

She fastened the cuffs and his insides began to chafe almost immediately. His muscles burned slightly and he tugged at the chains, just the way she'd expect.

"Relax," she said, putting her hands on his upper arms. But he didn't want to relax. He wanted to come, didn't realize how badly until he was firmly held down.

"Turn your head—look at me, boy. I need to make sure you're all right."

He did as told, raised his eyes and let the familiar feel of vertigo take hold of him, a side effect of getting someone else under his control. Rik stared at him, cocked her head in confusion for a second before reaching for the zipper on his pants.

Yes, she'd restrained him, but the chains would never hold. Nothing would, except his own will.

THIS ONE was going to be special. Ulrika could feel it. Smell it. And, when she ran her tongue over the pulse point in his throat, she could taste it. Power flowed through his veins, the currents as strong as those of the river Elbe, where she used to fish as a child.

But those days were as dead as her people, and in the years since she'd been taken from her German homeland, she'd learned to tamp down both the memories and the grief, and concentrate on nothing but survival.

A large part of her survival depended on what she was doing now, with Trance.

Her touch as she pulled down his zipper was featherlight, and unexpected, if his quick intake of breath was any indication. Her own breathing hitched as his cock broke free from the soft black pants, and she resisted the urge to take it in her palm.

The man was a magnificent creature . . . broad shoulders, rugged features, muscles carved from stone. A light dusting of blond hair coated his chest, which was as deeply tanned as the rest of him. Longish blond hair, shot through with darker brown, framed eyes as blue and clear as an Austrian mountain lake. Eyes that fascinated her, drew her in when he should be keeping his gaze averted a lot more than he was.

It had been a long time since she'd encountered anything like him. Usually her customers were either handsome or fit, but rarely both, and never to such extremes.

And before this life . . . she didn't want to think about it. Yet for some reason she couldn't help it. The full moon always brought out the beast's fiercest urges, and her worst memories. Such as how Itor had destroyed her clan, had wiped her kind from the face of the earth with experimentation that only she had survived. Now they wanted her dead. After subjecting her to years of hell and forced service, they were tired of playing.

She, however, wasn't. The beast in her needed to play. If the beast wasn't kept sated, it came out, a rabid, uncontrollable thing that raged hard, killed indiscriminately and wouldn't give back her body until it wore out. She'd wake in strange places, aching and covered in blood that wasn't her own, her memory a black hole.

Sex kept it calm. Meat kept it fed. The act of dominating humans kept it happy.

She'd just eaten three rare steaks. One down, two in the works.

"Mistress?"

Her gaze snapped to his. "Did I tell you to speak?"

His blue eyes gleamed, and she held her breath, unable to do or say anything until he dropped his gaze. "No, *Mistress*." His crisp American accent was like a velvet whip on sensitive skin, and she felt it all the way to her sex.

This man was not a sub.

The realization found its way into her bloodstream as a rush of adrenaline. Excitement stirred the beast; nothing fired the blood like dominating an alpha, but warning bells clanged in Rik's head. Her mind raced. Itor wouldn't toy with her like this—they'd simply take her out, just as The Aquarius Group would—payback for her attempt at killing one of their senior agents. No doubt ACRO would want in on the action as well. Heck, she had to assume everyone wanted her dead.

Caution had kept her alive for weeks, and she couldn't ignore her internal alarm, even if this turned out to be a false one.

Lightning fast, she pushed his face around so he couldn't look at her, and she scraped her teeth over his ear, not lightly or gently. "Tell me why you're here."

"To submit to you, Mistress."

"I don't believe you. Why do something so against your nature?"

His muscles tensed, and she smelled surprise rolling off him. "I want to know what it feels like to submit," he said smoothly, "and I hear you're the best."

"I am." She pressed against him harder, letting her stiff nipples rub against his chest through the fabric of her top. "I can make you love to be dominated. I can make you learn to crave it. To beg for it."

"Then teach me."

The underlying steel in his voice sent a shiver of feminine appreciation through her even as it raised the beast's hackles. She drew his head around and nipped his bottom lip, enough to cause pain but not draw blood. " 'Teach me, *please*.' Say it. Now."

His moment of hesitation lasted no more than a second, but she once again made the mistake of looking into his mesmerizing eyes, the distraction so intense that she barely heard him say, "Teach me, please."

Nodding, she stepped back and allowed herself a leisurely scan of his body, from his bound hands to his chest, his slim waist where muscles strained, to his erection that jutted like steel from where she'd peeled back his fly.

"You will do as I say. Always."

"Yes, Mistress."

His tone was better, properly subdued, and she heated all over. As a reward, she slipped her fingers between his legs and drew his heavy sac forward so it bulged over the top of his fly opening. Hunger consumed her, but she'd ignore her need until Trance had been properly schooled.

"You will come when and *if* I allow it," she said, as she drew one long nail up his cock, tracing the deep blue veins that circled the shaft like thick vines.

He breathed out a curse, and at her arched brow, he said, "Yes, Mistress." Though he'd responded through clenched teeth, his voice had deepened, and she knew his hunger had climbed.

"Good boy," she murmured. "Very good." She scraped her nails over one nicely developed pec. "You should know that after tonight, someone else will have to instruct you. I don't do this for your pleasure, but for mine, and mine alone." She tweaked his nipple, enjoying his barely controlled intake of breath. "I don't do the normal exchange of trust and power. This is about power only. My power. Do you understand?"

"That's highly unusual, Mistress."

She stepped away. "It's how I work. If you object, I'll send you away now."

Several heartbeats ticked by before he finally gave her a slow nod. There was so much fight in him, and so much restraint. He was magnificent beyond belief.

Her loose clothing grew tight, confining, her skin aching for the hot, smooth contact of male muscle. She would touch him, but he would never touch her. No man would touch her with his hands, ever again.

Slowly, she stripped out of her blouse, noting the way Trance's gaze darkened at the sight of her breasts. They were bigger than they looked beneath the top, the nipples hard and stiff within the gold rings that circled them but didn't pierce.

She now wore only her skirt, high heels and the radio collar, a leather-wrapped steel casing full of electronics—a homing locator and a nasty shock mechanism a handler could activate with different intensities to either control her behavior or force her to shape-shift.

The good news was that outside the ten-mile radius of a handler in possession of a controller, the collar didn't work either to give away her location or to shock her. The bad news was that the collar couldn't be removed without the tiny bomb inside blowing her head off.

So yeah, she could tell herself that she could tamp down her memories, but every time she looked in the mirror, they looked right back at her.

Right now, though, her sub was looking at her, and she wasn't going to disappoint either of them.

Watching him, she cupped her breasts, pushed them together so he could imagine his cock between them, rubbing and thrusting, each upward stroke allowing her to swipe at the head with her tongue. She circled her peaked nipples with her thumbs until sensation swept from her breasts to her sex, which flooded with her juices.

Trance's throat muscles worked on a hard swallow, his nostrils flaring, and when his tongue snaked out to moisten his lips, she knew he was ready for the next step.

Dropping to her knees, she brought her mouth close to his cock so he could feel the stirring of her breath on his skin. No touching, though, except to peel down his pants. But when he rolled his hips toward her, nearly catching her mouth with his shaft, she sighed and reached for the leatherbound box behind him.

"Naughty boy," she murmured. "Time for your first lesson."

CHAPTER
Two

Trance wasn't going to like this lesson.

Kira had warned him that his hypnotic powers might not fully work on Rik—especially once the beast within her emerged. If he could keep her calm and peaceful during these sessions, he could slowly win her over.

Still, it wasn't going to stop him from having to become Rik's bitch over the next few minutes.

Fuck. Just fuck.

"Did you say something?" Rik asked him.

Well, hell, no one said the job of an ACRO agent was easy. Definitely not, especially after seeing the cock ring she'd taken out of her bag of tricks. She wrapped the stiff leather around the base of his cock—it would keep him rock hard and stop him from coming.

"My boy doesn't like to be told what to do," she purred. "Doesn't like not being able to do exactly what he wants to, when he wants to. But in my world, you only get to do what I want."

"Do you want to come, Mistress? Because I can make you come if you put your hot, wet pussy on my cock—"

A squeeze and twist to his balls, coupled with a hard pinch to his nipple effectively shut his mouth. "You are not in charge here."

A drop of pre-cum had formed on the head of his cock—when he didn't say anything else, Rik took a long finger and spread the moisture, then pressed it lightly into the slit.

"So many possibilities—whips and chains—your skin would look so pretty marked with red."

Safe. Sane. Consensual. Those words had been such a big part of his life for so long. But there was nothing safe, sane or consensual about this. He squirmed under her words, her touch, and she slid her tongue into the slit of his cock. When he gasped, she did it again and again and then stopped as if confused by what she'd done.

"Maybe some sounding. I think you'd like that—the cold metal sliding inside your cock until you lost all control of yourself." She slid a finger along his ass. "Or maybe—"

No. No fucking way. He'd almost let the words slip out, but he held them back, held his breath and finally said, "Anything you want, Mistress."

With that, she took his cock in her mouth and tortured him some more by stroking a slow, intimate rhythm.

"Yeah, oh, yeah, baby . . ." he ground out.

"What did you call me?" She squeezed his balls in her palm again—hard enough to make him wince, and whimper with pleasure at the same time.

She was good—good enough to make him forget that this was a mission and just let himself go.

But this *was* a mission, and he had no desire to go back down this road again for real. Pretend was far safer—for him, for everyone involved, including the beautiful wolf woman who held his life in her hands. Being a submissive took a measure of control Trance did not have in these situations—his strength was better served when he was the one in charge of the scene. Otherwise, his reactions were far too volatile, and hurting anyone when he was in the throes of orgasm wasn't anything he wanted to do.

"Mistress," he said through gritted teeth. "Make me come, Mistress."

She chuckled, a sound that went up his spine, and then she stopped everything.

She was tugging at her collar. The collar in and of itself was an odd thing for a Dom to wear, but Trance knew exactly what the collar was all about. It was Itor's way of keeping her down, and they must've just sent through a major shock to her system. She was thrown off her game, and while that had saved his ass, literally, for the night, it made him angry enough to want to snap some necks at Itor.

It also made him realize that Itor might be closer than any of them thought. He'd have to work his magic, and fast, because she was ready to freak. If the beast came out now, he'd have no way to stop it—as strong as he was, he wasn't sure he could conquer Rik's wolf side.

But the beast didn't come out. Instead, she rose, her voice still steady and calm, and said, "Unfortunately, I have a prior engagement. I'd forgotten all about it."

And fuck it all if Itor was going to step on his game now, not after he'd been strung up like this. "I understand, Mistress."

"I can have someone come in—finish up here," she offered, but he shook his head. She undid the restraints quickly, but before she could unsnap the cock ring, he locked his gaze on hers.

"I don't want anyone but you, Mistress," he murmured, summoning just a thread of his hypnotic powers. "Want your permission to come. Please, help your boy."

She tugged at the collar again and then cocked her head and stared at him. He had to make her believe this was all her idea—giving her a command this soon would break the delicate balance of power he'd achieved thus far.

"You have my permission," she said softly. "Watch yourself, not me."

He lowered his gaze—his cock was bulging, begging for relief, the head red and angry as he began to touch himself.

"That's it, stroke yourself. Tell me how it feels."

"Feels so good, Mistress."

"I know you, boy. Know what you want—what you need."

"Yes." His breath was fast now, his hand moving quickly, and he'd burst the cock ring off of himself if she made him wait much longer.

With one flick of a finger, she unsnapped the leather restraint, freeing him. He shot his load almost instantly, creamy, thick ropes of come hit his chest as he closed his eyes briefly and prayed he'd done the right thing.

He licked his lips and his voice was hoarse when he spoke again. "Mistress, thank you for letting me come."

"You were a good boy," she whispered.

"I'll return. If you'll have me."

There was a long pause, and he held his breath, kept his eyes to the ground, as she hadn't told him he could look up as of yet. This was a time to follow orders.

"I'll have you—any way I want you," she said finally. "Tomorrow night. The room at the end of the hall."

When he heard the door close behind her, only then did he let himself sag to the ground.

LIKE ALL OF The Dungeon's staff, Ulrika left through the back door. She hadn't finished her shift, and the beast was raging with need. It was probably a huge mistake to not give it sex tonight, but she just couldn't do it.

Something was wrong.

During her session with Trance, a mild buzz of electricity had vibrated through her collar, something that hadn't happened in the three months since escaping Itor. The only reason she hadn't bolted out of the club in a panic was that when Itor shocked her, there was nothing mild about it.

Chances were that the collar had developed a short or maybe someone nearby had a cell phone or MP3 player that operated on the same frequency. Still, the jolt had been enough to stun her right out of the play with Trance.

Which had sucked, because something about him made her all jittery and hot, as if she were coming down with the mother of all fevers. She'd even taken him into her mouth, something she *never* did with any sub. And when he'd stroked himself off, it had taken a lot of discipline to keep from touching herself as she watched.

Not all of her clients—males and females—were looking for an orgasm. Many desired only to be dominated, to give in to a part of themselves that needed to please. Others wanted to get off, and for the most part, she could make them climax without ever touching their genitals with her hands.

As for her own orgasms, often she achieved completion by doing no more than spanking a sub. Rarely did she allow her clients to pleasure her, either with their tongues or cocks, but when she did, it happened while they were bound and helpless.

Funny, because even when Trance had been stretched out and tied up like a hunter's deer, there hadn't been anything helpless about him. His gaze had seduced her, his voice, smooth as brandy and a hundred times stronger, had intoxicated her, and his body, all hard flesh and silky skin, had robbed her of breath.

He wore sensual promise like a glove. She'd make him live up to that promise tomorrow. Sure, she never played with a client twice, but they hadn't completed their session tonight, and she was dying to get her hands—and toys—on him again.

Lifting her face to the night air, she sniffed, an instinctive action that went back to her childhood living in the mountains, and then later to Itor, when scenting, and identifying, a person before they arrived at her cell had helped her mentally prepare for whatever horrible thing they were going to put her through.

Now she smelled nothing but the faint odor of old grease from a corner fish-and-chips shop and the usual stench of vomit and piss from the alley behind the club. She moved toward the street, which, at barely midnight, still ran loud with cars and pub-crawlers.

"Mistress?" A man stepped out in front of her from the shadowy recess of another building's doorway, blocking her.

She smiled tightly, recognizing him from the club. She'd played with him once, weeks ago, and he'd been back every night since, trying to get her to play with him again. He'd been a satisfying enough sub, had liked his fun on the rough, humiliating side, which got the animal inside her off as much as anything, but his scent had been wrong, sour. With him, she'd fed her need to dominate, but hadn't taken sex. This one had made her nervous in a way few people did.

"I don't socialize outside of the club," she said, moving to the side with the intention of stalking past him.

He blocked her path again. "I've tried to talk to you inside. Please, Mistress. I need you."

Cold dread settled over her like a shroud. She'd dealt with nuts before, and they were generally easy to handle as long as she stayed in Dom mode. But this man . . . Robert . . . he didn't strike her as a harmless nut as much as someone who was balancing on the edge of sanity.

"I'm sorry, Robert. But I can't help you."

His hand closed on her upper arm, and in a flash of violence she was dragged behind the club and slammed against the side of the building. The back of her skull cracked against the brick, momentarily stunning her. Robert's heavy body held her in place, while one hand circled her throat. Panic welled up, her heart beating so hard she heard her pulse pounding in her ears. She could handle this, easily, if she allowed the beast out. She'd tear Robert apart, but it wouldn't end there. Who knew how many innocents she'd kill before she regained control?

"I love you, Mistress," he purred, his teeth scraping her cheek. "I need you to punish me. I've been very, very bad."

It took everything she had to keep from trembling. His hands . . . she couldn't bear them on her body. No man had touched her since *that day*.

The day she'd killed a man while in human form. The day that haunted her every night.

Now *she* did the touching. She had to do something, and fast, or the beast was going to rampage.

"Robert!" she snapped in her hardest Dom voice. "You will get down on your knees and bow your head to me while I consider how I'll punish you. Now. *Do it*."

His breath caught, just a little hitch that told her he wanted to follow her command. His erection slammed into her belly, and a low groan vibrated his chest. "Yes, Mistress," he whispered, his eyes glazing over with anticipation.

Slowly, way too slowly, he went down to his knees before her, and bowed his head. This was good, but she couldn't get her hopes up. He'd be on his feet and on her before she could get out a scream.

Her mind worked quickly, measuring the distance to the street and the back door to the club. If she could knock him off balance, she had a shot at escaping.

"Kiss my shoe, worm. Lips only. No tongue."

With a shiver of pleasure, Robert doubled over. The moment his mouth touched her foot, she brought it up, crunching the toe of her walking boot into his face. She whirled, dashed into the alley as his roar of rage and pain followed her.

Something that felt like a bus hit her from behind. Her skirt tripped her up, and a scream lodged in her throat. She hit the pavement hard, and even as she rolled and jammed her knee between Robert's legs, his fist caught her in the jaw. Stinging pain bit into her cheek, and she tasted blood.

"Cunt," he spat through bloodied lips. "Who's getting punished now?"

Terror and too-fresh memories froze her muscles as he yanked up her skirt, but rage flew in on its heels. A curtain of red came down over her vision and her skin tightened as the beast clawed its way out. Oh, God . . . it was coming and she couldn't stop it—

An enraged snarl echoed in the alley. For a split second, she thought the sound had been hers, until suddenly, Robert jerked. A hand yanked him upward so hard his head snapped forward and cracked against her temple. In an instant, Robert was facefirst in the side of the building. Trance had him in a headlock, and Jesus, the bloodcurdling snarl had been his.

"You fucking piece of shit." Trance's voice was a low, nasty drawl. "Come near her or this club again and I promise you, the cops will never find what's left of your body. Do you understand?"

Robert went deathly pale, and even more so when Trance jerked him back and then slammed him into the wall again.

"*Do. You. Understand?*"

"Y-yes."

Panting, Rik scrambled backward until she hit the bricks. She couldn't control her trembling as she sat there, trying to keep the beast at bay while Trance sent Robert packing, more than a little worse for wear. Later, she'd appreciate his brutal competence, the controlled, lethal power in his muscular body, but right now she needed to keep it together. The scent of Robert's blood in the air and the taste of her own in her mouth weren't helping things.

"Rik?" Trance eased toward her, slowly, as if she were a feral cat he didn't want to frighten away. Too late she realized that her eyes had probably changed, but she couldn't look away. His gaze ripped into hers, holding her captive in a way no rope, chains or manacles had ever done. "He's gone. Are you okay?"

His voice soothed her, brought her down gently and easily, until she no longer felt the itch to turn inside out and into a monster. A few feet away, he crouched on his heels. She watched him warily, managed to drag her gaze away to eye his hands, which she'd seen handle Robert with efficient skill, but which now rested tamely on his knees.

"I'm not going to touch you," he assured her, and she cursed herself for allowing her fear to show. "I just want to make sure you're all right."

She scrambled to her feet. "I—I have to go."

"I'll walk you."

"No!" She sucked in a shaky breath. With the cool night air came Trance's scent, earthy and male. He smelled like strength and power . . . and safety.

She shook her head, because that was insane. There was no safe place for her on earth, and certainly no man could offer her that kind of haven. "Thank you. I'll take a cab."

"I'm walking you to a cab, then. No arguments."

She nodded, allowed him to walk her to the street, where he flagged a taxi that had been parked down the block. Only after she'd gotten in did she realize that he'd given her a command.

And she'd followed it.

CHAPTER
three

Devlin O'Malley shut down the computer in his office and contemplated going home, where the constant needs of the agency weren't ringing his phone, beeping on his computer or slamming into his office.

He'd been contemplating this for the past four hours—now it was almost midnight. And still he knew that even in the silence at home the constant needs of the agency would be bouncing around in his head, because thinking about work was a hell of a lot easier than thinking about Oz.

Closing his eyes, he leaned back in his chair, let the squeak of the leather comfort him. He was as at home here as he was in his house, but at least here he had a shitload of distractions.

Like the latest status reports from the dozen operatives on missions around the globe. Or the request for rare supplies from the Mystic Research department in the Paranormal Division. Or the scores of other issues from ACRO's other thirteen divisions, and countless departments functioning under their umbrellas.

Fuck.

He stood and stretched and grabbed a pile of folders to take home with him. The halls were cool and quiet—deserted save for security posted at every entrance and exit, a necessary means of keeping ACRO and her operatives safe. The men and women who kept him safe simply nodded as he walked past, knowing their boss didn't appreciate extraneous conversation—more often than not, Dev's head was too filled with plans and he found greetings to be a distraction.

His car was waiting for him at the entrance to the building, brought around and checked thoroughly by ACRO staff who'd been alerted by the push of a button on his desk before leaving his office.

He drove the black bulletproof Hummer home, well aware that security followed him. Since getting his sight back last year he sometimes refused a driver, forcing himself to enjoy all the things he'd wanted to do when he was blind. He parked the big car in the driveway and looked around before letting himself inside his big, empty house and closing the door, surveying it more out of habit than worry—the ACRO compound had fortress-tight security, but that didn't mean he could get sloppy.

These days, it was all about forcing himself to do everything. None of it was working, although he put up a hell of a good front. ACRO was running as smoothly as could be—beyond Ryan Malmstrom's MIA status, all operatives were alive and accounted for at the moment. Granted, the situation changed on a daily basis, but Dev slept better knowing the whereabouts of all of the men and women in his charge.

Still, even with that knowledge, if he got into bed now, all he would do was stare at the wall of the guest bedroom. Since Oz died, Dev hadn't moved back into the master bedroom, but he had thought more than once about razing the entire house.

Marlena, his personal assistant, advised against it gently, as was her way. For now she'd persuaded him. But on nights like tonight, he wished he could tear it down himself, brick by brick.

The clock chimed at the same time the doorbell rang and he cursed as he stubbed his toe getting to the door. He fucking tripped more now than he ever did when he was blind, although his second sight hadn't diminished when his sight came back.

A total stranger waited there on the other side of the door, impatience radiating off him even though he leaned against the door frame as if he hadn't a care in the world.

The man was take-your-fucking-breath-away good-looking, in a rugged, I'll-kill-you-if-you-look-at-me-wrong way.

Dev was pretty sure he was looking at him wrong.

How he got past security—and Dev's own second sight—was the first thing to enter Devlin's mind. In fact, the phrase *rip someone a new asshole* was at the forefront, and he reached for his cell phone to make a few calls. "Who the hell are you?"

"I'm a new recruit. The guy at the gate dropped me here."

"What guy?" Dev growled as he dialed.

"I didn't get his name. He had dark hair. Dark eyes. Just said, 'Devlin will be expecting you.' "

The front gate answered Dev's call before Dev could respond to the stranger. "What can we do for you, Mr. O'Malley?"

Dev could barely breathe, but he forced his voice to remain neutral. "I'd like to know who authorized a new recruit to be dropped here."

"New recruit? Sir, that would never happen. There was a new recruit waiting here for transport, but he disappeared."

"Well, he's reappeared. At my house."

"We'll send someone immediately."

"Do that." Dev hung up so he didn't have to listen to any more of the man's excuses. "Gate security says you weren't given a ride. He says you simply disappeared."

"Some dude drove me here. Oh, yeah, he also said to tell you that it's spring. Like you wouldn't know that or something."

"Fuck. Me," Dev breathed. The man with the tousled blond hair just stared at him with gunmetal-colored eyes, as if some strange, electrical current connected him to Dev. By the groin.

After midnight. Spring. Motherfucker.

"I can't do this now," Dev said, heard the rawness in his voice.

That rawness had been there since Oz died last year. His lover had promised to send Dev someone when winter was over, and *fuck me*, winter was over.

He swore he could hear Oz's chuckle as he went to shut the door.

The man's palm slammed it back open. "Hey—fuck that. Can you just point me in the direction of the housing? Is it close to here? I don't want to get anyone in trouble."

Fucking, fucking Oz. "The *guy* at the gate will be reprimanded. No one gets dropped off here."

"Maybe you could just lighten up and help me."

"Did you just tell me to lighten up? Do you know who the fuck I am, boy?"

"Yeah, a cranky asshole. And don't ever call me *boy*."

"What did you just say?"

"You heard me, unless you're a deaf cranky asshole. *Asshole*." The man turned to walk away but Dev yanked him around and shoved him against one of the Colonial-style columns that flanked his front door.

"I'm not just some guy who works at ACRO. I'm your fucking boss."

"I'm supposed to be impressed by that?" The younger man's nostrils flared slightly—it wasn't because he was intimidated by Dev's title, though. This guy wasn't used to being threatened, not with physical force, and he seemed about to retaliate with his own.

"You're supposed to show some goddamned respect. I'm assuming that you came here for a job."

"Look, I just want to get some sleep. I didn't ask to be here—I was recruited by a few of your people. Against my will. So now I'm here and I've got no place to sleep and what the hell do you want me to do?"

Dev knew exactly what he wanted the cocky boy to do . . . and there was no point in denying it anymore. But it wasn't going to happen. No way. "What's your name? Never mind, don't tell me, that's not important. Wait here—someone's coming to take you to the trainee quarters."

He finally slammed the door in the young man's face and let his body sink to the ground on the other side.

TRANCE HADN'T SLEPT well—hadn't slept at all really, merely tossed and turned and stared at the ceiling. He could still feel the light scrape of the leather bindings on his wrists, even though he'd been long released, felt the pulsing pressure of the leather wrapped around the base of his cock.

He'd had to get himself off three times last night after he'd sent Rik safely away in a cab. Would've followed her all the way home too, but she'd have sensed that, and he couldn't afford to blow things now.

He was lucky as hell she'd agreed to see him a second time.

Still, he was going to wear his leather pants tonight. Didn't give a shit that he was supposed to be the pretty little unassuming submissive—Rik already knew he wasn't pretty or unassuming, and after last night, he was done playing around.

Kira understood Rik, maybe better than the woman understood herself. And while Trance had asked his boss to allow Kira to come along with him on the trip, Devlin had refused.

"She'd probably sense me." Kira agreed with Dev, told Trance so the second she'd opened the door of her house last month. "I would spook her and then she'd be lost. I could talk to her, woman to woman, but until we know if the animal inside can communicate when she's in human form . . . well, I just can't deal with her the way you'll be able to."

With Trance's excedo powers and better-than-average vision, he could bend a person's will. He was a sideshow hypnosis freak of nature who had to be careful of his own powers because he believed wholly in free will, never wanted to convince people to do things his way just because.

Occasionally, in his former life as an MP, it had come in handy, but honestly, it helped the prisoners more. He'd rather stop them with his mind than have to subdue the men physically.

"You're going to have to let her be the alpha for a while. That's the best way to gain her trust," Kira had lectured him, while her husband, fellow ACRO agent and excedo, Ender, unsuccessfully tried to hold back a laugh.

Unfortunately, Ender didn't try all that hard. "Dude, you're going to have to be the submissive. You, the big bad leather daddy again."

"I was never a leather daddy," Trance said through clenched teeth as Ender doubled over at the idea, and Trance mentally cursed the day he ever fucking agreed to this assignment.

He also wondered when in the hell Ender got a fucking sense of humor, because last time he'd looked, the asshole seriously lacked one.

"Tommy, stop." Kira pushed at her husband's chest. "Go—now."

To Trance's surprise, Ender did what she asked. Probably because he was laughing too hard to contribute anything more to the conversation.

Kira had shaken her head before turning back to Trance.

"Listen, Rik needs to feel in control—that's the beast," Kira explained. "But according to the cryptozoologists, her tribe was peaceful and nurturing, so deep down, that's who she is. Chances are, she's got a soft spot for those who are strong but not in control of themselves. It's something she understands. She doesn't like fear but she appreciates someone who needs true protection. Like a momma bear, she'll take you in if you play it right."

"Fuck," he'd muttered.

"You're going to have to fight every single natural instinct you've got," Kira said. "I know how hard that's going to be for you, but the fear could actually work in your favor—"

His knee-jerk reaction was to tell Kira that he wasn't scared. His fear was actually something deeper—based on the way Kira spoke of Rik, the Dom would sense it. Her protective instincts would be fierce.

"As long as she knows you're strong, she'll respect that," Kira continued.

Trance wondered if Rik knew what it was like to be both strong and afraid.

In his first career, he'd dealt with that combination of forces quite a bit.

When he'd first entered the Army, he hadn't cared what Military Occupational Specialty he'd be slotted for. But when it became apparent during basic training that Trance had a gift for stopping the drill instructors in their tracks and calming them with his hypnotic gaze, he'd been flagged for the law enforcement field. Following basic and twelve more weeks of specialized police instruction, he'd been assigned to Leavenworth.

While working as an MP in corrections at the prison, he'd completed most of the special tactics training and had been privy to all Special Forces training, had gone through Ranger School, done the Delta thing and BUD/s, as well as Force Recon and PJs. Any school that taught men how to escape from the enemy, Trance had learned those tricks. He was big and he was strong and most of the prisoners respected him. Those who didn't tried to fight him or were scared shitless of him.

Thing was, he didn't want Rik to be afraid of him. He told himself that he could only imagine what it must be like to have that beast living inside of her, waiting restlessly for a chance to break out, and then he called himself a liar. He knew exactly what it was like, had a similar beast inside of him—an inhuman strength that had been the bane of his existence since he was a young boy and discovered just how powerful—and lonely—his gifts left him.

He wasn't sure exactly what it was going to feel like to completely surrender to her tonight. He hoped that Rik wouldn't give him more than he could manage.

But as he sat in the club's lounge and watched her work the place while ignoring him, he started to think she was already giving him more than he could handle.

She hadn't acknowledged him once in the hour since he'd arrived, had left him in an infuriating holding pattern. And all around him, memories kept him on edge. The erotic moans coming from all sides, the sharp cracks of leather on skin, the smell of hot candle wax and sex . . . His stomach churned.

Watching Rik walk around in studded leather while touching other men only heightened his anxiety. He burned to take her beneath him and show her exactly why he should be in charge, but a bigger part of him knew that Rik could hold her own against him in bed, without restraints on either of them—and that part of him wanted to test his theory.

Which was seriously fucked up. She was an HVT—a high-value target—and he was playing a role. Just a role.

Of course, when she finally turned in his direction and crooked her finger at him in a come-here-now gesture, his dick led the charge, because it wasn't buying the whole it's-just-a-role thing.

CHAPTER *Four*

Ulrika never ever saw a client twice, and yet here she was with Trance again. Granted, they hadn't finished their first session, but still. She'd sensed his strength, his utter lack of submissive genes, had known he'd be trouble. She should have ended last night's session and left it alone. Instead, she'd told him to come back. She wasn't entirely sure why she'd done that—maybe it was because she enjoyed a challenge. Maybe it was because he excited her more than she'd been excited in a long time.

Maybe she was growing stupid and soft.

She fingered the whip in her hand. No, not soft. Definitely not soft.

Then again, last night's incident in the alley filled her with doubt. Robert's attack had left her prowling her flat all night long, afraid to sleep. Itor hadn't given her the usual agent training, which included evasive techniques and combat instruction. They hadn't wanted her to either defend or take care of herself should she escape. Though she'd been surprised at her resourcefulness when it came to survival, she cursed her inability to effectively defend herself in a life-threatening situation. Her only means of self-defense was the beast, which she couldn't control.

To make matters worse, Trance had compounded an already bad situation. Sure, he'd saved her from Robert, but he'd brought with him his own brand of danger. The underlying tone of command in his voice, even when he was saying "Yes, Mistress," rang through her body and split it in half. The beast bristled with irritation, but the woman responded with appreciation.

The woman had responded last night by obeying his order not to argue with him.

The beast wanted to punish him for that.

Slowly, Rik walked around Trance as he kneeled before her, now naked except for the slave collar, head bowed, hands bound behind his muscular back by a collar-wrist restraint. She trailed the whip over his skin and prickled with satisfaction when he shivered.

He was beautiful . . . all sinew and tan skin, long limbs, rolling shoulders. Everything about him oozed *alpha*. The beast in her wanted to challenge it, crush it. The woman in her wanted to roll over and let him take her as a dominant, powerful lover.

That would never happen, though, so instead she'd make him her slave.

"Follow me." She smiled at the sound of him scooting across the floor on his knees.

Her stilettos cracked on the cement, harsh reminders that she was in charge. She'd worn her one outfit that screamed *dominatrix,* and she'd even pulled her long hair back into a severe ponytail.

There would be no doubt as to who was in control tonight.

When she reached the bondage altar, a large cushioned table with iron rings welded to all sides, she sat on the edge and waited. Even on his knees, he moved with unimaginable grace, until she stopped him with one high-heeled foot on his shoulder. When he raised his gaze, she pressed the heel into his skin.

"I didn't give you permission to look up, boy."

He looked down again, but she didn't let up with her foot. She pushed harder, forcing his spine straight, and then she kicked off her other shoe.

"Look at me." He did, the defiance flashing in his eyes making this even more fun. "I want you to kiss my foot. Lick it. Suck it. Do it well, and I'll reward you."

Holding her gaze, he leaned forward, bracing himself against her shoe, which must have been painful, but he didn't even flinch. Instead, he opened his mouth over the sole of her offered foot. His tongue flicked over the sensitive skin there in her arch, circling, licking, mimicking something much more intimate.

Sensation flooded her, and she threw her head back, let him suck her toes, nibble her arch, lick her heel . . . God, he was good. Moisture flooded her sex, and damn, she could come from this.

It was *that* good.

"Suck my toe now," she murmured. "Suck it the way you like your cock sucked."

His lips closed around her toe, and he began a slow, sensuous slide in and out of the hot, silky depths of his mouth. As his tongue laved the sensitive tip, she could imagine her tongue swirling around the head of his cock as he fucked her mouth. He must have been picturing the same thing, because a low moan accompanied a gentle scrape of his teeth, the sound vibrating all the way up her leg to her core.

"Harder." He obeyed her instantly, adding suction and speed. She bit her lip and spread her legs as wide as her tight skirt would allow. "Good boy. Look what you've done. Look how wet you've made me."

Trance's hot gaze dropped, and she swore she felt the heat of it on her exposed, throbbing flesh. His nostrils flared in a primal response to her arousal. She recognized the flash of animal instinct, the moment when human conventions fled and all that remained was the most basic urge to rut, to unleash the lust.

Oh, she wanted the same thing, wanted to start with his tongue easing her ache, but not yet. She had a big night planned for him.

"Enough." She stood, slipped on her shoe, and pushed the call button on the wall. "You've earned a very nice reward."

She came around behind him, let the tips of her fingers smooth over his broad shoulders. His tight bindings made the muscles of his back bunch up and his arm muscles strain beneath his silky, tight skin. So powerful. Beautiful. She wanted to climb on him and ride him until he was completely slick with her desire.

Tugging her skirt up, she crouched behind him, allowing her inner thighs to rub against his buttocks. She reached around and wrapped her palm around his shaft. He tensed with a hiss, and she knew he was on the verge.

"You will not come without my permission, of course."

He thrust into her hand, but gritted out, "Yes, Mistress." She heard him swallow. "Mistress?"

She nipped his earlobe as punishment for speaking out of turn. "Yes, slave?"

"Will you let your hair down?"

Her body reacted with a warm stirring, something it had no business doing. "Would it please you?"

"Oh, yeah."

She nipped him again. "I seem to remember telling you that I'm in this for me. And right now, your cock pleases me," she murmured. "It will feel so good inside me. Filling me with heat." His head lolled back, and he rocked gently to her rhythm. "That's good, my boy. Get yourself nice and worked up."

She smiled and dropped her hand to his balls, which had drawn up tight and firm, a perfect fit for the cup of her palm.

"Mistress Rik." Syndee's sultry Welsh accent floated into the room. Rik stood as the other woman entered, her body encased in a crotchless red leather bodysuit unzipped at the chest to reveal her large breasts, which sported nipple clamps. She sized up Trance immediately, appreciation gleaming in her eyes. "Need some help with this one?"

"A reward." Ulrika seized the strap attached to his restraints and tugged. "You will stand."

He came to his feet, and Syn practically drooled. So did

Ulrika. His erection was enormous, fully engorged and dusky rose, the plum head so ripe she wanted to taste it. Again. Which was weird, because she never sucked men off. Doing so irritated the beast.

Syn came up behind Ulrika and pressed her breasts to her back. Rik fought the urge to break away as Syn's hands came around front to remove Rik's leather bra and cup her breasts. She never allowed men to touch her, and while she tolerated female attention, she didn't necessarily enjoy it. When a female touched her, it was all about the job, not pleasure.

Surprise and a hunger flickered in Trance's eyes for a split second before they shuttered. Even when Syn hiked up Ulrika's skirt over her waist and dropped one hand down between Ulrika's legs, Trance's expression remained unreadable.

His cock, however, betrayed him. A pearly drop beaded at the tip, and though she'd thought he couldn't get harder, he had. His erection strained upward, curving hard into his belly. And his breathing grew harsh and shallow the longer Syn played.

Rik lifted one foot onto a bench to open herself up and enhance the view. Syn took advantage, adding another finger to the sensual massage. Two fingers slid through Rik's swollen folds, back and forth before plunging inside her weeping core. Squeezing her eyes shut, Rik imagined Syn's fingers were Trance's.

She moaned, thrust her hips into Syn's touch. Her senses flared as her pleasure climbed. Trance's panting breaths mingled with her own, and a heartbeat later, Syn's labored breathing joined in as she rolled her pelvis into Rik's ass.

It could be Trance's pelvis doing that.

Heart racing, clit throbbing, she pulled away from Syn and bent over the spanking bench. Padded leather cushioned her stomach and hips, but smooth, hard wood gave her purchase for her feet and hands. Her thighs quivered in anticipation, and she had to take a deep calming breath before she could speak without sounding overly eager.

"Boy, you're going to fuck me now. But you will stop when I tell you to. Understand?"

"Yes, Mistress."

Syn led him to her. God, Rik was so ready her arousal was dripping down her leg. With his hands bound, he couldn't enter her, which was one of the reasons she'd called Syn. The other woman rolled a condom over his cock before taking it in her hand to guide him to Rik's entrance. A soft noise came from him, so soft she probably only heard because of her superior hearing. But it excited her.

"You can thrust now," she said. "Slowly."

He pushed his hips into her, and she moaned at the exquisite stretch of his cock sliding home. He was so large that her tissues burned at the invasion, but the pain enhanced the pleasure, threatened to dissolve her into a mass of liquid orgasms.

Inch by agonizing inch he filled her. Sweet, spiking friction engulfed her as he withdrew and plunged deep again. She clawed at the wooden hand grips, gritting her teeth to keep from coming. She wanted to, but not yet. The longer she dragged it out, the more sated the beast would be.

"Cease," she demanded.

Trance's thighs went taut against the back of her legs as he froze. "Back up."

The heartbeat's span of hesitation was her only warning before he began to grind against her, scraping his cock over sensitive tissue inside that screamed with her impending orgasm.

"Stop!" Her snarl echoed through the room as she struggled to escape, but she was pinned between the bench and Trance, who began to jackhammer into her with ruthless, short strokes.

Oh, God, her body tightened to the point of pain, her pussy clamping around Trance's shaft as he fucked her like he had something to prove, and by the time Syn got him off her, it was too late.

Her orgasm blasted through her, even though he was no longer inside her. It overwhelmed her nerve endings, fired a series of little implosions all over her body. She pumped herself against the spank bench, her hips moving on their own, her moans vibrating the padding.

When it was over, fury lit her like a match.

"You fool!" She spun. The look on his face, the arrogance and satisfaction, nearly sent her into a beast-rage. "Idiot!"

Syn watched as Ulrika grabbed the leather strap connected to his bound wrists and dragged him to the standing stocks. With a flick of the wrist, she freed his hands, forced them and his head into the stocks, and locked it down.

A cocky smile turned up his lush lips. She locked his ankles into the base as well.

"Syn, hand me a leather gag."

Trance's smile faltered, but his eyes still gleamed with amusement as she gagged him. "Now the ball spreader." As she fastened the device to his balls, his amusement faded. And she wasn't even close to being done. She stripped off the condom.

"Now a paddle."

A low sound came from deep in his chest. Good. He was finally getting it. Oh, and he was going to get it good. She sent a gentle whack across his buttocks.

"Did you enjoy that?" she asked, but he didn't make a sound. "Because I did. You have been very, very naughty." She paddled him again, the smart smack of the rubber on skin ringing in her ears. Inside, the beast urged her to hit him harder, but she resisted.

"I could make you come now. While I'm spanking you."

The slightest tensing of his muscles told her how much he'd hate that. "Yes, I think I might. I think I might prove to you that you could enjoy being punished." She palmed his ass, right where her strikes had heated his skin. "It would bother you, wouldn't it? Knowing that you got off on submitting to someone else's strength."

She trailed a finger down the crack of his ass, felt him clench. "Touchy, are we?" Featherlight strokes over his puckered opening made him clench harder and his shoulders heave. She leaned over him, brushed her lips across the small of his back.

Fresh desire built in her core again at the contact. She couldn't remember the last time—if ever—that she'd been so ready again so soon.

"You know, I've made straight men come while being fucked

by another man. Perhaps I should treat you to the same experience. Syn? Is Jacob with a client? Trance, you'd be in for a treat. He has a big dick, and a big hand made for reach-arounds."

A low, controlled growl rattled Trance's hypertense body. "Is that a no? Because make no mistake, this is my show, and if I want Jacob to fuck you, he will." Trance remained statue-still, but she got the feeling that she'd brought him to the absolute brink of tolerance. She wanted to push him to his limits, not break him, so she sighed in mock resignation. "Back to the spanking, but only because it will bring me more pleasure than watching someone else fuck you."

A knot of lust throbbed in her gut as she gave him several whacks, again and again, until his fine ass turned a lovely shade of pink. "More?" She reached beneath him, barely contained a gasp of approval at how hard he was. He might think he didn't enjoy being bound and at her mercy, but his cock said otherwise.

Slowly, she stroked him, teaching him to associate pleasure with the burn of the spankings. Still, when she dared a peek at his face, this time a gasp escaped her.

Fury and lust burned in his eyes, and she knew that if she let him go right now, he'd be inside her in half a second, and she'd know the meaning of rough and raw. Part of her wanted to release him, wanted to know what being taken—out of pleasure rather than violence—felt like. She was so tired of always being the one in charge. She was tired of these games. But what she wanted didn't matter. She couldn't know how the beast would react to being dominated like that. She couldn't risk changing in the middle of angry, rough sex. The beast would rip everyone in the club to pieces.

"You aren't suitably subdued, boy," she said. "So stubborn."

Tingling with anticipation, she selected a toy from the assortment of dildos hanging on the far wall. Syn fetched a bottle of lube, and Rik took her time slathering the clear gel on the crystal wand. Trance couldn't see what she was doing, but she sensed his growing anxiety. He wasn't afraid, though. She'd have smelled that, and she'd stop.

Smiling, she introduced the tip of the wand to his anus.

Trance went apeshit. His roar of rage was like a cold draft blowing through the room. The scent of his anger was so strong she tasted it on her tongue, a spicy, acrid burn.

She watched his fingers for the safe gesture he'd chosen before undressing, but he didn't make it. Instead, he made fists and tried to break free of the stocks, his biceps bulging and straining. The crack of wood shocked her; he had to be incredibly strong.

"Easy, boy," she murmured, unable to contain her appreciation for his fire and strength. She quickly but gently pushed the dildo inside him while at the same time stroking his cock.

His breath came in harsh pants, but his struggles eased as she thrust in and out with the wand, up and down with her hand. Her subs always liked this, but this man was no sub, and she doubted anyone had ever done this to him. If they had, it had been because he ordered it, but even then, she couldn't see him asking to be fucked with a dildo. No, alphas like him didn't want to be invaded in any way.

She angled the wand to strike his prostate on each stroke, drawing a ragged groan from him. Gradually, his struggles ceased, and he began to rock into her thrusts.

"You've been a very bad boy," she said softly. "I don't know if I should let you come or not." Still thrusting into him, she reached around and unsnapped his gag, letting it fall to the floor. "Are you sorry for disobeying me earlier?"

"Yes . . . *Mistress*." His voice was low, guttural, so thick with need that her own desire whipped through her, making her clit swell and her breasts grow achingly heavy.

"Then I'll release you. When I do, you'll climb on the bondage altar and lay on your back."

"Whatever pleases you, Mistress."

This was too easy. "Given your past behavior, I'll be taking some precautions."

He groaned as she removed the anal wand and fetched a cock cage. He didn't seem angry anymore, but she'd definitely pushed him to his limit, sexually and emotionally, and no way was she going to risk him either finding release with his own hand or jumping on her.

She locked the device, a tube shaped of wire and leather, in place, removed the ball spreader, and released Trance from the stocks. For a moment he stood there, nostrils flaring, chest heaving, and his wild gaze boring into her. Shadows lurked in his eyes, and she knew he was trying to decide how much further he wanted to take this. The internal battle waged in his expression, and she wondered why he was here, doing something so against his nature, and why it was so important to him.

"Do it," she said. "Do it now, or we end this."

The vein in his temple throbbed, but he padded to the altar and lay back as ordered. Quickly, she fastened his arms and legs to the table, for which she earned a brief glare.

Syn ran her hand up his thigh. "This one is worthy of extra attention." Her voice was husky, dripping with desire, and a savage streak of jealousy shot through Rik. "Let's play with him together. You can fuck him while I let him eat my pussy." She grasped his jaw and tilted his face toward her. "Show me your tongue, boy."

Trance nailed Syn with a fierce stare. *"You are not my mistress."* His voice was like gravel tumbling over ice.

He should have obeyed Syn, and Rik should be furious that he didn't, but satisfaction curled through her instead. She swatted Syn's hand away. "He's mine. For tonight," she amended, at the other woman's cocked eyebrow.

Syn huffed. "If you need an extra set of hands, call me."

Once Syn was gone, Rik turned to Trance. "Look at me." He obeyed, but nothing had changed. The battle raged on in the shadows of his eyes, the severe line of his jaw. Something in her melted a little at the sight of a war she understood far too well.

"Why are you doing this, Trance? Why are you forcing yourself to do something you don't want to do?" Her voice was soft as she placed a hand on his chest, felt his heartbeat pound into her palm, coming faster with each passing second. She knew what it was like to go against one's nature. Each time she played the hated role of dominatrix, she lost one more piece of the peaceful, happy girl she'd been before Itor took her. "Did you hurt someone during play? Is that why you're doing this? Penance?"

"I told you—"

"Yes, you said you wanted to learn to submit. I don't believe you. You don't want to learn. You don't want to be here. But you are. Why?"

"My reasons are my own." His voice lowered, throbbed with challenge. "If true confessions are part of this deal, then let me up and I'll go find Syn. She has no interest in my soul. She only wants my tongue."

Jealousy spun up again, and was ruthlessly squashed. If this were a true Dom-sub relationship, she'd push, would spend weeks, maybe months earning enough trust to go deep into his psyche and learn what he needed and why he would force himself to push so hard against his nature. But ultimately, for a one-night stand, she didn't need to know. And she wasn't sure why she even wanted to.

She did, however, know that she didn't want him anywhere near Syn.

"We'll finish what we started." She removed the cock cage and put some steel into her voice once more. "Do you think you've earned an orgasm?"

His lids lowered as he watched her stroke him. "Yes, ma'am."

"Ma'am?" She circled her thumb over a drop of pre-cum at the tip of his shaft. "Were you always so polite?"

A sharp intake of breath made her look up and wonder why the hell she was asking him questions as if she were serving him coffee instead of getting ready to mount him. "Yes, Mistress. Sorry. I slipped."

"I liked it," she said, with no damned trace of the hard edge she'd aimed for. "You can call me ma'am."

Heat bloomed low in her belly as he arched his back into her touch. She should punish him for that, but need consumed her all of a sudden. She needed to fuck him, needed to come.

She fetched the wand once more, climbed up on the table, and straddled his hips. Too late she realized she'd forgotten a condom, though she used them for the sub, not for her. The club provided birth control, and thanks to Itor's experimentation and genetic enhancements, she'd become immune to most human-borne diseases.

Trance didn't seem to mind the lack of protection. He watched, teeth clenched, as she lowered herself onto his hard cock, and when she reached behind and penetrated him with the wand, his eyes rolled into the back of his head.

Satisfaction and warmth sighed through her. He'd gentled to anal penetration, something he'd probably never thought he'd want or enjoy.

For the first time, she wished she could allow herself to continue seeing a sub. She'd like to be the one to tame him, to make him want to serve her. But she didn't have the patience, the trust, or the gentle touch necessary for such work, not when nearly every move she made was calculated to bring *her* pleasure.

Such as now. She rode him slowly, savoring the feel of the thick column impaling her. Her juices coated him, creating a slick, hot friction that made her whimper no matter how hard she bit her lip. A sheen of sweat dampened her breasts as she rocked, putting delicious pressure on her clit with every forward roll.

God, how many sessions had she orchestrated in different clubs? So many, too many, but not one had come close to bringing her the kind of pleasure she'd found with Trance.

And they weren't even finished.

The tendons in Trance's neck strained as he punched his head back on the table. His shaft swelled inside her, but before he blew, she stilled, not quite finished with the torture, even though her womb quivered with the need to find release.

"Beg for it," she said, and though the very idea must have grated on every fiber of his being, he did it. Through clenched teeth.

"Please, Mistress. Fuck me. Make me come."

"That was pathetic." She turned the wand a little, wiggling it to stimulate his prostate, and he gasped. "Tell me again. Tell me what you want."

His gaze caught and held hers, bored into her with an intensity that stole the air from her lungs. "I want to break free of these bonds, bend you the *fuck over* and rail you so hard you scream." He arched up as much as he could, forcing a breath of shock out of her in a rush. "And when I'm done, I want to spank the hell out of you before I tie you down, make you suck my cock and swallow every last drop of my load. Now, will you *please* let me come?"

Holy shit. If she weren't already on her knees, she'd have been knocked to them. No one had ever spoken to her like that. Her body shook with desire even as her mind screamed a warning. This man would never be tamed, and trying to do so would only result in tragedy.

Her body didn't give a rat's ass and began to move of its own accord, finding a punishing, grinding rhythm. "I'm in charge," she ground out, breathless already. "Say it."

"You're in charge," he groaned.

"You like it when I take you. You like to be bound and helpless while I fuck you. Say it. You can come if you say it." She tweaked one of his nipples, encouraging a response. Her own response made itself known in a rush of moisture flowing down his shaft.

His body strained against the bonds, his muscles bulging, his joints popping. "I like being bound. Like when you take me . . . oh, yeah, oh, *fuck!*"

Hot blasts filled her, licking her sensitive inner walls until she flew apart, her entire nervous system lighting up like a stormy sky. Beneath her, Trance jerked and shuddered as she milked the last of his orgasm. Heat poured off him, heat and relief and a touch of irritation. Mixed with those, the scent of blood.

Her eyes flew open, and she nearly cried out at the sight of his chest, scored by her fingernails in deep gouges. A rush of hunger struck before she could be too horrified. It had been too long since she'd let the beast out to hunt, to kill, to rend something apart and eat it raw. She could tamp down the urges with daily meals of uncooked meat, but sometimes, like now, instinct reared its ugly head.

A wicked tugging sensation drew her mouth toward his skin, her mouth watering. Just a taste. That's all she wanted . . .

"Mistress?" Beneath her, Trance bucked. "Mistress! *Daddy*."

She froze at the safe word, her mouth closed over a cut. The heady, coppery taste of his lifeblood coated her tongue and shot through her like an illegal stimulant. Lightning sizzled through her body, making her muscles twitch and her skin tighten until she thought it might split. Inside, the wolf howled, wanting out.

Oh, God. With a muffled cry, she scrambled off Trance. Her breath came in ragged puffs, and her hands shook. Trance was staring at her like she'd already grown fangs.

"No blood play, I guess," she said, hoping she sounded a lot more casual than she felt, hoping to hell he didn't notice the tremor in her voice or the fact that she'd been about to turn into a monster. There was a reason she left blood play to other staff members.

"Not into that."

Quickly, she released him and scooted as far away as possible. "You need to go. And don't come back."

He cocked an eyebrow at her. "But—"

"Don't." She hugged herself tightly, as though to keep her other half contained. "Submission isn't in your DNA. You want to try, you find some other Dom to help you, because my way will take you places you don't want to go. Now get out." She bit her lip and then added, "Stop at the medic room on the way out and have them look at your scratches."

Surprisingly, he didn't argue, merely dressed, though he didn't button up his shirt. Probably because he was still bleeding. He moved toward the door, but paused at the threshold to look back over his shoulder. "You don't want this."

"I know." She blinked. Why had she just said that? Of course she wanted this, wanted him to leave and never come back. So why did she suddenly not want it? She shook her head, trying to clear it, and when she looked at the door, Trance was gone.

CHAPTER
Five

Trance hadn't bothered with the medic—his skin would heal faster than he'd like anyway, and he'd need to keep the wounds open so Rik could track him. And she would—he was sure of it.

He wasn't sure if his psyche would heal all that well, though. His ass burned from the wand she'd used and his balls ached, still sore and heavy in a way that was supposed to remind him he'd been used—and used well.

It only served to remind him that he could never totally give himself up to another person—or animal—like that. His will was strong but his body was stronger, would resist until he broke the bonds and hurt someone. Maybe even himself.

The beast inside of him was angry and strangely satiated.

In the relative safety of the town house ACRO had rented for him, he stripped off his shirt and attempted to calm himself down.

He'd been with ACRO for four years—had been pulled out of the military at twenty-eight, after hearing about the agency from an unidentified source who called to tell him that there were others like him. That he could have a home and continue to help people. That he didn't have to hide his skills all the time.

It had been an invitation he'd resisted, up until two Convincers—also excedos—had come to get him and bring him in by force. From that day on he'd literally never spoken his given family name again—that was locked up tightly with the ACRO files, along with everything else from his past. He'd been on his own for so long that even the military, with its camaraderie, hadn't been able to spark him away from his loneliness. Which was why he'd embraced MP work once he realized the isolation didn't lend itself to making connections. He wasn't supposed to connect with the prisoners anyway, and the other MPs typically burned out after a few years working the prison scene and moved on to combat duty.

No family, few friends and a gift of freakish strength that kept him from even the simplest of relationships that didn't include control.

He'd never known his father and Trance always wondered just how big a piece of his own genetic puzzle the man really was—imagined, when he was still a very young boy, that his father would walk back into his life and fix everything. It never happened and he spent a lot of time vacillating between hating the man and wishing to hell he could find him. In fact, he'd asked the ACRO people to look into tracking his father down, but so far they'd had no luck.

Growing up, he used to tell people that his dad was a secret agent—a powerful man who helped the world. Of course, he got the irony in the fact that today he himself was a secret agent who helped the world.

Trance's mom was only sixteen when she'd had him—she refused to say anything more about his father than to call him *the bastard who left me*. He was only ten years old when she died of a drug overdose. He'd been sure that somehow his father would know this, would finally come forward to claim him.

He didn't and Trance, having been deserted by both parents, was moved around from cousin to aunt to other distant relatives, mainly because he always seemed to get into trouble without meaning to. At the time, he didn't know—or understand—his own strength. Being the new kid at school, he'd always end up in fights.

For as long as he could remember, women couldn't get enough of him, and for a while, he contented himself with the D/s scene. As much as it entailed trust, it also allowed him to keep most women at arm's length.

Now he was inviting one inside. Literally, inside.

He ripped at the scratches on his chest again, not allowing the skin around them to pucker and close. A thin line of blood seeped out and he tried to regain his composure and remember where he'd hidden the tranq gun Kira had given him before he'd left for London.

In case the beast comes out.

According to ACRO's intel, Rik couldn't control the beast once it had emerged. It would attack and feed on anything and everything in its path. That's what made her such a danger to society. It was also why ACRO wanted to try to harness that power. In the right hands, Rik was an asset.

But with that damned collar on, she was a loose cannon. And she was headed directly to his lair.

The problem was, he'd been warned not to use the tranq on her unless she was already chained—with *her* chains, the ones she no doubt had at her apartment, the ones that she would use to control herself when the beast attempted to come out. Since Rik was one of a kind, the vets and docs at ACRO had no idea if the tranq would work at all, and they wanted safety measures in place.

Which was why Trance was at once predator and prey.

His muscles tensed and he stretched them out, felt where he'd been bound hard earlier. And although he knew the knock at his door would be coming, it still made him jump.

He opened the door with his heart pounding, prepared to do whatever he needed to do to subdue the beast, and found Rik on the other side. One look in her eyes and he saw the beast fighting for control. But the woman, she was still there.

Without saying a word, he moved to the side and she strode in, still in her thigh-high boots, a long leather coat swishing around her legs as she moved.

"I came to check on you. To make sure you were all right," she purred, the sound making his cock harden and twitch in seconds. He'd been in a half-aroused state since he'd left the dungeon, despite the intense orgasm.

"I'm all right."

"Why do you keep lying to me, boy? I know you enjoyed yourself tonight, but I also know you're far from fine." She raised her head slightly, closed her eyes and breathed in. The wounds on his chest were closing quickly now that he'd left them alone, but not quick enough. The struggle for control poured off her in waves.

He wanted those mile-long legs wrapped around his waist, wanted his cock so deep inside her that she couldn't think of her collar or the beast—couldn't think of anyone or anything beyond him. And as he wondered where the hell that urge came from, she pushed against him with a flat palm to his chest. She was adrenaline-filled, stronger than she'd been at the club, and he smelled the power and the fear wafting off her skin.

Once he closed the door, she hooked her hand around the back of his neck to pull him close. He complied because that's what she wanted, what she expected.

He complied because he no longer knew what he needed anymore.

ULRIKA WAS going to kiss him.

She'd only kissed one other man, an Itor Seducer whose job it had been to train her in the sensual arts. Her time with Masanao had been pleasant—he had been one of the few people at Itor to show her kindness. But ultimately, she'd been a job to him, and he'd been a welcome break from the experiments and tests that seemed to go on twenty-four seven.

Now there were no tests, no Itor and no sex club. Just Trance and his stark flat, and his lips an inch away from hers.

She hesitated at the last moment. She didn't remember getting here, didn't truly understand why she'd come. In her culture, blood was sacred—not to be drawn lightly. And never, ever did one draw blood without a life-or-death reason. You either killed what you'd bloodied . . . or you mated with it.

Until Trance opened the door, she truly hadn't been sure what she'd intended. The beast wanted to finish off what it had injured. The woman . . . well, she might want sex, but a true Blooded Mating, complete with a ritual to bond them together in marriage? Not so much. Oh, she wanted that, but she had long ago given up the dream.

"Kiss me, Rik."

"Yes . . ." She brushed her lips across Trance's hard, firm mouth—and then realized he'd given her another order. And she'd followed it. With a curse, she shoved away from him. "You do not speak like that to me."

A flash of some emotion she couldn't name crossed his face, and then he was in hers, one hand gripping her upper arm with gentle strength. "We aren't at the club. You're in my house now."

Alarm tripped through her. God, this had been stupid. She shouldn't have come here, shouldn't have risked letting him take the upper hand. That she didn't remember getting here didn't matter. It was just more proof that she couldn't control herself and shouldn't be making any kind of attempt to live around humans. She should have made her way to the wilderness a long time ago, let the beast reign, survive or die as nature willed it.

"Remove your hand," she ground out. "Or you lose it."

"And then what?" He leaned in, so close his lips brushed her ear. "Will you let me do to you what I said earlier? Will you let me spank your pretty little ass, or will I have to just take the initiative?"

She didn't have a chance to so much as gasp in outrage, because he spun her, took her down to the floor on her belly. His arm came around to take the brunt of the impact, but then he was straddling her thighs and pushing her coat up around her waist. He left her skirt covering her butt, but his warm palm came down hard on one cheek.

"Don't," she yelled, even as a shock of pleasure lit into her. "Please. I—I can't."

"I seem to recall saying the same thing." His hand came down again. "And you didn't listen. So why should I?"

"You don't . . . you don't understand." Oh, no . . . no, no, no . . . inside, the fury was building. She had to get away from him.

As if he knew, he shifted his weight and eased his big body over hers, pinning her. Strangely, it was a comforting hold, not restraining, the latter of which would have had the beast exploding out of her skin.

"Make me understand." He nuzzled the back of her neck while stroking her arm, and she felt herself loosen up as the beast settled down, warily, as if it were trying to decide if it liked being petted or not. It definitely hadn't liked being spanked, and tension vibrated her organs even as her muscles relaxed.

"I can't explain," she whispered.

He rested his forehead on her shoulder and sighed. "I know what it's like, you know. To need the control because you've got something inside that's always fighting you. Always haunting you. Sometimes, you just have to let someone help."

"Is that why you've come to me? For help?"

"Yeah." His voice was rough, and she squeezed her eyes shut as if that would close off her ears too. She didn't want to hear any kind of emotion from a man she needed to stay away from.

"Well, I don't need any help. So let me up."

"Only if you promise to see me again."

She jerked in surprise. "Fuck, no."

"Why not?"

"*Let. Me. Up.*" She began to buck as panic frayed the edges of her control. Trance put more weight on her, and squeezed her thighs between his strong ones, effectively immobilizing her lower body.

"Give me a reason, Rik," he said smoothly, as if he gentled wild animals for a living and knew exactly what tone to use. "Make it a good one."

A sob fell from her lips, a humiliating sound she hadn't made in front of another human being in years. "Too many reasons," she said, wishing she could be more specific. She was too dangerous, too damaged, too scared.

Too *not* human.

"That's not good enough."

"Damn you," she croaked. She began to tremble, so afraid she was going to shift into a monster and tear him apart. "Please. *Please!*"

He inhaled raggedly and rolled off her. Immediately, she tried to scramble away, but he dragged her into his arms. The sheer pleasure of being held took the fight out of her momentarily, and she let herself just sink into him, feeling broken and so very tired as tears spilled onto her cheeks, and his shoulder.

Several minutes later, she realized she was crying. On a client. Whom she'd had no business hunting down. Son of a bitch, she was weak. She tore out of his grip, struggling with the half of her that wanted to rip out his throat for daring to touch her. When he reached for her, she hissed, spun on her knees and slapped him hard across the face.

"Don't touch me," she growled. "Don't ever touch me again."

She left him sitting on the floor, the startled expression on his face branded in her mind. She felt so torn in half, angry yet sorry for hitting him, joyful at the moment of comfort he'd given her, yet fiercely pissed off for allowing it.

Making matters worse, she had a feeling he wasn't going to let this go. Running off to her flat wasn't going to be enough. She needed to give notice at the club and move on.

She definitely had to get away from him.

CHAPTER Six

The file was sitting in the middle of Dev's desk the next morning, on top of the pile of paperwork Marlena had left for him. Dev was more than aware that a new recruit shouldn't be taking up his focus—no, he had bigger troubles in the form of Itor Corp and the man who ran it. The man who'd given life to Dev and used him last year in order to gain knowledge about ACRO.

Dev had been making plans—he and Oz had been making plans to wage a war against Itor, the likes of which they'd never survive. Dev had just begun to concentrate on his mission again. And now he was focused on a fucking folder, scared to touch it because he didn't want to know what it held.

He'd spent an uncomfortable night after the guards had come to pick up the wayward operative, spent his time roaming the house and trying not to imagine what the young man would feel like under him.

He fought the urge to bang his head on the desk and gulped his coffee instead.

"Rough night?" Marlena slid a second cup next to him.

He looked up at the beautiful woman who'd been by his side

for nearly six years now. Although it didn't show on her face, she'd had a rough night too. He was as finely tuned in to her as he was to himself.

He'd been woefully neglecting her feelings over the past months while he'd been mourning. She understood, but he had a lot of making up to do.

She glanced at the file. "New guy."

"You've looked."

"Would I do that before you with classified information?"

"Every single time." He couldn't help but grin. "Do we have an intake sheet yet?"

"He filled it out late last night after we got him settled into the trainee quarters." She pulled the papers out of the appointment book she carried with her.

Dev knew if he held the pages between his fingertips, he'd know too much. Having something the new recruit had touched made it much easier for him to get a read. He motioned for Marlena to put it down on the desk instead, and she complied, albeit with a quizzical look.

He picked up the second cup of coffee, took a long sip, and then, "This operative was dropped at my house last night. Any idea who gave those orders?"

"No clue. Did you call the gate?"

"They said he walked away—he claims he was driven to me."

Marlena raised her eyebrows. "I'm assuming reprimands are in order."

"Perhaps even dismissals," Dev growled in agreement. "That's a complete breakdown in protocol."

"I agree. Let me pull the gate records and bring in everyone who worked last night."

Dev rubbed his head, even as Marlena moved behind him to rub his neck. "Thanks."

"I'm here to make your life easier," she said, as Annika slammed into the office without bothering to knock. It didn't matter—Dev had sensed her presence as she rode the elevator to his floor.

"The new guy is a problem," she announced without so much as a "Good morning." She wore her PT uniform—black sweats and black T-shirt, and her blond hair was pulled back in a ponytail. She looked every inch the drill instructor she was.

A drill instructor with the ability to shock people to death.

"Tell me something I don't know." Dev leaned back in his chair. "I didn't call you here to talk about the new guy. He's not my concern now. I have a jet on standby to get to Trance. You'll leave in less than forty-eight hours if all goes as planned, less if it doesn't. You need to be packed and ready to go."

"I'll be ready," Annika told him—she was one operative he didn't have to worry about. Annika had it together when it came to her job. And, of course, if the new guy didn't fall into line immediately, it would annoy her to no end.

"Can we talk about the new guy?" Annika asked, and then continued without waiting for him to answer. "He's giving his handler hell, and he's got attitude out the ass. I know he's had a fucked-up life, but he needs to chill. He's too dangerous to be with the other trainees right now."

A fucked-up life. Dev didn't have to read his file to know it would show desolation. Loneliness. Foster care, juvie and jail. Dev could've exchanged it for over half of his agents with special abilities.

Could've exchanged it for Oz.

Dammit, he didn't want a replacement for his lover. There had to be something more here for Oz to send this operative to him.

Which was crazy, that he was even considering Oz was sending him someone. "Let me talk to Zach about him—maybe time with the animals would do him some good. In the meantime, give him a wide berth."

Annika nodded and left. He prepared to go back to work, except that Marlena was staring at him. "What?"

"You don't know the new recruit's name. You don't want to know it."

He didn't answer. "I thought you were going to get me a list of the guards who worked last night."

She nodded. "Okay, will do, Devlin."

"And take this with you—file it away," he growled, handing her the new recruit's file. She didn't say another word, just took it from his hand and walked out of the office in a huff, and yeah, it was going to be a hell of a day.

THE MAN who'd been told his name was Ryan might be thirty-two years old, but his entire life amounted to eight months of un-remarkable memories, several migraine headaches and two homemade DVDs of fetish porn, starring him and no fewer than six gorgeous, bound women.

Thing was, none of his eight months' worth of memories in-cluded any of the sex he'd had on those DVDs, which was a total fucking bummer, because it looked like he'd had a pretty good time, even if the kind of kink he'd apparently been into didn't look like fun now.

The utter lack of memories was the reason he'd ordered Itor's pilot to take a quick side trip to Frankfurt before continuing on to his final destination.

Ryan ignored the turbulence as the jet descended into its final approach to the German airport. He was too busy flipping through the pages in one of two files he'd brought with him. One file detailed his official mission: capturing or killing a rogue Itor operative named Ulrika Jaeger. The other file detailed his per-sonal mission: finding a woman named Meg Lapp and discover-ing why, when he couldn't remember anything about his past, he remembered her name. Or, at least, the name he'd known her by.

Coco.

And what the fuck kind of name was that?

He pulled her picture from the file, a familiar sensation wash-ing over him as he did so—a bizarre combination of hatred and lust. He had no idea why he might hate her, nor did he know why he threw wood every time he looked at the photo. Maybe they'd been married or something. Itor claimed he'd never been married, and while they hadn't ever given him reason to doubt them, in-stinct told him not to buy into everything they said. That instinct was also the reason he'd kept his search for Coco under the radar, even though he'd covertly used Itor's resources to find her.

Good thing too, because Coco would never have been found by conventional means.

No, his Coco was a clever little thing, whose shady cyberspace dealings kept her on the move and underground.

He ran his finger over the image of her dark, pixie-short hair as though he could smooth the windblown locks. The picture had been taken from a distance while she'd been sipping coffee and pounding away at a laptop at a Parisian outdoor café. Her funky, red-framed glasses sat low on the bridge of her nose, and he'd bet that right after the photo was snapped, she'd pushed them back up.

If the women in his DVD porn were any indication, he was attracted to tall, big-breasted blondes, but something about Coco fired his imagination. She was hot in a nerdy way he shouldn't find sexy if he was the bastard on the DVDs. Then again, his brain had been scrambled and rewired, and he didn't know what he found attractive anymore.

According to Itor, eight months ago he'd suffered a traumatic head injury while on an assignment, resulting in amnesia that left his entire life a big, black hole. Itor doctors had repaired his body, but no matter how hard he tried to remember his past, all he could come up with was the name Coco, something he'd kept to himself.

Itor had showed him evidence of his past . . . gruesome photos of the kills he'd supposedly made, and videos of his sex life that, apparently, he'd recorded. Christ, his life before the brain injury had included a penchant for torture and a seriously fucked-up BDSM habit that went beyond *safe, sane and consensual*.

Which was, in part, why he'd been tasked to bring in Ulrika. The shape-shifter seemed to have found a way to keep her animal side under control by taking sex to an extreme level.

The other reason he'd been given the assignment had more to do with his special abilities than anything else. When Ulrika had been an operative—though rumor had it she'd been less an agent and more a leashed attack dog—he'd been assigned as her comms agent.

She'd had handlers, men and women who operated the device that controlled and tracked her radio-shock collar, but when she went on a mission, she wore a mic to communicate with her handlers and Ryan. Ryan's special ability, electrokinesis, allowed him to see through her eyes, see what she saw, as long as they were in contact via an electronic device. So he knew her, but she'd never seen him. Handy, since he'd have to handle her capture delicately.

Itor had lost one of the only two remote controls when her handler was captured by enemy agents, leading to her escape, but apparently the remaining device was enough to locate her. It had taken months, but they'd finally narrowed down her location to somewhere in London. Unfortunately, they couldn't isolate her exact position, which had seemed odd to Ryan, until his mission supervisor, Miljenko Zoko, explained.

"We made modifications to the device to allow for a larger range than the ten-mile limitation. We were able to increase the collar's range to fifty miles. Unfortunately, the modifications ruined the device's capability of pinpoint accuracy."

"And you want me to track her down?"

"We know she frequents BDSM and fetish clubs. That's where you come in. You're familiar with the lifestyle and the lingo, so you'll fit in. And there can't be that many in London. You'll have her in no time, especially if you have the remote. Turn it on, and you should be able to see what she sees. If she looks at a street sign, a storefront . . . You get the picture. Find her club, and with your background, you're set."

Yeah, well, he couldn't remember the lifestyle or the lingo. Not that he was about to tell Zoko that. He'd been itching to get the hell out of the island Itor compound he'd been stuck in for months. Especially since he'd tracked down Coco, and who the hell knew when she'd up and move again.

"One other thing," Zoko said. *"Our modifications caused some power surges . . . it's possible that she's felt a mild buzz or shock in the collar. She may be extra-alert or even ready to run. Be careful."*

That conversation had taken place this morning, and now he

was on his way to London, but not until he had a little chat with Coco. Or, more accurately, a long, involved interrogation that would require her to accompany him while he hunted down Ulrika. He had a car waiting at the airport, Coco's address in hand, and he was taking her from her apartment if he had to kidnap her—which he was fully prepared to do.

Because he'd had enough of not remembering his past. The people at Itor had told him all about it, had told him how he'd served in the U.S. Marines, using the military to illegally sell arms, and when he got busted, Itor had picked him up. He'd been with Itor ever since, and the things they said he'd done for them . . . Yeah, he was a coldhearted scumbag, even if he didn't recall any of it.

But something didn't feel right, and he needed to know why. Somehow, he knew Coco was the key to his murky past, and she was going to unlock it, no matter how terrified he was that his past might be better left forgotten.

"WHERE HAVE YOU been? You were supposed to check in with me last week."

"Don't get all big brother on me, big brother." Meg pushed the glasses back up on her nose before taking a sip of her Caramel Macchiato and glancing around the outdoor café in Frankfurt, where she'd been spending the past month. "Obviously, I'm fine."

Mose—or ML, as he called himself these days—sighed on the other end of the line. Nothing she hadn't heard before from him, the same way she'd heard it from her mother and father years earlier. "You're never fine. Don't you think you've been on the run long enough?"

"I don't consider it running." As she spoke, she typed in the code that allowed her to access the bank accounts of some of the richest men in Germany. She had no plans to change their status, but knowing she could satisfied her almost as much as the caffeine.

Why she did it was more of a mystery than the how—numbers

had always been her thing, had come as easily to her as breathing from the time she was a little girl. When her formal education ended in eighth grade, as was the tradition in her Amish sect, she'd continued studying everything she could in mathematics and science, using books and papers smuggled to her from other Amish teens, fresh from their *rumspringa*. Mose helped her with this—had made friends with a group of older boys who roamed through the Amish areas riding their dirt bikes. He'd sneak out with them at night and come home with various gifts for Meg, like the laptop he'd brought her.

At night, she'd connect to the single working phone line in the house—used for emergencies only—and she'd learned about the world beyond her narrow one.

Her earliest memory was of wanting independence so fiercely it made her teeth ache.

Growing up, she and Mose never seemed to fit in with the community. At times, her parents would stare at them as if they were aliens.

They'd done the same to her sister, Mary. Like their sister before them, Meg and Mose had left their community and been ostracized.

The big difference was that they were alive. Mary had gotten sick—cancer—and her parents had refused to help her. To even take her calls.

Meg spoke to her once—Mary's voice was barely a whisper. And then their mother had come by and hung up the phone.

Later, Meg caught her mother crying, and Meg's young mind couldn't rectify believing in something that forced you to act so cruelly.

"How can something that professes to be all about goodness have so much bad in it?" she'd asked her brother once, after they'd been on their own for five years.

"It's their belief system, Meg. Sometimes people need something to hold on to," Mose had said.

"You don't hate them anymore?"

"For years, I thought I did. But then, well, everyone needs something to believe in."

Everything she did for a long time was to defy her parents and her old faith—these days, it was all about repenting for her own wrongs.

When she and Mose finished their *rumspringa,* they'd chosen not to go back and be baptized. Which meant they were both shunned by their family and the entire community, as was the tradition. As painful as that break was, for Meg—for Mose as well—there had been no other choice.

And so, she'd been freed—free, scared and exhilarated at the same time.

The woman Mose loved did return to the community, no matter how hard he'd tried to convince her not to. Meg knew that had broken Mose's heart—that he still didn't trust any woman, beyond Meg, to keep her word.

They'd waited six hours for her to show before Mose finally started the old car he'd rebuilt from scrap and headed toward Florida.

The easygoing surfer-boy attitude covered the man of steel, the one who'd always needed to prove that he could be good enough. And he had proven it, the way he'd learned from Abe Goldman, a man he'd met as soon as they'd gotten to Miami.

Abe's pawnshop fronted a money-laundering operation in the back. At first, she and Mose only worked the front of the store, but eventually Mose was let in on the illegal business.

Abe left the store—the money operation—to Mose when he died. Had thought of Mose like a son, and in turn Mose learned from Abe everything he could about money laundering and various other activities that weren't exactly aboveboard. And so, ten years after they'd left their roots and their home behind, Mose had turned himself into ML, one of the most successful money launderers on the East Coast—and one of the hardest to get to as well. And Meg had spent her time playing with other people's money—and ultimately, their lives.

"You've got people on your tail, Coco." Mose used her call name, the one she utilized when she was hacking. "I think you should come here—I'll send a jet for you."

She could fly to Florida and spend her days behind Mose's gorgeous, gated-wall mansion. Right now, her biggest concern was Interpol and a man who'd been tracking her to the ends of the earth.

Possibly, a man she'd thought was long dead.

There were many, many people she'd stolen money from over the years, all of them pissed off beyond belief, not the least of whom was the ultrapowerful Itor Corp, who her brother had been forced to tell her the truth about after she'd inadvertently interrupted a deal they'd been making with the Taliban. But most of her targets were wealthy, corrupt individuals, and as far as she knew, none of them had ever had their lives threatened because of what she'd done, except for Ryan. That transaction had happened nearly five years earlier—and to this day she had no idea if he was dead or alive.

The thought that she might have been responsible for a man's death—even a man who'd betrayed her as badly as he had—haunted her daily.

You were stupid to trust him anyway, she'd told herself fiercely, time and time again. Because a man had once promised to take care of her sister, Mary, and that man had dumped her sister at a city hospital, where she died in a room stuffed with eight people and the minimum of medical care. So for Ryan to convince Meg that he could be there for her—that he wouldn't abandon her, had taken almost a year. A year of talking every day, sometimes for hours, online.

He knew everything about her—about her religious upbringing, her fears, her past.

Ryan had given her enough erotic fodder to last her a lifetime of dreams, had made her blush and laugh with his frank descriptions of what he wanted to do to her when he finally met her. He'd loved her shy descriptions of what she wanted to do with him, and gradually, she'd gotten bolder.

So yes, he'd known it all, and then, on the day they were supposed to finally meet, face-to-face, he hadn't shown. She'd sat at a café very much like this one, and she'd waited. For six hours—just the way Mose had for his girlfriend, and then she'd gone home and she'd stolen money right out from under him—a big transaction she'd promised she wouldn't touch.

Twenty-five million dollars.

When she'd intercepted the money transfer to Ryan from the gunrunners who were making a trade, it had been thanks to a tip-off from Mose.

According to ML, Ryan had arms dealers and terrorists after his ass immediately following the transfer—and then neither of them heard anything. For all intents and purposes, Ryan had dropped off the face of the earth.

From that time on, much to her brother's dismay, Meg gave all her money to hospital charities. Lately, it was getting harder to top herself, to get the thrill she used to from stealing from the extreme rich. Yes, it still gave her pleasure to know the money went to good use, as she never owned more than she could carry with her at any given time. It was how she'd grown up, and how she traveled with such ease.

She'd also never given up on prayer, even though in the Amish tradition it stated that prayer and God had given up on her when she left the faith.

She chose not to believe that she'd been abandoned that easily. She'd heard in recent weeks that Ryan was alive—and that his eye was on *her* ass.

"I'm not planning on staying here much longer—I've got a flight out tomorrow." Changing locations and her personal style each trip kept the heat off her. Since arriving in Germany, she wore her short cap of dark hair with no hints of color other than natural highlights. She dressed high-end—Chanel. Manolo Blahniks that killed her feet, but gave her the haughty air of a woman who wasn't to be bothered. The large, dark sunglasses she wore, rain or shine, indoor or out, rounded out the look.

She enjoyed playing dress-up, but deep down, she'd already

found herself—a no-nonsense, jeans and T-shirt woman who wondered if she'd ever get away from the online world to live in the real one again.

In her parents' eyes, she was most definitely beyond redemption. In her own, she wasn't so sure.

As she typed, and listened to Mose giving her advice—all of it unsolicited—someone sat down across from her—a man, from the look of his hands on the small table. She didn't look up at his face at first, because this happened quite a bit. Men saw a woman sitting alone and instantly assumed she was lonely.

Okay, well, she *was* lonely, but not desperate. But when she finally glanced up, said desperation ran hot through her body, tightened her throat. She pressed her thighs together and wondered if the man knew he was beautiful.

She wondered why he bothered sitting here with her.

He had dark, fierce eyes—his body was strung tight, like he could hit the ground running at any second. Definitely not your garden-variety computer geek. Not by a long shot.

"Interpol is at your apartment right now," he said, instead of the more traditional nice-to-meet-you greeting she'd been expecting. At his words, her back straightened and she closed the lid of the laptop with a crisp snap and waited for him to continue. "There's a note there, from you, in your date book, with the name of this café penciled in. So I'm guessing that in about five minutes or less, they'll be here, looking for you."

"Meg, are you listening to me?" Mose asked.

"I'm going to have to call you back," she told her brother calmly and then clicked the phone closed and asked the man sitting across from her, "What is it you'd like me to do?"

"Come with me, Coco. You've got some explaining to do."

Coco. Suddenly, she knew, without a doubt, that the man in front of her was Ryan. And that she was, in a word, screwed. To the wall. "And why would I do that, Ryan?"

He barely registered surprise, but his fists curled. "You know me, then."

She couldn't breathe. There was a time she'd known him—better, she'd thought, than anyone. But she'd been so wrong and wore the scars inside her heart to prove it. She wouldn't let herself be wrong again. "As well as you know me. Although you're five years too late."

He ignored that—or he seemed to anyway. "As I said, it's your choice. Me or the police." He grabbed her drink and took a nice, long pull from the straw. Out of the corner of her eye, she caught the familiar green-and-white car that always signaled trouble.

The police. Or Ryan—who, if given the opportunity, might strangle her.

After she'd left her home, she promised herself that she'd never live in a place with so many rules and regulations again. She'd rather take her chances . . . rather be dead than bound.

She stood and held out her hand to him, as if they were lovers leaving after sharing a lovely meal at an outdoor café. Ryan stared between it and her, and for just a second she swore she saw something behind those eyes . . . something that she'd dreamed about all those years ago. And then he took her hand, his palm cool and strong against hers, and she fought the fleeting urge to ask him to kiss her, to do things to her body that he'd promised so long ago. To ask him not to kill her.

So yes, Ryan it was.

SURPRISINGLY, COCO didn't give Ryan any trouble on the way to the airport. In fact, she didn't say a word. Which was fine, because he was still trying to figure out how to handle her. Even after she calmly buckled herself into a seat on the Itor jet, she just sat there watching him, looking all fucking brave, cute and innocent.

Innocent, my ass.

He still didn't know why he hated her, but he did know she was into some seriously illegal activities, which meant she was about as innocent as a street whore.

He cursed, unsure where to start the interrogation. He'd

hoped he'd see her face, hear her voice, and magically his memory would come back. A foolish wish, and one that hadn't come true.

As the jet taxied on the tarmac, he settled himself in the seat across from her, tempted to cuff her to keep her from trying something stupid, but decided to let her try, if that was the way she wanted to play it. He'd show her exactly why he was in charge.

But for now, he said nothing. Just watched her until she began to squirm in her designer clothes. Nice stuff, with the labels all right there for the world to see and admire and envy. He didn't give a rat's ass about an outfit so expensive the money spent on it could have fed a small country. He just wanted to know if he'd seen the body beneath the clothes.

"So," he said, sprawling casually back in his seat, "why do you think you're here?"

She took the glasses off. "I have no idea."

"Oh, I think you do." At least, he hoped she did, because he was pretty clueless himself, but he didn't want to give away his memory issues until it became absolutely necessary.

"Are you going to kill me?"

He had to give her credit; she looked him straight in the eye and spoke with an even, strong voice. Too bad he needed her to be rattled. He leaned forward in his seat, braced his forearms on his spread knees. "Now, why would I do that?"

Maybe because they'd been married and he'd come home to find her in bed with another man.

"Unless I get you your twenty-five million back, you mean."

Okay, so maybe she hadn't fucked the pool boy. But twenty-five million? What the hell had he been doing with that kind of money? Hold on . . . the arms dealing. Of course.

He leaned in even closer, so their knees were almost touching, and probed a little more. "Can you get it?"

"My brother can." She squeezed the chair's armrest as the jet started its takeoff. He couldn't tell if she didn't like flying or if the whole money-brother thing was making her nervous. "No problem. I just need to call him."

"I'll bet. And while you're at it, you can tell him who I am so he can use the money to hunt me down. I don't think so." Not that he was worried. He had Itor at his back, and no one fucked with them. "It's not the money I'm after anyway."

"Then what? It's a little late for a date."

A date? For what? "You aren't my type." More bluffing.

He could have sworn hurt flashed in her eyes, but then it was gone and she was frowning. He could practically hear the gears in her brain working overtime to figure out why he was here. He knew when she'd come to the worst conclusion, because she paled, making a light sprinkling of freckles pop out across the bridge of her nose. "You want revenge."

"Do you blame me?" Man, he was talking out of his ass here.

"It's not necessary. You aren't dead. So you've escaped the arms dealers . . . unless . . . did they hold you prisoner all this time? Were you in hiding? Did they do something to you?" She flushed, looked out the window for a moment, and then turned back to him. "I mean, my point is that they didn't kill you, and I can get you the money—with interest—so there's no need for revenge. You can pay those guys off—"

"So you think this is about money. And arms dealers." Made sense, because he'd probably been homicidally pissed about losing that much money. Still, he wanted to make sure there wasn't more to their relationship. She'd said something back at the café about it being five years too late . . .

"Well, gee, since all you seem to care about is money and arms dealers, I don't see how I could believe you'd kidnap me for any other reason. *Since I'm not your type.*"

Touchy. "Did we ever fuck?"

Her gasp of outrage pretty much answered that. "Do you sleep with so many women that you can't remember whether or not *we* slept together?"

He shrugged. "Maybe it's you who doesn't remember." He

trailed one finger over her knee and smiled. "Nah. You'd remember if I'd taken you to bed."

"You arrogant ass." She slapped his hand away. "You were a mark. That's all you ever were to me."

He got the impression she was lying, but why? "Hell of a way to speak to a guy who wants revenge, don't you think? I'm amazed that with that mouth, none of your other *marks* have killed you."

Yeah, that put the fear back into her big brown eyes. It only lasted for a moment, though, before she just looked tired. And maybe a little guilty. Was it possible that she felt bad about stealing his money?

"Just...please...stop playing these games and tell me what you want," she murmured.

Good question. He'd hoped to learn more from her, but so far, she'd only confirmed what Itor had told him about being an arms dealer. The twenty-five million she'd stolen from him was new information, but now it made sense why Itor had said they'd saved his life. If arms dealers had been after him because he'd lost their money, he'd been in a shitload of trouble.

So now what? He was stuck on a plane with a woman who didn't know enough about him to help...but then, she was some sort of genius with a computer. And she owed him. He could use her. He eyed her slim ankles, long legs, perfect breasts.

Oh, yeah. He could use her. In more ways than one.

CHAPTER
Seven

Trance had worked out for four hours after Rik left his house last night. No matter how much weight he lifted, how far he ran, how much he jerked off, he couldn't get the sound of Rik crying from echoing in his ears or the feel of her hand on the back of his neck.

Unconsciously, he rubbed a palm over the skin that she'd touched—it still tingled, much like the lingering afterburn of a cat-o'-nine-tails. He wondered if her ass felt the same, and, Christ, the feeling of her under him, pinned to the ground . . .

Yeah, he wasn't thinking like a sub at all now, but the way Rik had acted brought out his dominant tendencies—his protective ones too.

There was so much pain trapped inside of her along with the beast who lurked . . . and he'd nearly pushed her too far last night. Had felt the stirrings, the strength rise up in her. If she'd been his sub, he'd have pushed her—but with Rik, she'd have shifted and he wouldn't have survived.

As it was, he knew survival of any kind with Rik wouldn't come without a price.

"Welcome back." The guy at the door gave him a once-over as he scanned Trance's card and let him into the discreet alleyway entrance.

The club was more crowded than he would've liked. Couple that with the fact that he'd gotten no assurances from Rik that she'd play with him again, and his body rode the knife's blade. Coming back into this world was not good at all. For him, acting the part of the dominant had been the best way he could think to handle his strength, to temper himself enough not to hurt someone accidentally. It had been a delicate balancing act, but this, the submission, was excruciating.

He'd spoken with Kira earlier—thankfully, she'd answered the phone and not asshole Ender.

"I'm screwed," he'd told her. "Rik's refusing to use me a third time."

He winced as he thought about saying that, but remembered that her voice had been gentle when she told him, "That's not a bad sign, Trance. Rik's had you twice—broken her rules. At heart, she knows she's getting attached, and so she's pulling back. But she's also an animal with animal instincts, so when she wants something, she wants it and doesn't know or care why. If you've bonded with her on any level at all, she's going to see you as hers. She won't like seeing what's hers flirting with other females. If you've gotten to her at all, animal instinct is going to override her human common sense."

Play on Rik's animal side . . . Yeah, he could do that. Wanted to, actually. When he'd arrived and saw her circling another man, his own animalistic tendencies reared up from nowhere.

It was in his nature to be protective, but he'd never felt that on an ACRO mission. This wasn't the time for emotions—just cold, hard logic.

Man, he was fucked.

"Trance, are you here to play tonight?" Syndee sidled up to him at the bar and he turned his body to her, catching her between his thighs.

"I might need some convincing."

Her hands ran up his leather-clad thighs. "I've got plenty of practice in convincing. But I don't want to step on Mistress Rik's toes."

"I don't see her next to me—do you?"

Syndee looked at him, her head cocked, before she ran a long fingernail across his cheek, ending at his lower lip. "If you were mine, I'd never leave you alone."

Even as she spoke, two other women circled him. "Would you mind sharing me, though?" he asked, and Syndee motioned the other women over.

Even though he wasn't enjoying acting like an eighth-grade boy in a room full of naked women, he could practically feel Rik's reach. She'd moved closer to where he sat, her teeth slightly bared, and when one of the mistresses put her arms around his shoulders and leaned in to nibble his neck, she walked toward him.

There was something in her stride, the way she moved so purposefully, that made the women back away. He forced himself to stay where he was, leaning lazily against the bar. He kept his legs spread, making sure she could see the bulge in his pants.

It hadn't been there a few minutes ago—only started when she came toward him.

"What are you doing, boy?"

"Syndee asked me to play." He could've sworn he heard a low growl.

"You're not in charge of yourself anymore—you don't get to make those decisions," she told him quietly as she moved in closer, between his thighs the way Syndee had.

"Who is in charge of me, then? Because when I asked you last night, you refused the job."

"You were out of line last night."

"You came to see me, remember? No one in here's made you feel the way I do."

"You're very presumptuous. Perhaps Syndee would be better suited to your attitude."

"That's bullshit and you know it. You're suited for me."

She sucked in a breath and he wondered if he'd taken it a step too far. But then she glanced over his shoulder—he did the same, saw Syndee staring at him.

"Are you going to save me from her, Mistress?"

"I didn't realize she was the big, bad wolf." Her eyes flashed briefly, and he found himself sucking wind at how beautiful she looked. "You'll do whatever I ask of you, boy."

"Yes, ma'am," he breathed against her cheek, felt her stiffen as though his words produced an orgasm. Her hands clenched around his wrists, human bonds.

"You won't resist."

"No, ma'am."

"Go to room four. Strip and wait for me. I've got plans for you."

ULRIKA STOOD outside the door to the room where Trance waited, afraid to go inside. Right now it was all she could do to stand up, let alone walk in.

She'd become aware of his presence the moment he'd entered the club, and for a while, she'd honestly believed she could ignore him. Could let him play with any other Dom. But out of nowhere, a possessive urge had risen up, and the only thing she could think when she'd seen Syndee with him was *Mine*.

Didn't matter that the reason she'd come into the club was to tell the manager she was quitting. Trance had walked in and instead of leaving like she should have, she'd stuck around, half-heartedly playing with other men, when the one she wanted had been right in front of her.

Why was she so incredibly weak when it came to him? She shook her head, because it didn't matter. Time to buck up, do the job, feed the beast, and get the hell out of there. This was the last she'd ever see of him. The last she planned to see of any man. Because today she was heading for the hills, where nature would just have to take its course.

Time to be strong.

TRANCE LAY flat on his back and waited as Rik began to strap him to the metal table.

He closed his eyes for a second to get himself to that mental place he needed to be, because he'd known exactly what she planned once he saw the medical tray and steel tools.

"Eyes open, boy. Or do you need a stronger reminder of who's in control of your body?"

The straps that locked his wrists to his sides, and his ankles so his legs were slightly spread, were strong—needed to be for what happened in this room. He tested them discreetly and knew he'd break them in seconds.

"I asked you a question." Rik placed a finger under his chin, her nail firm against the soft flesh. Her other hand trailed down his chest, fingertips squeezing a nipple until he arched up as far as the bonds should've allowed.

If he couldn't restrain himself from that touch, he had no shot for what was about to come. "I know who's in control of my body, Mistress."

She laughed, a low, throaty sound. "I'm sure you think you do. I'm here to show you so you'll have no doubt."

She took her hands off him and he forced his breathing to slow, told himself that it would be all right as he watched her snap on surgical gloves and lube up one of the objects on the tray.

Jesus Christ Almighty—she was going to use the sounds on him. Medical play wasn't something he used as a Dom, and he'd always known he wouldn't be able to hold himself still enough to let a metal wand be put down his urethra to massage his prostate. It was supposed to be intense—incredible—and required an inordinate amount of trust in the person wielding the instrument.

She grabbed his cock without warning, a firm grip under the head, and used a talented finger and thumb to stretch the skin over the head of his cock tight before inserting the cold metal dittle sound into the small hole. Instinctively, his body surged upward and his eyes screwed shut.

"Eyes open," she commanded. "I want you to watch while I do this to you."

He did as he was told, swallowed hard as the sound began to travel down his urethra.

A long, low keening moan escaped his throat—he hated himself for it, for the total loss of control, the way his mouth dropped and his skin broke out in a sheen of sweat, hated the way Rik knew how much pleasure she was giving him.

She held a strong hand on his abdomen, and that would be enough for a few minutes at least. She manipulated his cock, let the sound move deeper, her ultimate goal to let the curved edge of the wand massage his prostate.

He wouldn't be able to stay still, to not hurt himself. He was going to have to use his safe word, but he resisted doing so with every fiber of his being as the steel tip brushed his prostate and the jolt of complete and utter pleasure nearly drove him off the table.

"My boy likes this," she murmured. "This is just the beginning. We'll work up to the bigger ones."

"Rik," he said through his deep panting breaths. "I can't..."

"It's *Mistress*. And you will."

"No, please..."

"Relax. You can't go anywhere."

"He watched the sound drop more as he held his breath, his entire body turning into one long shudder. "Please, just stop for one second."

"You don't make the rules."

"Rik..."

"I don't hear your safe word, boy."

He held his body as steady as he could while he lifted his arm with no effort and took the bonds with him, metal rings and all. And then he stared at them, as if it had all been an accident. "I'm sorry, Mistress—the chains must've been weak."

She'd stopped moving the sound against his prostate but still held his cock in one hand and the sound firmly with two fingers so it wouldn't drop farther. And she stared at him, mouth open. When she'd composed herself, she whispered, "Excedosapien."

He kept his teeth gritted because his life was still literally in her hands, and feigned confusion. "What are you talking about?"

He remembered the first time he'd been branded with that

name—it had been a relief and a burden at the same time to know there was a term for what he'd always felt was an affliction.

"It's something that shouldn't be discussed here." She paused and lowered her voice. "It explains your strength."

"So you're going to give me some freak name and expect me to think that explains what I've been dealing with for my whole life? You think you understand what it's like?"

"I understand, better than you know," she murmured.

"No one understands me." He stared up at the ceiling, bracing himself for what would happen when she took the sound out. "We need to end this. Now."

It was sheer strength of will that kept him from flying off the table as she pulled the sound out slowly and the orgasm took him over. He didn't bother to hold back this time, let his body rip the other bonds from the table as his cock pulsed and his body strained from pleasure. And then he turned on his side, pressed his cheek to the cold metal and trembled with the loss of control.

Rik's hand touched his shoulder. "I won't let anything hurt my boy."

Play to the animal. Play hurt. "I'm not anyone's fucking boy." He shook off her touch and climbed off the table, grabbing for a towel to wipe himself down.

"Come back here."

He shook his head but he didn't go any farther, a small concession to her. Maybe she'd invite him to her house—there, in her own environment, her guard would naturally go down. And maybe his hypnotic powers would actually be less than useless. But there would be a bigger price to pay—he was actually submitting to her and a not so small part of him was liking it, and *fuck,* he was already nearly broken.

Until then, he was naked and vulnerable and, dammit, he felt stripped raw.

When she spoke again, there was an invitation but she wasn't willing to take him all the way. Yet. "I know you don't believe me, but . . . I can help. I have chains that will hold you. I can hold you and I can protect you."

For maybe the first time in his life, he actually believed that could be true, that she was strong enough to do both.

Whether he was strong enough to hold and protect her remained to be seen. He grabbed his clothes and headed for the shower without a look back at her.

CHAPTER
eight

Ryan sat at The Dungeon's bar, keeping an eye on everyone in the place. He'd expected to walk in and feel a sense of familiarity, but there was nothing here that stirred a damned thing. No, the only thing that had been stirred in months was his dick, and that was Coco's doing.

He thought about her, tied and gagged in the plane, wondered how pissed she was right about now. He'd hoped that seeing her would instantly restore his memory or something, but nope. Nada.

Fuck.

He stood, needing to stretch his legs. Needing to find Ulrika, because he knew for sure she was here. He'd turned on her collar's remote control unit the moment his jet had landed, and as luck would have it, she was within range of its signal. He'd instantly been given a view of some guy's hairy ass as Ulrika slapped it with a flog. A few moments later, she'd gone to the bar, and when her gaze lit on a box of matches, he'd gotten the name of the place. God, it was too easy.

"Jesus Christ. *Ryan?*" The deep male voice made Ryan's stomach drop. Friend or foe, he shouldn't know anyone in this dive.

Slowly, he turned. Saw a guy he didn't recognize, but who clearly knew him. The guy was pale as a ghost.

"Yeah. Hey, man," Ryan said. At this point, playing along was pretty much his only option.

"Jesus," the guy repeated. "I thought you were dead. Does Dev know . . . did he send you?"

Dev? That sounded familiar. But why? "Ah, yeah." Way to be smooth. And why would Dev . . . wait . . . Dev could be Devlin O'Malley. The head of Itor's enemy, ACRO. Suddenly, the pieces of the puzzle slammed together. This stranger was an ACRO agent. And it was way too coincidental for him to be in the same place as Ryan's target.

But why did the ACRO agent know him? Had Ryan been a double agent? Shit, he was in way over his head here and at a serious disadvantage. The only thing he could do right now was bluff, find out what this guy's exact mission was. Capture or kill?

"Look, Dev wants me to back you up. Just tell me what you need."

"I'm surprised he didn't tell me you were coming."

Ryan shrugged. "You know how he is."

"Yeah, I do. Which is why I'm surprised. And why you? Why not Annika or Akbar?"

Good thing it was hot in here, because Ryan was going to start sweating any moment. "My personal background," he said, casting a meaningful glance at the equipment room. "And I was in the area, now that I'm out of my deep undercover."

The guy's eyes narrowed, but then he nodded. "Whatever Dev says. I'm going to hit the shower. Why don't we meet at the pub next door in half an hour, and I'll explain everything."

"You got it," Ryan said, with absolutely no intention of meeting this guy anywhere. He was going to nab Ulrika, and if that didn't work, he had a little remote-controlled detonator in his pocket. Either way, he was going to accomplish his mission in the next thirty minutes.

RIK HAD WAITED until Trance left the room before sinking to her knees on the floor. She'd tried to play tough, to make up for yesterday, when she'd lost control at his flat. Fortunately, all she'd lost control of had been her emotions. If she'd lost control of the beast . . .

She buried her face in her hands and wished she'd been stronger when she'd seen him surrounded by Syn, Cher and Blaise. Which had pissed her off and made her go to extremes with him. The beast had wanted even more extreme treatment, and now she knew why. It had sensed something in him she hadn't.

Excedosapien.

Her mind had spun and her legs had turned to noodles. She'd never encountered a Special Ability type outside of Itor, and her first instinct had been to either kill him or run. But she'd sensed pain in him that couldn't be faked, and her suspicion had veered quickly to empathy. She knew how it felt to be an oddball, to feel so alone.

And now she knew why he was coming to the club. He was afraid of his own abilities, the destructive power of his strength, and he needed to learn how to manage it. She got that, wished she could be taught a better way to contain her own inner demon other than sex, domination and the occasional hunt.

She was out of luck, but Trance didn't have to be. She could help him.

She was an idiot for offering, and an idiot for considering it. So much could go wrong. But maybe if she stayed strong, kept their relationship professional and only met here at the club, it could work. Maybe . . .

The hair on the back of her neck stood up. Crouching, she scented the air. Something wasn't right. Her hand hovered near the top of her thigh-high boot as she crept toward the door. She always kept a concealed weapon on her, and today she had a razor-sharp stiletto tucked into her boot.

The hall was empty, save for a security guard. Heart kicking so hard her ribs hurt, she took the corner between the client-room area and the bar. Her senses were tingling, a strange sensation she'd felt before . . . every time she went on a mission for Itor.

The bar was packed. She hung back, looking for Trance. She saw him talking to some guy near an empty table. His posture was tense, his scent anxious. The other man . . . he was the source of the danger sensation.

She backed away, her lungs constricting. She might not know how to defend herself, but she had one hell of a flight reflex, and it was screaming for her to get out of there. Clumsily, because in her panic her feet didn't seem to work right, she raced to the employee room.

Coat. Purse. Keys.

She tried to control her breathing, tried to think, failed in both. Oh, God, she was in trouble. She'd kill herself before she let anyone capture her. Then again, those Itor bastards could blow her head off at the touch of a button if they were close enough, so maybe she'd die anyway.

Trance caught her as she whipped open the door and stepped into the hall. "Rik, what are you doing?"

"I-I'm sorry," she mumbled. "Have to go." She started past him, but he captured her wrist, his hold firm and unyielding.

"What's going on?"

She swallowed hard, felt the scrape of the dreaded collar on her skin, an ever-present, horrifying reminder that she was on the run, never safe. Never free. Trance's clamp on her arm only magnified her terror.

"Let go of me." She struggled against his hold, wishing her voice didn't shake. That her knees weren't doing the same.

He blinked as though he hadn't even realized he'd grabbed her, and then he released her. "God, Rik, I'm sorry. Did I hurt you?"

"What? Oh, no." His strength . . . he'd been worried he'd injured her with his strength. Didn't matter. Nothing mattered but the danger sensation that still crawled over her skin like ants. "Who was that man you were talking to?"

"I don't know." His voice lowered. "But he was asking a lot of questions about you. I think he saw us together. Are you in trouble?"

Oh, shit. Shit, shit, shit. "It's nothing." She inched toward the exit, her panic starting to cloud her mind. The dark-haired man might be a nobody, maybe just someone who'd come for her reputation, but if she was building a rep . . . that was bad too. Itor could find her.

"Bullshit." He moved with her, a mass of lean muscle and sudden anger. "Don't lie to me. Is someone trying to hurt you?"

A buzz of pleasure replaced the fear for a split second. Trance cared. She felt it in his fury, smelled it in his anger. Damn, she was scared, had been alone for so long and just this once she wanted someone to care whether she lived or died.

Then there was the fact that Trance was . . . special. Enough to put him in danger. She hated this, but maybe it was time to let someone in. Just a little. She couldn't run off and leave him to Itor—if the newcomer was, indeed, an agent.

"Look, this is going to sound crazy," she blurted. "But yes, there are some very bad people after me. They use people like us . . . I mean, like you. You aren't safe if they know what you are."

One blond brow arched. "That does sound crazy, but we can talk about that later. Right now . . . the guy strikes me as trouble, even if he's just a stalker."

"He's more than that." She measured the distance to the side exit. Twenty steps, at the most. "We have to get out of here."

"I told him I'd meet him next door in half an hour."

"Why?"

Trance grinned, like all of this was a game. He didn't understand the gravity of the situation, and she wasn't sure how she'd explain, but she'd work that out later.

"To give us time to bail," he said, taking her hand and pulling her toward the door. "I'm hoping he'll either head over there or think he has a little time to get to you while I'm waiting for him."

"Thank you." She had to choke out the words, because as grateful as she was, she couldn't—wouldn't—forget that the last person who helped her had paid with his life.

THEY HIT the door at a run and exploded into the alley where Trance had saved her the other night.

"This way," she said, heading for the street. "We can take the tube to—"

"I have a car."

He took her hand and dragged her in the opposite direction.

They dashed up a side street and behind a block of apartments. Ahead, a black BMW flashed its lights and beeped. "There," he said, keys in hand as he opened the passenger door for her. He hopped in the driver's seat, and in moments, they were on the road.

She kept an eye out for a tail, and she noticed he did the same, calmly, probably because he still didn't realize the danger they were in.

He wasn't the one with an explosive device around his neck.

She didn't know what range the bomb's signal had, but she did know the shock would turn her into a beast within a ten-mile radius. If the agent back at the club had the remote, he could turn her into a monster right now, and she'd rip Trance apart there in the vehicle.

"Where are we going?" he asked, as he approached a multilane roundabout.

She hesitated. Instinct made her want to keep her lair secret, but then, if Itor was here, it wouldn't stay secret for long. "My place. I need to grab some things. After that . . ."

"We'll figure something out."

"Take the first right, then." She eased around in her seat, making sure no one turned with them, and breathed a sigh of relief. "Nice car. What do you do for a living?"

"I'm an accountant for a law firm."

She snorted. "You're not an accountant."

"I'm not?"

"You're too . . . hard."

His mouth tightened, and she swore she heard the grind of teeth. "Maybe I wasn't always an accountant." He shot her a sideways glance. "Were you always a dominatrix?"

No. I was an assassin.

"Touché." She brushed some invisible dirt off her boots. "So what did you do before? Take the second left."

He shifted gears smoothly, his legs working the pedals with the same easy motions, like he was one with the vehicle, a pilot who knew his aircraft. A stir of feminine appreciation warmed her insides, because a man who could make a machine purr could definitely do the same to a woman.

And she really needed to get her mind out of bed. "So? You going to answer?"

"No."

"Then you can pull over and drop me off."

"Rik . . ."

Anger sparked, anger that she was rapidly losing control of this situation. She needed to get it back, and fast, before her inner animal decided it could do better to protect them both. "This is my fucking life, *boy*, and I need to know something about you if I'm going to spend time with you outside the club." Still, he said nothing. She leaned over, palmed his crotch.

"What the hell?"

"You came to me for a reason," she said. "You need to learn restraint. Which means you need to learn to obey. Tell me what I want to know." She rubbed a little, smiled when she felt him begin to harden. "Tell me, and I'll reward you. Or you can drop me off. Your choice."

She felt as much as saw the battle that raged within him. He slowed the car, and she held her breath, waiting for him to pull over and kick her out. He'd nearly come to a stop, when he cursed, hit the gas and shot back into traffic.

"I was a cop," he muttered. "In the States."

Now, that was more like it. Accountant, her ass. "Why aren't you a cop now?"

"I don't want to do this, Rik—"

"Mistress," she said softly. "And you *will* answer." She gave his cock a squeeze, and he sucked air between his teeth.

"I hurt someone," he ground out. "Robbery suspect. I didn't mean to, but . . ."

"Your strength."

"Yeah."

"And that's why you're playing the sub instead of the natural Dom you are."

He gave a sharp nod and glanced out the rearview mirror.

"Left at the roundabout and then straight for two kilometers." She removed her hand—reluctantly—from his crotch, and settled back in the seat, though she didn't relax. That Trance had been a cop made her feel a little better; he could obviously take care of himself. But no matter how much training he'd had, he couldn't stand up to a trained operative. She had to prepare him. Protect him.

Which was a joke, because she couldn't protect herself, let alone someone else.

"I need to know what's going on," he said quietly. "What's an excedo . . . sapien? Isn't that what you called me?"

Closing her eyes, she dropped her head against the headrest. This was going to sound so incredibly insane, and she wasn't sure how much to say. "It's a term for humans with exaggerated natural abilities. Like superstrength or -speed. Or extraordinary eyesight or hearing. Some scientists are saying that humans are suddenly evolving rapidly, but they don't know why. One theory is that it has something to do with Armageddon. Whatever it is, there are a lot of people like you in the world."

"Okay, that's interesting, but how the hell do you know all this?"

She opened her eyes, but didn't look at him. Just gazed through the sunroof at the starry sky, broken in places by low clouds. "There are these agencies . . . sort of like the CIA, Mossad, SIS. Except they are supersecret, and their agents are . . . special."

"Special how?"

Oh, science-fiction special. DC Comics Justice League special. Except these agencies were evil, and there was no justice involved. "They employ people like you. People with unusual abilities or areas of expertise. Psychics, pyrokineticists, people who glow in the dark. Or can see in the dark. And those are just the tip of the iceberg."

He snorted. "That's, uh, unbelievable."

"I told you."

"All right, let's say it's true. You haven't explained how you know all this."

She actually began to tremble. Her nerves were shot; she was being hunted and now she had to tell this man, whom she had actually started to like, that she was a monster. Taking a deep breath, she rocked her head forward. "Second right and straight again."

"Got it. Now, you going to explain?"

"I was part of one of those agency's programs."

"How?"

Her skin began to tighten and itch, and inside the beast stirred. It didn't like that she was confiding anything in Trance.

"They thought my family had special powers," she said quickly, before she could change her mind. "So they took us from our home. They killed everyone. Everyone but me. I escaped. But that man you were talking to . . . I think he was looking for me."

"If everyone has special powers, what's yours?"

The sensation of claws scraping the inside of her skin had her grinding her teeth. "I didn't say everyone has power. A lot of the people who work for these agencies are regular people. But they're the best in their fields, or they have special knowledge or unique skills."

"You're stalling. What's your special ability?"

She looked out the window at the run-down neighborhood where she'd rented a trashy town house. "I have a terrible temper," she snapped, letting a little of that temper out. "And let's leave it at that." She pointed to the curb. "Pull over anywhere. My place is right there."

He did, but after he shut off the motor, he turned to her. "I need more."

"Not now. After we're safe."

"Safe? If what you're telling me is true, it doesn't sound like you'll ever be safe."

A shiver ran up her spine, because he'd just voiced what she'd been too afraid to admit to herself. As long as she was alive, she'd be hunted, always in danger, and never, ever would she be safe.

She leaped out of the car and darted toward her front door, the instinct to get out of the open and inside her lair too strong to fight.

"Rik!" Trance caught up with her when she hit the top step of her porch landing. His hand closed on her wrist, and she swung around with a snarl.

"Don't touch me!"

He jerked his hand away, but it was too late. Overwhelmed by the danger, the loss of control, and now, a very alpha male she'd confided in far too much, the beast wanted out. Ulrika surged forward, teeth bared and· a film of red coming down over her vision. She slammed him into the porch post with a forearm against his throat.

"Never touch me without permission. Never. I've warned you before."

"Okay. Just take it easy. I wasn't going to hurt you." His voice was low, strong yet gentle, and his eyes were intensely focused on hers, the pupils narrowing to pinpoints. She felt a strange calm come over her, just enough to keep the beast from popping out of her skin. Still, it wanted out, and it wasn't going to be lulled by a soothing voice.

"Inside," she growled. "We're going to finish what we started at the club."

"We don't have time—"

"We'll make it." She released him, cursing herself, because he was right, but she couldn't risk leaving the house without regaining control. It was only a matter of time before she could no longer keep the beast contained. She had to do it *now*. "I need sex. And you need to realize that I'm the one in charge here. Not you."

His stare turned dark, full of conflict. She knew what he was thinking, that they weren't in the club, and he didn't have to submit to anything. But he probably also realized that if she was telling the truth about crazy supernatural agencies, he might need her. After a long moment, he gave a slow nod, barely a bow of the head.

She dug in her purse for her keys, dread making a sour ball in the pit of her belly. She hated this, hated having to waste time they didn't have, hated having to use him, hated having to need him. Especially away from the club. This was the closest she'd been to anyone since she'd been taken away from her home, and the closer she got to him, the more danger they were both in.

CHAPTER
Nine

Jesus H. Christ, there wasn't time for this. Trance touched his chest lightly, where Rik had drawn blood the night before. Those scars had long since healed, but what if she didn't stop this time?

She was on edge—even her eyes looked different, as if she was ready to make the switch.

But she was fighting it—and if sex with him would soothe her, he had little choice.

He looked around the neighborhood while she searched for her keys, and damn, the area was a cesspool. But then, Rik didn't really need to worry about thugs. Still, Trance moved close to her, as if he didn't know the true meaning behind her terrible temper, and acted the part of the protective ex-cop.

The cover story he'd used with her, about being a cop, was too close to the truth for him to be comfortable.

When she finally got the door open, he took a visual sweep of the place as he entered, and closed the door behind them both.

"No one bothers me here" was all she said before she grabbed his arm and all but dragged him down the hall.

Yeah, well, someone was about to start bothering them big-time. Dammit—he needed to let Dev know about Ryan, hadn't had time between Rik finding him talking to the back-from-the-dead operative and getting the invitation to her house. She'd been spooked as hell and he wondered if she actually knew Ryan when he was playing double agent at Itor. She didn't seem to recognize him, but she'd been playing with her collar. She did that when she was nervous, and he wondered why it was he felt like he knew her so well after such a short time.

The file, man—you read her file. But even as he reminded himself of that, he knew he was lying.

Still, Ryan's appearance had been a wake-up call, and fortuitous at the same time—it actually got Rik moving—and moving with him at her side. He couldn't have asked for a better stroke of luck.

She stopped at a door, and he noted her hand shook and her shoulders heaved with panting breaths as she opened a box on the shelf in the hall, and removed an old skeleton key. She fumbled it as she reached for the lock.

"I'll get it," he said, bending to pick it up off the floor, but a nasty snarl froze him, his fingers just inches from the key.

"I can do it myself." She snatched the key off the floor and jammed it into the lock. The door swung open, and he stepped inside the room, his gut doing a slow slide to his feet.

He'd been in private dungeons before, well outside the safety of a regulated club with cameras and guards that stopped things from getting too out of hand—had even had one in his place. But he'd never been on the receiving end of such a room, and he wondered if the nerves were more anticipation or expectation.

He should've tranqed her last night at his apartment. Even though it would've been going against the plan, even though he would've been risking life and limb, what he could lose here was far more intimate.

"Rik, I—"

"My name is 'Mistress.' Yours is 'boy.' "

His heart beat in a frenzy and, in his mind, he was ready for escape, looking for the exit. "I can't do this," he whispered. If she heard the words, she ignored them.

His breath caught at the sight of the heavy chains hanging on the wall—and at the look in her eyes. Even though she was in danger, he knew he was about to be bound with those chains, at her complete mercy.

What was more, that was exactly what he wanted. For the first time ever, he was going to truly submit and not just fake it.

"Touch them." She gestured to the nearest set. "Feel the strength. You're going to be intimately acquainted with them in a moment."

He did as she'd told him, and held their weight in his hands— heavy enough, no doubt, to hold her when the beast came out. Which meant they'd hold him tight.

He heard her whimper, and he spun around to see her tugging at her collar.

"Rik?" He stepped toward her, but she bared her teeth at him. Her hands curled into fists, and her eyes were gold fire. He immediately bowed his head and corrected himself. "I mean... Mistress."

"Good boy... very, very good." Her words of praise ran through him, hot and fast, his dick jumping with the approval in her tone.

"Clothes off. Now." She spoke in a barely controlled rasp that had become thick with a German accent, and he made eye contact with her briefly, to see if he could work any of his own magic on her. Like the first time, she cocked her head to the side and then shook it off, looking angrier than ever.

Shit. He stripped quickly, folding his clothes and leaving them on the chair in the corner.

"You're shaking," she noted. "Are you frightened?"

The words tumbled out before he could stop them. "Yes, Mistress."

"Are you frightened of me?"

"I'm frightened by what you can do to me."

"And what can I do?"

"Unravel me," he said, his voice hoarse.

"Yes, I can do that. I will do that. But you need to trust me to take care of you. I've done that so far, haven't I, boy?" Her hand trailed up his cock as she spoke and he fought a moan as her finger stroked the drop of pre-cum, working it into the soft skin.

"Yes, Mistress."

"Don't you want to fly?"

"I'm afraid I can't," he said honestly.

"Or maybe you're afraid you *can*. On the mattress. Now."

He complied, stretching out on the twin-sized mattress on the floor. She stalked toward him, and it was then that he noticed she'd chained one of her own ankles.

Ulrika shuddered at the sound of the chain scraping the floor as she moved. She hadn't wanted to do this, but she was too close to the edge. Often, the feel of the cuff around her ankle was enough to keep the monster at bay; she was larger in beast form, and the cuff hurt like hell when she shifted.

She tucked the key to the cuff's padlock into a special slot inside the toy chest next to the bed. The hiding place allowed her to retrieve the key while in human form, but was too small for her pawlike beast hands to manipulate.

Keys. Her life was so full of keys. But the one she needed most was the one she'd never have—the key to the collar.

Cursing under her breath, she turned back to the bed, where she often slept while chained. Heck, she spent most of her nights here, chained to the wall and hoping a nightmare didn't trigger a shift. She tried sleeping in the bedroom sometimes, so she could pretend she was normal, but ultimately, that's all it was—pretend. She wasn't normal, would never be normal, and she definitely didn't deserve the simple comforts normal people enjoyed.

Not after all the evil she'd done for Itor.

The mere thought spun up more anger, and her vision grew sharper as her human side began to fade. She looked at Trance through eyes she knew had gone glowing amber. The wolf wanted to hurt him. To make him pay for everything humans had done to her while she'd been held captive.

He watched her, his body tense, as though he knew he was in some serious danger.

And then, in an incredibly brave—and intuitive—move, he relaxed and slowly lifted his chin toward the ceiling.

He'd exposed his throat, acknowledging her dominance.

He'd probably just saved his life.

The alpha canine inside Ulrika settled down, just enough for the woman to gain control once more. Thank God she hadn't physically shifted, but that was the closest she'd been without it actually happening.

Still, the beast wasn't completely satisfied. It wanted to know that Trance understood who was boss. Giving in to those desires was easier than denying them, and Ulrika was too weary to try.

Silently, she clapped wrist and ankle restraints on Trance and secured them to the chains attached to the cement wall—chains she used on herself when she was feeling the call of the full moon, which had a tendency to heighten her wild blood.

"Tell me," she said, in a voice that didn't sound like hers, "when you make love to a woman, do you worry about hurting her?"

He stiffened. "I'm careful."

"Careful. That must be fun." She trailed a finger over his muscular chest. "Or not. It sucks to use restraint, doesn't it? To not let yourself go."

She knew how that was, because she'd never once made love to a man. She wanted to, but tender feelings, gentle touches . . . no, those didn't work for her other half.

"But now you can let yourself go. I'm going to take you to the edge again, Trance. You're going to have to watch me do it. I know you'll try to control yourself. You'll try to stay calm. But you won't be able to." She stroked the metal cuffs around his wrists. "So we have these. Now," she said, as she pulled a sounding kit out of the chest that held her key, "it's time for you to fly."

Trance jerked out of reflex, making the chains holding him rattle. He tried to picture Rik chaining herself—maybe when the moon turned full and she didn't want to be running loose and vulnerable with the Itor collar around her neck. He wanted to rip it off of her, to free her.

Wanted to free himself too, and he probably could if he really, really tried, but the chains were reinforced and Rik was really holding him down as she coated the metal sound with lubricant. When she was done, she took his cock in her hand and introduced the cold metal end to the tip.

She was soothing him, soft little growls, telling him that he was such a good boy, her sexy boy. That he was safe.

Safe. Could that ever be true?

Within minutes, she was sounding him and he was aware that he was yelling, something about *holyfuckingmotherofgod* and attempting to tear himself away from the mattress in order to meet the sensations that twisted his body inside out. "Rik..."

"Let it go," she commanded, pulled the sound out slowly and he began to come in hot, white spurts that seemed to overflow from his cock while he thrashed and gasped for air.

As promised, she released his arms and legs from the chains while he floated in that white zone, not wanting to ever come down. It was rare, if not impossible, for him to get into subspace, and he'd always watched his own subs with a hint of jealousy when he could help them achieve it.

And he was there. With Rik.

ULRIKA BACKED AWAY as Trance lay there, his body and mind in that place all subs sought. She'd been clueless about the BDSM lifestyle when she'd first come to it—heck, she'd been clueless about everything for weeks after she'd escaped from Itor.

She'd grown up in an isolated wilderness village, had been taken as a child to Itor, and they'd kept her even more isolated. Tutors had taught her the basics she'd need to interact with her targets and the people around them, but their training had proved extremely inadequate when she found herself on her own.

Her first couple of weeks of freedom had been spent merely surviving. She'd had to break into houses to steal clothes and food, and she'd slept wherever she could find shelter. In the country, that meant barns and abandoned cars. In Manchester, where she'd eventually gone in hopes the mass of people would help her blend in and keep Itor off her tail, that meant abandoned buildings and park benches.

Unfortunately, the life she was living put her in contact with a lot of violence, and twice she'd awakened covered in blood in strange places, with no memory of what happened the night before . . . but the daily papers had filled in the blanks.

Some said wild dogs were on the loose in the city. Others cried werewolf. It had been only a matter of time before Itor or some other agency caught wind of it. She'd run, but on her way out of the city, she'd caught the heady, musky odor of sex and pain. The scent trail had led her to a seamy sex club, and what she'd seen had been the answer to her prayers.

She hadn't been able to stay in Manchester, not with the rumors that were already circulating about a vicious creature, but she'd learned that the BDSM scene was big in London, so she'd stolen bus fare and gotten herself there as soon as possible.

Things had gone well—until now. Now she was on the run again, and she had the added complication of having to ensure the safety of another person.

Legs feeling rubbery, she sank down in one corner and curled up on the cold floor. Sometimes she wished she could give up, just lie there and let herself fade away. But revenge and hatred were powerful fuel for the will to live, and the animal side of her would never allow the weaker human side to succumb.

She heard the squeak of mattress springs and then the rasp of clothing, knew Trance was getting dressed. Something rattled and creaked . . . The chest. The key!

She sat up, saw Trance standing just out of reach with the key to her ankle cuff. A sense of panic and dread reared up in her, shot through her veins in a cold tide. He could leave her here. He could hurt her.

He could turn her in to Itor or sell her to the highest bidder.

As long as he held the key, he owned her.

* * *

TRANCE WAS SURE she could hear his heart beating—the sound filled his own ears even as the rest of his body remained languid. He'd wanted to remain on that mattress, chained or not—wanted more from Rik.

More than she was prepared to give.

What were the chances of finding a woman who could actually handle what he had to give, only to have to turn her in?

She'd never forgive him. And still, this was the perfect opportunity, a way to be done with this before he got in further, before he thought any more with his dick than he already had.

It was for the mission. But still, no matter how many times he told himself that, he didn't quite believe it.

He drew a deep breath as he flipped the key back and forth between his fingers and prepared to grab his phone, to tell ACRO he needed transport.

"Trance…" Rik's voice was soft, the fear evident as she clutched her collar. She was shaking, pale, and he was by her side in seconds.

"What's wrong—are you sick?"

"I feel them," she whispered. "They're coming. Oh, God, they're coming."

Shit. If she was right, Itor could be coming in force, and then they'd both be screwed. "You're sure?"

She held the collar with both hands, trying desperately to hold it away from her skin as she nodded. "We've got to get out of here."

Without hesitation, Trance unlocked the shackle from around her ankle and massaged the warm flesh for a second. "I liked you tied up," he told her. "I had plans for you."

She swallowed, hard. "Would I have liked them?"

"You'll have more chances to find out." He helped her up.

"We've got to leave town. Right now. I think it would be best if you came with me. I told you I'd help you—but you don't just need help submitting, Trance. It goes so much deeper and I don't have the time to explain right here."

"I'll call in to work, tell them I need a few days off."

"It might be longer than that."

"They don't need to know that now. Where are we going?"

"I haven't figured that out yet."

He nodded, because that was good. He'd figure it out for them. "Can we stop by my place so I can grab a few things?"

"Maybe. Just hurry and make that call. And watch the door." She waved her hand distractedly as she began to throw things from a drawer into a bag she'd pulled from the closet.

He leaned against the wall next to the window so he could see the street and anyone approaching as he dialed his cell—Devlin O'Malley was on speed dial.

"Hey, it's me. Listen, I'm going to need to take a few days off from work," he said when Dev answered the phone.

"Keep talking, Trance." Dev sounded sleepy, but Trance knew he was a man used to running on empty, used to his operatives calling in with strange requests and languages and was quick to decipher what the hell they were talking about.

"I know the boss will be pissed, but I've got a friend with an emergency," Trance continued. "You know how that goes."

"You're with Rik."

"Yeah. Oh, and before I forget to tell you, guess who I had dinner with tonight? Our long-lost friend."

"Long-lost friend . . . *Ryan?*"

"It's been a long time—took him a while to recognize me." Rik went into another room, closing a heavy door behind her. "Something's off. I'm not sure he actually recognized me or if he was just playing along. If I were a betting man, I'd say his memory isn't intact. In any case, he's spooked."

"Do you think he's after Rik?"

"I couldn't tell." He raised his voice to normal levels. "So yeah, cover for me. I'll be traveling—might not be in touch for a few days. I didn't want you to worry."

"I'll send someone in to look for Ryan. You need to get to the southern safe house and stay there. I'll have a plane there by tomorrow. And stay in close touch, Trance. This is where it gets tricky." Dev clicked off and Trance did the same, closed his phone and slid it into his pocket.

Rik came out of the bedroom with a bag slung over her shoulder. "I'm ready," she told him, cocked her head to the side with that look she gave whenever he tried his hypnotic powers on her.

"I've got a place. A friend relocated to the States for six months—I've got free use of his house." Trance kept his eyes steadily on hers.

"No one will know we're there?" she asked without breaking his gaze.

"No one but us," he told her, the lie sitting uneasily in his gut.

DEV ARRANGED Annika's flight to England—and to Trance—seconds after hanging up with him. Those pressing matters made him late to a post-dinner meeting with the psychics, but he assumed they'd know that and adjust accordingly—which was far more efficient than a phone call.

Marlena was still pissed at him for being so abrupt, and so he'd planned on stopping by the caf to pick up her favorite cookies.

Walking around ACRO during the day wearing the black BDUs every other agent wore was one of his favorite parts of the job. Two bodyguards trailed him no matter where he went, but they didn't follow closely enough that he felt hemmed in. Truth be told, he barely noticed them, especially at times like this.

The caf was busy—and it appeared there was some kind of commotion going on inside the large room. Devlin waited just outside the doorway and scanned the area for the source.

Even before doing so, he knew exactly what the problem would be.

Or, to be more specific, who.

The new recruit was like a bull in a china shop, pushing his way through the line and not heeding any order.

Heads turned—women, because he was handsome as shit, and cocky enough too to be the object of a quick fantasy or two, and men because they were assessing what kind of powers the man might have.

Excedos were considered dangerous—as dangerous as any new recruit. Coupled with the young man's get-the-fuck-out-of-my-way attitude, the place had begun to buzz with tension.

There was something so magnetic about the kid, so fucking fresh—arrogant and yet vulnerable—that made Devlin want to take him on one of the caf tables. Instead, he dialed Creed's number—Creed, who would be taking over the new recruit's training while Annika was in England.

Creed was also one of Dev's best friends at ACRO—and Oz had been his brother. Both Creed and Dev had been grieving in private and propping themselves up for each other in public.

"Creed, I've got an eye on your trainee—he's in the caf. And he's not ready for public venues."

"Shit, I told the guys at the excedo house to keep an eye on him. They were supposed to call me if he left. I'll come grab him right now," Creed said. "You don't like this kid much, do you?"

"I don't know him" was all Dev said before he hung up the phone. He waited, watched until Creed arrived a few minutes later and went up to the blond man. They began to walk out of the caf, the new recruit following behind Creed, seemingly without argument.

And then suddenly, the young man turned and stared directly at Dev. Creed hadn't noticed, but the look hit Dev in the gut . . . and then traveled lower. Much lower, until Dev was forced to stick his hands in his pockets.

The new recruit simply grinned when he saw Dev do that, and then turned and continued following Creed out the door.

CREED WASN'T a complete idiot—he had eyes and senses and, best of all, he had Kat, the spirit who'd been attached to him since he was born. A spirit that his brother, Oz, had put in place to protect him, along with the tattoos that ran the entire length of the left side of his body—head to toe.

Gabe was into Devlin. And, based on the gruff way Devlin asked about Gabe, the same also held true for him.

The fact that Devlin put him in charge of Gabe meant that Dev was feeling protective. Because, yeah, even though Ani could shock the shit out of the new recruit, she was a much better choice than, say, Ender.

"I was just trying to get some fucking dinner," Gabe was telling him now. "What the hell—do I need a babysitter every fucking step of the way?"

"Yeah, you do." Creed shoved him through the outside door. "Dinner's waiting for you in your room."

Devlin had been mourning Oz for what had seemed like forever. Creed understood, because it felt like just yesterday that he'd lost his brother. Oz hadn't tried to contact Creed at all, not even through Kat, and still, over the past couple of days, Creed had been sure his brother was close.

Probably wishful thinking.

And speaking of wishful, now Creed just had to find out if Gabe felt the same way—or if he was simply trying to get in good with the boss. He didn't get that vibe from the kid, but there was no way in hell he would let anyone hurt Devlin.

So here he was, stand-in trainer and matchmaker. Annika would tell him to leave it alone—so would Dev. But from the way Kat hummed in his ear about it, Creed knew he was onto something.

CHAPTER
Ten

Meg cursed herself for choosing Ryan over the police as she struggled uselessly against the bonds. She'd been left alone on the private jet—with no pilot and no lights—for two hours now, by her count. He'd taken her cell phone and her bag and locked them up tight.

If she'd told Mose that, yes, she needed to hide out in Florida for a while, he would've been meeting her now, would've known that she was in trouble when she didn't show.

But something was . . . wrong with Ryan. He came across as a big tough guy—and she had no doubt that he was—but something in his eyes held a desperation she recognized.

Plus, he didn't seem to know what she'd been talking about—had been taking her cues about the missing money. And he couldn't remember if they'd had sex, never mind an Internet romance.

At one time, he'd told her that he'd never be able to forget her. And she'd believed him, but obviously he'd been promising himself to a lot of women.

She'd never thought of herself as memorable beyond a few

minutes behind the computer screen anyway, but somehow she'd been certain that Ryan had seen her differently.

When she'd told him earlier that he'd only been a mark to her, it had taken everything she'd had to force out that lie. He'd been the furthest thing from a mark, but having him find out why she'd really taken the money would be too humiliating to bear.

A few more tugs on the ropes and they loosened, but nothing more. It was no use—the bonds were tied too well, by a professional.

When Ryan got back, she'd find a way to throw him off his game a bit, maybe bring up the money again.

The door swung open—Ryan stood there, illuminated by the lights of the runway. His face was slightly flushed, his hair was tousled, like he'd been running his hands through it, and he looked . . . turned on.

She swallowed hard and tried to pull it together. This man had the same effect on her he'd had when they'd played computer games together years earlier—the thrill of trying to one-up each other had always made her pulse race. In person, he was even more devastating and even though these thoughts were completely inappropriate, given the situation, being face-to-face with the consequences of her actions made her feel more alive than she had in years. "Can you please untie me? I'm starving and I have to pee."

He strode toward her, moving easily in his black boots, the leather jacket swinging open to reveal the holstered gun he wore. He stopped right in front of her, his crotch in her face, and she was forced to strain her neck to look up.

"You're a real tough cookie, aren't you?"

"Not so tough. And my name isn't Cookie."

"Right. It's Coco."

She took a chance. "It's actually Meg."

He leaned in close, his breath warm on her cheek—smelling faintly of whiskey and mint. "Is that what you want me to call you when I'm fucking you?"

Her mouth opened at the explicitness of his words...words she'd heard before from him, albeit on a computer screen.

What do I call you when I'm making love to you? When I'm fucking you so deep you'll lose your mind?

Meg, she'd told him. *Not Coco. Meg.* "Meg," she said, her voice barely registering above a whisper. "I want you to call me Meg."

She swore she saw a flicker of something in his eyes when she spoke, but when he smiled, it was wicked, and it made her stomach clench.

RYAN SMILED FIERCELY at Coco—Meg—whatever the fuck her name was. *Is that what you want me to call you when I'm fucking you?*

He didn't know what had come over him to make him ask that, except that he was highly frustrated and beyond pissed at having lost Ulrika. He'd spent hours searching for her after she disappeared from the club, had tried activating her collar to see through her eyes, but all he saw was her with the guy he'd spoken to at the club. There had been no way he could tell where she was, and now he just had to wait until she was looking at something a little more telling than that guy's dick.

Itor was going to have his ass for this. But how could he have anticipated that ACRO would already be sniffing around?

Motherfuck.

He looked down at Coco—he'd go with that name for now, since it was the only thing he remembered from his erased past. She looked back at him, her gaze strangely serene, as if being kidnapped were just another day at the office.

An office where she spent her time ripping off people.

The reminder that she'd stolen from him pissed him off, and he released her, yanked her out of the seat and took her down to the floor. "So, you like to be called Meg when you're being fucked, but what about when your marks are throttling you? What do you like to be called then?"

She struggled futilely beneath him, her glower as hot as her skin as it rubbed on his. Which worked for him, because he was in serious need of something to take the edge off. He was as coiled as an unpinned grenade, ready to blow.

So much had happened lately, and hanging out in that sex club had been the final straw. He was supposed to be familiar with the lifestyle, to be turned on by all the leather and restraints and sounds of pain and pleasure. And yeah, he'd been turned on, but was it because he'd been in the club, or because he'd been picturing Coco in place of all the women there?

Frustration screamed through him. He'd snatched Coco in order to learn something about himself, but if anything, he was more confused than ever. Because for the past few months, he'd felt nothing, and now, after being at the club, and with her writhing beneath him, he definitely felt something.

Obviously, being a bastard worked for him, just like Itor said.

He wasn't letting this opportunity go to waste.

"This might hurt a little, Coco," he said, as he stretched her arms above her head and cuffed them to the leg of a seat. "But don't worry. You'll like it." He nipped the top of her ear. "I'll make sure of it."

Snarling, she bucked her hips and tried to bite his arm. He jerked away from her just in time to avoid having a chunk of flesh taken out of his biceps. Annoyed, he grabbed her chin and held her face still.

"That was stupid," he said, his voice deep and rough. "Anyone else would break your jaw for that. Me? I'm more into the spankings. And that earned you a good one." He reached down and palmed her ass beneath her skirt. "Right here, on both cheeks, both thighs, until the skin is so hot and red you need ice with your orgasm."

She squealed in outrage and bucked more as he moved down her body. The Doms at the club had been all hard-bodied leather mamas, but Coco was softer, a little rounder, and a hell of a lot hotter. She kicked at him until he straddled her knees.

"Don't make me have to bind your ankles too." He ran his

palm up and down her leg. "Though apparently, I like doing that, so maybe I'll do it anyway." He squeezed her thigh, knowing the Ryan in the DVDs would be rougher, but her skin was so smooth, so soft . . . he didn't want to bruise her. Not even to spank her like he'd threatened.

Dammit, what was wrong with him? His body was willing—his cock was hard as a steel pipe—but his brain was screaming that this was all wrong.

Fury shot through him as the last eight months came crashing down on him. According to Itor, he was a cruel, abusive, amoral scumbag. He'd lost Ulrika. He'd lost his memory. He'd lost his fucking mind.

He had to get it back. The only way he could think of doing that was to do what he supposedly used to like, and if that meant bondage and pain, then so be it. Besides, the anticipation of being inside Coco's hot little body gave him all the inspiration he needed.

Roughly, he shoved her skirt up and practically drooled at the sight of her tight pink boyshorts. He'd never seen anything so sexy. The soft cotton outlined the hills and valley of her sex, and when he pulled her thighs apart as far as he could between his legs, the tiny pearl of her clit pushed up against the fabric. He nearly groaned. Fucking her wouldn't be enough. He wanted to taste her, to make her scream while he tongued her deep and hard.

No.

He shook his head, trying to clear it. That wasn't how he used to work. He made women suck him while they were bound. He fucked them while they struggled against their bonds. He never went down on them. At least, he hadn't in any of the videos. Oh, they came . . . they always came, but only while being fucked by his dick, or a dildo, or the handle of a flog.

That was how he'd play it with Coco. Maybe the rough stuff would spark a memory.

"You ready, little thief?" He reached into his jacket pocket and removed his Ka-Bar Mule. The folding knife flipped open with a soft scrape of metal that nearly drowned out Coco's sudden breath. "Hold still...I don't think I'm into blood play." He winked. "But I'm willing to find out."

Contrary to his words, he carefully slid the flat of the blade inside the leg opening of her boyshorts at the hip, and with two flicks of his wrist, he cut them away, and then it was his turn to feel the catch of his breath. She was beautiful, all open to him, her slit glistening through a soft, thin veil of dark curls.

His hand shook as he closed the knife and slipped it back into his pocket, next to the condom he'd stuffed in there earlier. He flipped the packet onto the floor next to her and released his straining erection. It kicked free of his fly as if it couldn't wait to get inside her, and yeah, no more playing. He couldn't remember the last time he'd had sex, because he hadn't been with a woman since he lost his memory.

"Please don't do this." She tried to jam her knees into his groin, but he pinned her legs with his while rising up to cover her.

"You'll love it," he growled, and took her breast in his mouth, sucked it through the thin fabric of her blouse. No bra. Nice.

It took a moment to realize that the fight had gone out of her. She lay there beneath him, trembling, a tear squeezing between closed lids.

He should be getting off on her anxiety. Fuck. Now he was really pissed. "Dammit, Coco, what the hell is wrong with you? You're not some fucking nun I abducted from a convent. You're a goddamned criminal wanted by several international agencies. So don't give me the innocent little flower act. Are you upset because I didn't spank you first? Shove a gag in your mouth? Because all that can be arranged."

She turned her head to the side and shook even harder. Seeing red, he grasped her chin and forced her to face him. "Look at me." When she didn't open her eyes, he raised his voice. "*Look. At. Me.* What is your deal?"

Her eyes popped open, and his heart took a dive. Pain swirled in them, pain and sadness and fear. "I just...I didn't want to... to..."

"To what? Spit it out." His words were harsh, but his voice had lost its edge. Appropriate, since he'd lost his erection too.

"To lose my virginity this way," she whispered.

A sucker-punch of oh-shit hit him right in the gut. "You can't be," he rasped. "Ah, fuck . . ." He trailed off, because he believed her, and oh, man, what had he been about to do?

I'm a virgin. Do you still want to meet me? The words flashed in his mind, but not in his ears. In his memory. Typewritten words on a computer screen.

Where had that come from?

"Ryan . . . please . . ."

Rattled to the core both by what he'd been about to do and the strange, broken fragment of memory, he scrambled off her, panting, his head spinning. With clumsy fingers, he released her from the cuffs and then got as far away from her as he could. "God, I'm sorry, Coco. Shit, I'm sorry."

She stared at him like he'd grown a snout, but he had to give her credit: she calmly tugged down her skirt and then tucked her legs beneath her to sit quietly. She didn't move away, but then, where could she go?

MEG GAVE HERSELF credit, knew she appeared much calmer than she was. She could still feel the heavy weight of the bonds on her wrists—the delicate undersides showing a pattern of blue-black braceleted bruises. She rubbed at them with the opposing thumbs, as if they were mere smudges she could get rid of and thought about how close she'd come to being violated.

"I'm sorry—I hurt you. Shit." Ryan ran his hands through his hair. They shook. "You can go, Meg. I'll call you a car—get you a plane back home where I found you."

"That wasn't home." She wondered if he would've gone through what he'd planned if she hadn't announced her virginity. In her near-panic, she'd noted a hesitancy, but since she'd never gone quite as far with any guy—not even close—she could've just been missing the signals.

I'm a virgin. Do you still want to meet me?

Do you know what a turn-on that is, to know I'll be the first—the only—guy to have ever touched you, the only guy to ever make you come?

"Meg, look, I don't know what I was thinking. I mean—fuck, this is hard to explain. But that guy who just did that to you—it wasn't me. It's supposed to be, but it's not."

He wasn't making sense, but he was contrite. Completely and utterly devastated too, by the look on his face.

None of this made any sense. "I stole from you. You're angry . . ."

"No." He shook his head hard. "That's not it. I'm supposed to like that stuff . . . and I don't. I was supposed to get turned on by hurting you. And I was turned on—fuck, I was turned on. I wanted to have sex with you—but not like that." He lowered his head into his hands. "You should go. You need to go."

She certainly wasn't going to argue, and moved quickly to grab her bag. Her feet were still asleep and she ignored the pins-and-needles pain as she headed to the exit.

She was out the door when she heard the heavy thud, turned from habit and saw Ryan on his hands and knees on the floor holding his head in his palms.

Go, she told herself fiercely.

Ryan groaned and she dropped her bag and walked back to him. She sank to the floor next to his prone body and spoke softly. "Ryan . . ."

He was unresponsive, his fingers digging into his scalp, his eyes screwed shut—his face bearing the obvious mark of severe pain.

"Ryan," she tried again. "What's wrong? Is it a migraine? Is there medicine I can get you?"

He still didn't answer.

"Ryan, look, maybe I should call an ambulance—get you to a doctor."

With that, his hand shot out, circled her wrist with an iron grip. "No doctor."

"But you can't move. Shit." She looked into his eyes, darkened with pain, the pupils dilated. "Tell me what to do."

"There's nothing . . . just have to lie here until the pain goes. Old injury from some bad people."

She needed to leave this place and the man who'd almost raped her. But he'd stopped himself. Hadn't hurt her.

The guilt of what she'd done to him—of what he'd become over the past five years—overwhelmed her. "I'm staying with you, then."

"Don't. Get out of here. I may be a bigger bastard than I think I am."

"Somehow I don't think so. Does this happen a lot with your head?"

"Yes." He lay down on the floor of the plane and began to rub his temples. "For as long as I can remember. Which is only the past eight months."

Wait a minute. The man had amnesia? Suddenly it made sense now, the way he hadn't been able to remember her or anything about the stolen money.

"What happened to your memory, Ryan?" She rubbed his head where he'd been clutching it and he groaned in appreciation.

"It hurts there—always hurts right there," he mumbled. "They told me it was a traumatic brain injury. I was in the hospital for a long time—almost didn't make it. Docs tried everything to get my memory back but I've only got the past eight months."

"Who are you? What do you do for a living now?"

His eyes were focusing better, the pupils smaller. "It's better you don't know. You don't want to mess with the people I mess with."

"I think I already have," she murmured.

"You might want to stop, then."

"You were really going to let me walk away just like that, after all the money I took from you?" she persisted.

"I don't know what you did to me. I don't know what anyone's done to me. Don't know if I've got a mother or where I grew up or if you really took money from me or some other guy named

Ryan. Fuck, I don't even know if my name is Ryan Matthews or not."

"It's Ryan Malmstrom," she said. "At least, that's what you went by before."

He repeated his last name, over and over again, as if testing its fit. "How do you know this—any of it?"

Her throat tightened. "I stole money from you." She wanted to keep the intimate details of what had happened between them to herself for the time being. The fact that he didn't remember that part was both humiliating and a relief. Soon enough, he'd remember dumping her—and she'd have to admit she stole the money because he'd hurt her. "I'd tried several times before to take money from you but I was never able to crack your code."

"How long ago?" He was no longer on the floor, but rather in front of her on his knees now. "Please, this is important."

"The first time we met was almost six years ago. I took the money a year after that."

"Can you tell me anything else you remember about me then? Anything I told you?"

You told me you loved me—that I was special. That you were going to make me call out your name when I came with your cock inside of me.

She drew a deep breath and tried not to let her voice shake. "You told me . . . you said you would kill me with your bare hands if we ever met in person."

RYAN PACED the length of the plane, Meg's words ringing through his aching head. *You said you would kill me with your bare hands if we ever met in person.*

Had he meant it? Probably. The Itor files he'd read had painted a gruesome picture of his life, his job, his hobbies, and the photos attached to the mission reports had confirmed it. He was a violent criminal with no conscience.

She'd planted herself in one of the seats, but he had no idea why. He'd said she could go. For her own safety, she should go. Before he hurt her.

"I might be able to help you," she said, and he whirled around, mid-stride.

"Why? Why would you want to help me after I kidnapped you, bound you, and then practically . . ." He couldn't say it. "Just go."

"And that will help both of us, how?" She tossed her head and gave an imperious little sniff he shouldn't think was cute but did. "You don't know who you are, and I don't know where we are."

"We're in London." He sighed. "I had a job. Fucked it up." He felt in his jacket pocket for the remote to Ulrika's collar. It was about time to check on her again. "Just be quiet for a minute, okay?"

She shrugged and flipped open her laptop. "Whatever."

Ryan kept one eye on her computer screen to make sure she wasn't e-mailing the police—or her brother—for help, as he turned on the remote. Instantly, his vision filled with the interior of a vehicle. Rain on the windshield. The guy who had been at the club was driving.

Ulrika was staring out at the road . . . the M3. They were on the move. A road sign showed the distance to Winchester. So they were heading west. Time for Ryan to get moving.

He flicked off the remote, wincing at the twinge of pain behind his eyes. Ever since the accident, he felt pain whenever he used his electrokinesis. But then, maybe he experienced pain before as well.

"I need to rent a car," he said. "I'll drop you off wherever you want." She didn't answer, just kept her fingers and gaze glued to the laptop, where she was playing a game of solitaire, and on the verge of winning.

"I never had the patience for that game," he muttered.

She looked up, her eyes glittering with impending victory. She looked a little bloodthirsty, and he realized she must have one hell of a competitive streak. Sexy. "I know."

"How?"

The tiny hitch in her breath made her breasts push against her top—and, sure, he was a jerk for noticing, but her admission about being a virgin made him wonder if any man had caressed them. Kissed them. Sucked them until she was ready to come from oral loving alone.

"I just know," she said, so quickly that he knew there was more to the story than her "just knowing." "You're the type of man who wants instant satisfaction. If you can't get what you want in three moves, you hire someone to do it for you."

How nice that she knew him better than he did. He snapped shut the lid of her laptop. "Sounds to me like you did a lot of research when you were staking me out."

She made a frustrated sound. "Maybe I'm just a good judge of character." She crossed her arms across her chest, which made her breasts overflow from the top, and made him grind his teeth.

"And maybe I'm a green-blooded space alien." He tore off his jacket and threw it on a seat. "And why the hell is it so hot in here?"

She muttered something, but he ignored her as he dug into his jeans pocket for his cell phone, made arrangements for a rental car from the nearest dealer at the airport, and requested several maps of the area.

"Okay, we're done here—" He broke off as Coco stood up, holding the remote to Ulrika's collar.

"What's this?"

"Nothing. Give it to me."

She jerked it away. "You're involved in something a lot bigger than arms dealing."

"Because I have a remote control unit?"

"Because it belongs to Itor."

He swallowed. Hard. "I don't know what you're talking about."

"Don't bullshit me, Ryan. If you want me to help you, you need to be straight with me."

Unbelievable. How many times had he told her to get away from him, and here she was, acting as if he'd begged her to stay. "I want you to forget you ever saw me."

"Well, I don't have the luxury of amnesia, like one of us here. So spill."

"How do you know it belongs to Itor? How do you know about Itor?"

She sat and crossed her slim legs at the ankles, looking all prim and proper. He wondered briefly what she'd think about getting messed up—good and sweaty, delicate designer clothes so torn that she'd have to wear her lover's shirt around the house. The very thought made his loins stir, but would probably disgust her. No wonder she was still a virgin.

"As you can imagine," she said, slapping him out of his ridiculous thoughts, "I deal with a lot of people who run outside the law and under its radar. The name Itor comes up every once in a while, and once I found someone who knew what it was, I started paying closer attention when I came across it." She pointed to the symbol at the base of the remote. "The weapons-development company that made this, Global Weapons Corporation, is affiliated with Itor. Supposedly, they have both legitimate and illegitimate dealings, and all of the best weapons and technological breakthroughs are swept right down the pipe to Itor." She held up the remote. "I'd be willing to bet this isn't legit."

"Give it to me" was all he said, but she just cocked an eyebrow and tucked it behind her back. "Remember what I said about killing you with my bare hands?"

Sure, right now she was in more danger of him ripping her clothes off than she was of him strangling her, but she seemed to believe him, and changed her mind. He took the remote, stuffed it back into his jacket pocket and threw the jacket over his shoulder.

"Come on. I need to get the car."

"What about me?"

"What about you?"

She lifted her chin and stared at him through fiery eyes. "I know too much for you to let me go."

Okay, this was officially the weirdest thing that had ever—in the last eight months anyway—happened to him. Who in their right minds tried to convince their kidnapper to keep them?

"You're the worst kidnap victim ever," he muttered, and she grinned, as if what he'd said was a compliment. "Fine. You can come with me. You might be useful." Actually, he was sure she would be. If she knew that much about Itor ... hell, she probably knew more than he did about his life.

"So," she said, as she gathered up her laptop and bag. "Where are we going?"

"To kill a woman."

She fumbled her laptop, and he caught it just before it hit the floor. "What did you say?" Her hands shook a little as she took the computer from him.

"You heard me."

"What did she do?"

"No idea."

"You're just going to kill her for no reason?"

"You changing your mind about coming with me?"

She raised that chin again, her mouth set in a stubborn line. "No. I'm going to find out who you are and prove you aren't as bad as you say."

In a move that surprised both of them, he leaned down, cupped the back of her head, and brought his lips to hers. Her outraged gasp opened her mouth, allowing him access. He slid his tongue against hers in a hot, penetrating kiss. It only lasted a second or two, but it was enough for him to know it was going to be really fucking hard to keep his hands off her. Cursing, he stepped back.

"I hope you're right, Coco. Because if you're wrong, I'm the last person you want to trust with your body. Or your life."

CHAPTER
Eleven

Ulrika would have offered up a prayer that she was doing the right thing by going with Trance to his friend's house, but she'd given up on prayer a long time ago.

So now she just had to hope this wasn't the dumbest thing she'd ever done, and hope Trance didn't discover what her chains were really for.

He set me free.

God, she couldn't believe he'd done that. He'd had power over her, had held her life in his hands when he'd held the key to her ankle cuff. She'd cursed herself for being so stupid as to allow him to get the key in the first place, her mind taking her back to all the times her handlers had kept her on a leash—a virtual one, but a leash, nevertheless.

Trance had set her free when he could have used her in so many ways. Even her inner wolf was warming up to him now.

"So where are we going, exactly?" she asked, as she looked out the passenger window of Trance's BMW, which still had a faint new-leather scent to it. She'd never had a car...didn't even know how to drive.

Maybe he'd teach her if they got a chance—in the time between the running for their lives and the sex she needed to control her homicidal urges.

Idiot.

"Plymouth." He turned on the windshield wipers to sweep away the buildup of drizzle that made the night even darker. "Is that far enough away for now?"

"It'll never be far enough," she murmured.

Trance touched her leg lightly, but it made her jump. "You need to tell me what we're up against."

"I already did."

"You held back. You never said why these people are after you."

"I told you I have a temper."

He hit the brakes to avoid rear-ending someone who'd pulled over but still took up part of the left lane on the M3. "I know a lot of people with bad tempers, and they don't have any secret agencies chasing them."

She turned away, unsure how much to say. He deserved more than vague half truths, but how much would he believe? And how much would potentially put her in danger if he realized what she was worth not only to Itor, ACRO and TAG, but to several terrorist organizations that either wanted her dead or who would love to use her as a weapon?

"I told you they grabbed my entire family. Itor. That's what they're called." She closed her eyes and pressed her forehead against the cool glass. She hated talking about her family, which actually meant nearly a hundred members of her clan. But her immediate family had included a mother, father, two older brothers . . . and a betrothed, an arranged match with a clan-mate two years older than she was. "My people believe that animal spirits exist in us all, but few can feel it. Communicate with it. Become it. We can. We can mentally shift into our animal soul—it's not a physical transformation, but more of a . . . joining."

"So, what, you take on animal habits? Behaviors?"

"Something like that." It was weird talking about this, because although her lifestyle and spiritual beliefs had been normal for her, she wasn't sure how someone on the outside would react. "We had a lynx-shifter who would become one with his animal spirit to assist in hunts. His sense of smell was an asset. And Horst?" She smiled at the memory of the elderly gray-haired man who'd always had cookies for the kids. "His was the soul of a squirrel. When he shifted, he'd run around collecting nuts and climbing trees like he had suction cups attached to his hands and feet. It was funny to see an old guy digging up acorns and scampering for tree trunks."

She risked a glance at Trance, but his handsome face was expressionless as he drove.

"What's your animal?" he asked.

"A wolf." A very, very angry wolf, though at the moment, she was calm.

"And this agency wanted your people because of these abilities?"

She nodded. "They wanted to harness the animal part of our souls. They wanted to twist it and mutate it, and make it manifest physically. They killed everyone but me in their failed experiments."

The nightmare had begun within days of her arrival at the Itor labs. Her father was the first to die, her mother had gone just weeks later, and though she'd never seen her brothers again, she'd heard they'd both died around eight months after their mother passed away.

"Were you a success?"

"No," she said truthfully, because she didn't consider what they'd done to her to be a success. "But I escaped, and they want me back. To put me down and put their experiments to bed."

He muttered something that sounded like a curse, and then blew out a breath. "I'm sorry you had to go through all of that."

"You believe me?"

"I've lived my life with this insane strength, so yeah, I'm willing to go out on a limb with this."

She turned, locked eyes with him. Even in the dark they were gorgeous, piercing, and they weren't full of bullshit. He believed her. He must have seen some crazy shit as a cop. "Thank you."

He nodded, went back to driving. She reached for the heat, a sudden chill in the air wrapping around her like an icy blanket. It filled her chest and numbed her fingers so she couldn't turn the knob.

Her senses tingled and her collar itched, and oh, shit, she was feeling that Itor sensation again.

"Rik?" Her name floated in the air around her head, never really making it inside her skull to her brain. "Rik!"

She gazed out at the M3, at the passing signs and cars. There was no sense of immediate danger, like there had been at the club, but the feeling was still familiar, the one she'd felt a couple of times since her escape, especially lately, but most memorably, every time her Itor handler had turned her loose to kill.

"Rik!"

She'd start out in human form, would be dressed to play whatever part she was supposed to play. Maybe a high-priced call girl. Maybe a businesswoman. Maybe a maid or a take-away delivery person. Then, once she made contact with her target, the shock would slam into her through the collar, and within seconds, she'd be a slavering, raging wolf-creature that would rip apart everything in sight.

"Goddammit, Rik, what's wrong?"

Eventually, they'd shock her again, turning her back into a woman, but her clothes would be shredded and she'd probably be hurt. Twice she'd been shot, and she'd lost track of the stab wounds and broken bones.

The sensation melted away, leaving behind aching lungs from a held breath. Raggedly, she took in oxygen, practically panting. Her eyes stung with unshed tears, and she was shaking uncontrollably, more from the bad memories than the actual sensation of being in Itor's clutches again.

"Rik." Trance's voice was rough, sounding strangely rattled. "Tell me what just happened. Did you feel them again?"

"Yes," she whispered. "Just like at the club and at my house."

"Do you feel them often?"

"When I was with Itor." She hugged herself, rubbed her arms. "Before I escaped. And then not again for months. But recently I felt them again."

"You were tugging at your collar. Like you wanted to tear it off. Is that part of it?"

She didn't answer. Just stared blindly into the night and thanked God that car engines tended to lull the beast.

The growl that came from her then was from her, not the wolf. "I won't let them catch me. And I won't let them have you either. I'll die before they—or anyone—take either one of us," she swore fiercely.

Trance's response was barely audible, but she totally agreed when he muttered, "This really fucking sucks."

RIK HADN'T WANTED any music on while driving the nearly five hours to the southern safe house. Instead, she'd urged him to drive not only faster, but rougher.

She still tugged at that damned collar too. And if Itor was after them, he would have to push up the timetable for the ACRO pickup that Dev promised. It wouldn't leave him much time to convince her to let him chain her again.

"We're here, Rik," he told her gently. She relaxed slightly, even as she turned to check their tail again.

The house was gated—he punched in the security code and then pulled up the winding drive to park in the attached, steel-reinforced garage.

"Your friend has good taste," she remarked, her fingers still tugging at the collar.

"Come on, you need to eat something."

"I'm not hungry." Her voice was irritable. Understandable, of course—her back was up. But making irritable women relax had been his specialty, and he would have to revive that piece of him that enjoyed watching a woman break down in the most enjoyable of ways.

He'd build her back up. And then . . .

And then he'd have to turn her over to ACRO. And she'd hate him forever. It wasn't like he hadn't gotten used to that as an MP. No matter how much the prisoners might've respected him, they still hated him for the one thing he had that they didn't—freedom.

It would be the same for Rik.

She was ahead of him, headed for the doorway that led from the garage to the house. He slapped a palm against the door, blocking her entrance. This time, he wouldn't be the one baring his throat in submission. "You'll eat."

She smiled a little. "That's the Dom coming out in you."

"Trust me, you haven't seen anything yet where that's concerned."

"This isn't your show, Trance. Just because you found the house—"

He stopped her with a finger on her lips. She looked as if she wanted to rip his finger off, but she didn't. "Why don't you let me help you, the way you helped me?"

She did pull his finger away then. "It doesn't work that way."

"It'll work, Rik," he told her as he pressed her to the wall, bringing his mouth down on hers in the kiss he'd wanted to give her since she'd unlocked him earlier, his tongue playing along the roof of her mouth. A tender, seductive kiss. When he pulled back, he growled against her ear. "It'll work when you're all tied up for me. I promise you, you'll love it."

She had nothing to say to that, and she'd stopped touching the collar. A good sign.

"Let's go." He brushed past her into the house, not looking back.

She was following, though—he heard the click of her booted heels on the marbled flooring.

ACRO didn't skimp on safe houses—this one was no exception. Meticulously designed so that a casual visitor—and some even not so casual—wouldn't notice the touches that said this was a haven for agents with special abilities. The glass on all the windows was bullet- and bomb-proof, the basement hosted a variety of camera controls—the best in security that ACRO had to offer. There were also several escape routes from the house, extra cars with unremarkable plates and secured phone lines.

And there was food too. His stomach growled as he slipped off his leather jacket and headed for the kitchen. He grabbed eggs and bread—breakfast would be the easiest and quickest food to fix.

"I'd like to use the loo."

He turned at the sound of her voice—it was softer, almost asking permission, and yes, she'd responded to him, whether she'd wanted to or not. "Go ahead. Breakfast will be ready shortly."

He turned away from her, not wanting to hear another protest, and this time, she gave none. He set the alarm perimeters quickly so no one could get either in or out without his knowing about it and then he phoned Devlin.

"Trance, you're at the safe house," Dev said instead of hello. And yes, Dev would know that, since any activity got transmitted directly to him.

"Yeah, but we've got company. She's been freaked the entire ride, tugging at the collar."

Silence, and then, "Itor uses a remote to track her. Someone could be tracking you that way, but we don't know the range. So if someone's tailing you, they could be close."

Shit. He'd been afraid of that. "We'll move up the time line—send the jet now, have it waiting."

"Annika's already on her way. Trance, do you think it's Ryan following you?"

"It makes the most sense." Ryan had been undercover at Itor when he'd dropped off the map. ACRO had listed him as MIA, and who knew what those bastards at Itor did to him. "He was definitely hunting someone at that club—he wasn't there for fun."

"Then he could be using the remote to see through her eyes. Get her chained and controlled, Trance. Work some magic. It's going to be close."

"Got it." He clicked the phone off and slid it into his pocket as he finished preparing the food.

A few minutes later, Rik appeared. She sat at the table and ate the eggs he put in front of her, quietly, but as if she hadn't realized how hungry she really was.

He refueled as well, watching her carefully. Finally, when she took a long sip of juice, he pushed his plate away and sat back in his seat. "Better?"

She nodded, licked the juice off her bottom lip as she placed the glass on the mahogany table. "Yes. Thanks."

"Not a problem. Maybe later you can cook for me."

"I don't cook, Trance." She took a piece of toast and he watched her strong, elegant hands as she spread butter and jam on the bread. "I have no desire to do so."

"Desires can change. Where did you say you grew up?"

"I didn't. Germany."

"Whereabouts?"

"Why? Have you been there?"

He had—numerous times with the military and a few times with ACRO as well. "No. I keep meaning to travel more but—"

She reached a hand out to him, covering his forearm. "It'll get better, Trance. Now that you know what you are, you can control it."

His gut twisted from the guilt as he placed his other hand over hers, locking her cool palm between his large ones. "I'll make it better for you too, Rik."

She attempted to pull her hand away, but he didn't let her. She was strong in human form, but no match for him. "You want me to make it better for you. Just the way you feel full and satisfied now, you're going to let me satiate you in the bedroom. Any way I want. Splayed out for me in chains on the bed, unable to move while my tongue finds all the places that drive you crazy."

"I won't let that happen," she breathed.

"You already have. You've let me lick you. I swear I can still taste you—sweet. Addictive." He smiled. "I can already hear you moaning. Letting go. Submitting to me."

"Jesus. Jesus," she whispered, and this time he allowed her to take her hand away. Then she stared at it, rubbed one palm with the other before she spoke. "I need to shower."

"Yes, I'd like you clean. Wet."

She jolted in her seat as he continued, "Hurry, Rik. I don't like to be kept waiting."

She stared at him for a second, obviously torn, before she rose and fled toward the guest bedroom.

JUST BEFORE DEV left the office for home that evening, Marlena had assured him that security had no knowledge of the new recruit's trip to Devlin's house last night. The men and women who'd worked night detail had been thoroughly questioned.

"Apparently, they'd been waiting for him to arrive—he was being allowed to bring himself to the ACRO gates, his Convincers following behind his cab in their car. Jack said he saw the recruit get out of the cab, and just like that, he was gone," Marlena explained.

Jack, one of his best Convincers, had been roaming around the ACRO grounds looking for the guy when Devlin called security to come and pick him up.

"So he's some kind of fucking Houdini, then," Dev muttered.

"Would you like Jack reprimanded for leaving the new recruit alone?" Marlena asked, knowing full well Dev would do no such thing. He knew, better than any of them, that sometimes a man— or woman—had to walk through those gates on their own terms. He understood the pride that came with that decision, and even though many of the ACRO operatives were far too unstable to be trusted to do so on their own, the ones who were always came back to thank Dev for that later.

"That's all for tonight," he told her instead of answering her question. There was a brief pause, as if she was waiting—hoping— for him to invite her over. But when he didn't say anything, she simply said, "Good night, Devlin," and hung up.

He felt slightly spacey, almost dizzy, and realized he hadn't eaten anything today after his morning workout. It had been an intense one—he'd trained with Annika and afterward had been too busy to do anything but glance at the plates Marlena kept bringing him. And so he headed to the kitchen.

He stared into the refrigerator and then closed it. He was hungry, yes, but it wasn't for food; it was the persistent, sexual ache that had begun when he met the new operative the night before.

Kira would help the kid, and Annika would do the rest once she got back from England. He was sure of it.

But when the doorbell rang at exactly midnight, he groaned and cursed and then stood on the other side of the door praying he was wrong about who he'd find when he opened it.

No such luck. The nameless new recruit waited there, his arms crossed. And he didn't look happy.

"What the hell are you doing back here?" Dev demanded. Security would hear about this—loud and clear. Heads would fucking roll.

The young man sighed loudly, not bothering to hide his temper. "I'm so fucking sick of this shit. You called for me. I was sleeping—that same guy woke me the fuck up and told me you needed to see me to discuss some crap about the animals I worked with today."

Dev clenched his teeth and ground his words out. "I don't discuss things with new recruits. You'll need to be trained before you've got a shot at going out on a mission for ACRO, never mind talking with me." He sounded like the ultimate asshole, but it was true. The only operatives he talked missions with were those he'd known the longest and the higher-ups. For the others, he depended on their sups.

"Look, I don't need to be here. At ACRO. I've got places I can go."

Dev smiled at the cocky stance. "Like where—jail?"

"Ah, fuck you. What, you know everything? You've read my file?"

"I don't have to read your file—I can read you, clear as day. I'm psychic."

The young man smirked. "So tell me what I'm thinking right now."

Dev hesitated and then, "I'll need to touch you in order to do that. Just hold out your hand, palm up."

It was the young man's turn to hesitate, but he did what Dev asked. Dev put his own palm on the warmer one and closed his eyes.

He didn't need the closed-eye bullshit, but he always found it a nice touch. Plus, he didn't want the guy to be able to read his expression. Lately, Dev hadn't had much of a poker face.

I want you to fuck me. Hard.

Now, that made Dev's eyes open fast—his mouth dropped too as he stared into the younger man's eyes and wondered if this was all a game to him. "You shouldn't ask for things you don't want delivery on," Dev said finally.

"That's a generic answer if I ever heard one."

"You want me to fuck you. Hard."

The man's eyes blazed, cheeks flushed at being caught. He yanked his hand away but Dev grabbed his wrist. "Isn't that what you were thinking?"

"No," the man said hoarsely, but he was lying just the way Dev had lied to himself last night.

There was no point in denying it anymore. "What's your name? Never mind, don't tell me—that's not important."

With that, Dev curled his hand around the back of the younger man's neck and pulled him in, brought his lips down on the incredibly full ones, hard and fast. Because there was no other choice for Dev now.

The young man's chest heaved, and he held his hands away from Dev's body as if he wasn't going to let it happen. But Dev's kiss was insistent, and finally, finally, the man moaned into his mouth and grabbed Dev's shoulders. Responded with his own tongue, let it play against Dev's in a fiercely sensual kiss that lasted until neither of them could breathe.

Until Dev could barely hold himself up. He pulled away from

the kiss, went to pull away from the embrace, but the other man's strength held him there.

Excedo. No doubt about it. Even the ones who didn't have superstrength were still much stronger than average. But the way the man held him, Dev knew the new recruit hadn't a clue just how much strength he had.

The young man panted out, "It's Gabe—Gabriel. My name. You asked before—shit . . ."

Gabriel. Like the archangel. Oz always did have a sick sense of humor.

But somehow, here with Gabriel, the ache didn't feel so hopeless. "Are you coming in, Gabriel?"

Gabriel's forehead remained against his. "Fuck."

"Yes," Dev murmured.

"I thought you didn't want me here."

"There's a lot I *do* want right now, and all of it requires you being here." Dev put his mouth back on Gabriel's.

This is for one night, Oz. And only for you.

Why the little voice in the back of his head told him he was a liar was something he wasn't prepared to ponder.

COLD. SCARED. PISSED. Gabe had been all those things and more as he waited outside the cranky asshole's house last night for fifteen minutes until another official black ACRO Humvee pulled up.

He'd shoved his bag into the backseat and climbed into the front.

"What the hell were you thinking, coming to Devlin's house?" the man demanded.

"I was dropped there. I didn't know he was God fucking Almighty and never to be disturbed. I don't know shit about this place."

"You'd better get up to speed fast."

Gabe stared out the window into the dark, could almost hear the clank of the cell door closing and another man giving him the same advice—better get up to speed fast, son. Won't live long in here if you don't.

He'd been about to go back to jail when two men intervened, grabbed him—kidnapped him from the police, actually, and told him he was special.

"You'd be surprised how many of your kind we find in jail," one of them commented.

"My kind?" he asked.

The men had glanced at each other. "Don't worry—they'll explain everything to you soon enough."

Tonight, Gabe was a little less lonely and still scared, but it was a different kind of fear. Sure, Gabe knew he was strong, but Devlin O'Malley was much stronger than he was in so many ways—Gabe had felt it last night when he'd stood on the man's front porch for the first time. Dev's presence had been like a punch in the gut, and Gabe had been unable to erase his boss's face from his dreams.

Now he was in Dev's arms—Dev needed him. He could tell by the rough way the man handled him, like he was trying to lose himself in the sex.

Gabe wasn't about to object, not even when Dev dragged him inside and pushed him roughly to the first couch they stumbled across. Facedown, he let Dev strip his shirt over his head and yank his pants down around his ankles until that panicked feeling of being held down began to overtake him. Especially when Dev called him *Oz*, muttered it against the back of his neck as he lay helpless on the couch.

He rolled, easily pushing Dev off him. "I can't—not like this."

Dev sat back on his heels on the end of the couch, staring at him as if he were crazy. Which Gabe probably was, refusing this man—refusing his boss anything—but he would never be able to let himself relax like that again during sex.

He stared at Devlin—the man's eyes were intense and he was as aroused as Gabe himself was. "I just . . . need to take it slow."

Well aware that he sounded like a fucking, *fucking* idiot, he attempted to pull Dev's body down onto his. Dev resisted until Gabe put more strength behind it.

He kissed Dev, but the man didn't respond at first. After

another attempt, Dev finally did—a long, hard, breathless kiss that he took over from Gabe.

When he pulled away, he told Gabe, "Turn over."

"No."

"I'm in charge—we're doing things the way I want them."

"You're in charge of me when we're working. Not here," Gabe shot back.

"You have so much to learn, Gabriel." Dev was off him swiftly, tugging at his clothes to right them, running his hands through his hair. "Get up and get out."

CHAPTER *twelve*

The moment Ulrika was out of Trance's sight, she broke into a sprint down the hall and hit the loo at a run. The beast was clawing at the inside of her skin, furious at Trance's suggestive, dominating talk. But the woman she was had damn near climbed up on the table and offered herself to him.

This was never going to work. The idea that she could protect him from Itor was ludicrous. And even if she *could* protect him from them, she couldn't protect him from herself.

Right now, the biggest threat couldn't even be identified. She could rip him to bits, or Itor could break in and take them both.

She touched her collar, which had stopped tingling, but it still felt like a two-ton weight around her neck. She'd sensed Itor's presence for most of the drive, and only now did she realize that if they were somehow tracking her, she was putting Trance in danger from them as well. She wasn't protecting him; she was making him a target.

Swallowing sickly, she closed the door behind her and braced her fists on the sink, needing a moment to compose herself. A look in the mirror told her more than she wanted to know about her physical state. Her hair was a wild tangle, her makeup so smudged she looked like a raccoon and the hollows in her pale cheeks gave her the appearance of a half-starved street urchin.

Only her eyes sparked with energy and life, but that was the wolf in her. It wasn't comfortable in this house it didn't know, wasn't comfortable with Trance at all. It wanted to run.

And, if Ulrika was honest with herself, she did too.

Staying with Trance would be a death sentence. For him.

"I'm so sorry I got you into this," she whispered. He was the first person she'd learned to like in years. The first since Masanao, and even that hadn't been a true friendship. He'd been nice to her, and in a world where everyone else had been vicious or cold or simply apathetic to her circumstances, he'd been a godsend.

But ultimately, he'd paid for his kindness, and she couldn't risk that, or worse, for Trance.

It took her about two seconds to shove open the window over the toilet and slip through it. As she hit the ground, an alarm blared.

The place was wired with alarms? *Shit!*

Adrenaline and fear sent her scampering across the expansive yard to the fence, which she scaled effortlessly. A childhood spent climbing trees and mountains paid off, big-time.

On the other side, she hesitated long enough to scent the marine air and get her bearings. Instinct told her to head for the country, to a forest, and right now instinct and the knife tucked into her boot were all she had in her defensive arsenal.

She tore through yards and between houses, kept off the streets and sidewalks as well as she could. Using her heightened sense of smell as a guide, she headed for clean air that didn't reek of humans. As she ran, her wolf spirit sang, loving the freedom, loving the run. It still wanted out, to run as an animal and not a human, but this was better than nothing.

Ulrika's terror climbed every time she saw a human, but soon, maybe an hour later, she finally found herself traipsing into rugged country terrain. She leaped over a stone fence and headed for the opposite edge of a meadow filled with sheep. The wolf quivered, wanting to hunt, but now wasn't the time. She needed to reach the forest just beyond the rocky outcrop ahead.

She gave herself a moment to rest, sinking down on the damp ground and bracing her back against a tree. Her legs were rubbery and her lungs burned after nonstop running. Exhaustion set in; she hadn't slept at all during the five-hour overnight drive to Plymouth, and now the early-morning gloom was sitting heavily on her. She needed a nap, but she'd have to make do with a few minutes of rest.

Closing her eyes, she wondered what Trance was doing. No doubt, he was searching the city streets, probably expecting her to head for crowded areas where she could blend in. Or maybe he thought she'd head to the water, where she could stow away aboard a moored boat.

The bleating of a lamb startled her, had her leaping to her feet, confused, blinking, realizing she'd fallen asleep.

And standing in front of her, looking extremely pissed off, was Trance. "We tried it your way," he said, in a deep, sharp voice that cracked through her like a spanking on bare skin, "and now we're doing it mine."

She swallowed dryly and backed up a step. "How . . . how did you find me?"

He moved forward with her. "I was a cop. I'm a good tracker."

"Stay away," she whispered.

"That's not going to happen."

"I'm doing this for you. You're in danger." She whipped the knife out of her boot and held it in front of her. "From me as much as from the agency."

He cocked an eyebrow, his gaze flickering to the blade and then dismissing it completely as a threat. "We can do this the easy way or the hard way, but the end result will be the same. You're coming back with me."

"Damn you, Trance." She put the blade to her jugular, because, yes, she was willing to slit her own throat if it meant not getting captured. Or if it meant keeping him safe. "Don't you get it? I thought I could protect you, but if they're tracking me, I'm only putting you in danger. You're better off on your own."

Apprehension flickered in his dark gaze. "Take it easy. Hurting yourself isn't going to help anything."

Tears stung her eyes. She was tired, so tired of running and fighting and being so desperate that death was starting to look good. "It'll keep me out of their hands. You don't understand how far I'll go to never be caged again."

"I do understand, Rik. I've arranged a flight out of here. We'll get out of Britain and away from the guy at the club. We can go anywhere you want. We just need to get back to the house until the plane gets here."

She narrowed her eyes at him. "How could you have done that?"

"My friend who owns the house has a jet. He owes me a favor for some creative tax help."

"I don't know..."

Trance's offer sounded good. A way out. Right now she had nothing but the clothes on her back, was in same situation she'd been in three months ago when she'd fled from her handler and the powerful telekineticist who had nearly killed her after she attacked the TAG agent. She didn't relish the thought of scrounging for food again, living like a vagrant and always worrying about hurting humans.

Trance made the decision for her. He struck like a snake, uncoiling in a lethal blur and disarming her with a flick of his wrist. He caged her against him, her back to his chest. His voice in her ear was a low growl. "We're in this together now. You can't do this on your own, and it's about time you trusted someone. That someone is me. You're coming back with me, and I'll take care of you. This isn't negotiable."

She began to tremble, a combination of fear, the beast's fury and her own desire to let him take control. "I don't...I don't know if I can give you what you want."

"You can, and you will." He spun her around, gripped her

shoulders, and captured her gaze with his. His pupils dilated and then contracted to pinpoints, and she felt a strange calm fall over her. "I released you from those chains back at your place. If I'd wanted to, I could have hurt you. Badly. But I didn't, did I?"

"No," she rasped. And by letting her go, he had to know he'd laid the foundation for her to grow close to him. To trust him. And now he was demanding even more. He had every right; his life was in danger, and to save themselves, they'd have to trust each other.

She'd betrayed his trust by running, and he needed to build it back again.

He dipped his head and kissed her, hard and fast, leaving no doubt about what he wanted. He wanted her trust and her body, and he intended to have both.

THE RIDE to Plymouth had been . . . interesting, mainly consisting of a high-speed chase of what seemed like nobody. But Ryan held on to some sort of remote control and barked out directions to her, and Meg had driven like the wind, liking the feeling of not knowing where she was going.

She could still feel his mouth on hers, his tongue stroking her . . . the kiss held so much promise that her body still tingled, hours later.

He hadn't asked her any more questions but she did have more answers. Several more, actually, but she held those in reserve for a time her life might need saving from the man sitting next to her.

The heavy cloak of guilt at holding back the connection she'd thought they'd once had was something she hadn't been able to shake off during the ride. She'd thought several times about telling him everything she knew about his past, but good old common sense, laced with a dose of fear every time she remembered Ryan's last words to her forced her mouth shut on that subject.

If you're wrong, I'm the last person you want to trust with your body. Or your life.

At one time, she'd been more than prepared to trust him with both.

"We're about forty-five minutes out," he told her finally as he plugged in some coordinates into the GPS tracker. "Just follow the directions."

He finally put down the remote for a second and closed his eyes. A small sigh of exhaustion escaped his lips and she realized it had been a long time since she'd slept as well.

"You can sleep when we get to the hotel."

She glanced at him. "You read minds?"

"No, I read people." And that was his last comment until they arrived at the hotel—in half an hour, thanks to her lead foot.

She waited in the car while he checked in and then walked with him into the small suite—a bedroom with a queen-sized bed and bathroom on one side and a couch and chair, TV and kitchenette on the other.

"Don't get too comfortable—we're not staying long." He didn't say anything else, and went to shower, closing the bathroom door behind him.

In order to assuage the restless feeling that invaded her now that they were stopped, she opened her laptop to see if there was any information on Interpol looking for her, but strangely, she couldn't get online. Annoyed, she dialed her brother, because being out of contact with Mose for more than twenty-four hours at this point guaranteed a freak-out on his part.

"Where. Have. You. Been." Mose was past freak-out, having moved on to furious some time ago.

"I'm, ah, in Plymouth. England."

"And I was at your apartment. Which had been gone over thoroughly by Interpol," he told her.

"I've lost that tail for now." She peeked over her shoulder toward the bathroom and the sound of running water. Being with Ryan was one way to ensure she stayed clear of them. If they'd been close, Ryan would've let her know—he didn't want to be bothered by them any more than she did. "I told you not to come for me."

"Tell me where you are right now. I'm coming to get you."

"I'm not alone. I'm helping someone out—he got me away from Interpol."

"Who? Give me his name—I'll check him out."

"He's someone from my past, Mose. Someone I took money from."

"Name."

She lowered her voice. "Ryan Malmstrom. He's suffering from some kind of memory loss. I think . . . I think he's an agent."

"ACRO?"

"Itor."

"Shit, Meg. How the hell you manage to get yourself involved in this shit . . ."

"Mostly it's been helpful to you. The money I took from Ryan was for you—five years ago. That twenty-five-million-dollar job I pulled."

"I'm calling my source at ACRO. While I'm on the plane coming to get you."

"I won't tell you where I am. I can't compromise what Ryan's doing."

"What kind of shit is that? You're kidding me, right? You're not any kind of superagent, Meg. You're a computer geek."

His words cut her—they were true enough and nothing that would've insulted her in the past, but today she didn't want to just be that computer geek hiding behind fashionable clothing from Interpol. "Screw you, big brother."

She hung up the phone and turned it off for good measure. She probably should tell Ryan that ACRO would be investigating him, but then again, she was tired of telling people things. She wanted some answers.

She couldn't help but rummage—put her hand inside his overnight bag and came up with two DVDs labeled RYAN in big, black lettering that was almost ominous. Quickly, she popped one into her laptop and gasped out loud at the sight of Ryan dressed in all leather and doing some extreme BDSM.

He seemed to be enjoying himself—the women were crying

out, their flesh red from the whips. Her stomach churned—is this what he'd meant to do to her in the plane?

Would he have really? Because the Ryan on the screen didn't mesh with the way he'd touched her in real life, his face so close to the curls between her thighs . . .

"Haven't you heard it's not polite to look at things that don't belong to you?" Ryan growled, catching her by the wrist and pulling her to him. "No, of course not. You like taking things that don't belong to you."

His chest pressed against hers, her shirt wet from the dampness of his body. He didn't even have a towel on, and she'd caught a glimpse of his heavy manhood between his legs. That arousal now rubbed her belly. "That's right. It's more fun to take things that don't belong to you."

Ryan actually smiled a little, more when she licked her lips and flushed at the sounds of the female moans emanating from the computer on the desk. "*I* don't belong to you, Coco. You want to take me on? Is your little virgin clit twitching for me?"

She didn't know what was happening. She was angry—so angry at Ryan, and at her brother for treating her the way he had. She'd been good enough to remain above the law, and yet somehow he still thought she was unable to function without him in the real world.

She had got along fine. But right now, she wanted something more. Without hesitation, she put her arms around Ryan's shoulders, feeling their broad strength flex against her own bare forearms. It forced her body closer to his, and his nostrils flared.

"Do you really like that, Ryan? Tying women up so they can't touch you? Or do you like to be touched?"

"Are you going to touch me, honey?" His hand was firm on her buttocks now, holding her in place.

"Yes," she whispered.

He watched her when he pulled back, and for a second she thought he would let her. But when she dropped her hand to his erection, he grabbed her wrist. "I don't want you touching me. I have one use for you and then we're done."

Her cheeks flushed, a combination of anger and humiliation as he let her go and went back into the bathroom.

RYAN DRESSED in silence, and thankfully, Coco didn't interrupt. She just tapped away on her computer—the one she'd been watching his sex videos on.

He supposed he should have been angry, but the look of shock on her face had been satisfying enough. Shock was better than disgust, which was what he felt every time he viewed them, looking for clues to his past, but he never saw anything new. He was always dressed in leather and chains, and the women were always begging for mercy as he hurt and humiliated them.

He glanced at Coco while he threw on his jacket, and wondered why she hadn't run away screaming after seeing the sex. No, she'd done the opposite, had actually come on to him.

Which had to be a fucking joke. She was either an innocent virgin trying to get something from him by playing the temptress, or she was lying about the virgin thing and really was a temptress. He'd have bet on the latter, because in his world, the former didn't exist. But something about her just dripped sweet and pure, with a touch of hot spice deep inside. He'd tried a chocolate-covered jalapeño once, had sucked down the smooth sweetness while wiping the sweat off his brow.

That was Coco.

Then again, maybe she was a great actress.

Either way, she was trouble, and now he was stuck in a hotel room with her. At least, he was stuck until he either captured or killed Ulrika, or Itor arrived to do it. He'd called them while in the bathroom and told them where she was. It had been easy to follow her—Coco had driven while he stayed connected with the shape-shifter through his remote and her collar. Everything Ulrika saw, he saw, including street signs and addresses.

"I'm going to get us some breakfast," he said, as he tucked the car keys in his pocket. "Stay here."

She didn't look at him. "Don't know where else I'd go."

Well, that was something they'd have to work out eventually.

He wanted her help getting his memory back, and since she seemed to know so much about him, she could be invaluable. But at the same time, he didn't need the complication of having a civilian with him, and he definitely didn't want Itor to arrive and catch him with her. Sure, he could tell them she was just some chick he'd picked up for sex, but if, for some reason, they knew who she was, they might nab her for her skills.

Or for something much worse, if she'd ever stolen from them.

He hurried down to the hotel's restaurant, not at all worried about her trying to get help. She'd volunteered to come with him, and besides, when he'd closed her laptop on the plane, he'd used his gift to rewire her modem so she couldn't get online. She could use a phone, of course, but being covert in front of him where he could hear would be a lot more difficult.

He ordered two full English breakfasts to go and waited outside in the cool spring air, letting it wake him up. It had been a long night, but he couldn't afford to sleep. Too much was at stake.

When the food was ready, he took it back to the room, and they both dug in, him sitting on the bed, her at the desk where she'd been nose-to-screen with the computer when he'd walked in.

She ate like she'd never seen food before, but then, he hadn't eaten in over fifteen hours, and it had been at least twelve for her.

"I love English breakfasts," she said, as she piled her fork high with eggs. "Rasher and beans and tomato . . . yum."

Ryan grimaced. He liked the thick strips of bacon, but he'd never gotten the tomato-and-beans-for-breakfast thing, but then, he'd grown up eating cold cereal.

He blinked. Cold cereal . . . how did he know that? He searched his memory, which was mostly a big, dark hole, but a flash came through—a lady . . . his mom? She was pouring Trix in a bowl.

"Damn," he muttered.

"What is it?" Coco took a break from shoveling food into her mouth to stare at him.

"I remembered something. From when I was a kid. Nothing important. Just that I liked fruit-flavored cereal."

Coco's smile tugged at his groin. "Well, that's better than nothing. Even if you have terrible taste in cereal."

He lobbed a packet of jam at her, and then wondered why he'd done that. Was he the playful type? He wouldn't have thought so, based on what Itor had told him.

When the packet came sailing back at him, he caught it one-handed, and tore it open with his teeth. "Your choice, Coco—should I put this on the toast, or on you? Either way, I'm going to eat it."

The smile fell off her face, and her lips parted in the tiniest of gasps.

"What's the matter?" he teased. "You came on to me earlier, and now you're shocked at my suggestion?"

"Of course not." She sniffed and went back to eating, but he couldn't touch his food. Not now that he had the naughty image in his head, the one of her, naked on the bed, smeared with jelly in all the sensitive places. He could picture himself licking every bit off, starting at her breasts and working his way down.

Cursing, he set aside his plastic container and fetched the remote to Ulrika's collar. He'd need to keep an eye on her, make sure she didn't go on the move again. He was guessing that she and the blond guy were going to dig in for a while, and if he was ACRO, they'd be waiting for extraction.

Which was why he didn't want to go in by himself. Not only did he not know what skills the guy possessed, but if more agents showed up, he'd be screwed. Better to wait for Itor if at all possible.

"What are you doing?" Coco asked as he sank back down on the bed and switched on the remote.

"Keeping an eye on my girl."

CHAPTER
Thirteen

Trance didn't want to pull back from the kiss, wanted to take Rik roughly against the hard ground. By the way she clutched him, he doubted if she'd resist. But they were far too vulnerable here—he needed to get them safely back to the house and Rik under complete control before the jet arrived.

He wanted time to be able to talk to her. To explain. But for now, he was done fooling around. Thankfully, Kira had given him some advice in case Rik did run, and Trance had followed it to the letter once he heard the alarms blare.

She was fast—speed wasn't his greatest gift as an excedo but he was definitely faster than most, so it wasn't difficult to catch her.

He tugged at her hair to pull her mouth off his, held her there for a second. "You're coming with me." He didn't give her another option or another way out, just stared into her ginger eyes until that small part of her that wasn't immune to his hypnosis tuned in. "You will not run from me again."

He'd parked at the edge of the forest—it took them less than fifteen minutes of walking fast through the brambled woods to arrive there. When he opened the passenger-side door, she stared down at the chains—her chains that he'd laid on her seat.

"Do I need to use them now?" he breathed against her neck, one finger running up her side to brush her breast and move toward a nipple. "Because they will be used sooner or later, just like I promised."

"I . . . don't need them now. I won't run again."

He believed her. She'd been running to save him, not running away from him, something that nearly broke his heart. Every fiber of his being wanted to take her home, chain her down and make her fly—wanted to bring her pleasures she'd yet to experience.

He would do that. And then he'd talk to her . . . make her understand. He went over his plan in his mind on the drive back to the safe house, until he pulled into the garage and locked and armed the house around them. Then he led her into the basement, where Dev had installed a wall strong enough to hold Rik, with the right chains. He'd helped Devlin design the dungeon so it looked lived in, as though it was used often, but this was the first time he'd seen it in person.

It made his blood run hot, seeing his old stomping grounds re-created here. He hadn't wanted to revisit his past, but this was different—this was where he'd thrived. It had gotten old for him because he'd wanted to settle in with one sub and couldn't allow himself.

But with Rik . . .

Fuck, no. With Rik *nothing* . . . she was Itor. She was dangerous—she needed to be captured and contained, and then she'd hate his guts so much there'd be nothing left but scraps of the time they'd spent together. If she survived ACRO and Itor fighting over her.

"So this friend, the one who owns the house . . . you play together," she mused, looking around the well-stocked dungeon. There was a St. Andrew's Cross and a spanking bench—two medical tables, and a large bed in the corner, plus various other toys. Whips and masks lined the wall, along with heavy chains that hooked to a stone wall.

He preferred to use Rik's chains—obviously, they'd been proven to hold her and hold her well.

"We've played together with subs, yes. My friend is also a Dom. He's rougher than I prefer, though."

"You don't like it rough?" She picked one of the leather belts up and ran it over her arm as if to test its weight.

"I like to give pleasure. Sometimes, that comes from pain, but I'm not into pain for pain's sake."

She turned into him, a palm on his chest. "You've had long-term subs before?"

"No. Never. I was always . . . it wasn't something I saw myself doing well." He put his hand over hers. "You're the first person I've been with more than once in any capacity, Rik. Now sit on the edge of the table."

"I'd rather stand."

"It wasn't a suggestion. Sit."

He actually saw her teeth grind together.

She looked as if she wanted to protest, but didn't.

Once she was seated, he caught her gaze. "Just look at me, and breathe."

"I can't do this, Trance."

"Call me *Sir*."

Her back stiffened. For a moment, her eyes went wild, and her breathing grew slow and deep, and he knew she was trying to suppress the beast. Then, just as the tension melted from her face, her eyes shot wide again, and she clawed at the collar.

Ryan.

He couldn't fully hypnotize Rik, but he could damn well hypnotize Ryan—if Dev's theory was correct and Ryan was using his gift to see what Rik was seeing. Trance stared into her amber-colored eyes and worked his magic.

The first time he'd realized he had this gift, he'd been six and he'd convinced the babysitter to let him eat junk food all day long. He didn't have real control of it until he was in his late teens—blamed the testosterone and the fact that he had more than normal, thanks to his excedo gene. But he'd used the gift sparingly, and once he joined the military, he used it only during times when he knew his muscle would get him in more trouble than his mind control would.

This time, he knew both his mind and his brawn would bring the trouble, and he was actively courting it.

He continued staring at her until she was calmer, and then he spoke. "Remember that time at the annual picnic? You took off all your clothes and went swimming in the lake and then most of the people at the picnic followed, including your boss. And then later we went to that club called Chaos and you picked up that woman with the purple hair. Remember you telling me about how you grew up in San Diego?"

"What are you talking about, Tr—Sir?"

"Lay back for me, Rik. No more questions." He waited for her to follow his direction—he'd maintained eye contact the entire time, hopefully taking out whoever was on the other end of the remote for a bit. And if it was Ryan, well, he'd given him enough reminders of ACRO life for the man to begin to suspect something. Even a total mind scrub couldn't take away memories forever, just make them so painful to access that the victim typically wouldn't bother.

But Ryan wasn't typical anything. He'd bother. And Trance had the chance he'd been working up to: Rik, submissive.

He locked the cuff around one ankle and then the other and then locked her wrists above her head. She gave a soft gasp each time the metal clicked shut until she was left splayed open for him. Still fully clothed too, but he'd have fun taking care of that detail.

First things first, though. "Itor are not your people," he whispered fiercely, the message for both Ryan and Rik. "Come home where you belong."

* * *

RYAN'S WORLD TILTED on its axis, and spun out of control. The guy with Ulrika was looking at Ryan. *Directly at Ryan.* He felt it all the way to his brain.

Remember that time at the annual picnic? You took off all your clothes and went swimming in the lake and then most of the people at the picnic followed, including your boss. And then later we went to that club called Chaos and you picked up that woman with the purple hair. Remember you telling me about how you grew up in San Diego?

Yes . . . he remembered. Swimming naked . . . But where? His boss . . . a guy named . . . Roland.

Chaos. He didn't remember that. Or the purple-haired woman. But somewhere in the fog of his mind he did remember San Diego. And his mother, who had been pouring the cereal. A warm wash of feeling came over him. He'd loved her. They'd been close, but she'd died just days before he graduated from high school. Cancer.

The fog closed in again, and Ryan floated, somehow aware that the blond guy—Trance, he thought—was doing this to him. Dimly, he felt Coco's hands on his shoulders, heard her calling his name.

Itor are not your people. Come home where you belong.

Pain blasted through Ryan's head, spiderwebbing across his skull, and then the connection with Trance broke. He sat, stunned and unable to speak or move, except to look down and see that he'd dropped the remote and was now clutching the headboard so hard it had cracked.

Itor are not your people.

Ryan's stomach churned up his breakfast. If Itor weren't his people, who were?

RYAN WAS getting all freaky again, nonresponsive even. This whole head injury thing sure got in the way of, like, his job.

"Ryan, dammit, please." Meg shook him, more roughly than she had when he'd collapsed on the plane. Nothing. She stroked his hair, moving it off his forehead—it was cool to the touch, so no fever. But his eyes were staring straight ahead and his lips moved, as if he was answering questions inside his own mind.

He sat up, hugging his knees to his chest—his breathing was fast, and when she touched him he barked, "Get the hell away from me."

"Sorry." She moved across the room, tried her best to become invisible. This was probably the stupidest thing she'd ever done, stayed with a man who'd kidnapped her—a man who'd once threatened to hurt her.

You took this man's life from him—you owe him.

But she didn't have to let him treat her like shit.

Slowly, she stood and walked over to him, bent down so her face was closer to his. "You're in pain and you're scared and fucked up—I get that, Ryan. But don't you dare treat me like some sorry-assed scapegoat for your problems."

"You're part of my goddamned problem!" he roared, catching her by the arm and pulling her toward him.

She didn't struggle out of his grip, but she didn't stop telling him off either. "Poor baby—you're money's all gone. Stolen by a girl. Money gotten by illegal means. Let's not pretend you were feeding orphans, asshole."

He released her, tried to turn away, but she wasn't having it. This time, she grabbed his chin, forced him to look at her. "Most women I know would've been long gone, would've left your sorry ass on the floor of the plane. Especially after what you tried to do to me. I didn't. You'd better start appreciating that."

He was breathing hard, eyes averted. When he finally spoke, his voice was still angry, but it wasn't directed at her. "I'm not who I thought I was . . . I'm not an Itor agent. I think I might be an ACRO Agent."

"How can you be sure?"

"I met a guy the other night—the one we followed here. He knew me but I didn't recognize him. But I swear, he was just talking to me, in my head." He stared at the remote as if trying to figure things out. "He was telling me things."

"While you were out of it, you mentioned San Diego again—the way you did earlier. I know some things about you," she said finally, wondered if he'd yell at her for holding back.

He didn't, just took her by the shoulders and told her, in no uncertain terms, "Stop fucking around and tell me everything you know about me. Now. Please."

Yes, she supposed that was only fair. "You grew up in San Diego," she started, and immediately his fingers eased up.

He muttered, "That's right, that's right," to himself before turning his attention back to her.

"And you're right—you don't work for Itor, you're an ACRO agent." She revealed what ML had told her—he'd called when Ryan had gone to get the food, confirming that Ryan was working undercover at Itor when he'd been discovered and captured. "I think Itor caused your head injury . . ."

"They did a mind scrub," he muttered. "Motherfucker."

"I don't know what that is, but it doesn't sound good." She leaned against the bed and watched him carefully, the way the dark hair fell over his forehead, tousled, like he'd just woken up from a long, deep sleep. In many ways, he had—but she wondered what had happened to him during those long months when ACRO had believed him to be dead.

He's probably all kinds of fucked up, sis. You need to get away from him. Wyatt said they're sending agents in to grab him.

She'd been trying not to think about the tapes of him she'd seen earlier, with him hurting the women. Although maybe *hurting* wasn't the right word, because, from what she'd read about the BDSM world, some people liked that kind of pain.

Ryan just didn't seem to be the type of man who enjoyed dishing it out . . . but she supposed she didn't know him very well at all.

"I've got to go." He was on his feet, rummaging in his bag, grabbing for the keys.

A big part of her wanted him to leave—she'd just sit here on the floor and let him go and then she'd catch a flight to Italy or Greece and hang out there until Interpol got too close.

She just wanted to go home, but she had no idea where that was anymore. "I can help you."

Ryan stopped, watched her even as his eyes darted frantically from her to the car. "I've got to move fast—there's not much time. Got to chase my past . . . the key to my future."

If she couldn't find her own, she might as well help someone find theirs. "Where are we going?"

"I need to find a way into a house—an ACRO safe house." He moved close, let his fingers rest lightly on her computer and rattled off the address to her. Surprisingly, the Internet came up. Quickly, she began to type, fingers flying, getting into places she shouldn't be. The familiar thrill began to ease over her body as she began to type in codes in an attempt to find the blueprints of both the house and the elaborate security system.

"Can you break it so I can get in? I've got to see the guy who's in there. Now. Got to warn him . . ."

"It's not going to be easy," she muttered, her fingers typing a mile a minute. "This system is far more sophisticated than anything I've ever seen. You need codes—security codes, things I might not be able to get access to."

"You've got something better than that. You've got an ACRO agent at your side—if what's coming back to me is right."

"Let's hope more starts to come back to you."

"Let's go—you'll work while I drive. Maybe, between the two of us, we'll be able to break and enter."

DEVLIN WAS at the office long before Marlena, a typical occurrence. Although this time, he'd arrived around two in the morning, after he had kicked Gabriel out of his house.

God, he was an asshole. He wondered how Ender did it every day, all day long, because being a jerk wasn't Dev's natural state of being. He'd been harsh—angry with Gabriel, even as he could see that the boy clearly had been traumatized in some way.

Everything was getting screwed up, no matter how hard Dev tried to control things.

Still, Ryan had risen from the dead—an ACRO operative

found alive was always reason to celebrate, and this was no different. But the heaviness settled into Dev's chest because he wished the same held true for Oz.

He smelled the fresh coffee brewing and it was only a matter of seconds before Marlena was in his office with a fresh mug of the hot liquid and her concern. "What's wrong?"

"Nothing." He ran his hands through his hair, knew that Marlena wouldn't let him get away with that. "I think my sight might be . . . off."

Marlena narrowed her eyes and studied him. "Interference?"

As in, a possible Itor problem. Now that the issue of his paternity had been solved and it was determined Dev himself was indeed the biological son of Alek, the man who rose to power as Itor's leader, Dev was always watchful to keep his mind—and his gifts—well protected. Having his mind broken into and ACRO secrets leaked to the enemy agency wasn't something he wanted to go through again.

"I don't think so."

She already had her hand on the phone. "Let me call Samantha, just in case." The head of the Medium department, and a woman who'd known his parents, she had helped to create a mental shield for Dev so Itor—and Alek—couldn't break into his head again.

"No really, it's nothing like that." He put a hand over hers and reluctantly she put the sleek black phone back into its receiver. "It's just that I read someone's signals wrong. And I never do that."

Marlena went to the couch, sat down, crossing her endless legs. God, she was beautiful—would make any man happy. The fact that she could never be happy herself tore Dev's heart out every time he was with her.

"I need more information," she told him.

Right, she did. There was no holding back anymore. "Gabriel . . ."

Her brows went up, lips formed a small smile, but she didn't say anything. Wise move.

He continued, "Gabriel came to see me again."

"Another problem at the gate?"

"He said . . ." He couldn't believe he was about to share this. "He said a dark-haired guy kept picking him up and dropping him off at my house, and . . . Fuck, do you think it's Oz?"

A few months ago he'd revealed to Marlena what Oz had told him about sending someone to him. He and Marlena had had sex and he hadn't wanted to be alone, had let her curl up next to him for the night.

"I think Oz was a very powerful man, but whether that extends from beyond the grave . . ." She shrugged as she trailed off. "The question really is, do you think it's Oz? Or do you think it's just time you felt something for another man?"

It was a question he'd rolled around in his mind as well, one he hadn't wanted to answer.

Apparently, he still didn't, as his fingers slid over to his keyboard to begin clicking on the morning's e-mail, and Marlena exited just as quietly as she'd entered.

CHAPTER
Fourteen

Gabe was still trying to come to terms with everything ACRO. He'd been poked and prodded by a team of doctors and he'd met with a shrink—although he'd refused to talk with her about anything until she answered his questions.

It had proved to be a short session in her office, and it left him feeling more unsettled than ever, especially after last night's fight with Devlin. He'd woken up in his quarters, surprised he hadn't been dragged out in the middle of the night or fired or whatever the hell they did to people they no longer wanted in this place.

But nothing of the sort had happened. Instead, he was supposed to follow his usual roster of training duties and try to forget that he'd fucked things up badly with the first man he'd actually wanted to be with in years. To say it had put him in more of a foul mood than usual was a grand understatement, and when he'd referred to the ACRO operation as a "team of assassins no one could legally touch," his new supervisor had tried to deck him.

And now he was at the outdoor gym with the ghost hunter named Creed—a grueling five-hour workout in which he had to fight every instinct he had and try to bring his strength back into the realm of normal.

But fuck, anything was better than being stuck with Annika—that bitch who could throw lightning bolts of electricity if he pissed her off. Which seemed to happen with excruciating frequency before she'd left him in tattoo-man's care.

Of course, he hadn't realized that Creed and Annika were, like, together. And so the first time he'd made a comment about her, he'd practically had his head torn off—but strangely enough, it hadn't been by Creed.

No, the large man with the tattoos over half his face and neck and left arm, from what Gabe could see, had simply stood there, staring at him before saying, "Enough, Kat."

"Who the fuck is Kat?" Gabe had asked, clutching his head and turning it from side to side to make sure it was still attached to his neck.

"She's my spirit guide. Annika's one of her favorite people. And mine."

Gabe had held up his hands in a show of surrender. "Point taken, man."

Now, after several sessions with Creed, Gabe realized that the guy was actually cool as hell. Which totally didn't explain how he and Annika got along.

That thought earned him a pinch on the back of the neck from Kat.

"Ouch. Fuck." Gabe rubbed the tender skin and Creed gave him a small when-will-you-learn grin.

Time to change the subject. "So, do Dev and Marlena date?"

Creed shrugged as he held the punching bag steady for him. This was part of getting him to realize—and control—his own strength. He'd been told that in the future he'd train with some guy named Trance, an excedo who had the same gift.

"It's complicated," Creed said finally.

Gabe kicked the bag hard—too hard, apparently, since Creed went flying on his ass. "Christ, no one can give a straight answer around this place."

Creed rose from the mat and dusted off. Gabe tensed for Kat's attack but none came. "Why do you want to know about Devlin so badly?"

"I need to get a handle on this place. Who's with who. It helps to navigate the system." He was a damned fine liar when he needed to be, but he didn't think Creed would buy his explanation. Mainly because it was complete and utter bullshit.

"Marlena's there for him but she's not his type," Creed explained, to Gabe's surprise. "Do you know what I mean?"

Gabe nodded.

"You're cool with that?"

Gabe was surprised as hell that Creed seemed fine with it. "Yeah, I'm cool. But it doesn't make sense."

Creed paused, and for a second Gabe was pretty sure the guy was going to walk away from him. And then, "Dev lost the love of his life less than a year ago. An operative named Oz. His picture's hanging on the ACRO memorial wall. So if Dev comes across as more of an asshole than usual, cut him some slack."

And that's when Kat chose to slam Gabriel from behind. He came to on the ground, breathing hard. Creed stood over him, studying him. "Devlin's one of Kat's favorite people too. If you hurt him or try to use him, she will kill you. And I'll help."

"And what if I can make him happy?"

Creed startled, as if that was something he'd never considered. "Oz was one of my best friends—he was also my brother."

Oh, fuck. "I'm sorry, man. I was just . . ."

Creed stared at him for a moment, his jaw clenched. "If you can make him happy, then you'd be all right in Kat's book. Mine too."

With that, he was gone, calling over his shoulder, "Training's done for the day."

Gabe hadn't hesitated in getting off the mat. Back in his room, he'd showered quickly, thrown on the usual uniform of all black BDUs, the only clothing he had since his bag had been confiscated the first night he'd arrived—for having too many creative weapons, he'd been told—and he headed out to find the wall Creed had spoken of.

It was on a far corner of the ACRO property—at the end of a long, winding path that Gabe supposed was somehow symbolic. It loomed large in front of him, a simple slab of stone embedded with pictures of people identified only by their first names. He scanned the memorial quickly, looking at the faces of the men and women who had served ACRO well. He stopped dead when he came to the picture of Oz, actually had to grab on to the wall to keep from crashing to the ground.

He didn't remember leaving the wall or taking the path back toward the main ACRO compound—all he could see was Oz's face in front of his eyes.

"You all right, son?" One of the guards had a hand on his shoulder to steady him. "You're awfully pale."

"Too much training," Gabe managed. "They're fucking killing me."

The guard nodded in sympathy. "I understand. You probably need a drink. Want a lift to the bar?"

DISORIENTATION LEFT Ulrika's head fuzzy as she lay on the table. She tugged on her wrist restraints, feeling the burn of panic spread from her gut to the rest of her body. She'd allowed Trance to do this, but she wasn't sure why. Her inner wolf was pissed as hell, was clawing at the inside of her skin so ferociously that she could practically feel her control start to shred.

She must have fallen asleep or hit her head or something, because she remembered him saying some strange things about a picnic and a purple-haired woman, and dear God, had she really called him *Sir*?

"Trance, you have to let me go."

He trailed a finger down her arm. "Let's lay down the rules now. From this point on, I don't respond to anything but *Sir*."

A low growl slipped out before she could stop it.

"I'm not going to hurt you." His voice was soft and soothing. "And I won't let anyone else hurt you. Do you believe me?"

She wanted to. God, she wanted to put her trust in him, to let someone else shoulder her burdens. Closing her eyes, she lay there, concentrating on her breathing.

"Let me go," she repeated, but with less conviction than last time.

"I didn't hurt you when you chained yourself at your apartment. I won't hurt you now. I only want to help you. Like you helped me."

Her eyes popped open. "I haven't helped you. I've put you in danger—"

"No." He pressed one finger to her lips. "I'm more a danger to myself than anyone else can be. No one has ever been able to do to me what you have. No one has forced me to control myself as much. And sure as shit, no one has known my secret and actually wanted me to lose control."

"It . . . it was my job."

"Tell yourself that all you want, but I know the truth." He grasped her hand and squeezed it gently. "There's something special about you."

She stiffened and then relaxed, because there was no way he could know how *special* she was. "I'm nothing. Nothing at all."

"Which is why some crazy, supersecret agency wants you. Because you're nothing." His voice held an underlying tone of don't-lie-to-me that at once chafed and made her feel guilty. "Why did you chain yourself up, by the way, if you're nothing?"

"I told you. My temper."

"Right. Your *temper*." He shook his head. "There's something you're not telling me." He dragged his warm palm down her arm, leaving behind pleasant tingles in its wake. "But I get it. You don't trust me yet. We'll work up to that."

She bucked when his hand skimmed over her breast. It felt good, too good, and it wasn't something she was used to. *She* determined who touched her, and when, and where. "I've changed my mind."

He paused, scrubbed a hand over his face, where a five o'clock shadow had darkened his skin, creating harsh planes across his angular jaw. "You think I'll hurt you? Be honest."

"No," she said, surprising herself by meaning it.

"No?"

No, Sir. She pulled in a ragged breath. She knew what he wanted, and crazily, she felt the need to give it to him. In the time she'd been doing the Dom thing, it hadn't been for the usual reasons, for the usual relationships. It had been because the beast liked the control. But she knew how it was supposed to work for a lot of people, knew the desire to please, and therefore be pleased, was a driving force. As a Dom, she'd fed off that. Now she wanted to give him something back. But to take that step . . .

"Just breathe," he said softly, locking gazes with her. "I want you to breathe, to regulate your heart rate. Listen to my voice. Let it move through you like a caress."

"Yes," she murmured, that strange calm falling over her.

"Yes . . . ?" he prompted.

"Yes, Sir." She swallowed hard. She'd done it. And the wolf wasn't freaking out. Better, Trance was smiling at her, his hand rubbing slow circles on her belly until he plucked one of the buttons open and slipped his fingers inside to touch her bare skin. An electric buzz shot through her, and wow, this . . . this was amazing.

"Nice." He leaned over and dragged his lips over her ear, his hot breath fanning across her cheek. "I'm going to take care of you. Do you believe me?"

She wanted to say yes, but he was so close, his lips like velvet on her ear, and all she could do was turn her head so her mouth met his. He flinched in surprise, but he kissed her. Hard. Hungrily. With a moan, she opened for him. Funny how, before Trance, she'd only kissed Masanao—the Seducer who kissed her only to teach her how—but now she couldn't get enough.

This was intimacy, what two normal people did when they cared about each other. After a moment, Trance pulled away, his eyes flashing with anger.

"That," he rasped, "was not acceptable. You get what you want when it's something I want."

"Oh, you wanted it." She smiled. "That's why you're angry."

She knew she'd hit on the truth when his mouth tightened into a hard line. Interesting. She had the sudden feeling that kissing wasn't something he normally enjoyed or wanted from the women he was with, and the fact that he'd been as lost in the moment as she had bothered him.

It might bother him, but it made her wiggle like a happy pup. She was bound, but she wasn't without a measure of control.

"I'm not angry." He unbuttoned her shirt. "This isn't the time for it. Anger never belongs in bondage play."

Funny, because it always belonged in hers. Her time at the club was all about the beast taking out its anger on humans.

He peeled her shirt away from her chest and unfastened her bra with a flick of his fingers. When his hand came down on her breastbone, her breath caught.

"There will come a point where you're going to think I've betrayed you," he said quietly, "but you have to know it's for your own good."

"I tell my subs the same thing." Well, maybe not quite like that, but when she stretched the torment out, not giving them the release they wanted, they might see that as a betrayal. The end result was always worth the delicious denial, though, and once she gave her subs the ultimate release, they glowed with worship.

He dragged his hand low, to the waistband of her jeans. He took a long time to unbutton them. "Lift your hips."

She did, and he slid her jeans and underwear down, unlocking one ankle at a time to remove them. When he'd refastened the second cuff, he gripped her calves and slid his hands up her legs. Slowly. Sensually.

Pleasure skittered across her skin, and as his hands smoothed up her inner thighs she had to fight the instinct to lift her hips so his thumbs would brush her core on their journey up her body. Still, he knew, and he smiled.

"What do you want, Rik?"

To change places with him, but she didn't say that. "I want to come."

"Right now?"

"Yes."

"I'm not going to fuck you." His voice was rough. "Not until you beg for it. And you will beg for it."

So cocky, so arrogant ... and so wrong. But she said nothing, was too choked up with need and with the enormous amount of restraint she had in place to keep from writhing into his touch.

To her surprise, he slipped his fingers between her folds to a rush of wetness.

"Oh, yeah," he growled. "You were so ready for this."

She was beyond ready, she realized. To have someone concentrating fully on her was an amazing experience, and when he began an easy back-and-forth slide through her sex, even the beast began to purr.

It liked this. It liked *him*.

The knowledge freed her in ways she couldn't have believed, and she felt a tear squeeze from her closed eyes. His thumb pressed against her swollen, aching clit, nearly taking her over the edge, but he stopped the delicious motion suddenly.

"Rik? What's wrong? Are you okay?" Tenderly, he wiped the tear from her cheek, and she opened her eyes. God, his expression was so full of concern, and maybe a touch of worry.

"Oh, yes," she whispered. "I'm more than okay. Just ... please ... keep touching me."

"I love touching you."

He moved his fingers lightly over the pad of her sex, stroking the cleft several times before dipping them between her folds again. He brought her to the edge over and over, until she couldn't control her body anymore, was arching her back and rocking her hips, and when he penetrated her with two fingers, her sex clenched around them and she screamed in release.

She pumped against his hand, knowing she could get a multiple orgasm out of this, but before she hit that peak again, he with-drew to caress her inner thighs, her belly, her breasts. She watched him dip his head and tongue her nipple, and the erotic sight nearly had her coming again.

But again, he knew, and he stopped. "What do you want now?" His hand dropped to his hips, where he stroked the mas-sive erection popping against the fly. "I'll give you anything you want. You have my promise."

"Another orgasm," she blurted.

"How?"

"Your tongue, your fingers, your cock, I don't care." She was starting to pant, her hips still rocking as if that could relieve the terrible ache.

She licked her lips as he unbuttoned his jeans. "You want me to mount you? To take you over and over until you lose your voice from all the screaming?"

"Yes. Yes, please."

It was only later that she realized that not only had she begged, just like he said she would, but that, when he asked what she wanted and promised he'd give anything to her, she hadn't asked to be released from the chains.

AFTER STOPPING at a small corner store, Ryan parked the rental car a block away from what he believed was an ACRO safe house, and he and Coco hoofed it the rest of the way. As they neared the gated residence, he grabbed her hand and told her to walk leisurely, as if they were a couple on a stroll.

"There are probably cameras on the surrounding area," he ex-plained. "Smile and pretend you're happy."

"Oh, I don't have to pretend," she said, and yeah, her sarcasm was duly noted.

"You didn't have to come."

"You need me."

That was probably true, but he didn't want to admit it. "Okay, so how do you plan to get us in?"

She tapped her laptop bag slung over her shoulder. "I need to find the nearest utility trunk."

He scanned the area, saw a grate in the grass a few yards beyond the far corner of the property. They'd be vulnerable while Coco worked, but there was no help for that. They'd need to hurry.

Ryan placed himself between the ACRO house and Coco as she kneeled next to the grate and opened it. He dug out the pack of cigarettes he'd bought at the store and lit one, doing his best not to cough. He wasn't a smoker, but he'd anticipated needing to play casual, so he stood there like he'd taken a much needed smoke break. Hopefully Coco was hidden well enough behind him, because if not, she was going to look really fucking suspicious.

After a few minutes, her curse startled him. He didn't think he'd ever heard her utter a harsh word.

"What is it?" He risked a glance back at her, saw her sitting on her heels, laptop balanced on her legs, a wire running from it into the grate, where it was no doubt plugged into an electric wire.

"These people have a top-notch security system. I've never seen anything like it."

"ACRO would have the very best," he muttered.

She cursed again. "I can get in, but they've installed a couple of backup measures."

"Like what?" he asked, though he was still amazed by the fact that she could get in at all. He'd had his doubts, had been running through alternate break-in-to-the-house scenarios in his head, but damn, she knew her shit.

"There's a broken relay between the cameras and the main control panel. It requires manual manipulation at the source to alter any settings. I might be able to get around it, but that would take hours."

Ryan threw down his cigarette butt and ground it into the dirt with the heel of his boot and then squatted next to her. She was so hot sitting there, her fingers flying over the keyboard, her intense expression what he'd expect from her during sex.

He mentally kicked his mind out of the gutter and put his hand on the computer.

"What are you doing?"

"I'm mildly electrokinetic. I can manipulate some electronic devices. I might be able to . . ." He trailed off as he let his mind travel through the circuits and electronic pathways until he found the gap Coco had been talking about. "Okay, I can bridge it, but only while I'm in contact with the computer. The moment I stop, it's gone."

"Wow," she breathed. "I think I love you." She tapped furiously, a smile curving her full lips. Man, she was beautiful when she got all excited. "Got it. Cameras are off." She grinned.

"Can I stop?"

The grin fell from her face, replaced by a scowl. "Crap. No. There's another safeguard in there." She glanced at him. "I can't do anything about this one. Not without a lot of time and a lot more sophisticated equipment than what I've got."

"What is it?"

"I can turn off the alarms, no problem, but the system is set to reboot after ninety seconds of being down."

"ACRO designed it to thwart exactly what we're doing."

"Yes."

"So we've got one and a half minutes to get in and find my guy."

"Yes."

"Shit."

"Yes."

Ryan glanced at the house and felt his stomach hatch some butterflies. This was either going to get him some answers . . . or get him killed.

He wouldn't be able to hold out. The only thing keeping Trance together at the moment was how beautiful Rik looked— half contented from her orgasms, the other half wanton and wanting more. From him.

He could only give her more for a little while longer. There was an expiration date stamped clearly on this mission—on this developing relationship—and he'd definitely stepped over the line.

Him, who'd never ever allowed himself to get personally involved with a sub when he was still Domming. Hell, he'd never allowed himself to get personally involved with any woman.

But here, with Rik, she'd already taken him in ways he'd never let anyone take him. And she was wet and willing and spread for him—the chains pulled taut with the force of her begging.

He pulled his shirt off, his pants remaining undone, but he didn't pull them down. Still, he enjoyed her gaze washing over him, taking him in the way she had those times before and wanting to see more.

It was different now—her eyes held the look of trust this time. In his heart, the severity of the betrayal he would soon commit threatened to burst open and for a second he pondered what would happen if he set her free, loosened the binds, sat her down and explained everything.

We can help you . . .

He hadn't believed those words the first time he'd heard them. No, he'd punched the agent and run off and he'd hidden deep inside the BDSM community until someone else had come for him. He'd listened then, mainly because the female agent had the ability to seduce the shit out of him, allowing two other excedos to tie him down and drug him.

He'd woken up at ACRO, scared out of his mind and angry—it had taken him days to calm down. But he'd finally listened to Devlin and the others, who'd explained, much in the way Rik had the other night, what he was. What he was capable of doing, and how he could help others with his powers.

Helping others—that's what he'd always done best. Helping himself, not so much, something Devlin gently reminded him the last time they'd spoken.

"Trance, please." Rik was breathing heavily from her last orgasm—it wasn't helping that his fingers still played with her nipples, that he'd mounted her and her sex rubbed his. It would be so easy to sheath himself inside of her and ride this whole thing out.

"Why do you want me so badly now, Rik?" he asked. "Before, you couldn't wait to get rid of me. Didn't need my cock to orgasm. Still don't. So why do you need me?"

"I don't need you," she panted. "I want you."

He pushed himself back, though he remained above her. "I can't do this."

She lifted her head from the mattress to stare at him, the soft clink of the chains sounding like guillotine blades to him.

"Trance, what are you talking about? What can't you do? I'm right here—I'm okay . . . please. Please don't stop now—this is good for me. You're not hurting me."

"Not yet," he muttered.

Trance allowed himself the luxury of taking one of Rik's nipples in his mouth, rolling first one hard nub and then the other as he ground against her.

"This is for my pleasure—you understand that," he told her when he lifted his head from her breasts. She nodded, but they both knew it wasn't entirely true. This had been about both of them from the second he'd walked into the club and found her.

"I'm going to take you—the way I've wanted to since we first met. And then we're going to talk. There are things I have to tell you." He'd tell her everything, explain about ACRO. About how he would be able to help her.

"Okay." She looked up at him, trusting. He wondered how long it had been since she'd trusted anyone but herself.

He reached down and prepared to sheath himself inside of her warm sex just as the house alarms began to blare.

He didn't have time to unchain Rik before pulling the semi-automatic rifle from its hiding place inside one of the basement's hollow wall panels. He pressed a few buttons to bring up the camera screens—most of them were down, except for the two backups that focused on the most vulnerable sections of the house.

Before he could do more, out of the corner of his eye he caught the shadows of two figures standing in the doorway. One was an unarmed woman who looked a little frightened. The other had a gun trained on Trance. They had breached the system, bypassed the cameras and now stood, in the flesh, in the basement.

Ryan stood there—angry, yes, but confused too, as if he wasn't sure he should be here armed. He faltered, and Trance noted what he held in his other hand—it looked like a remote and it was pointed toward Rik's collar. "Ryan, let's talk this through. You know I can fix this. I told you that already."

"I don't need fixing—I need answers."

Trance stared him down. "Right now, those two are one and the same."

CHAPTER
Fifteen

Ryan held his Sig in one hand, aimed at the ACRO agent, and the remote to Ulrika's collar in the other. "Stay right there, or I blow her head off."

"Take it easy, man." The agent held up his hands. "Just let me get a blanket to cover her up."

Ryan glanced at the wolf woman, who was fully bound, fully naked and shaking like a leaf. Goddammit. He didn't want to feel sorry for her, but obviously, she was scared to death.

"Please, Ryan," Coco whispered. "Don't hurt these people. At least let her have a blanket."

"Fine," he snapped, and nodded at the other agent. "Cover her. And tell me your name."

"Trance." Trance moved slowly toward the bed in the corner, took the comforter off it and placed it over Ulrika, who watched him with utter trust, and looked at Ryan with absolute terror in her gorgeous golden eyes.

"Unchain me." Her voice was thin, barely audible.

"Since I'm here to kill you," Ryan said, "that's probably not a good idea."

Trance's hands closed into fists. "Ryan, listen to me. You aren't an Itor agent. You're ACRO."

"Trance?" Ulrika was frowning at him, jerking at her chains. "How do you know him?"

Trance ignored her. "Listen to me. You went undercover to infiltrate Itor. They found out, and they scrubbed your mind. Whatever they've told you isn't true."

Ryan shook his head, his mind having trouble processing the information, even though he'd suspected it. He looked at Trance, saw the other man's eyes narrow, the pupils contracting and dilating, and ... *Fuck!* He looked away quickly, realizing what was happening. The guy was a natural hypnotist ... which was how he'd been able to get to Ryan while he was looking through Ulrika's eyes.

Fucking wonderful.

"Don't look into his eyes, Coco," he said, but when she didn't answer, he knew it was too late. Worse, not looking into Trance's eyes severely limited Ryan's ability to read the guy. This pretty much sucked. And was why both the Air Force and ACRO had drilled into him the importance of not running into a situation half-cocked ...

Hey ... he remembered something. Air Force training. It was vague, but there. Itor had told him he'd been a U.S. Marine, which had felt wrong for some reason. And ACRO ... man, he remembered being put through the wringer in training that was more intense than anything the Air Force had done to him. Some hot blonde named Annika had been the drill instructor from hell—

"Put the gun and remote down," Trance said, interrupting the memories that were both good and bad, but definitely welcome. "You don't want to hurt either of us."

Ryan snorted. "Not a chance."

"Why are you here? To kill Rik? To capture her and me? Because neither of those things are going to happen."

"I'm here to find out who the hell I am."

"I told you."

"And who's to say you aren't lying? Maybe Itor is telling the truth and ACRO is the one trying to fuck me up." Which could definitely be the case. ACRO could have put those Air Force and ACRO memories into his head.

"Trance?"

Again, Trance ignored Ulrika, who had begun to struggle against her bonds. "Do you really believe that?"

"I don't know what to believe. This could be some sort of elaborate setup by ACRO. Or an Itor test."

"Listen to me," Trance said, moving forward a step. Behind him, Ulrika had frozen, was staring at the ceiling while her chest moved with rapid, ragged breaths, and Ryan had a feeling she was trying to keep it together. "Look into my eyes—"

"Fuck that."

"Do it, Ryan. If you want to get your memory back, it's your best option, and you know it."

He was probably right, but this could also be a trick. Then again, at this point, Ryan had little to lose. He raised his gaze, and immediately, Trance's eyes locked on. Ryan's mind screamed in protest, but he couldn't look away. Couldn't fight the sensation of being violated.

"Remember," Trance said. "Remember your childhood." Instantly, years of his life slammed into Ryan's brain. Christ, he'd been a happy kid, full of life and with a laughing, perpetually optimistic mother. No father, but his mom, a schoolteacher, had made up for that, and he'd never felt like anything was missing.

"Good." Trance moved closer, but Ryan couldn't do anything about it. "Now remember your time in the military. Remember enlisting. Basic training. Your first mission. Your last mission."

Again, memories flooded his head, with such force that it snapped back on his neck. He'd feel that one like whiplash later.

He became distantly aware that his gun and the remote to Ulrika's collar had been taken away, and although he really wanted to fight, he couldn't. He just kept staring into Trance's eyes. He heard Coco pleading with Trance to release Ryan, and when her pleas failed, she threatened him. The little firecracker was actually swearing and telling Trance she was going to whack him over the head with her laptop. Even after Trance pointed the weapon at her and told her to cuff herself to the wall, she kept cursing, but Ryan heard the rattle of chains and knew she'd obeyed.

"Okay, Ryan, now think about ACRO. How you got there. Do you remember that?"

Ryan nodded, because yep, he remembered. He'd gotten involved in something bad while in the military, something he had been blackmailed into. Arms dealing. When the Air Force initiated an internal investigation, he'd gone AWOL and started working for the bad guys, mainly for survival. It had come down to live free as a criminal or live out the rest of his life in a military prison.

But when Coco interrupted the transfer of money he'd been sending to his bosses from the sale of weapons, he'd ended up running from everyone. ACRO had nabbed him just as the bad guys were closing in, had saved his life and given him a new one.

Ryan didn't know how long he stood there, letting his past weave itself back into the fabric of his life, but eventually he felt almost whole. Almost, because there were still holes.

"Ryan, I need you to get on your knees."

Ryan did it. Like a well-trained dog. "Good. Now, I'm going to release you, and when I do, you'll stay there. Just like that. You'll let me restrain you. Got it?"

"Yes." Son of a bitch. Had he just said that?

Trance turned away, and a sense of relief washed over Ryan. A sense of relief and a sudden urge to do exactly the opposite of what the other agent had told him. Yes, his memory had come back, and he knew Trance was a friend. But he also wasn't going to sit around and let himself be tied up and transferred back to ACRO like a trussed-up turkey.

Or like Ulrika.

He launched himself at Trance, too late remembering the guy's excedo gift. He hit Trance squarely in the back, knocking them both into the wall.

"Son of a—" Trance cut off as Ryan's fist plowed into his gut.

For a second, Ryan thought he might actually stand a chance, especially when Trance rolled and groaned. But Ryan's victory was short-lived. As he moved in to put Trance into the wall again, the other man swept his legs out, catching Ryan in the chest so hard his breath blew out of his lungs. He lay stunned while Trance cuffed him.

"Sorry, man," Trance said, as if that was going to help his damned cracked ribs heal. "But until we get you back to ACRO, I'm not taking any chances."

Ryan wanted to cuss at him, but he still didn't have any breath. So instead he looked over at Coco, who was snarling like a wild-cat and leaping against the chain around her ankle as though trying to get to Trance. Man, if glares were lasers, Trance would have holes through his head.

How cute.

"Don't . . . hurt . . . her," he gasped between painful breaths, and Trance scowled at him.

"Do you ever remember me hurting a helpless woman?"

"I'm not helpless, you ass," she snapped, and Ryan would have laughed if it didn't hurt so much.

"Well?" Trance said, ignoring her.

"No," Ryan admitted. But then, not everything had come back to him. Sure, most of his life had, but some things were still gaping voids. Like his sex life. Why the hell could he not remember what was up with those damned videos. Although he couldn't remember Trance ever hurting a woman, there was evidence that said Ryan had.

"Jesus, Trance," came a new female voice, a familiar one. Annika. "I knew you were into some kinky shit, but damn. Two women and a guy? And hey, Ryan, I really didn't know you were into the dudes." Ryan craned his neck to watch the icy blonde strut into the room, somehow looking sexy in black BDUs and combat boots. She gestured to the table where Ulrika lay, but Ryan could no longer see her. "So this is the leashed assassin, huh?"

"Shut up, Annika," Trance snapped, but it was too late. Something about what Annika said set Ulrika off, and as the god-awful snarl echoed around the basement, Ryan realized what had just happened.

Trance had tricked her, and she'd finally just realized that, without a doubt, she'd been betrayed.

ULRIKA COULDN'T STOP screaming any more than she could stop the past couple of minutes from replaying in her mind.

When Ryan had burst into the basement with the woman, Ulrika had been terrified, especially when she saw the remote in his hand. But Trance had remained calm, confident, in control. She'd believed his law enforcement training had been responsible.

It wasn't until it became obvious that he knew Ryan—an Itor agent—that a cold shroud of dread had settled over her, and the wolf, which had been relaxed and content for the first time ever, stirred uncomfortably. Still, she chose to believe Trance and Ryan knew each other from somewhere else. *Hoped* they knew each other from somewhere else and that there was a good reason he hadn't mentioned it sooner.

Even when Trance mentioned ACRO, which she'd never brought up to him, she still couldn't quite make her mind go there.

But then the scary blond woman he'd called *Annika* had walked in, and her words had broken the wall of denial like a hammer on glass. *"So this is the leashed assassin, huh?"*

Trance had betrayed her. Panic and terror surged in her chest, building until all she could do to release the pressure was scream.

"Rik," he said, putting one hand on her belly. "Calm down. I can explain."

"You bastard!" She'd spent months evading capture by Itor— or any of the supernatural agencies—and in the end she walked right into one of their traps. Inside, the beast was clawing to get out.

"Listen to me." Trance's voice was low and soothing, but she wasn't buying it. Her Itor handlers had been good at fooling her with kindness... right before they did something painful to her. "We're going to help you. No one is going to hurt you, okay?"

She shook her head wildly, her hair whipping into her eyes. *"I hate you, I hate you, I hate you!"*

Hurling the words at him over and over, she tugged on her restraints and bucked until her bones cracked and she felt the sting of blood at her ankles and wrists where the restraints cut into her skin. The blanket had long since slid to the floor, leaving her naked and exposed, but she didn't care. At this point, her nudity was the least of her worries.

"Shit," Annika said. "You got a sedative?"

"There's a hypodermic in my bag. It's in the corner."

"No!"

The beast inside snapped. She couldn't stop it, didn't want to. Pain overwhelmed her as her skin stretched and her joints popped. Sharp teeth erupted from her gums as her jaw cracked and elongated. The transformation took only seconds, but it always felt like a lifetime. For the first time, though, she welcomed it, because she could let the beast handle things while she sank into the background, into the darkness and prayed for numbness.

"Holy mother of God," Annika breathed, as Ulrika heard herself roar so loud the air vibrated. She jerked one of the chains around her ankle so hard it snapped free of the table.

Yes. She was going to rip apart every one of those bastards, taste their blood, feel their bones crunch between her jaws—

"Annika, no!" But Trance's words came too late. Annika touched Ulrika's arm, and suddenly the world exploded in a cascade of colors and her body stiffened and seized under what felt like a million volts of electricity.

When it was over, Ulrika lay stunned, her brain scrambled, her vision blurry. Her ears buzzed, so she could hear voices but not words as someone restrained her loose leg. She felt a prick in her thigh, knew she'd been given that shot.

But all she could think about, even as Trance spoke softly and stroked the thick fur that now covered her arms, was that he'd lied again.

He'd said no one was going to hurt her.

"I TOLD HER that no one would hurt her." Trance tried to keep his cool with Annika, but it wasn't working. Together, he and the blond agent loaded the metal cage into the private jet. Better that his hands were busy, because they wanted to wrap themselves around Annika's neck.

After he'd given Rik the tranq, he'd ordered Annika away, told her to stand the fuck down. He'd tried to talk to Rik. He didn't know if she could understand him while she was in beast form—didn't know if her rage overtook any power of coherent thought, but figured it had to be worth a shot.

She hadn't responded with anything but gnashing of teeth and several lunges that came far too close for comfort. He hadn't moved away fast enough and she'd ripped a nice-sized gash in his arm. And he swore she smiled at that before she passed out.

That's when he gave up the explanation.

Annika dropped her end of the cage with a loud crash. Rik didn't move. "She's not going to care about your honey-baby mushy shit, Trance. She's pissed."

"She's pissed because you went after her."

Annika put one foot up on the metal and gave it a final shove toward the back and then shook her head as if he was an idiot. Which, in this case, he fucking was. "She's pissed because she thinks you betrayed her. But you had to. So get over it and get on the plane already. I've got a class to teach tonight."

Annika's attitude was one he'd always held as well—partially because of his days as a Dom, and also because he hadn't allowed himself to form bonds with anyone. Until now.

He was such an idiot.

"You should really stick with the non-beasts to date. I mean, going out with another agent, fine, but when they can change into a werewolf when someone makes them the least bit angry... well, that's just not cool." Annika pushed some hair off her face.

"I'm not dating her."

"Yeah, I know—the whips and chains were just for show." Annika smirked.

"You know I can take you out quicker than you can shock me, right?"

"And you know that's bullshit, right?" She sang softly, under her breath, "Trance and wolf girl sitting in a tree . . ." But she stopped once Trance locked eyes with her. It was nice, for a change, to watch her helpless.

"You will not shock me," he ordered, but he didn't take his eyes from hers—not yet. This would be the only peace from Annika he would have on this flight. From behind him, he heard Rik rattling the cage, and Ryan and the woman he was with—Coco something—were shifting around, trying to get comfortable while handcuffed to their seats.

Annika refused to take chances with Ryan until Devlin cleared the rescued agent. She was right—about that and about Rik, and the more he thought about the past days, the more he realized how deeply in he'd let himself go. How much he'd trusted her.

How stupid he'd been.

Rik would have to get over herself. Plenty of people were brought into ACRO against their will—and they all got over it. She would too.

"I'VE GOT to call my brother. Will these people let me do that?" Meg whispered to Ryan, even as the big man called Trance turned toward them as if he could read minds. And maybe he could—since the blond woman seemed able to shock people with electricity she produced from nowhere.

And then there was the woman who'd turned into a wolf-creature, currently housed in a cage in the back of the plane. A traveling freak show extraordinaire, and she was along for the ride. Albeit reluctantly, as the fact that she was handcuffed to her seat proved. Ryan was trussed up in the same fashion. "Although, on second thought, I guess you don't have all that much pull there anymore."

He gave her a small, weary smile. "I'm hoping to change things—to get my life back to the way it was. Back to normal."

"None of this is normal. I just watched a woman morph into a bloodthirsty wolf-thing and now I'm traveling with her, a woman who could shock me to death and a man who literally hypnotizes me every time I look into his eyes. It's a freak—"

She didn't finish her sentence as she saw Ryan flinch.

"Yeah, a freak show. Nothing we haven't heard before."

"Ryan, I'm sorry."

"Forget it. Look, you can call your brother and go back to your nice, quiet life of stealing money from people for kicks. Get your orgasms that way, at least."

"Screw you," she whispered furiously, felt the tears rise in her eyes. Trance and Annika had turned back to look at them at Ryan's last words and she blushed and contented herself with staring out the window and telling herself that she no doubt deserved what he'd said.

"I'm sorry, Meg. You're scared. And I'm not helping." Ryan eased closer to her and there was nowhere for her to go, nowhere to escape the press of his body to hers. He leaned in to whisper in her ear, "What I said wasn't fair."

She shrugged, like it didn't matter, but both of them knew it did. Reluctantly, she tore her gaze from the window to look at Ryan. "Once they get you back to ACRO, they'll know they can trust you, right? I mean, you remember . . . everything, right?"

He shifted. "Most everything."

"Good. Then you won't need me anymore. And I can get the hell out of this mess." She turned away, anxious to get as far from him as possible, because if he had his memory back, he had to remember what they'd had together. And he acted as if it hadn't been a big deal.

She wondered why, after all this time, he was still able to hurt her this much.

CHAPTER
Sixteen

It wasn't midnight—it was four in the morning, and this time the phone rang instead of the doorbell, and Dev barked a hello into the receiver.

It was the night guard. "Uh, Mr. O'Malley? Sir, I'm sorry to bother you. I didn't mean to call. I swear I'd dialed Creed's number, so I have no idea how I got you . . ."

Creed. This had to be about Gabriel. Fuck. "It's okay, Wheeler. What's going on?"

"Well, your new boy's causing a scene at the Town Bar. I was going to get Creed over here—"

Dev clenched his teeth so hard he swore he'd break them. "No, don't do that. I'll send someone. And how the hell did he get off the compound?"

"He has a pass, Mr. O'Malley—it's valid. Signed by you."

Fucking, fucking Oz. But there was no reason to let the guard know that Dev's life had suddenly gone insane. "I'll take care of it."

He called Marlena, because there was no way he would go down to the bar himself and court Gabriel in front of everyone who happened to be there. He had to maintain some sense of decorum. "Marlena, I need you to stop Gabriel from making an ass out of himself—he's at the Town Bar. Please go pick him up."

There was a pause on the other end of the line and for a second he swore that Marlena would tell him no. But then her voice, still sleepy, whispered, "I'll get him and bring him home."

Yes, home. To Gabriel's home at ACRO, not Dev's. "Please. And I don't want to hear any more about it."

That was so far from the truth that Dev could barely get the words out.

"Why do I fucking care about this?" he asked the ceiling after he'd hung up, but no answer came.

HEADS TURNED when she walked into the bar in the middle of the small Catskill town ACRO was located near, something Marlena was always keenly aware of whenever she entered a room. The irony of the situation never failed to both amuse and sadden her.

She was gorgeous—yes. She could both see and agree to that as impartially as someone who looked at a work of art and declared it perfection. But it didn't matter what she looked like outside because she knew the reality of her own situation—few others did, and to tell them would mean exposing herself to pity. So she took the glances and the come-ons with a grain of salt and tried to tell herself that many great people had lived great lives without being loved.

She was never going to be truly happy, and instead tried to content herself in making others that way. Like Devlin. And now a very drunken and upset Gabe.

Gabe, who was currently circled by three large, non-ACRO biker types who would have no shot against the young man. And that's just what Gabe was after tonight—he wanted to lash out, to hurt someone.

He was beautiful—handsome, masculine—but there was something about him that simply shone. Marlena could see the attraction right away.

When she stepped directly in front of him, his eyes locked on hers, and his hand grabbed her shoulder, as if he meant to throw her out of the way.

"Listen to me—if you hurt me, Dev will absolutely kill you on sight," she told him, keeping her voice low. He settled down immediately at the mention of Dev, and yes, something was there. The connection had tugged at her when she'd first come across Devlin refusing to read Gabriel's file the other day, more strongly when he'd spoken of losing his instincts this morning.

She turned and nodded to the men Gabe had been ready to fight. They were used to Marlena's presence, and out of respect for her—and because the bartender had his own brand of justice out, a well-worn metal bat—they backed off into the crowd.

She moved Gabe toward the bar, where she ordered two waters. "You know, there's a bar on base."

"The guy who brought me here told me this was the kind of crowd I would be comfortable in. I told him I didn't want to be around anyone from ACRO right now."

"Dev sent me here to get you."

"Why the fuck would he do that? Dev hates me," Gabe muttered.

"The problem is that he doesn't."

"Yeah, because I was sent to him like a fucking sex gift from some man named Oz." He studied her reaction, and as much as she tried not to have one, he saw the surprise. "Do you know what that's like? To be attracted to someone who's only attracted to you because of some fucking afterlife manipulation?"

"Yes."

He snorted drunkenly. "Yeah, that's what they all fucking say. I didn't think you'd be condescending, but hell, I've been wrong before. And fuck it—you and Dev have something going on, I don't give a shit what Creed says."

She grabbed his arm and held it roughly—stupid to do to an excedo, probably, but she'd learned a long time ago that they were actually more conscious of not hurting anyone than were mere mortals. "My stepsister cursed me," she told him, her voice low enough that he had to lean in to hear her above the noise in the bar. "No man will ever love me, but I'll love any man I sleep with. I'll always be alone. I'm no threat to you and Devlin."

Gabe touched her arm, such a sweet gesture that she almost pulled back, not able to bear it. But there wasn't pity in his eyes, as she'd expected. No, there was pain and a great deal of understanding, as if he'd spent his entire life being the only screwed-up one. "I'm sorry."

"Don't be, it's not your problem." She took her hand away and kept her eyes on Gabe. Other men at the bar had begun their ritual circle, trying to gain her attention so they could buy her a drink, dance with her, attempt to take her home for the evening. There was only one bed she'd go to tonight, and that would be her own. "Come with me."

Gabe followed, actually put his arm around her as they left, as though he instinctively knew she wanted a shield between her and the men. They got into her car and she drove down the backroads and onto ACRO's guarded compound.

"You're taking me home?" he asked.

"I'm taking you where you need to be," she answered. It wasn't the first time she'd deliberately disobeyed her boss's orders, so she did something that Devlin would not want her to do but was still the best thing for him. She turned up the radio as she left Gabriel standing outside of Devlin's front door and drove away.

DEV HADN'T MANAGED to sleep more than an hour before he was back up, actually showered and ready to go into the office at motherfucking five in the morning. He'd resisted the urge to call Marlena and make sure things were okay with her, that Gabriel hadn't put up too much of a fight, but resisting had taken its toll on his patience.

So when the pounding on his door began in earnest, accompanied by yelling, he flew down the stairs and nearly took the door off its hinges when he slammed it open.

"What the fuck is going on?" Gabriel was demanding loudly before Devlin could even get a word out.

Dev yanked him inside, hard and by his shirtfront, prepared to have a talk with him that involved protocol, most possibly while using his fists in conjunction with his mouth, when Gabriel said, "Oswald Jameson Hughes drives a '76 Olds with a white convertible top."

Dev let him go and took a few steps back. "What did you just say?"

Gabe repeated his statement.

"How the hell did you know that?"

"Because he drove me here two nights in a row. Tonight, Marlena dropped me off—after she left, I saw that he's parked across the road from the house."

"Where?" Dev strode to the window first and then the front door, slamming it back open and staring into the night. He scanned the area. Nothing.

"It's gone," Gabriel said quietly from behind him. "Why does your dead lover keep bringing me here?"

A valid question, one Dev didn't plan on answering. "Who do you think you are, coming here and asking me these questions?"

"The man you almost fucked last night, that's who," Gabriel spat—and yes, the boy was angry.

"Yeah, that went really well. What, I wasn't gentle enough for you? Were you looking for flowers and candles? You don't like to sweat? Are you really a romantic under the tough-guy swagger?"

Gabriel straightened. "No, but Oz says that you are."

That made Dev stop in his tracks. "What else did Oz say?"

"That you're an asshole, and not to let it bother me too much. That eventually you'll come around." Gabriel headed to the door, but turned one final time before he left. "And for the record, I don't mind getting sweaty. What I do mind is you calling me by another guy's name."

With a final, definitive slam of the door, he was gone. And Dev knew with certainty he would not be back, that it was his turn to chase the boy. Because that was most definitely something Oz would do to him.

"You're not getting your way!" he called down to the floor,

just to piss Oz off. He waited for thunder, lightning—an apparition. Anything.

None came. And so he sat on the floor and pulled his knees up to his chest and whispered, "Damn you, Oz," even though the only thing he could see in his mind's eye was Gabriel walking down the lonely path, alone.

CHAPTER
Seventeen

Ryan didn't think the flight from England could have been more tense. Trance hadn't sat still, kept glancing at the crate where Ulrika lay in a state of half sleep, half snarl. And every time Trance looked, the beast snarled louder, and Annika, who wasn't pleasant on the best of days, pounced all over Trance's not-so-covert attention to the crate.

Trance, who had always been intense but calm and in control, had been on the verge of exploding out of his skin.

Annika had antagonized the situation with her teasing.

Then there was Meg, who had continued to shoot death glares at both Trance and Annika. Ryan hadn't helped her mood by being a total asshole when he should have tried to reassure her that everything would be okay. She'd been incredibly brave in the face of being bound and shoved on a plane headed for a location she didn't know, with people she didn't know. She was a tough little thing, and he admired the hell out of her.

He'd admired her even more when, after Trance sat down across from her and hypnotized her into telling him who she was and what she did for a living, she kicked him in the nuts.

Annika had laughed her ass off. Trance had limped back to his seat, cursing, but he'd left both Meg and Ryan alone for the rest of the flight.

Yep, the tension in the cabin had been so bad, the pilot probably felt it through the closed cockpit door, and Ryan heaved a huge sigh of relief as he and Meg stepped off the jet and onto the familiar ACRO tarmac.

Yes, familiar. He remembered it.

He also remembered how armed security guards would always be standing at the base of the stairs if an enemy or potential operative was being brought in. Sure enough, they were waiting, a couple of them eyeing him and Meg, but the rest watching as Ulrika's crate was unloaded.

"What now?" Meg crowded close to him, her eyes wide as she took in the huge old military base.

"I have no idea," he said, and didn't that just chap his hide. He hated feeling so out of place in his own home. Hated feeling like the enemy.

Trance came up behind them and unlocked their cuffs. "Security is taking you to Dev," he said, as a black Hummer pulled up. "And hey, welcome home. It's good to have you back."

"Thanks." Ryan shook Trance's hand and then took Meg's. "Time to meet the boss."

She shot Trance one last glare, and then hopped into the back of the vehicle, where a security guy sat. Ryan climbed into the front passenger seat for the short ride to headquarters, where he and Meg were escorted into Dev's outer office.

"Hey, Marlena." Ryan smiled, because damn, it felt good to recognize someone.

Dev's secretary came out from behind her desk and gave him a hug. "I'm so happy you're safe." She pulled back, gave Meg a smile and gestured to the leather couch. "Have a seat. Ryan, Dev is ready for you."

"Thanks." He squeezed Meg's hand, sort of an apology for being such a dick on the plane. "I'll be right inside the door, okay?"

She nodded and sat, and he headed into Dev's office, where his boss was doing something with a PDA. Annika and Trance had caught him up on ACRO stuff, but the biggest shock had been the fact that Dev had regained his eyesight, and now Dev looked up, his brown eyes flashing with what Ryan swore was relief.

"You have no idea how glad I am that you're safe, Malmstrom," Dev said with a grin. "You had us worried."

"*I* had me worried." He still was, truthfully, but he'd keep that information to himself for the time being.

Dev put down his PDA, and his expression turned serious. "How are you? Doing okay?"

"Yeah," Ryan said, as he sank into a chair across from Dev. "My brain is still a little scrambled, but it'll work itself out."

He hoped. His memories were there inside his skull, like a box containing all of the pieces of a jigsaw puzzle, but they hadn't been put together to form a finished product yet. He blew out a long breath, feeling a release of tension that had been coiled inside him since the day he'd awakened in the Itor med lab with no memories except the false ones Itor had given him. He might not be whole, but he was home, and he was safe.

"What happened, Dev?" he asked quietly. "How did my cover get blown?"

Dev was always in control, never showed weakness on the job, but for a split second, his eyes skipped away, coming back to meet Ryan's so fast Ryan wouldn't have seen it if he'd blinked.

"Dev?"

"It was my fault," he said bluntly. "I gave you up."

Ryan's breath rushed from his lungs. "It was . . . how?"

"My mind was breached." Dev looked down at his hands, seemed to realize he'd clenched them, and splayed them flat on the desk before looking back up. "There's not enough time in the world to tell you how sorry I am."

"*Sorry.*" Ryan's body and brain went numb, and he sagged back in his chair. "They tortured me," he murmured. "They came for me one night, tortured the fuck out of me for days and then scrubbed my memory. And you're sorry."

Dev said nothing, though Ryan knew he was being unfair. His

blown cover might technically be Dev's fault, but how could he have prevented it? Dev had taken extreme precautions to keep Ryan's mission a secret by making sure he was the only person at ACRO who knew about Ryan's insertion into Itor, so it wasn't as if his boss had been negligent. But Ryan also wasn't ready to apologize for being unfair. Not when he'd had needles jabbed into his joints.

"How?" Ryan demanded. "How could that have happened? Don't you have one of the strongest minds in this agency?"

"Let's just say it was an inside job." Dev shoved his fingers through his hair. "I know you're angry—"

"Fuck you." Cursing at his boss wasn't the brightest thing he'd ever done, but he was tired, confused and his nerves were shot. "Sorry. It's just... I knew the risks when I signed on, but..." He trailed off, afraid he'd say something that he couldn't take back. He didn't trust himself to be logical right now, so he bit out, "What now?"

There was a long silence, and Ryan had a feeling he'd gone too far, and Dev was trying to decide just how hard he wanted to come down. Finally, he said mildly, "The usual. You need to check in with your supervisor for a debriefing, and then check into Medical."

Fun. He'd be subjected to medical tests, psych evaluations and then finally, he'd have to get run through the Paranormal Division so the psychics could sweep him for psychic tags, mental programming and a variety of other crap. The entire process would take months.

"What about Meg?"

"She'll be handled."

Which meant she'd be interrogated—nicely, but still, she'd be subjected to a battery of questions by trained interrogators and psychics. Then, depending on a huge variety of things, including her skills and background, she'd either be asked to stay on at ACRO, or she'd be released back into the wild—with or without some memory modifications.

"I'm not ready to let her go." The words popped out as if someone else had said them. Ryan cursed. "Ah, what I meant was, well . . . could you take it easy on her? She's here because I sort of kidnapped her . . ."

One corner of Dev's mouth tipped up. "I know."

Of course he did. Trance would have called from the jet after he got the info from her. "Are we done? I could use a shower. And a beer. Bad."

Dev nodded. "Get some rest, but make sure you're checked into Medical by ten A.M. And send Meg in."

"Yes, sir." Ryan left the office, which had started to close in on him after his stupid I'm-not-ready-to-let-her-go crap. He was an idiot.

Meg was chatting with Marlena in the outer office, and she stood when she saw him. "Are we done?"

She looked so hopeful, like they could leave the office and he'd put her on the plane for home right now. "Dev wants to see you."

She frowned. "Oh. Then what?"

His stomach turned over. "I don't know."

"Okay. You're going to wait for me, right?"

Shit. "I can't. They're going to take you somewhere after this."

The color drained from her face. "Where? Why?"

"They have some questions for you."

"Will . . . will I see you again?"

"Why would you want to?" Christ, after everything he'd done to her, he couldn't imagine her wanting to be anywhere near him. She should be grateful for the opportunity to get away from him. But deep down, he knew. He was the only familiar face in a strange, scary place.

She stiffened, her spine going steel-rod straight. "You know, I have no idea. Thanks so much for . . . well, nothing." With that, she turned on her heel and stomped into Dev's office.

Marlena looked at him like he was a total ass.

"Yeah, yeah," he muttered, as he sauntered past. Figured that even Marlena, who had a tendency to get along with men but not women, would come down on Meg's side.

He must really be an asshole.

KIRA KNIGHT WAITED impatiently at ACRO's animal facility as the steel crate was unloaded off the truck. The jet had landed half an hour ago, and once Ulrika had been taken off the plane, she'd been delivered to the huge facility that featured kennels, stables, pastures and habitats for several species of animals—many of which had arrived after Kira had. She had a way of picking up strays, and not all of them could go home with her to the country house she shared with her husband, Tom, and their three-month-old triplets.

Triplet girls who were, at the moment, at ACRO's new day-care facility until she finished getting Ulrika settled in. Today was supposed to have been the start of her monthlong vacation, since her spring fever was due any day now, and it was becoming harder to work with the distraction of her heightened sexual state. Not to mention the fact that every man who came near became instantly aroused and extra-attentive to her. Fortunately, with the exception of her supervisors and husband, no one understood why.

Tom definitely knew why, and he'd glued himself to her for the last couple of days, was even now on his way back here after being called away by Dev for some sort of meeting. He'd be taking the month off with her, because once her heat started, she'd need him almost constantly.

A black Hummer pulled into the parking lot and next to the truck, and Trance and Annika got out. As Trance walked past the crate, a vicious snarl came from inside, and the whole thing rocked violently.

"We sedated her," Trance said, looking like he hadn't slept in days, "but it isn't very effective."

Kira nodded. "It was hard for the vet to estimate the dosage without knowing exactly what Ulrika is, so we had to go light with the meds." She walked with him and Annika toward the building while four security guys carried the crate. "Is she still wearing the collar?"

"Unfortunately. I was going to mess with it while I had her restrained, but Ryan said any attempt to take it off could detonate the explosive charge inside."

"Dammit," she breathed. "Those sick bastards." Not that this was news to her. Itor had wanted to do some seriously twisted things to Kira too.

A bloodcurdling wail came from the crate, and a wave of pain blasted through Kira's brain, making her stumble. Trance caught her just before she cracked her knees on the pavement.

"Kira? Hey, you okay?" Trance held her up, which was good, because her legs felt like rubber.

"She . . . Ulrika . . . hurts."

Trance drew in a sharp breath, and Kira swore she saw a flicker of worry in his eyes. "What's wrong? Did she hurt herself?"

"No." Kira shook her head, trying to clear it. "It's emotional. She feels trapped. Betrayed. And she's terrified."

"She needs to get over it." Trance's voice was harsh. He dropped his hands and backed away from Kira. "If that's all you need, I'm out of here." He didn't wait for her to say yes or no, just walked away without a backward glance.

Annika shrugged, gave Kira an apologetic look and went after him.

"Where do you want her, Kira?" Sancho Rodriguez, one of their new animal handlers, called out to her from where he held open the door to the facility.

"Put the crate inside the largest of the cages in the east bay." The east bay had been emptied out in preparation for Ulrika's arrival. They hadn't wanted any other animals to be disturbed, nor had they wanted her to be unsettled by other animals.

She followed the men inside, and as they pushed the crate into the cage and attached a chain to allow the door to be opened from outside the twelve-by-twelve structure, she ignored their heated glances, the casual brushes against her, the light, friendly touches. Thank God Tom wasn't here. He wouldn't care that her pheromones were affecting them, and he'd be breaking some fingers. Or worse.

"Thanks, guys," she said, when they'd finished and closed the door to the cage. They all smiled and offered to stay. "I'll be fine."

They left, but as the last one walked out the door, a tall blond guy came in, his blue eyes focused on her, a cocky smirk turning up one corner of his mouth. She'd never seen him before, but the orange name tag pinned to his black BDUs identified him as a trainee.

Gabriel.

Zach Taylor, her boss, had told her about him, said Dev had assigned the guy to work at the animal facility as part of his training program. Apparently, Gabriel was a little high-strung, and Dev thought that working with animals might help settle him down.

"You're Kira, right?"

She sighed. She'd argued with Zach over the wisdom of this— it didn't seem like a good idea to have someone work with animals if they didn't want to—but her protests fell on deaf ears. "Yes, I am."

"I'm Gabe. Zach told me I should see if you need help with the . . . beast thing."

"She's not a thing," Kira said. "And no, I don't need any help."

He shrugged, leaned against the wall, but didn't leave. Whatever. She tugged the chain hanging from the ceiling, and the crate door swung open. Immediately, the beast inside scrambled out and lunged at her. Her long claws missed Kira by no more than an inch.

"And I thought I had anger-management issues," Gabe muttered.

Kira ignored him to squat down on her heels, putting her in a nonthreatening position, and she gestured for Gabe to do the same. Ulrika stood on all fours in the middle of the cage, growling. Her huge jaws, something like a cross between a wolf and a bear, were open, revealing long, sharp teeth. She was massive, would probably stand seven feet tall on two legs, with thick, red fur and wicked claws as long as Kira's pinky fingers.

She was beautiful, the way a tiger was, and every bit as deadly.

"Hey, Ulrika," she said in a low, soothing voice. "Can I call you Rik?"

"Can she understand you?" Gabe asked, scooting closer.

"I don't know. I communicate with most animals through images and scents, but since she's human, I figured I'd try this way." Kira tried again, this time using her mind to send the message.

Rik. I'm Kira. I'm here to help you.

No help. Only pain.

Horrifying images punched Kira in the brain with such force her head snapped back on her spine. The poor wolf-beast had gone through hell in Itor labs. God, they'd experimented on her, tortured her, beat her until she couldn't stand. Tears sprang to her eyes.

"They hurt her so badly," she whispered.

I'm sorry they did that to you. So sorry. Kira pulled in a ragged breath. *We're not like that. We want to help, not hurt.*

Another image came to her, of Rik in human form, locked in an intimate embrace with Trance, kissing him, her head thrown back in pleasure. And then again, chained to a table and Trance standing over her. And then she was in beast form and Annika was shocking her, and Trance was jabbing a needle into her thigh.

"Damn," she breathed.

"What is it?" Gabriel asked.

"I don't know if I'm going to be able to get her to understand. We need the woman, not the animal." Kira wiped her damp palms on her BDUs. *I know you're confused, but I think we can work this out. If you'll let your human come back, we can put you both in more comfortable quarters. Won't that be better than a cage?*

Liar! Rik snarled and lunged, crashing into the cage hard enough to make the floor vibrate.

Gabriel jerked back. "What's her malfunction now?"

"You're a real sensitive guy, you know that?" Kira huffed and tucked her hair behind her ears.

Gabriel cursed softly and slid her a hesitant glance. "You know, you're not my type, but for some reason—"

"Yeah, yeah," she muttered. It was so time for her vacation. "Okay, I'm going to give this one more shot, and then I think we need to leave Rik alone for a little while."

I know how hard this is. I didn't want to come here either. But they've treated me really well, and I'm very happy.

Let us go! Rik threw herself against the cage again and again, working herself into a frenzy. *Let. Us. Go!*

Kira's heart broke wide open. God, she wanted to help, but she was only making things worse. Quickly, she came to her feet and tapped Gabe on the shoulder. "Come on. Hurry. She's going to hurt herself."

They dashed out of the room, and once the door was closed, a mournful howl echoed through the building.

"What the hell was that?" Gabe asked, and Kira collapsed against the wall, unable to stop the case of the shakes that came over her.

"The beast is protecting the human. I don't know how to get the human out. That's not really my thing."

A door at the end of the hall opened, and Zach approached. "How'd it go?"

"It didn't."

He peeked through the window in the door and grimaced. "We'd better tranq her."

"No. That'll make things worse." Kira bit her lip, remembering the image of Trance touching Rik, kissing her—and then chaining and drugging her, and Kira realized a lot of the pain she'd sensed had its roots in how Ulrika had been captured. "Let's give her the night to settle down, see if she shifts back by morning."

"If not?"

"If not, we'll need Trance." And something told her that Trance was not going to be happy about that. Not one bit.

CHAPTER
eighteen

Dev didn't trust himself to bring Gabriel to his house, but he needed the privacy. A trip from the boss to the training quarters would cause a stir, and so he had Marlena bring Gabriel to his house after dark.

He hadn't bothered reprimanding Marlena for bringing the young man to him last night—if he was totally honest with himself, he'd wanted that.

He was sitting out back by the pool when Gabriel came through the sliding glass door. With the light from the kitchen shining behind him, the boy looked like some kind of handsome, angry angel. The black BDUs fit him well, and he let his eyes roam over the hard body.

Gabriel flushed but stood there under Dev's appraisal for a few seconds more before he asked, "I'm flattered as hell, but I don't think you brought me here to stare."

Dev opened his mouth and closed it. He'd rehearsed what he would tell Gabriel about Oz, short and sweet and that would be the end of it. Once the younger man knew that this was all some crazy manipulation from the great beyond, he'd be out of here.

But Dev couldn't say a word, sat there like an idiot, until he realized that Gabe was kneeling on the ground by his feet.

"I know who Oz was to you," Gabriel said. "Marlena told me—so did Creed—but even if they hadn't . . . well, you were whispering his name that night . . . when I stopped you."

Shit. "It's not what you think."

"So your dead lover isn't trying to set us up, then?" Gabriel had one eyebrow arched, spoke as if Oz picking him up in a ghost car was a normal, everyday occurrence.

Maybe he fit in here more than Dev thought. "I don't know what in the hell he's trying to do."

"And you think I'm attracted to you because Oz wants me to be."

The more Gabriel spoke, the stupider Dev felt. "I never said that. But this—whatever you think is happening between us can't. Won't."

"You can't stop how I feel."

"You stopped yourself the other night."

"I wouldn't now . . . now that I understand."

"You don't understand anything," Dev told him fiercely. "It's complicated."

"You're in mourning. Not so fucking complicated."

"There's so much more to it. Things I don't want to share."

"I'm tired of secrets," Gabe muttered.

"No, you're not. You've got a lot of your own, so don't give me that bullshit."

Gabriel's head snapped back, so his chin jutted stubbornly. "You've read my file. You know everything about me."

"I don't think so." Dev stood, forcing Gabriel to do the same. He put his hands on the younger man's shoulders, slipping under the collar so he could put his palms on the warm skin.

Gabriel tried to take a step back and throw Dev off, but Dev wouldn't be deterred. "You were violated."

"I—"

"I wasn't asking," Dev barked, put his hands back on Gabriel's shoulders. The young man sat still for a few minutes in silence, but he couldn't hold the pose for long. God, there was so much in there—pain, fear and hope, all mixed together and piercing through Dev's fingertips. "It started when you were young . . . your mother's boyfriend. You didn't know what he was doing exactly, but you knew it was wrong."

Gabe's breath came in a harsh, stuttered rush, like he was trying his best to keep it all together and not succeeding at all. Gabriel's life played out before Dev as though projected on a screen. It was black and white, grainy, like an old movie that was slightly out of focus because Gabriel was trying desperately to block Dev.

It wouldn't work. "You ran away—lived on your own. Let your body be used for money, but you never let anyone hurt you. You were able to stop things if they got too rough. Until . . ."

God, there were four or five men—they'd used drugs and chains. The flashes showed Gabriel on his hands and knees. Even worse, Dev heard his cries. "Dear God . . ."

Gabriel had had enough, jerked himself away from Dev with more strength than he needed. He stood a few feet away, breathing hard. He opened his mouth and then closed it and finally, "I didn't want you to know that. Any of it. You had no right."

"And I didn't want you to know about Oz. So now you know what it's like to have your life spilled out to a stranger," Dev said, more anger in his voice than he'd meant to let leak through. Because reading Gabriel wasn't about tit for tat, or at least it hadn't started out that way, but now his temper had built unreasonably.

Dev wasn't the only one with an uncontrollable temper now, though.

"I didn't want to know about Oz either—or you or this fucking place—I didn't bring myself here, you and Oz brought me here!" Gabriel yelled.

Dev knew what the younger man would do, but that didn't mean he'd have time to stop it. In seconds, Gabriel was on him, pushing him hard to the ground, angry as hell that his life had been revealed to Dev so easily. He pinned Dev to the ground, his knees on Dev's shoulders.

And that's when Dev saw it—or rather, when Gabriel simply disappeared. He'd been staring at Gabriel when the man just . . . flickered. Became invisible for a split second, and then he was back, in solid form—and still very pissed.

Gabriel had the power to make himself invisible. By the look on his face, Gabriel knew he'd done it, and looked ashamed, as if it was something he didn't have any control over. Obviously, the anger had brought it out.

It's about the anger . . . make him angrier . . .

Dev bucked as if trying to get away, bared his teeth, which made Gabriel tighten his grip. This time, the flicker was longer— wasn't over in the blink of an eye. One instant, he saw Gabriel on him, and the next, he only felt the strength of an invisible force holding him down.

Seconds later, Gabriel flickered back, must've realized what had happened because he scrambled off Dev and looked ready to bolt until Dev stopped him.

"Has that happened before?" Dev demanded.

"The invisible thing? Maybe a couple of times. It's not a big deal—I can control it," he lied, then shrugged as if it really were no big deal, but Dev saw the fear in his eyes.

He laid a hand gently on Gabriel's shoulders, keeping it there even though Gabe flinched. "It's all right if you can't control it. That's why you're here. But the more we know . . ."

"The more ammunition you'll have to put me back out on the street." Gabriel's eyes blazed with fear and a thousand betrayals, beginning with his mother. "Then again, that's probably what you want anyway, so maybe I'll make it easier on both of us and go before I'm asked to leave."

"No one's asking you to go."

"No one's giving me a reason to stay either," Gabriel shot back.

"You haven't given ACRO a chance."

"I don't have any chances left to give."

GABE FOUND HIMSELF at the same goddamned bar—the only fucking one within reasonable walking distance from ACRO. He wondered why no one gave a shit that he'd left the grounds—as a trainee, he was supposed to stay within the compound, but maybe Devlin had given other orders.

Devlin. Fuck.

He'd only been there long enough for two shots when Marlena walked in. The woman turned heads, for sure, and if he wasn't completely solid as to which way he swung, he'd definitely be hitting on her.

Or he would have if he'd met her before Dev.

Devlin. Just fuck.

"You're muttering to yourself," Marlena pointed out. She took the third shot from his hand and downed it, then dropped the glass to the bar and slid it back to the bartender. "Dev told you about Oz."

"You already told me what I needed to know. I just kind of . . . I don't know, fucked things up. Again."

She sighed. "I'm sure Devlin didn't help matters."

"I'm leaving ACRO." He motioned to the bartender for another. "You want?"

"No. What do you mean, leaving?"

"I told you—I really screwed things up. Dev pissed me off and I kind of . . . jumped him. And not in the good way."

Marlena shook her head. "I haven't gotten any orders to kick you off the property. Just the opposite, in fact."

"He sent you to babysit me again?"

She smiled, pushed the shot away from him and threw a fifty-dollar bill on the bartop. And then she took him by the hand and led him outside. "You have training tomorrow with Annika. She's back."

"Fuck me," he said roughly, taking a long, deep drag on the

cigarette that tasted so much fucking better when he was half in the bag.

"If you're going to stay at ACRO, you can't go out and party every night."

"If I'm going to stay at ACRO, the only way I can get through this bullshit is to party every night," he countered. "And I'm not making any promises."

CHAPTER
Nineteen

"Fucking forget it." Trance punctuated his feelings by kicking the door before attempting to walk out of Kira's office.

"Don't you dare leave." Something in Kira's voice told him she wasn't fooling around, that as angry as he was, she would be more so.

Still, he didn't turn around when he spoke again. "I'm not the one to help you. Rik hates me—doesn't trust me, and for good reason. My part of the job is done—I brought her in. I can't be responsible for her."

"Whatever happened already bonded the two of you. It's too late to try to slink away from what you've done."

"I did my job."

"Maybe a little too well."

He finally swung around to see Kira, arms crossed in front of her, eyes blazing. Ender would fucking kill him for making his wife this angry, but Trance was beyond caring.

"She's safe here, isn't she? She's out of Itor's clutches. We've got the fucking remote."

"We need the woman, not the animal. We gave it all night, but the beast won't give Ulrika back."

"Why is this my problem? I thought you could reason with the beast."

Kira shoved him. "Get out. You're an insensitive bastard—not at all who I thought you were."

"Yeah, I'm not who Rik thought I was either," he muttered, not counting on Kira having animal-like hearing, because suddenly she was grabbing at the back of his shirt as he walked down the hall and away from her.

"You fell for her."

He refused to turn around. "Kira, I'm not talking about this with you."

"I know what you're going through. Tom would know too—"

"I'm sure as hell not speaking to your husband about this shit." He stared down the empty corridor, saw himself making a quick escape. But to where? Dev would haul his ass back here in no time—his boss had made it clear earlier that this was where Trance needed to be. That the job wasn't over yet.

He'd come to the animal facility straight from Dev's office late this morning after Devlin made his feelings clear.

"So things went well." Dev had his feet propped up on the round table in the corner of his office, files on his lap. He looked distracted but somehow still locked Trance with his gaze.

"Yes, great." Trance didn't sit down and Dev didn't offer him a seat. *"Rik's a wolf and refuses to change back."*

"But she's here and not with Itor." Dev's feet slammed to the ground. And he stood.

"I'm not in the mood for a fucking pep talk, Dev."

"I wasn't about to give you one."

Fuck. *"Sorry, Devlin."*

"Kira needs your help."

He forced himself not to think anymore. *"I heard."*

"You heard hours ago."

"I've been busy."

"Bullshit." Dev stared him down. *"I don't give a shit if you like*

Ulrika or not, if you fucked her or spanked her or let her into places you never knew existed. You are not done with your job. Not until I say you are."

His reverie broke when he heard soft footsteps and watched Kira walk down the hall, away from him, without looking back once.

He stood outside the door that led to Rik for a long time—until he didn't hear any movement from inside, no clanking metal. Nothing. He cracked the door as quietly as possible, but the sound didn't escape Rik's notice. No, the wolf lunged for the door of the cage, rattling it hard enough that the entire room seemed to shake.

Yeah, she was still pissed.

Drawing on what he once knew best, he marched over to the cage with a purposefulness that made the wolf stop growling for the moment. "Ulrika, come out and see me now."

The wolf bared her teeth and growled.

"Do you remember what I told you, Rik? That I was your master—that you needed to obey me? That there's great pleasure that comes from obeying me?"

It wasn't working. He sighed and dropped his head and for a second, the wolf stopped. Subtle, since it still held the cage with its claws, but his instincts told him to do what he most dreaded.

He walked up to the cage and bared his throat, raising his head up and placing his Adam's apple close to the bars, much in the same way he'd done when he'd submitted to her at her house.

It was a gesture of faith—or stupidity. He grabbed the bars tightly so Rik wouldn't see his hands shaking and he closed his eyes as he heard the low, throaty growl at his ear. The heat of the wolf's body radiated toward him even as his own body grew cold.

"You've got to give this place a chance, Rik," he told her, his voice nearly breaking. He'd been up against bigger and badder, but somehow this was different. "Come on, I know you want to get out of the cage. Kira can help you—she's good. She's been there. We all have."

Nothing was happening—at least in the way of his throat being ripped out. Tentatively, he opened his eyes and saw the wolf staring at him, with one paw resting on the collar.

Shit. "Okay, yes, we've got to figure that out. But Itor needs to be within a certain distance to work it, and we don't allow them to get that close. If they get close, we know about it. What other choice do you have? You can't run for the rest of your life."

A low, mournful howl tumbled out of the wolf's mouth—head pointed toward the ceiling, down now on all fours, she howled over and over, until he wanted to cover his ears and scream with her. Instead, he closed his eyes again and he waited for what seemed like an interminable amount of time.

This wasn't going to work—Kira would have to find another way.

He opened his eyes and moved away from the cage momentarily—long enough to scan the room, and see the keys to the cage hanging on a hook in the far corner of the room. He grabbed them and the wolf stilled as the cool, heavy metal weighed his hand down. Drawing a deep, resigned breath, he went back to the cage, and without pausing put the key in the lock, turned it and stepped into the cage.

The wolf stilled. She'd moved to the far corner of the cage, unsure of what exactly he was doing.

I don't know either, honey.

He closed the door behind him with a definitive click and he threw the keys to the middle of the room, outside the cage. If Rik killed him and remained in wolf form, she wouldn't be able to escape. If she changed back, someone would be in to check on her soon anyway.

"I'm here, Rik. I know you're pissed, that you want to hurt me. I'm strong as hell and I don't know for sure who'll win this one, but I owe you this."

He swore the wolf smiled as it began to move—within seconds they were circling each other until, without warning, the wolf leaped gracefully into the air and pounced on him, knocking him to the ground.

He fought as best he could, attempted to throw her off him, to grab her jaws and lock them, and for a minute he gained the upper hand—until her strong claws raked down his chest and he let loose his own howl of pain.

THE BEAST REVELED in the sound of Trance's pain. The tang of blood was in the air. Victory—and revenge—was so close. She slammed her paws into his shoulders and held him down with her weight. Their gazes locked. In his eyes, she saw death. He knew she would kill him.

There was no fear. Just acceptance. Snarling, she dove for his throat.

No! Awareness broke into Rik's mind, into the dark place inside the beast's body where the human hid while the animal was in control. This couldn't happen. Ulrika hated Trance, but she couldn't allow him to die.

With every ounce of mental strength she had, she screamed at the wolf. She yanked its head aside so its jaws snapped closed on empty air next to Trance's neck. An inch to the left and he'd have been missing his jugular.

She threw herself to the side, knocking the beast off balance. It howled its anger even as Rik clawed her way back. The beast fought for a long time, and she became aware that their body—half beast half human—was writhing in the corner, neither willing to give in to the other.

Distantly, she heard voices, the cage door opening, Trance's angry voice, Kira's soothing one.

Rik didn't know how long she battled for control, but when it was over, she was lying naked on the cold floor, quivering with exhaustion, and Trance was sitting inside the cage, propped against the door, naked from the waist up. His chest had been bandaged.

Rik nearly choked out an apology, but then the reason she was here in the first place came roaring back, and she just closed her eyes and tried to pretend none of this was happening.

"Go away." Her voice was shredded, as if she'd been

screaming for hours. Inside, she supposed she had. "You did your job. I'm human again."

Silence stretched. "I was going to tell you," he said finally. "Before Ryan busted into the basement. I was going to explain everything."

"Is your conscience eased now? Is everything all better because you *planned* to do the right thing?" She sat up and reached for a blanket that had been placed near her. "Go to hell."

"I know this is hard to believe, but we're here to help you."

"What part of *go to hell* didn't you understand? No doubt you're used to hearing it."

One corner of his mouth turned up—just barely, and just for a second. "We're here to help you," he repeated, wincing when he shifted. "You were a danger to yourself and others while you were loose. And Itor had a price on your head."

"I'm aware of that," she snapped.

He shook his head. "I don't think you know the half of it. They put the word out—five million euros for anyone who brought them your body."

Her stomach rolled. She hadn't known. "Why doesn't ACRO want me dead? Why help me? I've killed ACRO operatives." Not a wise thing to say, no doubt, but the elephant was in the room, so she might as well acknowledge it.

"You did what you had to do."

"So that makes it okay? Is that how you justify lying to me? Shocking me? Drugging me? Shoving me in a crate?"

"Yeah."

She'd have laughed if her throat didn't hurt so much. "I actually liked you. I trusted you." She ran her fingers over the satin edge of the blanket she'd pulled up to cover her breasts, and wished she hadn't admitted that fun tidbit of information.

"You need to trust me now."

"Are you kidding me?" she asked, incredulous.

His eyes gleamed with intensity, because he was dead serious, and as he moved toward her on his hands and knees, shoulders rolling like a giant, stalking cat, she felt his sincerity in a wave of heat.

"We want to help," he said, crouching in front of her. "We're going to help you control the beast, and we're going to get that collar off you."

It sounded good. Too good. "And after that will come the poking and prodding and cutting me open to see how I work."

He took her hand, and when she tried to jerk it away, he held tighter. "I'm not going to lie to you—"

"Well, that would be a change of pace," she snapped, but he ignored her.

"ACRO will want to study you. But they aren't going to cut you open or subject you to torture. You'll be informed of every step, and if you're uncomfortable with anything, they'll stop."

"Why?" She narrowed her eyes at him. "If you expect me to believe ACRO is full of humanitarian intentions and is doing this out of the goodness of their hearts, you're delusional."

"We're in this for the big picture," he admitted. "We want you on our side, and we won't earn your loyalty by hurting you. That's how ACRO works. They'll use the hell out of you to get the job done, but they'll take care of you too."

She became aware of his thumb stroking her fingers, of her blanket having slipped down to her waist when she wasn't paying attention. She knew Trance had noticed too, because his eyes flickered down, and when they met hers again, they'd darkened.

She didn't bother covering up. He'd seen—and touched— every inch of her. Besides, let him look. He wouldn't be doing anything more than looking, ever again.

"They can really get the collar off?" Her voice was husky and low, everything she didn't want it to be. "Without killing me? There's a bomb in it . . ."

"We have the world's best explosives experts here," he said, and she was happy to note that his voice had gone just as deep and morning-rough. "We've also got top-notch electronic technicians, and people with other skills who might be able to help." He pulled his hand away and tugged up the blanket to cover her. "There's an ordnance guy and an el-tech outside the door right now. They want to inspect the collar. Will you let them?"

The beast, which had been sitting on a slow simmer while Trance touched her, went berserk, and Ulrika hissed a breath between her teeth, trying to keep it from coming out.

"Rik? Are you okay?"

"Yes," she ground out. "Just . . . give me a minute." She took long, deep breaths, kept telling herself—and the wolf—that the men coming in would be here to help, not hurt.

They'll find a way to take off the collar.

Slowly, gradually, the sensation of claws digging at the inside of her skin faded, and she nodded. "Let them in."

He stood. "Do you want me to stay?"

"Yes," she whispered. How could she hate him as much as she did and yet want him to stand by her side? And why did she want to trust him again?

Maybe it was because even though he'd lied to her from the very beginning, he hadn't truly hurt her. If what he was telling her about ACRO was true, then he'd saved her life by getting her away from Itor. Maybe they would give her a shot at a new life.

The door opened, and inside, the beast growled.

Then again, maybe they'd only prolonged the inevitable, because she didn't think she'd ever gain control of her animal half, and someone would eventually be forced to put her down.

Trance watched as the men from the bomb squad cautiously approached the cage. Rik bristled beside him, but she remained in place, actually let him put a hand over hers.

He shifted and winced, and immediately her attention diverted to him. "You're hurt, Trance. Do you need a doctor?"

He shook his head. "I'll heal fast. These are just . . . deep."

She nodded and looked up at the men. "You can come in and look at the collar."

"Trance, we'd like you to step out," the man Trance knew as Lucas said as he unlocked the cage.

"I'm not going anywhere. Dev promised this part wouldn't be dangerous." Trance sat up, daring them to say another fucking word.

"It's not, it's not." Lucas held up his hands in surrender and he and the other man, name tag reading BRETT, headed toward Rik.

"It's okay," Trance told Rik for the thousandth time. She didn't believe him—or any of them—and right now he couldn't damn well blame her.

Neither Lucas nor Brett actually touched Rik—instead, they peered at the collar and shined their penlights onto it. After a moment, they dug various machines out of their bags and used them for measurements, X-rays and a bunch of other crap Trance could care less about.

"How many fingers can you fit between the collar and your skin?" Lucas asked finally. Rik obliged by pushing two thin fingers under the collar and yanking it as far as she could away from her neck.

A look passed between Lucas and Brett, and Trance knew there was no way to get the collar off—not by them anyway. They'd have to resort to plan B, which was something Devlin was working on right now. But the operative who would be involved in that plan would not agree easily, if at all, and with good reason.

"They can't do it," Rik whispered.

"We're sorry," Lucas told her. "Anything we try puts you—and us—at too much risk."

"Could you jam the signal at least?" Trance asked.

"The way this thing is built, it would have to be unlocked." Lucas shook his head. "It's a damned fine piece of machinery too."

Trance swore he heard a wolf's snarl, and he couldn't blame Rik for reacting. He wanted to shove his fist down the man's throat and collar him—and not in the good Dom way either.

"Get the fuck out now," he told the men. "And keep your observations to yourself."

"You know as well as I do that we need to study that collar if we're going to keep up with Itor's technology. If it comes off, we want it," Lucas said.

Trance surged to his feet, ignoring the ripping pain in his chest. He stood toe-to-toe with the man. "You're either really brave or really fucking stupid, or both. This isn't something you talk about when a woman's life is on the line—she's my first concern."

Rik stared up at him. "It's never going to happen. I resigned myself to that a long time ago. But maybe if I stay here, I can be safe."

"You mean here, in this cage?" Trance looked around. "That's no life for you, Rik."

Her voice shook when she asked, "Why do you care so much?"

He could spill his guts, tell her how she'd touched him—helped him. Instead, he said, "It's my job."

She didn't say anything after that, just stared at her hands blankly.

"There's someone else who could help you get the collar off," he said finally, when the silence had become deafening.

"If your best people couldn't do it—"

"Those were our best tech people. But we have other resources." He knelt on the floor next to her. "I'm going to find a way to get that collar off of you. That's been ACRO's goal from the start. But I'm going to have to leave you here for a while—and then I'll bring back someone who can help."

She looked up at him, her amber eyes liquid. "Hurry, Trance. I don't know how much longer I can stand this."

"Don't do anything stupid, Rik—please."

She gave him a wry smile. "I couldn't detonate this myself, even if I wanted to."

CHAPTER
Twenty

Ryan had every intention of staying away from Coco, but as he walked past guest quarters on the way to Medical . . . well, all his good intentions flew the coop.

The guest quarters were set up like military billeting—basically, a casual hotel. Except the front desk personnel at this hotel carried weapons—either on their person, or their person *was* a weapon.

He got Coco's room number from the front desk guy, and then had to take a couple of deep, calming breaths before he knocked on her door. He had no idea why he was so nervous, except that he knew somehow she was still a key player in his past. Yes, he remembered most of it, but there were some holes. And she was a big one.

She answered the door wearing a robe, hair wet and water dripping down her legs. Instantly, his body hardened and he wanted to sink to his knees and lick every drop off her smooth skin.

He was such a bastard.

"Um . . . hi," she said.

"Hi." So he was a bastard *and* he was lame. "So, ah, can I come in for a minute?"

She shrugged and stood aside. He brushed past her—intentionally rubbing up against her. He didn't miss how she sucked in a harsh breath.

"So why are you here?" She shut the door and stood there, arms crossed over her chest.

"I still need something from you. I don't have any right to ask—"

"No," she snapped, "you don't. You kidnapped me, tied me up, attacked me and broke my heart."

"I know, but—" He shook his head. "I what?"

She realized what she'd said, and her eyes flared wide before she closed them and let out a long sigh. "You really don't remember."

His heart kicked hard at his chest. "There are still things that are fuzzy."

"That's why you're here." She strode past him and sank down on the edge of the bed, kept her gaze cast at her feet. "You don't remember how we knew each other."

"I know you took my money. I was furious. I was being hunted by some serious bad guys, and then ACRO picked me up. But everything before that..." He shrugged. "It's just bits and pieces. Like, I remember your name. Coco. I can see it on a computer screen, for some reason."

"That's because we'd flirted for months online."

Okay...he hadn't seen that coming.

"Flirted? As in, romantically, or cat and mouse, for our jobs?" *I'm a virgin. Do you still want to meet me?* He saw the words on the computer screen again. His computer. He'd been chatting with her...and he broke out in a cold sweat, because he suddenly knew that their *flirting* had been so much more than that, if only on his side.

She finally looked up at him. "It all started out because you were trying to hunt down someone who was hacking into illegal transactions, though I didn't know all of that until much later."

"Who was I working for?"

A drop of water plopped to the carpet, and she prodded it with her toe for a moment before speaking. "I don't know. I got the impression that the people you were buying arms for were losing money, and they paid you to find out who was siphoning money out of their accounts."

Okay, yeah, that sounded right. After leaving the military, he'd built a reputation as *the* guy to hire for spy jobs and investigations, thanks to his ability to see through other people's eyes when connected via electronics. It had been great having a second job when he wasn't dealing illegal arms.

"So how did you fit in?"

"I was the one siphoning money out of the accounts. Somehow—must have been that gift of yours—you managed to pop up a chat box on my computer, and you let me know you were onto me."

She looked so vulnerable sitting there, wet, barely clothed, her feet rubbing against each other almost playfully, and he hated to ask the next question.

"Were you afraid?"

Her head snapped up, a cocky smile curving her mouth. "You were good, but not that good. You'd never have found me."

He wanted to kiss her. Instead, he cleared his throat and asked, "What then?"

"We played cat and mouse for a long time, and eventually we just started playing. I don't know how it turned into a game like it did, but we flirted and stuff and . . . Man, this sounds stupid."

No, it didn't, because this was starting to sound familiar. "We had sex, didn't we?" He couldn't help but smile at her shocked expression. "Online sex. Yeah, it's coming to me now." He grinned. "Who'd have thought a virgin could have asked me to do some of the things you wrote?"

She turned about ten shades of red. "Yes, well, that's not important. What's important is that I actually liked you. We were supposed to meet. In Milan."

"We were?"

"Oh, sure. Selective memory now?"

He shook his head, because the memory sat on the edge of his mind, so close he felt like he could touch it if he reached out far enough. Closing his eyes, he searched the corrupt files in his brain, tried to connect the wires . . . but, nothing. Dammit, nothing. Frustration shorted out his patience, and his eyes popped open.

"This is bullshit, Meg." He grabbed the fuzzy collar of her robe and yanked her to her feet so they were face-to-face. "You used me. You played all that flirty bullshit so you could get to my accounts."

She slammed her fist into his chest, but he didn't let go. "Screw you, Mr. Selective Memory. I could have taken your money at any time, but I didn't do it until you screwed me over. Left me waiting like a loser for six hours on a park bench." She hit him again, and this time he let go. "Why didn't you show up? Were you married? Involved with someone else? Were all those e-mails telling me how you'd never felt as close to any flesh-and-blood woman as you felt to me just one big lie?"

"*What?* No, I wasn't lying when I said that. I—" Holy shit, he remembered. Remembered the excitement he'd felt the morning of their meeting, remembered taking a cab to the park.

Remembered telling the cabbie to keep going once they arrived.

He swore, long and hard. He'd chickened out. Never in his life had Ryan been involved in a serious relationship, and just the night before, he'd gone out with a couple of buddies who had been really damned vocal about why a relationship was a bad idea, given their line of work.

"You can't trust anyone, man. You should know that by now. No matter how well you think you know her. Women fuck you over just for the sport of it."

Ryan hadn't believed it, but they'd freaked him out enough that he'd changed his mind. He'd gone to the airport, caught a flight to Greece, finished an arms transaction and then drank himself into a two-day hangover. When he came out of it, he realized what a huge mistake he'd made, and he'd tried to contact Coco.

Only to learn that she'd intercepted the money transfer. Hurt, furious and knowing he now had a price on his head, he'd told Coco he'd kill her with his bare hands, and then he'd gone on the run.

"Well? What do you have to say for yourself?"

Right. Like she'd done nothing wrong in all this. "I freaked, okay? I got an earful from friends who said I couldn't trust you." He narrowed his eyes at her. "Guess they were right."

Coco stood there, little hands clenched into fists like she wanted to deck him, but after a moment, her chin began to quiver. When her eyes started to water, his anger swirled right down the drain.

"You're right," she whispered. "What I did was vindictive and mean."

"Dammit." He pulled her into his arms, and she came willingly. "I'm sorry. You didn't deserve that." Doing his best to soothe her, he stroked her hair, which had started to dry into soft curls. "I guess neither of us has a pretty past. But at least now I know why I threw wood every time I saw your picture when I was searching for you through Itor." Which actually didn't make sense, because they'd never exchanged photos.

She made a strangled, choking sound. "Do you ever filter your thoughts before they come out of your mouth?"

"Nope. That's part of my charm."

She drew back a little to look at him. "I'm not sure *charm* is the right word . . ."

He laughed, his first real laugh in months. The first real laugh since he'd left ACRO to infiltrate Itor.

Man, it felt good to be home, to know who he was . . . and to be holding a woman in his arms. Still, a touch of sadness brought him back down to earth. "Look, I'm sorry I was such an asshole to you. That I kidnapped you and—"

She pressed a finger to his lips. "Stop. We can keep feeling guilty about everything we've done, or we can start over. I know which one I vote for."

Warmth bubbled up inside him, filling spaces that had been so cold since the day those Itor bastards had taken his memory. He curled his hand around hers and kissed her knuckles, enjoying how her eyes darkened and her breath hitched.

"I like the way you think."

"I'm thinking you should kiss me."

"Oh, yeah," he breathed. "I definitely like the way you think." He dipped his head and brushed his lips over hers, wanting to take things slow, but she would have none of that. She cupped his head with her palm and met his mouth with a hungry, punishing kiss.

This was stupid. Crazy. He still hadn't gotten his shit together, didn't know if she was staying at ACRO or going home, didn't know what the future held for either of them, but dammit, he'd been drawn to her for months, and he wasn't going to turn back now. Not when she was rubbing against him so hard the friction was causing them to both start smoking.

He lowered her onto the bed, gently, but urgently. Her robe fell open, and a crimson flush settled across her breasts. She was shy and embarrassed, but eager, and she didn't cover herself. In fact, she pushed aside the loosened sash and let the robe fall completely open.

God, she was beautiful. Creamy white skin, small but perfect breasts tipped by apple-red nipples that tightened as he watched. He wanted to suckle them until she begged him to move his mouth lower . . . and yeah, buddy, he'd take that route at a hundred miles per hour.

Stretching out over her, he took her mouth again, and this time he was so worked up he groaned when her tongue met his. He reached between her legs, found her wet, hot, and when his fingers slid over her clit, she cried out.

"Please," she whispered, arching against him. "Please . . ."

The thought of being inside her, of taking her virginity and making her his and his alone, reached up and grabbed every primal male instinct he had. The unevolved caveman in him grunted, *Mine,* while the more civilized side of him screamed that this was wrong. She was better than this. Better than him.

But that didn't stop him from ripping open his pants and letting out "Little Ryan," as she'd called him during their online sex sessions.

"Ryan." Meg was panting, pleading, rocking against him so his cock slid through her slippery folds and he was about to fucking lose it. Just one thrust, and he'd be home, buried in heaven and shouting to the angels.

He hadn't done that in ages. Not that he remembered anyway. He thought about the DVDs, the women on them, the rough, nasty sex, and his stomach churned. He now knew that the things Itor told him he'd done for them weren't true, but he had DVDs to prove that his sex life had been real enough.

"Can't wait," Meg whispered. "Five years was too long to wait." She slipped her hand between them and wrapped it around his shaft. He groaned, but when she angled her hips and shifted so he was poised at her entrance, something broke inside him.

Five years. Five years he hadn't remembered until mere hours ago. His memory still wasn't complete, and until he figured out how his sexual past fit into his memory puzzle, *he* wasn't complete.

It wasn't fair to give this woman less than a whole man, not after all she'd been through because of him.

"No," he rasped, "no." He rolled off her, pulling her with him so they were on their sides, face-to-face.

Dazedly, she blinked at him. "What . . . what's wrong?"

"I can't." And man, it hurt to say that. Physically too, because his balls were freaking throbbing. The confusion and hurt on her face hit him right in the heart, and he smiled as reassuringly as he could, though his own pain probably turned his smile into a grimace. "I want to make you feel good."

She stroked him again, and he nearly bit his tongue off. "I want that too."

"Then let me. Just lay back and let me." Gently, he removed

her hand and placed it on her stomach. Her mouth fell open in protest, but he pushed her hand down until her fingers spread her sex. Slowly, he slid his own finger between hers, loving the little gasps she made against his neck as he began to work her.

Long passes through her slit made her pump her hips, and slow circles around her clit had her straining, pushing into his hand for more.

"Ryan . . ." She trailed off on a moan as he pushed a finger into her tight sheath.

Her slippery satin walls clenched around him, and he shuddered at the erotic sensation, as well as the fantasy of how great it would feel to replace his finger with his cock. He added another finger, turning his hand so he could draw his fingertips back and forth, as though calling her with a gesture. Each pass over the swollen pillow at the top of her passage made her blow little puffs of air, faster and faster, until her entire body flushed and her hips came off the bed.

She came with a muffled shout, and he damned near shot his load all over her stomach. Instead, he held her until her breathing evened out, and still, he didn't let her go. He needed to, he knew that, but for now—

Something beeped. His pants. Shit. He drew away, couldn't hold back a smile at the drowsy satisfaction in Meg's eyes as he dug into his pocket. The ACRO-issued cell phone his supervisor had shoved into Ryan's hand flashed a text message.

He was late for his appointment at Medical, and if he didn't get there in the next ten minutes, his sup was going to call out the hounds. *Fuck*.

Time to do what needed to be done, no matter how much he didn't want to.

He pressed a kiss to Meg's forehead. "I gotta go." Wincing, he buttoned his pants and avoided looking at her. She tugged her robe together and sat up with him.

"So, um . . . what now?" Her voice was morning-raspy and so freaking hot. He'd love to hear it every morning.

It was so tempting to tell her he wanted to see her again, but not until he got himself back. "Now I go back to work, and you go back to what you were doing before I kidnapped you." He'd made his voice as gentle as possible, but the way hurt flashed in her eyes told him it wasn't enough.

"That's it?" She stood, jerked the ties of her robe around her waist with shaking hands. "After all of this—not just the sex, but . . . *everything*, you're just casually walking away?"

He came to his feet in an instant, grabbed her shoulders and brought her hard against him. "There's nothing casual about it," he growled. "But you're so much better than me, and I can't risk hurting you. So yes, that's it. But dammit, don't *ever* think there was anything casual between us."

With that, he swept out of the room.

And he didn't look back.

ULRIKA SAT in the corner of her cage, waiting for Trance to come back. He said ACRO would find a way to remove her collar, and she believed him. Kira had been in too, had tried to convince Rik to come out of the cage, but she'd refused. Until the collar was gone and she could be sure that no one would use a remote to force her into beast form or blow her up in a crowd of people, she was staying put.

Kira had brought her food, blankets, clothes, even a few magazines to read. Then she'd tried to communicate with Rik's inner wolf, but that hadn't gone so well. The beast was furious at having been stopped from killing Trance, and right now, it wanted to strike at anyone who came near.

The door opened, and Trance walked in. He was wearing black BDUs and combat boots, and Rik's mouth watered. He wore the uniform as if it had been custom-made for him, and she had the sudden urge to lick it right off him.

"Hey." He approached the cage but didn't unlock the door, and her heart dropped a little. Especially because the expression on his face said that something was not good. And he smelled like irritation. And anxiety.

She came to her feet. "What is it?"

"Dev found someone who might be able to remove your collar."

Good news. So why did he look like he was announcing a funeral? "But?"

"He doesn't want to do it."

She blinked. "Oh. It's the explosive charge, isn't it?"

"No. He can stand back several feet, so that's not the problem."

She frowned. "Then why?"

Trance didn't have time to answer before the door opened and a tall, dark-haired man walked in. Instantly, a cold sweat broke out over her skin, and her lungs seized. She stumbled backward, slamming into the cage bars.

The man who walked in wanted her dead. The look in his eyes revealed nothing less than murder.

Her mind flashed back to the day she'd escaped from Itor, the day she'd been tasked for the assassination of TAG's chief, Faith Black.

Rik's handler had activated the collar as Rik approached Faith in a park, turning Rik into a raging monster that attacked the operative. The beast had delivered a fatal blow and had nearly finished with her when the dark-haired man came out of nowhere, his bellow of rage something that haunted Rik's dreams to this day. Without touching her, he'd thrown her several yards away. She'd crashed into a tree, felt bones crack.

As the man tended to the woman, Rik had shifted back into her human form and crawled off, somehow managing to climb into the back of a farmer's truck several miles away. She'd covered herself with hay and made her escape, but never knew how things with the woman had turned out.

From the expression on the ACRO operative's face . . . not good.

Trance moved to him, grasped his shoulder. "It wasn't her, Wyatt. It was the beast."

Wyatt's green eyes drilled into her. "Ulrika." He'd said her name, but his tone said, *Die, bitch.*

She swallowed. Hard. "I—I'm sorry—"

"*Sorry?*" he roared. "You ripped my wife's throat out!" He shrugged off Trance's hand and slammed his own hands onto the cage bars. "If I hadn't been there, or if I'd been ten seconds later, she would have bled out and died. Her and the baby."

Baby? Faith had been pregnant? Rik wanted to throw up.

"The only reason they survived is that I'm biokinetic and I was able to repair on the spot some of the damage you caused. But she was in intensive care for weeks, you—"

"Wyatt!" Trance snapped. "Check the fuck up. Faith's okay now. And so is the baby."

Wyatt rounded on Trance, fists clenched. For a long moment they were nose-to-nose, the air between them roiling with tension. Finally, Wyatt shook his head. "I'm not doing this."

He stormed out of the room, and Trance went after him. "Dammit, Wyatt! She was under orders! Don't tell me you haven't done some questionable things to get the job done."

Trance's voice was muffled through the door, but she heard them both clearly enough, and her heart pounded while she waited. Maybe it would be better to not have the collar removed, because she wouldn't put it past Wyatt to detonate the collar *accidentally*.

"I don't care!" Wyatt said, and she heard the distinct sound of a fist hitting a wall.

"Come on, man." Trance's voice was calmer now, and barely audible. "They made her do it. They tortured her. Turned into an uncontrollable creature that did their dirty work. She couldn't do anything about it. It wasn't her fault."

There was a long silence, and finally, the door opened again. Trance and Wyatt entered, and though hate still gleamed in Wyatt's eyes, he looked a little less homicidal. Like maybe he'd kill her quickly instead of making it hurt.

She took a tiny step away from the back of the cage.

"Stand still!" he barked, and his eyes began to glow amber, the way they'd been when he'd thrown her against the tree.

Her whole body began to tremble uncontrollably. He was going to kill her. She knew it. "Trance . . ."

Trance's gaze tore between Wyatt and her, and with a curse, he entered the cage.

"What are you doing?" She backed away from him, bumped into the bars. But his arms came around her and he pulled her close. "What—"

"Shh," he whispered into her ear. "Just stand still. I'm here. I'll stay with you."

"No!" She struggled to get out of his grip, but his arms were steel. "If the collar detonates—"

"It won't. Wyatt won't let it explode if it'll kill me too."

"Goddammit, Trance," Wyatt snapped. "Get away from her!"

"Do it." Trance's voice was hard, but his hand stroked her back gently. "Hurry up."

Wyatt's curses flooded the room. She felt a brief tingling in her throat. Heard some faint clicking noises. Each one made her heart leap. Sixty seconds later, the collar sprang loose and hit the floor with a clatter.

Relief and joy struck her like a blow, and she collapsed. Trance caught her, held her as she sobbed against him. She was safe. No longer bound to Itor by a device that turned her into a monster at their will.

Sniffling, she turned to thank Wyatt, but he was gone, reminding her that even without the collar, she was still a monster.

TRANCE REMAINED on the floor with Rik in his arms while she cried quietly. As her breathing became less hitched, he shifted and stroked her hair, whispered that it was done and over.

He didn't want to let her go, because having her cradled against his chest was what he'd been thinking about since the last time he'd been able to have full body contact with her.

Tearing himself away wasn't easy, not when they were alone and he was aroused and all he needed now was her body under his, on his, wherever she wanted him, but it wasn't the time for that. He still had amends to make and he wanted to let Rik taste the freedom she'd now have.

She deserved nothing less, no matter Wyatt's opinion.

She looked surprised when he moved to her and stood, leaving her curled against the wall, one hand pressed against her now naked throat. There was a mark there that would fade over time, but he suspected the memories of what had happened to her would take far longer to heal.

"Come on, Rik—you can come out of here now." Trance held his hand out to her, but she ignored it, stared at the door Wyatt had left through as if all the ghosts of her past were there.

"No," she said hoarsely. "I can't. Don't you understand—I'm still the same inside. I can still change. I'm still a danger."

"We all are."

"Not like me."

"So you want me to have tea served at your pity party, then?" His voice was angrier than he'd expected it to come out, but it made her snap to attention, nonetheless.

"I'm not in the mood to play Dom/sub."

"And I'm not ready to leave you in this cage. You wanted that collar off—it's done. The rest—controlling the beast that lives inside of you—well, that's all up to you now, isn't it?"

"I haven't been in control in so long . . . I don't know what it's like," she admitted. "I'm scared."

He still held out his hand, and several agonizing heartbeats later, she accepted it, let him help her up from the ground. She stood in front of him unsteadily, as if having the collar gone had temporarily messed with her sense of balance.

With her hand still in his, he finally told her what he'd wanted to before Ryan broke into the safe house and sped up his time line. "I didn't lie to you about my issues with my strength when we first met, Rik. You have no idea what you did for me. I've never let anyone in the way I did you—never let my guard down. And I lied to you before, when I told you that the reason I care is because it's my job. And now you fucking hate me and I get that. But if I can make it up to you somehow . . ."

"And then what?"

"And then, if you don't hate me . . . I'd like to see you. In a non–work-related situation. Take you out. Maybe even make love to you, if you'll let me. But you don't have to agree to any of that now—let's just walk out of here together and get you moved into a trainee billet."

Her eyes studied him carefully—they were an almost brilliantly ringed topaz and he waited for what seemed like an eternity. Finally, she tugged her hand out of his and looked long and hard at the opened doorway before she exited ahead of him.

He understood that she had to do it on her own, without him. But once she was on the other side, she turned back to look at him and gave him a small smile and he knew that, somehow, everything would be all right.

Twenty-one

The next twenty-four hours passed quickly for Ulrika, and for the most part, her inner wolf behaved.

Trance had taken her to ACRO's training quarters, which were, to her surprise, not scary, gray cells with bars, but dormlike rooms complete with beds, kitchenettes, private bathrooms, desks, bookshelves and even a small television. An exotic, dark-skinned woman had arrived immediately after Trance left, introduced herself as Neema, a Tanzanian-born martial artist whose venomous bite could stun an opponent for up to ten minutes.

She would be Rik's primary trainer and handler.

Neema had taken Rik on an orientation of the base, had been patient and understanding when Rik would suddenly need to sit somewhere quiet for a few minutes and gather her wits after the beast grew agitated about something. It had never liked men, and it grew tense every time she walked by one. And the medical facility had sent it into a tizzy Rik almost couldn't control.

"We'll avoid Medical for now," Neema had said, in her lilting British accent.

After that, Neema had loaded Rik down with books. Apparently, every trainee had to learn the history behind ACRO, the rules they must follow if they wanted to work there, and the basic structure of the operation.

Rik figured she'd be reading for a month.

The cool thing? No one had poked her with a needle, threatened her or chained her up. They did lock the door to her room as a precaution, but she was okay with that.

Locking the door ensured everyone's safety.

She hadn't felt comfortable going to the cafeteria for meals, so Neema had brought them to her. This morning, she'd eaten enough extra-rare steak, eggs and pancakes to feed a dozen people, and now it was nearly noon, and she was starving again.

Kira, who had arrived an hour ago, smiled when she heard Rik's stomach growl. "Maybe it's time for a break."

Rik nodded. "I've been so hungry. First time I remember feeling this way."

"I think it's because you finally feel comfortable."

Rik's brow shot up. "I don't know about that . . ."

"Trust me. I haven't been able to get through completely to your other half, but I've sensed a huge change in her since you first arrived."

"How long is it going to take before I have complete control, do you think?"

Kira sighed. "I don't know. You've both been terribly abused. Your wolf is so angry. The abuse turned her vicious, and it could take some time for her to get over her hatred and fear of humans. Men, in particular."

And wasn't that the truth. Kira had come with her husband, but he'd had to stay outside the door, because the beast would not calm down with him in the room. Only Trance didn't agitate the beast now that the collar had been removed. Oh, it was still wary, but then, so was Rik.

"Kira?" She nibbled her lip, trying to decide whether or not she should risk asking the question she was afraid to have answered.

"Yes?"

Oh, screw it. "Trance said he would come back to see me. But..."

"He's either coming back to see you because he wants to, or because you're a job, right?"

"I'm that transparent?"

"I had a similar issue." Kira's gaze cut briefly to the door, where Ender's partial reflection shone in the glass. "Obviously, it worked out. Now I can't get rid of him."

Her tone was teasing, with an underlying affection that made Rik's heart beat a little faster. Those two were obviously dedicated to each other in a way Rik had been afraid to believe existed. Because if it existed, what were the chances that she could find the same?

"You are in heat." Rik sighed.

Kira blinked. "How did you know?"

"The wolf knows."

"Oh." Kira shifted in her seat. "Well, the truth is that I'm on vacation because I have, ah...special needs every four hours. And men go a little insane around me during this time. Which is why Tommy is here. He won't let me be alone without him right now." She glanced at her watch. "In fact, we'd better get going. But you should know that Trance was officially off the job the moment the collar came off. Anything else he does with you is on personal time."

A silly little shiver of pleasure broke over Ulrika's body at the thought, and she began to tremble in anticipation of seeing him.

The beast didn't exactly wag its tail, but it didn't growl either.

Maybe, finally, things were looking up.

RYAN HADN'T LOOKED back. Not once. And Meg had watched him walk the entire length of the hallway that led away from her room.

God, she was completely, utterly humiliated. He hadn't even wanted her to touch him.

She'd been kidding herself all those years ago and she'd done it to herself again. He had to give her an orgasm to get her off of him. And now she was stuck here at ACRO, and no one would give her any answers about what she was supposed to be doing and when—and if—she could leave.

You should've learned from what happened to Mary. She'd promised herself that she'd never get taken in so badly by a man, the way her sister had. Mary had died all alone because she'd trusted the wrong man, and the thought of that made Meg's insides churn.

"I told you that you were headed for trouble."

The voice came from behind her, and she recognized the slow, easy drawl of her brother even before she turned around.

"Mose!" Meg ran toward him—her brother had entered her room behind a really tall, dark-haired man, who he introduced to her as Wyatt before she flung herself into his arms. Mose accepted her hug easily, even though he muttered something about good thing she was alive or he would have to kill her for getting into this much trouble.

"Did that Ryan guy hurt you?" Mose demanded. Meg looked between him and Wyatt, who already seemed a bit wired—she felt like all she had to do was nod yes and they'd both hunt Ryan down like a rabid street dog. And though she was still angry at Ryan for involving her, she was even more angry at herself for going with him in the first place. For stealing his money years ago.

For not doing more with her life before this.

"Ryan didn't hurt me," she lied. Actually, it wasn't a total lie, because she was far beyond hurt—she was pretty close to devastated, but she'd be damned if she'd admit that in front of Mose and another ACRO agent.

Ryan was no doubt reacquainting himself with his old life, and maybe with some of the women from those videos, and not thinking about her at all.

"It's great to finally meet you—ML always talks about you. I'll leave you two alone, unless you need my help," Wyatt said, but Mose waved him off.

"I've got this, brother. But thanks."

"I can't believe you know these people." She rubbed her bare arms and then reached for the sweater Marlena had lent her—tall, beautiful Marlena, who if she hadn't been so nice would've made Meg feel like a total schlump.

She pulled the long, cream-colored cardigan on and tied it at the waist.

"These people saved your ass, Meg."

"That remains to be seen," she muttered. "What's Wyatt talking about, you needing his help? What are you about to try to talk me into?"

"ACRO—Devlin O'Malley, to be specific—wants you to stay on here."

"Stay here? And do what?"

Mose shrugged. "You've got talents—ACRO could use your computer skills. And then I wouldn't have to worry about you running all around the world."

"What about Interpol?"

"ACRO will take care of that for you, should you decide to join them."

"They have that much power?" She rubbed her hand along the smudged table, her fingers itching as if they missed her usual constant contact with the keyboard of a computer.

"They do."

"I don't know, Mose . . . Staying here, it's like being back with Mom and Dad. I don't think I want to be part of a group," she lied, because there was nothing more she wanted to do than stay here and be close to Ryan. But he'd made his choice—it was time for her to make hers, to move on. She'd done her penance, helped him to get his memory back. They were even.

"Then you're coming home with me."

"You can't give me an ultimatum like that."

"Christ, Meg, now's not the time to be stubborn."

"That's just it, I don't know what it's time for."

"You mean you don't just want to sit around and be a beach bunny?" he teased, and then grew serious again. "You're sure this Ryan guy didn't hurt you?"

She shook her head, refusing to admit how utterly stupid she'd been. "He didn't hurt me. I hurt myself."

TRANCE WALKED UP to the half-opened door of Rik's room—her back was to him as she leaned over her bed, fluffing the pillows and pulling the covers taut. He cleared his throat, and she turned.

"Hey" was all he could say.

"Hey yourself." Rik's voice was soft, but she looked stronger, more in control than she had the other night when he'd brought her into the training quarters and reluctantly left her.

Since then, he'd been attempting to train, to prepare for whatever jobs might come his way, all the while trying not to think about Rik every five seconds.

It didn't work, which was why he found himself in her room, holding a fucking picnic basket.

"Women like picnics—she'll think it's romantic," Kira had told him when she pressed the basket into his hands earlier. Ender had laughed so hard, finally Trance had to punch him, and the men ended up rolling around fighting until Kira threatened to turn the hose on them.

"I thought maybe you'd want to take a walk with me. The lake's beautiful this time of year . . . and I've got food," he said. He held tight to the picnic basket and waited, feeling like an idiot until Rik nodded.

"That sounds nice. I'd like to get out of here, get some fresh air." She paused. "Are you sure it's okay—do I have permission?"

"You're fine, Rik. You're free to go anywhere around the ACRO premises as long as someone's with you—and that's only temporary and for your own safety. After a while, you won't need anyone." Even as the words dropped from his mouth, he felt the tug at his gut and wondered if that would really be true—if she wouldn't need or want him now that her collar was off and she had freedom to be with anyone she wanted.

He refused to think about that further; instead, he opened the door and let her pass, and together they walked the half a mile to the lake, as Trance pointed out various buildings to her and explained their functions.

Once they got to the lakeshore, Trance spread out the blanket and Rik settled herself in, the questions began, like he'd known they would. He'd prepared himself, as he'd never much liked talking about his past, but if this had a chance of going anywhere, he'd have to spill.

Rik sat Indian style, rubbed her hands over her knees. "How much of your background—what you told me—was true? I mean, the cop thing?"

"I was an MP, so the cop thing was pretty close." He passed her a sandwich. "I don't know what it is—Kira made it, so it's probably vegetarian."

"This was Kira's idea?"

"The idea was mine. She just lent the necessary hand so the food would actually be edible. I'm not the best cook."

Rik chewed slowly and then, "These are just sandwiches."

"You'd be surprised how helpless I can be in a kitchen. Although I'm good to have around if you've got a tough can to open."

She laughed and continued to eat her sandwich as he laid out the fruit and cheese and crackers that Kira had packed thoughtfully, and yes, much better than he would've done. His first choice would've been a restaurant, but, as Kira had pointed out, Rik wasn't ready for real-world encounters just yet, and the ACRO caf wasn't a place Trance was taking this date.

"It's so beautiful here." Rik was gazing across the lake, which was like glass. "I haven't had a chance to look around much—I'll have to remember this is here."

"There are hiking trails too, just beyond the bend over there."

She turned back to him, her face serious. All business. "Have you brought other women here?"

He really, *really* liked the fact that she was jealous, but he wouldn't point that out to her. Not now anyway. "No. Never. I don't date much, especially since starting with ACRO. Before that, well, the military makes it really easy to fool around and real hard to settle down. And then there was the whole excedo issue."

"You didn't know what you were until you came here?"

He shook his head. Man, he didn't like remembering those days. "I knew something was up, but no, until those men—the Convincers—came to find me, I had no clue that I wasn't alone. That a place like this existed. That I could do some major good for the world."

"You were my Convincer, then."

"Yeah, well, there weren't many men here who would've been able to handle you."

"So they sent out the resident Dom to come fetch me."

"I'm not a Dom anymore." He lay on his back in the cool grass, let his eyes drift up toward the puffed clouds that lingered across the sun. "In my military days, that's when I did most of my Domming. Once I got to ACRO, and I understood everything, I pretty much gave it up."

"Why?"

"Once I knew for sure that there most likely wasn't a woman who could actually handle my strength, I figured why bother?"

"Aren't there other excedos?"

"Males. And we both know I'm not swinging that way. If I did, my life would've been a hell of a lot easier in some ways."

By now, she'd eaten several of the sandwiches. It was nice to see her appetite coming back to life. But it didn't stop her questions. "What about your parents?"

"My dad was an excedo. Or I'm guessing he was. My mom was normal, and excedo isn't exactly a recessive gene."

"You didn't know him?"

"He left my mom when he found out she was pregnant. Growing up without a dad pretty much sucked." The painful memories flooded back to him far too easily. No matter how hard he tried to push down the feelings of utter desertion by the man who'd made Trance into what he was, they always came back. "Sorry, I didn't mean to get heavy."

She put her hand on his arm. "You can talk about it. You

should talk about it. It must've been confusing for you, the not knowing why you were so strong."

"Yeah, it was."

"You told me that you left your job because you hurt someone—was that true?" she asked hesitantly.

"No, it wasn't. Not once I got into the military anyway. I learned to control it. Had to, for survival."

"Did your mom help?"

"Not really. She was too young, got addicted to drugs. After she died, I bounced around a lot as a kid, looking for a place to fit in."

"And you found that here?"

"I'm considered normal here. That's really nice." He paused. "I haven't been happy, though. Not completely. I've been alone for a long time, Rik, just like you."

Her eyes flickered with surprise and then recognition. "Of course—you know everything about me already. My background, my parents . . ."

"I don't know everything. But I'd like to." He shifted so he was closer to her—attempting to gauge her mood and make sure he wasn't pushing the wolf too hard. But she seemed calm, even though she appeared to be having trouble sitting still.

He couldn't sit still either, wanted to roll with her in the grass until they were both hot and sweaty and naked. "You started out as a job, but you ended up being so much more. It was completely unexpected. Scary. And wonderful."

She smiled shyly, ducked her head for a second before letting her gaze settle back on him. "I want you to kiss me."

"It's about time." He gathered her against him and kissed her, hard enough to make her grasp at him and push back with her mouth against his. His hands tugged at her hair, loosening it from the clips she'd worn, letting it tumble over her shoulders. Her hands were bolder, reaching for his pants, his zipper, until he took his mouth from hers. "We can't do this here. I don't want you on display. Ever. You're all mine, Rik. I'm going to be the only one who sees you naked from now on."

His tone—his possessiveness—surprised him but seemed to amuse her, because she laughed and then she growled into his ear, "The same goes for you. I owned you the second you let me tie you up."

He pulled back, startled, mainly because she was completely, utterly right, and that was something he hadn't wanted to fully admit to himself. She didn't let him get too far into his own thoughts, though, before she began to stroke his hair. "Do you know what a turn-on that was for me—especially now, knowing how you could take me, hold me down, capture me, to know that you let me take you in the same way?"

He put his head on her shoulder for a second, overwhelmed by his feelings. And then he gathered her into his arms to walk with her to her quarters, leaving the picnic and talk of their pasts behind.

CHAPTER
Twenty-two

Rik's heart pumped crazily as she and Trance headed back to her quarters. She was going to make love to him. Over and over. She slowed when a building came into sight, because as much as she wanted to get back to her room and undress him, she wanted to be free with him more.

Smiling wickedly, she all but dragged Trance in the opposite direction, toward the woods. The scent of trees, ferns and wild-flowers made her nostrils tingle, and the sound of birds chirping and small animals scurrying at the approach of what they sensed was a predator made the wolf in her get all squirrelly.

Her wild blood rose in a tide, wanting to bond with nature as it joined with the powerful male animal next to her.

Something had happened after her collar had come off, and the beast inside, while still wary of female strangers—and downright snarly around male ones—had accepted Trance.

Whether or not it actually liked him was still up for debate.

Rik cast a sideways glance at him and decided that for her, the woman, there was no debate. No more denying her attraction. She liked him. And she thought there could be so much more.

"You know," he said, pulling her to a stop on the trail they were on, "we don't need to head into the next county."

The breeze ruffled his hair, and she didn't fight the urge to tame it down with her fingers. "It feels good to run. To be free."

Closing her eyes, she raised her face to the wind and inhaled the fresh, clean air. Here, the scent of nature was untainted by the odors of man, reminding her of her childhood in the mountains.

Only days ago she'd not have believed she'd ever feel free again. But here she was. Trance had given her a gift beyond measure.

She opened her eyes, grinned and poked him in the shoulder. "Tag, you're it."

"Rik, wait—"

But she was gone. Laughing like she hadn't done since she was a little girl, she sprinted through the trees, weaving and dodging boulders, leaping over fallen logs. Behind her she heard Trance crashing through the brush. He was faster, but she was more nimble, and she kept him from gaining on her until she was ready.

Spinning, she skirted a thick tree, pinched him on the arm and shot down an incline toward a trickling stream. Her inner wolf was ears-back, tongue-lolling and having a great time playing with the male back there. He was cursing up a storm as he came after her, but a shift in the wind brought the heady scent of arousal.

He was as worked up by this little game as she was.

Maybe she'd let him catch her.

She glanced over her shoulder, saw him closing in on her as she leaped the stream. His expression was hot, intense, predatory. And at the same time, amusement glinted in his eyes, because he was enjoying this and was probably a little surprised by how much he liked it. Laughing, she slowed, waited until he was close enough . . . and pounced.

They went down to the soft forest floor in a tangle of limbs, with Trance uttering a breathy "Oof."

She nipped his earlobe. "Gotcha."

"You think?" He flipped her so she was on her back and his thigh lay across hers, pinning her down. "Maybe I let you catch me."

"Male pride is such a funny thing," she teased, as she threaded her hand through his hair and brought his mouth down to hers. His lips were firm, soft, and tasted like the lemon-lime soda he had drunk at their picnic.

The kiss was chaste, affectionate and playful. Still, Rik's body heated, and inside, the beast wagged its tail. As if Trance sensed a change in her, he pulled back a little.

"How's Cujo?"

"Cujo?"

Trance's grin took her breath away. "Famous name for a really mean dog."

She cocked an eyebrow. "Well, *Cujo* was feeling pretty good until that crack. Now she's ticked off."

"Hmm." He brushed his lips across hers. "And how can I make her happy again?"

"She likes to be petted," Rik said, surprised at the way her voice had gone husky and take-me-baby rough.

"Is that so?"

"Mmm-hmm." She sighed as his hand came up to stroke her hair, her face, her throat. Even though he'd settled himself between her thighs so his erection sat heavily against her core, he kept his hands in G-rated territory and made no move to take things further.

She wanted more, but this was nice. She'd never been touched like this before. Her entire sexual past was so dark, full of pain and tears even before she'd started working at The Dungeon.

"Hey." Trance stopped petting her. "What are you thinking about?"

"Nothing worth talking about."

Trance rolled off her, pulling her with him so they were lying on their sides, facing each other. "Tell me."

His words weren't a command, not with the way they'd been spoken in a soft whisper. But still, her inner wolf balked at dropping that one last barrier, the secrets she'd cemented into a wall that shielded her from having to feel anything.

But it was that same barrier that kept her from gaining complete control over the beast, and she knew it. As long as her fears governed her life, so did the angry animal.

Still, her mouth wouldn't open.

"You're not used to talking to anyone, are you?" he asked, using one finger to trace the shell of her ear. Made her leg twitch like a dog getting scratched.

"I've never had anyone to talk to. I was pretty young when Itor took me. After that, I was caged alone. The only people I saw were trainers, handlers and scientists, and they didn't exactly encourage meaningful conversation."

Trance's expression set into something hard and cold. "Was anyone ever nice to you?"

"Masanao." The half-Japanese Seducer had been kind and patient, the closest thing she'd had to a friend. Ever. "They sent him to teach me about sex. I think they wanted me to be a Seducer, even though I have no psychic abilities." Most Seducers could read minds to an extreme even very powerful psychics couldn't, but the catch was that they could only do it when their partner orgasmed. So their skills, while useful, were limited.

"And how did that go?"

She dropped her gaze to his broad chest. "He refused at first. I was a virgin, and he thought I was too young . . ."

Trance went taut. "How old?" When she didn't answer, he tipped her chin up, and she nearly gasped at the fierce, protective light glinting in his eyes. "How. Old?"

"Fourteen," she whispered.

"Those bastards." He tugged her closer. "So what happened?"

"They punished him for disobeying orders." She closed her eyes and swallowed the lump in her throat. "Two excedos cuffed him to a chair and made him watch as they . . . um . . ." She trailed off, because there were no words for what those men had done to her. They'd each taken turns with her, and by the time they were finished, there was nothing virgin about her.

"Man, I want to kill someone," he growled, and she couldn't help but smile. No one but Masanao had ever wanted to protect her like that.

Masanao had gone crazy while the men abused her, and when they were finished, he'd comforted her as well as he could. Eventually, they'd taken him away, and two weeks later, he'd been sent back again to teach her about sex. This time, he didn't refuse. But he'd been gentle and patient, and then one day, he'd tried to help her get free.

His kindness had gotten him killed.

"Didn't your wolf protect you?" Trance asked, his hand running in long strokes down her arm.

"They hadn't gotten that far in their experimentation yet. They were close, but not quite there. I shifted for the first time about six months later."

Her shift had been an accident, a surprise to her and Itor. They'd hooked her up to machines that monitored her vitals, her brain activity and even her electrical output. Something had gone wrong, a short in one of the machines, and the shock she'd received had brought the beast out. The shift had been excruciatingly slow and painful, and though she didn't remember much about that first time, she could still feel the agony when she thought about it.

Trance's curses were soft, barely audible, but the string of them lasted for a long time. "So I'm guessing they changed their minds about using you as a Seducer. Made you an assassin instead."

Anger swirled through her. They'd turned her into a killer, all right. When she'd refused to be their leashed hound, they'd tortured her until the wolf went rabid, only too happy to kill humans. As long as they could control the beast with the collar, they could have their monster assassin.

"I'd rather have been a Seducer," she said. "They made me . . ." She shuddered, and Trance pulled her tight against him.

"It's okay." His voice was low and soothing, and she felt her muscles starting to relax. "It wasn't your fault."

"That doesn't take away the guilt." She pushed back from him so she could see his face. "I know some of the people I killed were scum, and honestly, those people didn't bother me. But what about Wyatt's wife? I could have killed her and an innocent baby."

"But you didn't." He frowned. "There's something else going on here, isn't there?"

"What makes you say that?"

"A hunch."

This time, when she pushed away, she sat up and scooted out of reach. Trance sat up with her, but he made no move to touch her.

"Rik? You can tell me."

"I killed someone," she blurted. "I mean, *I* did it. Not the beast." She slid him a glance, prepared to see disgust in his expression, but there was nothing but understanding.

"How did it happen?"

She swallowed hard, clenching and unclenching her fists. A fine sheen of sweat broke out over her skin as she recalled the steamy heat in the jungle where she'd been taken to root out an enemy operative. "Itor sent me to Ecuador. The target was an . . . an ACRO agent."

Trance swore under his breath. "Go on."

"The agent was looking for some sort of artifact. He was supposed to be deep inside a cave, so I was told to go in, and after thirty minutes, they'd trip the shock collar and turn me into the beast. But the agent was coming out of the cave, and he caught me." She picked up a leaf and poked it with her nails, making little circles for no reason other than that she needed to occupy her hands.

"What did he do?"

"Nothing, at first. I told him I was a tourist who got lost. But he didn't believe me. He tried to subdue me. And he was strong. Strong like you."

Her teeth began to chatter as the memory slammed into her brain. She'd not been able to bear a man's touch, and the ACRO agent hadn't been gentle about taking her to the ground to restrain her. The memories of the rape, of all the beatings she'd suffered, had blacked out her mind, and she'd managed to snag a knife from his belt. Without thinking, she'd stabbed him.

The man's eyes had widened in shock, and he'd reared back, giving her a chance to crawl from under him. The rage inside, the horror at what she'd just done and the smell of blood had combined into an explosive mixture, and the beast had come out to finish the job.

So yes, the beast had played a role, but she'd seen the wound she'd caused with the knife, and she knew the man would have bled out even without the wolf's help.

Trance's arms came around her once again, and she realized she'd been speaking out loud.

And that she was crying.

"Listen to me," he said fiercely. "You did what you had to do to survive. I know what that's like. But it's in the past. You have a new future here. A new beginning. So cry it out, but then let it go."

"I—I don't know if I can."

"I'll help you, Rik. I'll be right here to catch you. We'll work through it together."

She hugged him so tight he gasped. A strange, warm energy filled her, made her heart beat faster and her breath come hotter. It took her a moment to realize what the feeling was.

Happiness. For the first time since her childhood, she was happy. And, she suspected, she was also in love.

When Devlin walked through the ACRO compound, it was always with a purpose. Having his sight back had actually forced him to slow down, to notice more—but on days like today when he wanted to pass unnoticed, it was a real pain in the ass.

He shoved sunglasses on at one point, began taking long strides, forcing his bodyguards to rush to keep up with him.

They were nearly past the excedo training center when he heard Annika's laughter and turned in time to see Gabriel on his back on the mat.

"He's getting better," she'd told Dev grudgingly. Kira had given Dev the same information, saying how Gabriel was a natural with the animals. "They're really taken with him," she'd added. "I'm thinking of giving him a couple of the dogs once he gets his own place."

It was a definite change from when Gabriel had told Marlena that he might not stay at ACRO. Dev wondered what the turnaround point for him was, and then told himself that he didn't care, that he had an entire team of operatives to worry about.

That the young man's laughter did not affect him.

Fuck.

He watched from the side of the building as Annika took Gabriel down again with an electric shock—and he knew what she was trying to get Gabriel to do.

Suddenly, Gabriel was no longer there. Instead, Annika flipped feet over head and landed facedown on the mat. She tried to get up, but couldn't—most probably because Gabriel had a foot planted on her back; his invisibility must change his molecular structure such that he was immune to her electrical charge.

He'd come far in a few days. Dev wasn't surprised. It was amazing what some compassion and being surrounded by likeminded people would do to a person.

Suddenly, Annika was up and standing, hands on her hips, looking around.

Dev himself froze as hands traveled across his shoulders and down his arms. He couldn't tell if Gabriel was in front or behind, but one hand was slowly making its way down his chest toward his...

"You little son of a bitch," he muttered. But Gabriel was already gone from him, back to Annika. And back to his noninvisible persona.

He didn't even look in Dev's direction.

CHAPTER
Twenty-three

Rik was at his house. Trance grabbed a couple of cold beers from the fridge as he watched her look around the living room.

He'd had his choice of houses when he'd moved onto the ACRO compound—he'd picked this one because it had three floors and the top was perfect for a playroom/dungeon. But soon after, he'd retired that room and now it was empty. He'd moved everything to the basement he didn't use and could never quite figure out what to do with all the space. He was a big guy, yeah, but three bedrooms and three baths, plus the entire first floor, had always been too much. Too lonely, even though ACRO kept him busy enough so he had little downtime.

"I like your house." Rik turned and accepted the beer, holding the bottle by the long neck. "Do all agents get houses?"

"Most of the time, if you want. A lot of agents don't—they'd rather live in the old officer and enlisted dorms and have things done for them." He shrugged. "But I wanted my privacy."

She took a long sip of beer and then licked her bottom lip. "Privacy, huh?"

God, he wanted her. On the couch, the floor—it didn't matter. "I told you, I don't like to share."

That made her grin. "I don't either. That part was never an act." She turned almost shy. "It's hard without the persona. I've had it for so long . . ."

"I know. It's not easy for me either, Rik." He gathered her in his arms and pulled her to him and kissed her again, and God, he could kiss her for-fucking-ever and still not get enough. When he finally pulled back, her lips were red, slightly swollen, and she'd dropped her beer bottle to the ground.

So had he. And he didn't give a fuck. "I'd like to finish what I started, back at the safe house. Except I don't want you chained. I want to make love to you with nothing between us."

She reached up to stroke his cheek. "I haven't ever done that, Trance. Haven't let myself lose control with someone, because—"

"I trust you."

"What if I don't trust myself?" she practically whispered.

"What if it's time to finally start?"

"And you're willing to be my experiment?"

"Ready, willing and able." He'd already buried his face against her neck, his mouth nipping at the sweet skin behind her earlobe, her hair tickling his face. "Besides, you'll be mine too."

She pulled back, looked at him with her eyes wide because she'd forgotten about his issues with strength. "So we'll just go slow."

"Yeah, slow."

"There was nothing slow about those kisses," she pointed out. "If something happens . . . if the wolf comes out . . ."

"She won't." He led her up the stairs by the hand until they came to his room—one entire wall was windows that opened up to the forest.

"Oh, that's beautiful," she said. "It's almost like we're outside."

He was behind her, his hands traveling down the front of her BDU shirt, undoing button after button until he was able to pull the shirt off her shoulders, revealing her sport bra. As she faced the woods, he pulled it over her head and let it fall to the ground next to the shirt. He made quick work of her pants and underwear as well, and she sighed softly as his hands brushed her breasts and one moved down her belly toward the juncture of soft curls between her thighs. "Don't shave," he murmured. "I like it like this."

"I like . . . when you do that."

He stroked a finger against her clit. "That?"

"Yes." Her word came out as a long, stuttered moan, and no, he had no intention of stopping anything.

"You're so wet, Rik . . . so hot . . . Is that all for me?"

She could only nod this time as he stroked her folds, ignoring the swollen nub for a few minutes. Her hand circled his wrist like a tight handcuff as she attempted to bring his fingers back to where she wanted them. She was strong, but without the wolf, not even close to his match. Still, he liked her fingers on him, guiding him, and after a few more minutes, he let her do just that.

"Show me, baby," he murmured against her neck. They were both sweating now as she rubbed her bare body along the length of his fully clothed one. His cock ached, his balls tightened as though he could come right in his own pants watching her lose it.

With both of them working together, two fingers against her sweet spot, she was quick to release. Her orgasm made her knees sag. But his arm held her steady around the waist, and when she was done shuddering, he slid a hand under her ass and carried her to the bed. She faced away from him, on all fours, and as much as he wanted to explore her further, his needs were too great.

Besides, this position allowed her to see the woods still—she hadn't taken her eyes from the view, and he thought about her imagining her freedom and figured maybe that would be enough to keep the wolf happy.

It seemed to be working, as Rik was practically mewing as she remained in front of him, her hands fisting the sheets, unable to keep her body still.

He made quick work of opening his pants but he was too damned impatient to take them off, and simply pulled them down to free himself. Rik was already whimpering, pushing back against him and he didn't make her wait.

He entered her—she was slick, ready for him, and she arched

her back to allow him access. His hands splayed along the bare skin of her back as she pressed against him so he went deeper and deeper inside of her. He threw his head back, reveling in this feeling—no chains, no barriers, nothing at all between them anymore.

"Oh God ... Trance!" She was yelling in earnest now and his groans matched hers. He was pretty sure they could be heard outside the house and he didn't give a shit about that, about anything but this, this combination of fucking her and making love to her. It was tender and raw and neither of them were worried about keeping their guards up any longer.

He had no doubt that, although he was the one on top, she had all the control—she was taking him, had turned her head so she could watch him, could look him in the eye as he roared toward climax.

"Now," she told him. "Now, Trance."

He let himself come in a pulsating stream of release, held fast to her hips as she went over the edge as well, her contractions drawing out his orgasm until he half collapsed on top of her.

He dragged a tongue up her spine and she shivered as he tasted the salty and sweet from her body. And then he rolled off her, taking her down to the mattress with him.

He lay on his back and she turned into him. "You didn't even take your clothes off," she murmured. "And you're still hard."

He locked his gaze with hers. "I guess we're going to have to do something about that."

RIK LAY in Trance's arms, her heart swelled with contentment. And love. And, as he pushed his erection into her hip, horniness.

God, she'd never felt like this before. Always in the past, sex had been about keeping the beast happy. When Rik got off, her releases were exactly that—releases of tension that took a lot of sass out of both her and her inner wolf. But this ... the sex act with Trance was so much more than an orgasm. They were making love, expressing their feelings through touch and taste and whispered endearments. For once, her releases didn't exhaust her; they energized her.

She dragged her lips across his shoulder and spoke against his sweat-dampened skin. "Take me again."

She didn't wait for a response, instead climbing on top of him to straddle his hips. Between her legs, his shaft spread the swollen lips of her sex. His jeans rasped against her tender skin, and while she liked the contrast of soft and rough, she wanted skin on skin, with nothing between them ever again.

There had been too many barriers in her life and in their relationship already.

As though he heard her thoughts, he arched up and shoved his jeans down. She helped him remove them, and then his shirt, and in a few rapid-fired heartbeats, he was as naked as she was.

This was the way it was meant to be. Finally.

Inside, the wolf sang. Trance had taken Rik from behind, the way a wolf's mate would, and she was happy, perfectly willing to let Rik have Trance the way she wanted now.

Playfully, she kissed her way down his muscular chest, reveling in how good it felt to linger, to coax a response from a man with gentleness instead of pain or humiliation. She dragged her fingernails lightly over his rippled abs as she worked her way lower... lower... until her cheek brushed the tip of his cock. A little hiss broke from his lips as she nuzzled him, going even lower.

She laved attention on the sensitive area on his inner thighs with little kisses, tiny nips, and long sweeps of her tongue.

"God, Rik," he panted. "I thought we weren't doing the torture thing anymore."

She pressed the flat of her tongue against the smooth spot behind his balls, and grinned. "I didn't agree to that."

He sucked air. "Clearly."

"Are you complaining?" She opened her mouth over one of his testicles and blew warm air over his sac.

"Not even close... ah, *yes!*"

Her mouth watered as she dragged her tongue from his balls to the head of his cock. A crystal drop had formed at the tip, and she lapped at it greedily. This was something that normally sent the beast into a rage, but she remained calm and content, and Rik took advantage of the wolf's relaxed attitude.

Taking him deep, she wrapped her hand around his hard shaft and pumped as she sucked. Trance's hands gripped her head and his whispered curses drifted down to her, his naughty words working her into a frenzy. Moisture pooled at her core and her clit throbbed and this wasn't going to continue for long. She wanted— needed—him inside her.

"You'd better stop," he rasped, even as he thrust his hips upward. More pre-cum coated her tongue, tempting her to bring him off so she could taste him fully, but he made the decision for her by lifting her head away from him. "As much as I love this, I want you on top, like you were the first time at the club."

Her breath caught. She understood what he was saying—that first time had been rough and raw, and both had been playing a role. He wanted to wipe the roles away, to repeat the position and make new, better memories.

Emotion made her eyes water as she climbed on him and lowered herself onto his shaft. They both groaned at the delicious, slick friction. She rocked slowly, loving the way Trance's breathing came faster, how he moaned when she reached back to cup his sac. It drew up tight as she stroked the seam separating his heavy balls. She could still taste the bold, smoky flavor on her lips, an aphrodisiac that had her grinding against him with increasing enthusiasm.

She absorbed everything—the rough whoosh of his breath, the strain of his body beneath hers, the sight of him fisting the bedsheets, his thick biceps bunching and rolling against the wicked sensations that gripped them both. She wanted to remember this forever.

He swallowed hard and kicked his head back as she ground her hips. "God, this is amazing."

"Yes," she whispered. "But I want more. Bind my hands."

He froze, rocked his head up off the pillow. "What?"

"I . . . I liked when you bound me at the ACRO place in England," she said softly. "For the first time, I was able to let myself go and trust and just feel good. I mean, it all turned out messed up, but I want to do that again. This time, it'll turn out different."

"You don't need to control yourself like that anymore. I don't need to either—"

"Shh." She put a finger against his lips. "It's not about control, Trance. It's about pleasure. You remember, don't you? You remember how strong your orgasms were when I had you bound and helpless?"

One corner of his made-for-pleasure mouth quirked up. "I wasn't helpless."

She rolled her eyes. Men. "You know what I mean. When you had nothing to worry about but how you felt, it made everything better, didn't it?" She tilted her hips so he went as deep as he could go, and then bit her lip at the lightning strike of pleasure the motion caused. "Every sensation is magnified. Better."

His eyes darkened, and he nodded. "Oh, yeah."

"So don't be afraid of the bonds," she said, dragging her finger down his chest to tweak a nipple. He hissed a breath between clenched teeth. "Embrace them. I want to make love to you with nothing between us, but I also want to love you using the skills we both have."

"Well, when you put it that way..." He stretched for his nightstand and opened the drawer. Inside, he kept condoms, lube, a blindfold, and a long silk sash. His blue gaze was intense as he looked up at her. "Help yourself."

Her hand shook with anticipation as she pulled the black length of cloth from the drawer, but before she gave it to him, she brushed the tip over the rim of his ear, the sensitive skin of his eyelids, and down to trace his lips. By the time she was done, a new sheen of sweat had broken out across his body.

"Enough," he said roughly, but his hands were gentle as he tied her wrists with the sash. He let them settle on his chest and gripped her waist. "Kiss me. I want you to be kissing me when you come."

Oh, she wanted that too. She fell forward, bracing her forearms on his sternum so her breasts rubbed against his hard chest and her hair fell in a curtain around his face. One of his hands still rested on her hip, but the other slid up her back to the nape of her neck to bring her mouth to his.

The kiss was soft as a whisper. Trance slid his lips across hers, sometimes stroking them with his tongue, and sometimes pulling back so there was only a thin veil of air to caress her mouth. God, he was good, so skilled, and she never in a million years would have guessed that a man could nearly make her come by doing nothing more than kiss her.

But he was driving her to new heights with his teasing, made worse by the fact that she couldn't touch him with her hands, couldn't guide his ministrations to her liking. The denial was delicious, beyond anything she could ever have predicted.

And then, as though he couldn't take it anymore, he arched his hips and drove deep as he plunged his tongue into her mouth. The double penetration made her moan with pleasure.

She rode him faster, the heat at her core building so quickly and so intensely that she couldn't hold back, and when Trance bent one leg up for leverage, the new angle of his cock sliding into her slick channel sent her over the edge.

She shouted into his mouth. He shouted back. Locked together as fully as they could be, they rode out their pleasure until they were nothing but a quivering, panting tangle. Though Rik could barely think, let alone move, Trance managed to pet her hair and her back with long, soothing strokes. The attention felt amazing, like nothing she'd encountered before. Yes, the sex was incredible—beyond incredible—but the way he held her now was the most intimate act she'd ever experienced.

"Don't stop," she murmured. "Don't ever stop."

"I won't."

"Ever?"

Trance didn't hesitate. He drew back, looked deeply into her eyes and whispered, "Ever."

CHAPTER
Twenty-four

The look on Ryan's face when Dev had admitted he'd been the one to betray him to Itor kept flashing in Dev's mind. Ryan was a long way from forgiving him, if it ever happened, and there was nothing Dev could do about that. He refused to grovel—couldn't, really—not in his position.

But when he thought of the months of torture Ryan had gone through—the times he still had ahead of him . . .

Fuck. He'd never felt so alone in his life, despite the fact he was surrounded by hundreds of agents and staff and Marlena.

And Gabriel. Zach had reported that working at the animal facility was helping Gabriel. Annika reported that he seemed calmer, albeit distracted.

"You know why he's distracted," Marlena said after skimming the report.

"Because he's new. Because he has no idea how to deal with his gift." Dev had pushed the papers aside, not really wanting to get involved any more than he had. He'd let Gabriel's direct sup know about the basics of what Gabriel could do and left it at that.

"You can't do this to him—it's not his fault that Oz is keeping his promise."

"How do I know the kid didn't manipulate this entire situation? It's not that hard to find out about me and Oz. Not that difficult to find out what kind of car Oz drove," Dev shot back.

"You'd know," Marlena said calmly, and he bit back the urge to retort further. She didn't deserve the brunt of this. "ACRO is functioning at its most efficient level ever. Peak performance. All missions in the last six months have been accomplished with minimal injury to ACRO agents and very little collateral damage, except to Itor. You can't be this hard on yourself."

But he was, always would be. He'd watched his father go through the same thing—his mother too. It was why he'd gone into the Air Force instead of joining the family business when he'd turned eighteen. And right before Marlena left his office, he told her he didn't want to see Gabriel again, on any level, told Marlena the young recruit wasn't allowed near his office, finished with "And make sure to tell the guards to keep him away from my premises."

He was well aware he was past the verge of behaving like a complete and total asshole. He was pissed and horny, a horrid combination, and yet Marlena still wanted to be around him. She'd forced him home early, promising him the kind of surprise he enjoyed. And so now he waited in the guest bedroom, like Marlena told him to. He'd showered and he lay naked under the sheets, eyes closed.

But still, he knew when Marlena entered. She was alone, waiting by the door. "Turn it off, Devlin."

He knew what she was asking—she wanted him to turn off his gift of second sight and CRV. As much as he hated the vulnerability, he understood why she felt it important for him to do so. For him, it took away any element of potential awkwardness when he and the Seducers sat across from each other at a meeting. They were consummate professionals, but still, what he didn't know, in this case, couldn't hurt him. "It's done."

"Then sit up—come to the edge of the bed," she told him.

He was totally and completely naked now as Marlena shut the lights and stripped off her clothing. She was easily one of the most beautiful women he'd ever seen, and if he'd swung more that way, he had no doubt he'd marry her, love or no love. She had a way with men.

She tied a blindfold over his eyes, whispered, "Relax," as she bound his wrists behind his back with soft, black silk ties. They were all for show, of course, but his cock hardened instantly.

Marlena gave an appreciative moan as he took one of her nipples in his mouth and sucked hard—her hands wound into his hair as her naked body writhed in his lap.

And then, just as suddenly, they weren't alone anymore. The air changed as he heard footsteps come toward the bed. Clothing was unzipped, fell to the floor with soft sounds as Marlena moved behind him, her breasts pressing against his back.

Someone knelt on the floor between his legs. Jesus. His hands tugged at the soft bindings as a hot mouth worked his cock.

He was intimately acquainted with Marlena's hands, her mouth, and knew that it was a man sucking him, not her. The pace was different—harder, more knowing.

Lately, he'd resisted being with men, had allowed Marlena to bring in a male Seducer only once in an effort to banish Oz's ghost.

Now that ghost appeared to be gone. In its place was the young, chiseled face of Gabriel, and even though Dev tried to block out the face, he couldn't.

And so he pretended that whoever was down there was Gabriel, because no one would have to know that. The mystery man's tongue flicked over the slit on the top of his cock and then firmly pushed in and out of the small hole.

"Holy fuck." His body jolted as his voice went up an octave, and still hands held him down hard and fast to the bed. He couldn't move and he knew two things immediately—one, that Marlena had long since left the room, and second, that this was Gabriel holding him down. He recognized the touch of the excedo . . . the strength, and he heard himself say, "Take the blind-fold off me. I want to watch you."

Gabriel complied, taking only a moment to free Dev's eyes from the black cloth. By the time Dev blinked, Gabriel was back between his legs, deep-throating his cock, looking up at Devlin the entire time.

It was so fucking hot, watching that, feeling the way his balls throbbed, and no, there was no reason to hold out. He'd been too far gone from the second Gabriel had arrived on his doorstep.

He came—with a loud groan that made Gabriel tighten his grip on him. Their eyes remained locked until Dev stopped shud-dering from his orgasm and lay back on the bed on his elbows, his wrists still tied behind him. He was breathing hard, had come harder than he could remember, and he was still erect. Gabriel stood and climbed onto Dev—the young man's body was beauti-ful, carved and covered with a thin sheen of sweat.

"Are you going to be able to do this—to let me fuck you?" Dev asked.

Gabriel rubbed his chin as he balanced himself over Dev's thighs, his balls and long, hard arousal brushing Dev's. "I'm here, aren't I?"

"Untie my hands."

"No."

"I won't read you," Dev assured him.

"I'm not worried about that anymore. What more can you find out? I'm an open fucking book to you, whether you touch me or you read my file. No, I want your hands tied so you remember who's here with you. So you can't bury your head against my neck and think of another man. I want you to realize that this has nothing to do with Oz," Gabriel said fiercely. "This is you and me—no ghosts."

"No ghosts," Dev repeated.

"Oz wasn't outside tonight," Gabriel said. "I haven't seen him in days."

To be fair, Dev's every waking thought hadn't been about Oz either—he'd been strangely free to think about other things, like the man currently on top of him. "Untie me, Gabriel. I want to touch you, do things to you that make you call out my name."

Gabriel leaned against him, chest to chest, and finally did what Dev asked. While he worked the black ties, he kissed Dev's neck and shoulder, nipping the skin with his teeth. And when Dev's wrists were freed, he placed his hands on Gabe, who froze instantly despite his earlier speech.

"It's okay—it's just a touch." Dev ran his palms along the man's smooth shoulders, down his arms and back up his chest. Gabriel shivered but remained still, until Dev's hand circled his erection. And then he let forth a groan that intensified as Dev's strokes did.

"Jesus . . . you need to . . . I'm going to . . ."

"Just come, Gabriel. It's not going to be the last time tonight, not by a long shot."

Gabriel did, clutching Dev the entire time.

HOURS LATER, when both men were spent, Gabe stretched his lean, muscled form out on the bed, curling his arms around one of the pillows as his cheek rested on the soft white cotton.

Dev could kick him out now. Should.

Instead, he lay back and curled himself around Gabriel. The other man stiffened with surprise and doubt, until he felt Dev's erection. "I'm not ready for sleep."

"But when you are?" Gabriel asked.

"You can stay."

"Why now? What's changed? You still think I'm here because Oz sent me."

Dev shook his head. "Oz believed in free will. He sent you here for a different reason. I just haven't figured it out yet."

"Marlena told me . . ." Gabriel stopped for a second, no doubt figuring that Dev would stop him. But when he didn't, Gabe continued. "She said that Oz promised to send you someone."

"And you think you're that someone?"

"No, I don't. I'm not the kind of guy you'd wish on anyone. So what you said about other reasons seems right on."

"And you'll keep me company until the love of my life walks through the front door, then?" Dev asked sarcastically.

But Gabriel remained silent and so Dev put his arms around him tighter.

"I know who you are. I know who's in my bed."

"Are you sure?"

"Yes. I just needed...I needed to let him go. You let me do that." Dev rolled onto his back. "You let me do that in a way no one else has."

"You were together a long time."

"Yeah, forever." Dev turned to him. "That's not as long as it used to be. What else did Oz tell you?"

Gabe probably should've been freaked out once he realized that he'd been driven around by a ghost, but strangely enough, he wasn't. "He said...ah..."

"That I could be an asshole."

"Yeah, there was that."

Dev snorted. "I don't do apologies."

"Because you're the boss?"

"Because I make amends for my fuckups in other ways." Dev was back on him, straddling him, and for once Gabe didn't feel the familiar panic. "Trust me."

"I do. I don't know why...but I do."

Dev's hand trailed down his chest, farther, until he cupped Gabriel's balls. It didn't stop the man from speaking. "He said you liked taking care of people, but you needed someone who could take care of you right back. Someone who wasn't scared of your...bullshit."

"And you fit that bill?"

"Like I said, I'm here, right?"

"I'm too fucking old to court someone, Gabriel."

"Yeah, thirty-six is kind of ancient."

Dev rolled him. "I'll show you ancient."

Even with the young man's face buried in the pillow, Devlin could feel Gabriel's smile.

CHAPTER
Twenty-five

Marlena sat at her desk nervously. It had been nearly twelve hours since she'd brought Gabriel to Devlin's bed—if he was going to reprimand her, it wasn't too late.

But it *was* late—Dev rarely came into the office past six in the morning, and it was nearly nine now. She fielded calls and the questioning faces of agents who had morning appointments.

"He's fine," she assured each and every one even as the butterflies in her stomach grew more intense.

"Gabe never showed up for our morning appointment and he's not in his room," Annika announced loudly, and good thing they were the only two in the office at that moment. God, the woman could be so exasperating sometimes, speaking without thinking.

But before Marlena could say anything, Dev strolled in, his BDUs a little ... well, wrinkled. Almost askew. And he ran a hand through his hair, which looked messier than usual. His face was flushed, and he smiled.

He never smiled in the morning.

Marlena instantly felt better, even as Annika narrowed her

eyes and crossed her arms and stared between the two of them. "I think Gabriel's AWOL," she said.

"Really?" Dev reached for his coffee mug, which Marlena had filled for him.

"Yes. And you don't seem all that concerned."

Dev took a long slug of coffee. "I'm sure he'll turn up."

Gabriel did, about two seconds later, looking as disheveled as Devlin, and Marlena tried to bite back a smile.

"Where the hell have you been?" Annika demanded.

"I was, um, running," Gabe offered, and Dev turned away from him with a smirk of his own hidden inside his mug. "Sorry."

"You're nowhere near sorry yet—but you will be," Annika told him. "Let's go."

Gabe followed Annika out, with a quick look back at Dev. Marlena watched the men's eyes meet and knew that, somewhere in the universe, Oz was smiling.

"Rik's working well with Kira," she told him.

"I know. That's good." He ran his hands through his hair and suddenly he was all business again.

Devlin wouldn't invite her into his bedroom again. Marlena had resigned herself to that the moment she'd brought Gabriel into Devlin's house last night. She was fulfilling Oz's final promise, to make sure Dev was happy.

"If anything happens to me, you need to make sure Dev finds happiness," Oz had told her—again and again, and not only before his death. He'd been telling her that for years, even when he and Devlin weren't together. She felt a certain amount of peace at fulfilling his last wish, even as the sadness overtook her heart.

MARLENA LOCKED her desk and stared at the smooth, bare mahogany surface. She ran her hands over the cool wood, and then, before she had any more regrets, she stood and went into Devlin's office, left the keys on top of his morning reports.

She'd e-mailed him her letter of intent to transfer departments. He would sign it because she requested it but he would hate having to do so.

She hated having to make him, but he didn't need to keep his promise to her any longer—not when he had his chance of real happiness with Gabriel. Oz understood the relationship between her and Devlin, didn't mind it, and she probably would've stayed doing what she was doing forever if Oz had lived.

But he hadn't . . . and maybe, in some small way, he'd saved her too. Even though she'd never be free from the curse her sister put on her, she'd find a way not to care. If nothing else, she'd devote her life to ACRO, to saving the world any way she could.

She walked across the compound until she came to the house that the Seducer trainees lived in. The guard let her in and she made her way to the main office, a large, luxurious room. If nothing else, the Seducers liked excess—their lives revolved around seduction twenty-four seven, they lived and breathed sex in all its various forms, saw it as more of a function of a power play than a form of love.

They were able to separate the emotions from the act. And maybe, in time, Marlena herself would be able to do the same. Or the ACRO scientists could create a pill or a mind block or something.

Lourdes, a tall, bronze-skinned woman who was the department head and one of Marlena's closest friends, lounged on one of the plush couches, reading a file. She looked up as Marlena entered, and smiled.

Marlena didn't. "I'm ready for training."

Lourdes frowned and stood, dropping the paperwork. "Marlena, I thought you'd said . . . never. Dev said never."

"Dev will say yes now. Train me."

Lourdes wasn't convinced. Marlena couldn't blame her, as no one went against Devlin's wishes. "You need to trust me on this. Devlin will agree to it."

"What about your curse—has that been lifted?"

"No."

"So how can this work? You'll fall in love with every single man you seduce . . . and none of them will ever fall in love with you. You cannot do this job."

"I'll never know until I try."

"There must be something else for you to do here . . ."

"I have no special powers, other than my looks," Marlena said. "I don't want to be support staff any longer. I need to figure out what I was meant to do."

"And you're convinced it's giving away sex for intel?" Lourdes cocked an eyebrow. "This is one of the hardest jobs at ACRO. Do you know how many Seducers accidentally fall in love, especially when they're on an ongoing case? There are more broken hearts in this department than I care to think about."

"Then I'll fit right in." Marlena eyed her steadily. "You know I'd be an asset here."

"And I know that a woman in love can spill her secrets to the wrong man," Lourdes shot back.

"I would never—could never—betray ACRO. My pain is private. I've been hiding my broken heart from men for years. You can help me refine that ability." Marlena sat in one of the leather chairs.

Lourdes was out of arguments for now, but Marlena knew the road wouldn't be easy. "I'll call Devlin. And then we can get started."

CHAPTER
Twenty-six

It was time to meet the boss.

Devlin O'Malley had sent for Ulrika, and she had to admit her nerves were in knots. Trance had said she'd have to meet him eventually, but she'd been here only a week, and it seemed so soon to her.

But now she was standing just outside his office with Neema, and staring at the doorknob like it might bite.

"Go ahead," the secretary, whom Neema had said was a new girl named Christine, said kindly. "He's waiting."

Taking a deep breath, Rik entered. Mr. O'Malley was sitting at his desk, his spiky brown hair full of deep grooves that said he always had his fingers in it.

"Have a seat, Ms. Jaeger. Can I call you Ulrika?"

"Yes, of course." She sank into the comfy leather chair. "Rik is fine too."

"I'm Dev."

"It's, um, good to meet you."

"Are you settling in? Comfortable?"

She nodded. "The quarters are very nice. Trance was right, my room is much better than a cage."

Sympathy flashed in his brown eyes, and she instantly regretted the cage comment. She didn't want anyone feeling sorry for her. Especially not now, when she was starting a new life that made her past grow more distant with each passing day.

Trance had a lot to do with that, and she had to bite back a smile when she thought about how he'd been making sure every minute of her day was full of either training or him. He wanted her to have no time to dwell on the past, and he'd been doing a damned fine job of ushering her into the future.

"Neema explained why you're here?"

"She said you won't force me to do anything I don't want to do."

Dev leaned back in his chair and steepled his fingers. "You sound like you don't believe that."

"I'm not sure what to believe," she admitted. "If I don't want to kill people, then what will you do with me?"

"I'm sure we'll find something for you. The cryptozoology department is dying to acquire you."

Her blood ran cold as images of being strapped down to a table and poked and prodded flooded her brain. "Why?"

"To help find other cryptids. You're the only known shapeshifter. They'd love to use any of your special abilities to seek out all the creatures they are looking for."

"Oh." She relaxed, because that sounded really interesting. And nonviolent.

He considered her for a long moment, and she suddenly wondered what his talent was, because she got the distinct impression he was attempting to read her mind. "How are you doing? Kira said she's still having a hard time reaching your other half, but that it's calmer now."

She smiled. "Cujo."

Dev blinked. "Excuse me?"

"That's what Trance calls her. Cujo."

"Ah . . . do you know what Cujo is?"

"He said it's some sort of rabid dog from a horror novel." She shrugged. "I didn't get to read a lot when I was with Itor."

"Trance has an interesting sense of humor," Dev muttered. "In any case, your . . . Cujo is calmer?"

"Much. She still doesn't like any man but Trance, but at least she doesn't go nuts around them anymore." Like now. The wolf was wary, sort of pacing, but she wasn't all hackles-raised.

"Good." Dev gave a single, brisk nod. "Then are you up for a little work?"

And there went the hackles. "What kind of work?" she asked, narrowing her eyes.

He held up his hands. "Nothing dangerous." He pushed a fat book across the desk at her.

"What's that?" She reached for the book.

"It's a photo file of all operatives who have gone missing or turned up dead under mysterious circumstances."

Rik drew her hand back so fast she bumped her elbow on the arm of her chair. "Why are you showing me this?"

"We need closure. I'm sorry, Rik, but we do this every time we recruit someone who might have come up against us in the past. We need to know what happened to these agents. They deserve that." He gestured to the book. "Please. If you know something about any of these agents, tell me. We're not looking for revenge. Just the truth."

Her stomach churned so violently she looked around the office for a garbage can in case she had to throw up. She knew she'd killed one agent, but she suspected that there may have been others. Itor hadn't always told her who her targets were.

Finally, she reached for the photo album again. Heart pounding, she flipped it open. First page, a female she didn't recognize. Second page, male, same thing. And on and on.

Until page twenty. As if a nightmare had come to life, she saw the face of the agent she'd killed in Ecuador. Excedosapien. Arthur Scott. Handsome, with eyes that appeared familiar. Probably because she'd seen them up close when she'd buried the knife between his ribs.

Closing her eyes, she nodded. She heard a scratch of pencil on paper, and then Dev's calm voice, urging her to go on.

Her mouth was dry as she continued. Thank God she didn't find any more, but still, the one was one too many.

"Just the one," she breathed, as she closed the book. When she glanced at Dev, she saw in his eyes that she hadn't surprised him. "You knew."

"I suspected. We thought wild animals . . . but once we heard about you . . ." He trailed off, and mercifully didn't continue. But he also seemed to be looking inward, to a place she couldn't follow, and she was very glad of that.

Because he seemed to be very, very troubled.

"I'm sorry." Her voice was raspy and shaky, and she just wanted to slink away. But what she wanted even more right now was Trance. She'd give anything to have him swoop in and whisk her to someplace where only the two of them existed.

Dev came to his feet and moved to the door. "It's been good talking to you," he said, a dismissal if she'd ever heard one.

She stood. "I really am sorry."

"I know." He opened the door. "I'll be checking in with you every couple of weeks, just to monitor your progress. If you need anything, don't hesitate to ask. Neema or Kira can help you out." He pegged her with a somber stare. "We'll take care of you, Ulrika."

Strangely, she believed him.

DEV WAITED UNTIL Rik left his office before he buried his face in his hands. Elbows propped on the desk in front of him, he shielded his eyes from his surroundings and let his mind run wild.

You knew . . . what the hell were you trying to do, prove yourself wrong?

Yes, in this situation, he would actually enjoy being wrong.

There were so many secrets he'd kept—for the good of his agents, for the good of ACRO . . .

Now one of those secrets could potentially have a devastating impact on one of them. And one of them already did.

Fuck. Just fuck.

She'd been the one to take away the man who might've helped Trance come to terms with what he was sooner rather than later. She'd killed his father and now ...

Christ, it didn't take a genius, or a psychic, to figure out that Rik was falling for Trance. Dev had never expected Trance to follow suit, but based on the way Rik talked about him, he was pretty sure Trance was just as enamored with her.

He thought about only sending same-sex agents on missions from now on, and realized, with a sharp, barking laugh, that that wouldn't have stopped *him*.

No, he was failing everyone, including a young man who refused to think that Dev wasn't wide open to the prospect of falling in love. A man who currently stood in the doorway of Dev's office, even though it was long after hours and everyone, including Marlena, had already gone home.

And then he remembered that Marlena didn't work for him any longer—not on a personal level anyway. She'd slipped away from him, insisting he had to let her grow and make her own mistakes.

God, he hated himself for agreeing to let her go to the Seducers.

"You shouldn't be here," he told Gabe harshly.

"I work here," Gabriel returned. "What's wrong?"

"I just have a headache." He pushed his paperwork to the side and shut down his computer. For the first time in a long time, he didn't want to stay in the office all night, wanted Gabriel to drag him away from all of this shit and take him home.

Gabe approached the desk and leaned over it, palms flat on the mahogany, face close to Dev's. "What else is wrong?"

"I can't tell you."

"Then who can you tell? Who do you talk to, Devlin?"

The way the man said his name ... Christ. "It's a lonely job, being the boss."

The younger man shook his head slowly. "No, it's a lonely job being Devlin O'Malley."

"Gabriel..."

But Gabriel covered his mouth with a kiss, a long, hard, hot kiss that sucked the breath and the need for conversation away.

Dev had wanted to say, *You can't heal me,* but Gabriel seemed intent on doing so anyway. And after a while, Dev wasn't so sure of anything anymore.

DEVLIN HADN'T BEEN lying when he'd told Gabriel the other night that what was happening between them was for a bigger purpose. But still, he'd felt a heavy guilt about sleeping next to Gabriel. About enjoying having another man there and about feeling that thrill of excitement when you didn't know what would happen next, but you knew you were happy.

Dev had felt it the first time he'd met Oz. And then each and every time they'd gotten together beyond that.

"It's been a long road, Oz," he said as he stared out the front windows to the dawn that was just breaking. He'd left Gabriel upstairs, sound asleep, and Dev was actually thinking of cooking him breakfast.

He went to turn away, but a flash of blue brought his gaze back to the window. He rubbed his eyes. It was still there. With a pounding heart, he tore outside.

Oz's old blue convertible was parked in his driveway, rather than across the street, and Dev was pretty sure that the car would disappear the moment he approached it.

But it didn't, and he felt a strange flutter when he peered through the driver's-side window and found the seat empty. Hesitantly, he opened the door and climbed behind the wheel. The seat was cool and the keys were in the ignition.

They'd made some good memories in this car.

It was nice to be able to smile when he thought about Oz—to not be mired in grief any longer. To be grateful for what had been.

Oz had saved his life—more than once—and he was doing it again in the form of a young man currently sleeping in Dev's bedroom. The master bedroom, not the guest one.

It was time to get back to Gabriel.

He saw the note at the last minute—scrawled in black ink across a piece of paper. Oz's writing.

It was always meant to be this way. I'm not doing anything that wasn't planned for you on the day you were born.

—*O*

P.S. Could you make sure Trance gets this car? It's the same make and model Arthur used to drive when he was dating Trance's mom.

It wouldn't make up for a lost relationship between Trance and his father, but it was something. A tie to his past. Dev knew, with certainty, how important that was. And so he looked up at the sky and he mouthed a silent *Thank you.*

His own ties would always be there, but loose enough to let him be happy again. It was time.

AFTER THE PRIVATE jet took them from ACRO to ML's estate in Florida, Meg slept for what seemed like twenty-four hours straight. It might've been too, and she really didn't care. She stayed in bed with the blinds pulled and left her computer dark, until finally ML insisted she eat something. He even sent in one of his staff with a tray of her favorite foods—surf and turf and French fries—to tempt her.

It didn't, but she did get out of bed and opened her computer. The familiar feel of her fingertips on the keyboard comforted her and within twenty minutes, she was actually eating in between typing.

Until Ryan popped up on her IM screen. The fork fell from her hand, clattered on the plate and might've ended up somewhere on the floor. She didn't know, didn't care—closed her IM screen and shoved the computer away from her.

"Hey, sis, can I come in?"

She looked up at her brother, dressed in his usual Hawaiian shirt and long shorts, his blond hair loose. A surfer-dude, money-laundering millionaire who still harbored a heartbreak from when he was seventeen years old. "Why haven't you gotten over Rebecca yet?"

He avoided the question about his ex-girlfriend, which told her everything she needed to know. "I knew Ryan screwed with you."

"That's not an answer, Mose," she said as her brother made himself comfortable on the empty side of the king-sized bed. She shifted so he couldn't see her computer, since Ryan's name kept popping up on-screen, asking to speak with her. "I was there when you were waiting for Rebecca. When she didn't meet you—"

"It pretty much sucked."

"Mose, please."

He sighed. "Yeah, look, she broke my heart. I'd like to think I'm over it, but, man . . . she promised. And she broke that promise. I'm over her, just not what she did—all right?"

"It's just like what that guy did to Mary. Promised her the world and then left her in the hospital to die alone," she said bitterly, noted that Mose's hands fisted.

"Did Ryan promise you things?"

She could only nod.

"You should've let me kill him back at ACRO."

"Maybe." She shut the computer's lid. "I don't want to steal anymore."

Her brother looked stricken. "You're going straight?"

"Don't worry, I won't try to convert you."

"Will you stay here with me, at least until Interpol gets off your back?" The concern in his voice matched his expression.

"I've got no place else to go. So yes, I'm yours."

Twenty-seven

Devlin beeped Trance early—an urgent request to come to his boss's office. Within half an hour, Trance had showered from his early-morning PT, dressed and headed to see Devlin.

A woman named Christine manned Marlena's desk—an odd sight, but before Trance could ask if Marlena was all right, Dev was waving him into the inner sanctum.

"Come in, Trance. Have a seat."

Trance did so, on the soft leather couch even as Devlin remained on his feet.

The book of dead and missing ACRO agents was on the table in front of the couch—Trance recognized the book immediately by its black leather binding and red lettering.

Dev reached down and flipped the book open to a man named Arthur Scott.

"I remember seeing him at the gym, and at meetings. He was an excedo, right?" Trance said. His memory was slightly fuzzy on that—the man died the same year—and month—that Trance had been forcibly dragged into ACRO.

"Trance, this man, this agent—he was your father."

Trance stared at the picture as Dev's words swirled in his head. If he wasn't already sitting, he would've had to, as his world tipped violently upside down. "My father was a fucking ACRO agent..."

"Yes. He had the same superstrength you have. But your hypnosis effect, that's a mutation."

"Fuck talking to me about genetic mutations, Devlin. I was here when my father was here—why wasn't I told about this?"

"He didn't want you to know."

"Yeah, well, he'd never wanted anything to do with me before that, so it's not a surprise." Trance slammed the book closed.

"He was young when he got your mom pregnant," Dev said. "They were both only sixteen. And your mom didn't know your dad was an excedo—he was young and scared, the same way you were."

Trance spoke through clenched teeth. "Then he should've been there for me. If not at first, then once ACRO took him in. I would never do that to a son of mine."

"He figured you were better off without him."

"That's bullshit, and you know it."

"I do know it, Trance. But I couldn't force him to find you— he didn't know where your mom had taken you, if you were even alive. Until you walked through these doors and he saw you—"

"And why didn't he tell me then? I was brought here weeks before he died."

"He didn't know how to tell you. He made me promise not to say anything until he was ready." Dev paused. "He spoke to me before he left for his final mission. It was routine; he was supposed to be back within thirty-six hours. He was going to tell you then. And when he died, I didn't see the point of hurting you with what might have been."

"That wasn't your decision to make, Devlin."

"I know that now."

Trance bowed his head, because he didn't know what else to say. All he wanted to do was leave this office and go find Rik and lose himself in her arms. "So why are you telling me this now? You've kept it from me for years. Is he alive or something?"

"No, he died the day it says on that page. We were just never sure who was responsible."

"And now you are," Trance said, and Dev nodded. "And you want me to find that person? Because hell, I wouldn't mind the chance."

"That person is already here, at ACRO."

"Devlin, I don't understand—what the hell are you trying to tell me?" Dev was typically straightforward with his mission details, laying it out immediately so his agents had no doubt what their plan of attack needed to be.

This time, though, Dev looked like he wanted to be anywhere but here. "It's Rik."

Trance's world took another hit and he had to check to make sure he wasn't on his knees, because his entire body was numb. He heard himself ask, "Does she know?"

"She knows she killed an agent named Arthur Scott—she doesn't know he was your father."

Trance didn't know anything anymore, except the fact that his world had once again changed, irrevocably so, and not for the better.

RIK DIDN'T THINK she'd been so happy in her entire life. Trance had stopped by her room last night right before curfew, and he'd lingered long enough for one of the training center monitors to finally nudge him along.

This morning, Neema brought her breakfast, but she hadn't eaten more than a few bites of the rare steak and eggs when Kira arrived, looking exhausted, as though she'd been dragged forcibly out of bed.

Rik frowned. "What's wrong? You said you were on vacation and would only be here if absolutely necessary."

"I know." Kira sighed. "Dev thinks it's necessary." Kira pegged her with a look of concern. "We need to talk."

A feeling of foreboding tugged at Rik's gut. "Can we go

outside? I was just getting ready to take a walk before Neema drags me to the gym."

Kira nodded, and they walked out into the cool morning. She didn't say anything until they came to the little park that sat in the middle of the compound, where a pond full of ducks watched Kira warily.

"It's funny how animals flock to me, but they run from you," Kira said.

"The lion and the . . ." Rik cocked her head and studied Kira, because the woman was not a lamb. But neither was she a predator. Still, Rik had a feeling Kira could scrap with the best of them if she had to.

Kira shrugged and sat on one of the benches that lined the sidewalk circling the park. Rik sank down next to her.

"What's going on, Kira?"

"How in control of the wolf are you at this point?"

"Well, right now, she's pretty calm. Still wary and not willing to trust most, but she's learned to accept you and Neema. And Trance." For some reason, Kira winced. "Okay, I'm starting to freak out a little here."

"Dev wanted me to prepare you. Mainly because he doesn't know how Trance is going to react."

Rik's stomach plummeted. "React to what?"

"The news about his father."

Rik blinked. "Father? He said he never knew him. Has he been found?"

"He worked here at ACRO, but Trance never knew."

"Well, where is he? Where's Trance? What's going on?" Worry had her completely on edge, because the idea that Trance was upset was eating at her. She wanted to go to him, but she didn't know where he was or what she could do.

"I don't know where Trance is. But his father is dead." Kira took a deep breath and locked gazes with Rik. "You killed him."

Rik rocked backward so violently she nearly fell off the bench. "No." She stood. "That's not . . . I couldn't . . . *no*."

"You identified him to Dev yesterday," Kira said softly.

Yesterday came back at Rik like a bulldozer through the brain. The ACRO agent in Ecuador. The one she'd stabbed. The only one she remembered with such clarity that she could still hear the wet punch of metal through flesh.

"Oh, God." She wanted to throw up. "Trance. Does he know? Does he—"

"Yes." Kira took Rik's hand. "Dev is telling him this morning. That's why I'm here. We didn't know how he was going to react."

Rik jerked away from Kira, because she didn't know how *she* was going to react. What if Trance hated her now? Running her hands through her hair over and over, she paced. Kira was talking but Rik had no idea what she was saying.

Suddenly, the hair on the back of her neck stood up, and gooseflesh erupted all over her body. Awareness shivered across her skin. Slowly, she turned.

And locked gazes with Trance.

He stood about fifty yards away, near Dev's office building. For a second, she remained frozen in place. Then she took off at a dead run toward him. Kira called after her, but she didn't listen. She threw herself into Trance's arms. He caught her, but after a brief, stiff hug, he grasped her upper arms and gently put her aside.

In his eyes, she saw pain, confusion and something else she couldn't identify. Disgust? Disappointment?

"Trance—"

"Don't." He held up his hands and took a step back. "I can't do this right now. I can't even look at you."

Her eyes stung. She couldn't blame him, but she had to explain. Had to get him to understand . . . which would be quite the feat when she didn't understand herself.

"I told you what happened. You said it wasn't my fault and that I did what I had to do to survive." A tear rolled down her cheek, and she dashed it away. "You said—"

"I said a lot of things, Rik." He looked up at the sky and shook his head. "But it's different when you're talking about someone else."

"Isn't that a little hypocritical?"

"Yeah," he said. "It is." He started to walk away, but she grabbed him.

"Wait. You said you'd be there to catch me. We'd work through this together!"

He peeled her fingers from his wrist, still not looking at her. "You should be used to my lies by now, Rik."

Stunned, she stumbled backward as he strode away. Inside, the wolf howled for him to come back.

He didn't.

AT THE SOUND of Rik's mournful howls, Trance wanted to drop to his knees and cover his ears. He wanted to scream until his throat went raw in order to drown out the sounds and the images in his head, of Rik's wolf killing the man he'd never known as father. And he wanted to hurt the wolf for taking away his only chance of finally putting some goddamned closure on the situation.

"Trance, wait!"

It was Kira, and still, he didn't turn around—couldn't, for fear of seeing Rik's face and losing it.

"Trance, please." Kira was walking next to him, attempting to keep up with his strides.

"Not now, Kira. I walked away from her before I said something I might regret later. Please, just let me go."

But Kira got in front of him, so fast he almost tripped. "You can't do this to her."

"You don't get to tell me what I can and can't do."

"What if Tommy had judged me to be some kind of whore because of all the men I'd slept with during my seasons, before I met him. Would you have thought that was fair?"

"This is different and you damned well know it," he told her through clenched teeth.

"Give her a chance . . . She had no control over herself. Just like me." Tears stained Kira's cheeks, and fuck it all, Ender would kill him if he even thought Trance had upset his wife.

"This isn't about sex, Kira. I can handle anything that has to do with sex—I would've fucking preferred that. But this . . . this is about my family."

"You didn't even know him. He left you. Has Rik done that? No. Not when she thought you were some poor little excedo who needed help. She took you in even though doing so put her in more danger. What did your father do for you?"

He paused, sucked air as the empty feeling in his chest got bigger. "Don't you know better than to push a man when he's like this, Kira? I'm not Ender—I don't have to love you and forgive you and I fucking damn well don't have to listen to you."

Yeah, there was a fight with Ender in his future, but he didn't give a shit. He moved around Kira and took off at a dead run for the woods that would lead him to his house.

He could still hear Rik's howls, long after he went inside and shut the door.

RIK HAD SUNK to her knees on the grass and closed her eyes, unable to watch Trance walk away. Kira had gone after him, but Rik had no idea why, and worse, she knew nothing Kira said would make a difference. She'd seen the resolve in his eyes, knew he wasn't going to give in to any kind of pressure to make him stay anywhere he didn't want to be.

Or stay with anyone he didn't want to be with.

No, Trance's incredible strength was as mental as it was physical.

"Rik?" Kira kneeled next to her, but Ulrika sensed another presence. Male. An anxious, tense male.

She opened her eyes and looked past Kira to Ender, who hovered a few yards away. Menace radiated from him, obvious in his tightly coiled body and tense stance. He was ready to rip into her if she so much as twitched.

The beast wanted to twitch.

Stay calm . . . stay calm . . .

Kira's soothing voice treaded around the outskirts of Rik's consciousness, but the words were jumbled, indiscernible through the wolf's howls and growls. It mourned Trance, but was angry at the same time, and it wanted a piece of the man throwing off danger like a neon sign.

"Get away from her, Kira." Ender's rumbling voice rolled through Rik in a seismic wave, shaking the beast and making it want out more than ever.

"Hush." Kira framed Rik's face in her hands and forced her to look at her. "Hey, keep it together. You can do it."

Her skin stretched painfully tight, as if her muscles wanted to erupt right through it. "Can't . . ."

"You can. You're strong." Her fingers feathered over Rik's cheek—and inside, the wolf calmed a little. "You need to do this."

Rik became aware of another presence. Neema. "Kira, let her handle this herself."

Panic wrapped around Rik's chest. Kira was the only thing keeping her together. If she backed off . . .

Kira did exactly that. But not before she leaned in and said softly into her ear, "You can do this."

The moment Kira stood, Ender snagged her arm and pulled her away. Which, of course, set off the beast. Rik heard a godawful snarl emanate from deep inside her.

"Tommy, that's not necessary," Kira snapped, but Neema cut her off with a sharp hand signal.

"Ender, make a threatening move. Make her mad."

Before anyone could protest, he said something about crate training and Milk-Bones, and drew a pistol from inside his jacket. Rik had seen enough tranquilizer guns to recognize it, and so had the beast. Its pain and rage welled up inside her as memories of all the horrible things Itor had done to her hit her from all sides. She couldn't count the number of times she'd been shot with tranqs when her handlers couldn't put the beast back inside.

She knew this was a test, one she was going to fail miserably in about two seconds.

Failure . . .

She'd made so much progress since meeting Trance. The wolf

hadn't felt the need to hurt or control a human in days, when before, the need had been constant. She'd actually felt peace. Happiness. For the first time since losing her entire family, she felt like she might actually belong somewhere.

If she shifted now and attacked these people, all of that would change. They might never trust her, and her own guilt would lead to withdrawal and misery.

Kira was right. She had to be strong.

She *would* be strong.

In a firm, commanding tone, she barked out an order at her inner wolf to stand down. But with Ender moving forward, Cujo raged, throwing herself at the walls of Rik's mind.

Stand. Down!

Slowly, calmly, Rik stood. Sweat beaded on her brow as the effort to hold the beast in took its toll. She trembled, skin feeling like fire ants were biting her from the inside. But she held it together. Somehow, she held it together. Even when Ender grabbed her wrist as though he was going to throw her to the ground, she managed to keep from exploding into fur and fangs.

It wasn't easy, but she didn't think anything had ever felt as good as the realization that she'd remained in control. And when Ender released her, she nearly laughed at the victory.

She'd won. Just a few days ago, nothing could have kept her from shifting into a man-eating monster, but today, she'd kept it together. She couldn't wait to tell Trance—

Closing her eyes, she blew out a long breath, her joy tempered with sadness. She couldn't tell Trance, because after what she'd done to his father, how could he talk to her, let alone forgive her?

She stared off in the direction he'd gone, still tempted to go after him. But not now. Later. Later she'd find him, and she'd make him listen. Make him understand. Because she'd lost way too much in her life, and she wasn't about to lose him too.

CHAPTER
Twenty-eight

Ryan stood on Trance's front porch, waiting. He'd been pounding on the door for several minutes, and he was about to bust through it, because he knew damned good and well the ex-cedo was home.

Finally, Trance opened up. The guy looked harsh, unshaven, his hair standing up, dark circles under his bloodshot eyes.

"Wow," Ryan said, taking the excedo in from his bare feet to his worn jeans and wrinkled T-shirt. "Protesting showers?"

"Bite me." Trance stood aside and let Ryan inside, despite his growled words.

Ryan strode to the living room, went straight to Trance's DVD player, and inserted one of his sex discs.

Trance stood in the entrance to the living room, arms crossed, leaning against the wall as if it were the only thing holding him up. "I don't remember making a movie date with you."

"Keep your dick in your pants, Romeo." Ryan pushed Play and stood back. "What do you know about that?"

Trance's eyes shot wide, and he yanked himself off the wall. "I know you need an ass-kicking if you came to watch porn with me—oh, fuck me, *that's you.* Turn it off! I don't need to see that."

Ryan hit the Pause button. "Well?"

"Well, what?" Trance shuddered. "Christ. I'm going to have to gouge out my eyes now." He stalked to the kitchen, where he yanked two bottles of beer from the fridge, popped the tops and gave one bottle to Ryan before downing half of the other. "You going to tell me why you just gave me reason to make an appointment with a mind-scrubber?"

"Funny," Ryan muttered. "You know, or the guy who had his mind scrubbed."

"Ah, yeah. Sorry about that. Is that why you're here?" He eyed the TV. "I hope."

Ryan took a swig of his beer and sank down on a bar stool at the counter. "When did you find out I was inside Itor?"

"After you were pronounced missing, presumed dead, Dev let us know what happened."

That made sense. Though his boss probably left out the little detail about how Ryan's death was Dev's fault. "Dev told me that before I left on the Itor mission, I came to see you. I don't remember why."

Trance nodded. "I didn't know what your mission was, but you told me that for your cover, you were supposed to have an extreme BDSM fetish."

"Why would I come to you?"

Trance cocked an eyebrow. "Because I'm the go-to guy for that stuff."

"Oh." That put images in Ryan's head that had him considering his own mind-scrubbing appointment. "So . . . I wasn't into it before I came to you?"

Trance choked on his beer. When he recovered, which seemed to take for-fucking-ever, he said, "Man, when you came to me you thought candles only had one use."

"Bullshit." At Trance's I'm-not-shitting-you look, Ryan frowned. Maybe he was right. He thought back to all his relationships . . . there had been a few, mostly casual, and yeah, pretty vanilla sex.

Something flashed in his mind—Trance, taking him to a club, showing him videos, online sites. Lots and lots of research.

"You had to go beyond normal BDSM for your role, Ryan. Your sexual fetishes were supposed to cross the line of what's safe and acceptable. Obviously, a love of torture was supposed to lure Itor."

God, had he been able to separate his undercover persona and his real self during the time he'd been with Itor? How had he not gone crazy?

He now knew he hadn't tortured anyone to death—his job at Itor had kept him in a communications cubicle most of the time. Itor had only filled in the memory gaps with lies after they scrubbed his brain. But now he remembered how, before they took his memory and still didn't know he was undercover, they'd sent him nightmarish photos now and then, thinking he'd get all hot and bothered. Remembered how they'd send him women to play with—frightened women who hadn't given their consent.

What had he done with them? Were the women on the DVDs those women?

Trance gestured to the TV. "What are the dates on your, ah, porn?"

"Dunno. Never looked." Ryan went over to the DVD player and fast-forwarded through a few sessions. "They're timed before Itor says I had my accident."

"Before they wiped your mind."

"So I did those things as part of my cover."

"Looks like." Trance saluted with his beer bottle. "Gotta hand it to you—you really got into your role."

"Too well," Ryan muttered. "But something doesn't feel right. Like maybe Itor doctored the videos. They lied to me about everything else." Or maybe he was just hoping Itor had tampered with the evidence, because he didn't want to believe he was capable of the things he'd done.

272 • Sydney Croft

"Why is this a big deal?"

Ryan gave Trance an are-you-kidding-me look. "How would you like it if you could remember almost everything about your past except one big hole, and that one hole is filled by stuff that feels completely alien and out of character? And what if you were afraid you'd done things . . . to hurt innocent women? You ever made a woman cry out in agony, Trance? Because I gotta say, my soul weighs about a million pounds right now."

Trance exhaled slowly and nodded, looking more haunted than he had when Ryan arrived. "Yeah, I get it."

"It's driving me nuts. I can't concentrate on anything. Can't commit to anything." Anything or any*one*, which was the real problem. "Not until I know who I am. And that one missing piece is so not me."

"Have you been with a woman since they scrubbed you?"

Only Meg. "Yeah."

"And?"

"And what?"

"Did you have the urge to tie her up? Spank her? Maybe go beyond what's pleasurable to hurt her or humiliate her?"

"Fuck, no." Ryan had to ease his grip on the beer bottle before he shattered it in his hand. "I mean, I did, but that was before my memory came back. I thought I was supposed to be like that."

"But since you got it back?"

"No. Nothing like that. So why—"

"Look at me."

Startled, Ryan looked up, and instantly fell into Trance's hypnotic gaze.

"Think back, Ryan. Think back to your assignment."

"Itor," he murmured.

"Right. And the women. Think about the women you were with in the videos. Who were they?"

"Some of them . . . taken off the streets. Forced to . . . to . . ."

"Ryan. Tell me."

Ryan swallowed hard as the memories flooded his brain. He'd thanked the Itor guys who brought the women to his little play room he'd set up for his role, and then he'd dragged the women inside. He'd tied them up. And whispered in their ears that everything would be okay. He wouldn't hurt them, but if they wanted to get out of the situation alive, they had to act like he was torturing the living hell out of them.

He didn't realize he'd been speaking out loud until Trance swore.

"Good, Ryan," he said in a soothing voice. "You didn't hurt them. Were they all forced on you?"

Ryan's head throbbed as he searched the recesses of his memory. "No. Some I hired," Ryan said, and whoa, that was definitely something he hadn't remembered until now. "Hired from clubs."

Trance moved closer, still holding Ryan's gaze. "Why did you hire them? For sex?"

Ryan blinked, nearly breaking out of the haze he was in, but Trance grabbed his face and held him still.

"Why, Ryan?"

"Paid them . . . to act . . . hurt."

"So you didn't hurt them?"

"No," Ryan mused, relief making him light-headed. "I knew Itor was watching. I made it look like I was hurting them . . . like with the women they brought to me."

Suddenly, Ryan was out of the fuzz and everything made sense. He hadn't been into that shit. He'd faked it. Thank God, he'd faked it all. And now his mental jigsaw puzzle was complete.

Trance stepped back and finished his beer. "Well?"

"I'm cured, Doc." Cured, but still fucked up. Because in Meg he'd found something decent, something he knew he'd been looking for all his life. And he'd sent her packing. Sure, he'd weakened a couple of times and tried to IM her, but he hadn't gone as far as to visit her in billeting again. "Thanks, man. I owe you."

Ryan took off at a dead run, heading straight for guest quarters. He darted past the front desk guard, who looked at him like he was nuts, and pounded on Meg's door. When no one answered, he sprinted to the front desk.

"Where is she?"

The guard shrugged. "Gone. Checked out with some guy days ago."

Ryan cursed. This wasn't over. She might have left ACRO, but he knew exactly how to find her.

THERE WAS a knock on his door. This time, Trance had showered and cleaned up his house, mainly because he was tired of being a zombie. Or, more to the point, he didn't need another operative showing up at his door commenting on his zombieness.

"It's like fucking Grand Central Station around here," he muttered, swung the door open and stood stock-still when he saw Rik on the other side. "You shouldn't have come here."

She held out a hand to block the door. If he'd wanted to, closing it wouldn't have been a problem, but he controlled himself. For now.

"I need to talk to you, Trance. You have to give me that opportunity."

"No, I don't. I can't." This time, he did shut the door on her, got it almost all the way closed when she kicked it open viciously, enough to dent the wood.

He hadn't expected that, stood dumbfounded as she pushed her way inside his house. She demanded that he speak to her, and her words jumbled in his mind in a sea of anger and pain.

The last time she'd been here, in his house, things had been so different. Wonderful and gentle. And now they were back to this—the violence. The pain. "Please, just go," he begged her, because he knew if she stayed, things would get much worse.

He only had so much control and he knew from experience that so did she.

"You can't block me out—not after all we've been through. I gave you a second chance when you betrayed me."

"I never betrayed you, Rik. I saved your goddamned life," he said with a quiet but deadly edge to his voice that he hadn't heard himself use in a long time. Not since his days as an MP, when he was letting an inmate know they'd fucked with the wrong guard.

She noted the tone, he could tell, but she didn't back down. "I'm not leaving, Trance, not with things between us the way they are. That's not fair to do to me."

"Fair? Not fair to you?" He grabbed her, swung her inside easily and brought her down to the carpeted floor. "Is this what you want—to provoke me? Because I don't fucking think that's such a good idea."

Rik struggled for a second and then stopped. "If this is the way I can get you to listen—"

"You want me to listen?" he roared, the anger that he'd been holding deep down coming out fast and hard and nearly uncontrollable. The anger he'd worried about when he'd walked away from her the other day. "I've already listened."

"You're upset with me, I know that—"

"You don't know anything." He pushed himself off of her, leaving her sprawled on the floor. He'd wondered if the wolf would emerge when he was holding her down, pinning her to the floor with his full strength. Before this, since they'd been together in his bed, he'd stopped worrying that the wolf could come out to get him.

She wasn't angry, didn't seem scared of his strength. She was sad, so freakin' sad. But that wasn't his responsibility anymore.

And she shoved to her feet, slammed against his chest with both palms, hard. He didn't budge, didn't move until she did it over and over again, until he grabbed her. He pulled her close to him, held her steady even as she squirmed and struggled. "You don't know who you're messing with, Rik. You've only seen me one way—you don't get it."

"So what are you saying? That you're pissed enough to hurt me?" She snorted. "You could never hurt me. You're not capable of it."

"You want to see what I'm capable of? Really?" Fury shot through him, days of anger built up, and before she could answer, he yanked her along, dragging her down the dark basement stairs to his dungeon. The one that hadn't been used in years. Hadn't even been seen in years.

He shoved her into the center of the room, crossed to the wall, locked the chains around his ankles. "Do your best."

She blinked. "My best what?"

"I want you to bind me so hard and tight you don't think I could ever possibly escape."

"Trance—"

"Do it!" he roared.

With a curse, she obeyed. She fitted him with a leather harness that wrapped around his throat, stretched his arms behind his back, then forced him to lie on the floor as his legs were pulled painfully up behind him. In this position, the limbs had no leverage, and no normal person could possibly break free. Especially not with the way Rik's practiced touch bound him tight.

"More," he said, and though she sighed, she fastened more chains and cuffs to his wrists and ankles.

"Now back away."

Something in his voice must've told her to comply, even though she was the unchained one. The one in control.

Straining, he stretched his muscles, his joints. She'd bound him well, and this was going to be a challenge . . . for about five seconds. As his muscles screamed with heat and strain, he yanked his arms apart, snapping the leather holding his wrists behind him. His legs popped free a second later. With one easy movement, the chain pulled from the wall, cracking the concrete. The leather strap on the second one pulled apart like taffy. The cuffs that held him to the floor were cake for him—steel, double reinforced, buried in concrete, and those came up along with the spikes from the ground.

He picked up the St. Andrew's Cross with one hand and smashed it against the wall in a million pieces.

And he hadn't even broken a sweat.

"Stop it, Trance!" Rik grabbed his arm and yanked him around, her eyes sparking with anger. "All this does is prove that you're strong. Stronger than I thought, but still . . . So you can tear up your furniture. Big deal. You won't hurt me." Her eyes narrowed at him. "Or is it someone else you want to hurt? Do you want to hurt the beast? Is that who you want? The one who finished killing your father after I started? You going to hurt her? Take out on her your anger for your father never being around? Because *we* didn't take your father from you, Trance. Your own father did that, and maybe it's time you got that through your thick head."

"Get out," he rasped, pulling out of her grip so hard and fast she left scratch marks on his forearm. "Get out before I do something we both regret."

"You already have," she said softly. "You already have." With that, she fled.

A COUPLE of hours after Rik left, Trance was still on the floor of the basement dungeon, staring at the mess around him.

"Trance?"

He looked up to find Wyatt at the bottom of the stairs, staring at him. Wyatt gave a long whistle as he looked around the room and then again at Trance. "Orgy gone wild?"

Trance groaned. "Is there a fucking sign on my door that says 'Bother Me Now'?"

He stood and walked past Wyatt up the stairs, without inviting Wyatt to follow, knowing that wouldn't stop the man. He ended up on the couch, feet up and eyes closed, and Wyatt joined him.

"Drinking a little, huh?" Wyatt commented. Trance opened his eyes to see Wyatt staring at the collection of bottles strewn around the coffee table.

"Yeah, well, I'm trying to erase images of Ryan fucking from my mind," he said, because it was easier than mentioning what had happened with Rik. Wyatt raised his eyebrows. "Forget I said that. Jesus, forget I said that."

"I'll try." The dark-haired man stared up at the ceiling. "Ender wants to kill you."

"I figured. What, are you here to protect me?"

"No, I'm here to talk to you—about Rik."

"Now, that doesn't make any sense at all. You hate her."

"I don't hate her. I hate what her wolf did." Even now, Wyatt growled at the mention of what had happened to Faith and the baby.

Trance let out a long breath. "Right now, I can't separate the two. I don't know if I'll ever be able to do that."

"You love her."

Trance bristled, hating this conversation. "And how do you know that?"

"I'd never stand in a cage with a woman who was wired to explode if I didn't. But I guess that's just me."

Cursing, Trance kicked half the beer bottles to the floor—they fell with a satisfying crash and he turned the entire table over, just for good measure. Of course, it went farther than he'd meant it to, flying into the front wall and causing a nice big hole. But still he didn't say anything, and Wyatt continued. "She took someone from you—I get that. But you were the one who talked me into saving Rik's life when I would have much rather blown her to hell for what her wolf did to my family."

"You only had to free her, you didn't have to love her," Trance said quietly.

"That's true. But she wouldn't do anything like that now—you said so yourself. She was being tortured then. And as much as I wanted to hold her accountable for that . . . I couldn't. Neither could Faith."

Trance scrubbed his face with his palms. "I appreciate what you're trying to do—"

"You might be throwing away the best thing that ever happened to you," Wyatt interrupted.

"You don't know any fucking thing about it, Wyatt. Devlin lied to me. Kept things from me and then sent me out to—" No, Dev hadn't sent him out to fall in love. Trance had done that all on his own. And now he couldn't even bring himself to sleep in his own bedroom because the memories of having Rik up there—having her, over and over again—came back too strong. His sheets still held her scent.

The woods were off-limits too. At this point, he'd need blinders to walk through the ACRO compound. "She was just here."

"Ah, that explains the mess in the basement."

"There's no way it can work, Wyatt."

"Faith is thinking about forgiving her," Wyatt said. "I mean, she is forgiving Rik. She wants to tell her in person. Meet her face-to-face."

"That's some brave shit." Trance stared at his hands. Forgiveness from Faith would mean so much to Rik and he wondered if Faith would actually go through with it.

"Faith says life's too short to hate."

"What about you?"

"It's hard. I'm not there yet. But we're going to have to work with her, whether or not she stays here or goes to England."

"England?"

"Yeah. I'm supposed to talk to you about that. Dev wants to know . . . he wants to know what you want to do about Rik."

"What do you mean, what do I want to do?"

"You were here first. She committed a crime against ACRO."

"I promised her she would never be punished for anything she did for Itor while she's under ACRO's care."

"But Dev doesn't have to keep her here. She could work out of the British office. Be kept away from you."

Kept isolated. "I can't do that to her. I might not be able to forgive her, but I'd never forgive myself if she didn't get the full benefits of working here. Of being able to heal."

Wyatt stood, readied to leave. "You love her, man. The sooner you admit it, the sooner you can get past all this garbage."

CHAPTER
Twenty-nine

Coco was so predictable. She was on her computer twenty-four seven, and Ryan had used his own laptop to attempt an IM connection with her. She hadn't replied once, and yesterday she'd finally turned off her IM program, but by then it was too late. A couple of ACRO computers had been designed specifically for his skills—they grabbed a connection with a computer through any IM software, and as long as Coco had her computer on and was touching it, and Ryan was touching his, he could see through her eyes.

And her eyes had been looking at some guy. In a bedroom. The guy looked angry, and then Coco was shaking her head. She grabbed her laptop and walked through a screened door to a patio overlooking a beach. A moment later, the guy was there again, still appearing pretty pissed.

Looked like they were in Florida, which was where her plane had landed.

After Ryan discovered she'd left ACRO, he'd gone straight to Flight Ops at ACRO's airport, where the person in charge had given him information about recently filed flight plans. Since the private jet Meg had boarded was not an ACRO plane on a mission, the flight plan had not been considered classified. Even if it had, Ryan had ways of accessing the information.

Thankfully, he hadn't had to use them, because Dev would have kicked his ass.

He was going to kick Ryan's ass anyway, because Ryan had taken off without permission, boarded a commercial jet and was now driving to the private airport where Coco had landed. Yup, he was in a shitload of trouble.

It would all be worth it, though, if Meg forgave him for being such an ass.

Fortunately, between ACRO's resources and his electrokinesis, he'd been able to figure out approximately where Meg was staying. Problem was, from even the very little he'd seen, he'd been able to tell that the house was no ordinary dwelling. Not with the six-foot walls, electrified gate and armed guards.

Getting to Meg was going to be a trick.

Good thing ACRO's training was top-notch, because he'd really hate to die before he got a chance to tell Meg he wanted her.

MEG LOOKED UP from her computer to see Ryan standing about ten feet from her poolside.

It was apparent, however, that Ryan was too busy looking at her to notice the five armed security men who now stood in formation behind him, ready to take him down at a moment's notice.

"I should let them shoot you, you know," she called to him casually, even though she felt anything but.

Ryan stiffened, put his hands in the air and turned his head slowly to see the firing squad for himself. "Could you tell them I'm not here to hurt you?" he asked over his shoulder.

"No, you've already done that," she muttered. "Guys, you can put the guns down. He's all right."

"The hell he is." Mose had come up from behind her. He carried a simple Glock, but then, he didn't need more—his posse had him covered.

"I can handle this, Mose. I have to handle it."

Ryan had turned back to her, his hands still in the air. "I want to talk to Meg. To apologize. To explain."

"It's going to have to be one amazing apology for me to not shoot you for trespassing," her brother countered.

"Stop, just stop, okay?" She said to Mose, "Call them off and go."

"Meg . . ." Mose warned.

"I'm to blame here. I stole money from him and caused a lot of trouble because I was jealous and hurt. So please, just go."

Mose lowered his gun. A sharp wave of the hand and the men standing behind Ryan disappeared, along with Mose himself, leaving her and Ryan and a gorgeous Florida afternoon.

"You're not to blame, Meg." Ryan's voice was hoarse. "I fucked this all up . . . there were things I didn't know and I couldn't explain . . . I was in a dirty business, and what you did . . . I was fair game. And it was never my money to begin with."

"Yes, well, you've paid for that. You almost gave your life." She heard the break in her own voice and the tears were next and then Ryan's arms were around her. For a few minutes, she forgot about the embarrassment of Ryan's rejection and her broken heart, forgot about everything but her own discontented soul.

"We've all done bad things, Meg. But you can make things right."

"Yes, I've made things so right that you didn't want to be with me."

"I was an idiot to let you go the other day," he said. "And five years ago, I was just as much of an idiot." He paused, and then spilled his thoughts as though afraid he wouldn't voice them if he didn't hurry and get them out. "I was afraid to trust you. In that line of work, opening myself up, being vulnerable, well, let's just say that wasn't the way to go. And when I realized I'd been an ass for letting myself get talked out of meeting you, I tried to set up another time to meet. But by then—"

"I'd stolen the money," she finished. "You knew I was afraid to trust too, Ryan. I'd already told you about my sister . . ."

"Mary," he said, as if just remembering the name. He shook his head, his brow furrowed. "God, Meg, I'm sorry. I was an ass."

"Yes." She paused, because she wasn't being fair. They'd both been terrified to trust, but for different reasons. She'd been worried about her heart—he'd feared for his life. "But you were also scared. I was too. Agreeing to meet you, falling for you—those were things I never thought I'd be able to do. And I still believe in special, that there's one person you're meant for. Stupid, right? And naive and—"

"No, none of those things. Not even close." He leaned his forehead against hers. "Can you forgive me?"

She licked her bottom lip gently. "I think . . . I think I might be able to."

"Do you think, maybe, we could continue this someplace more private? Because I can see your brother watching us from behind the palm tree—and man, he's still holding that pistol."

"I want that. But Ryan, I can't be who you want me to be. In the bedroom."

"That's part of what I came to talk to you about." He blew out a long breath, and for a second, she thought she'd just said the wrong thing. "I let you go when we were at ACRO because that last part of my memory was a blank. This is going to sound stupid, but until I knew who I was, a hundred percent, I couldn't commit to anything. Not even to you. But I found out about my past—the S&M thing, the tape you saw. It was all a fake. My cover. I'm not into that. I mean, I'm not Gentle fucking Ben, but . . . if you need me to be . . ."

"No." She swallowed hard, shifted from foot to foot. "I want to make love to you, you have no idea—"

"Oh, I think I do." There was a glint in his eye as his voice dropped an octave that she felt like a shot straight into her belly.

"No, I mean . . . I can't do this unless . . ." She felt stupid again. "Unless you love me. And I know that you don't, can't possibly."

He sat back on his heels from where he'd been kneeling on the rough pool deck in front of her chair. "I remember falling in love with you, Meg. And the best part is, I'm doing it all over again, right now."

RYAN'S HEART POUNDED so hard he couldn't hear the roar of the ocean even though ML's house was so close to the surf he could practically throw a rock and hit the waves. He felt so freaking stupid exposing himself to Meg like that, but he'd seen the hardest ACRO agents turn into jelly when they were in love, so he supposed this was normal.

How nice that the natural, normal state of being in love was being stupid.

"Ryan..." Meg's whispered voice trailed off, and she swallowed repeatedly, as though trying to keep from saying something as revealing as he had. She was so much smarter than he was.

"I'm not just saying that to get you into bed," he blurted. "I mean, duh, I want to get you into bed, but I can wait. If you're not ready, I can wait as long as it takes."

Tears filled her eyes, and yeah, now he'd done it. She was going to tell him to go to hell. If he was lucky, maybe her brother would just shoot him and get it over with.

"Dammit," he breathed. "It's too late, isn't it? I'm sorry." He looked down at the cement deck because it was better that than see the hurt he'd caused her.

"It's not too late," she said. She grabbed his hand and stood, bringing him up with her. "Come on."

Too stunned to argue, he allowed her to lead him inside the house and down about a dozen halls.

"This is my wing." She made another turn down a hall.

"You have your own wing?"

"ML likes to give me privacy and space." She huffed and led him into the huge bedroom he'd seen through her eyes earlier. "When it's convenient for him anyway."

"Is that why we're here?" he asked, as he moved toward the sliding glass door that led to a deck overlooking the ocean. "Privacy?"

She closed the door. And locked it. "Unless you'd prefer to take my virginity by the pool, where everyone can watch."

He damned near tripped over his feet. He swung around to her, and though his brain was still having trouble processing what she'd said, his body had gotten the message loud and clear. The biggest erection of his life had popped a tent in his cargos and his heart was working overtime to keep the blood pumping to it.

"Are you sure?"

She stood there, her green-and-pink tropical bikini highlighting her tan skin, and then there was nothing but tan skin, because she'd untied the top and shoved down the bottoms.

"I'm sure."

Meg was going to be his. A primal surge of pride swelled up in him that he would be this woman's first. And only. He wished he could give her the same, but he'd screwed that up—literally—a long time ago. Now the only thing he could offer her was his promise that she would never regret this.

He went to her, framed her face in his hands and kissed her to seal the promise he didn't want to say out loud for fear of ruining the moment. Her palms rested on his pecs, so the only contact between them was through their lips and hands and pulses. It was the most erotic thing he'd ever experienced, and they'd barely begun.

The kiss lingered, until Meg leaned in so her breasts rubbed against his chest. He might have been okay, might have been able to keep the kiss going on even longer, but then she brought her stomach into contact with his erection, and that was it for him.

A raspy sound of need came from deep inside him, and he swept her up in his arms. Still kissing her, he took her to the bed and laid her down. Only then did he break contact, in order to undress.

She watched as he stripped down in record time, and when her gaze darkened and her lids grew heavy at the sight of his naked body, pride wasn't the only thing that swelled.

"You're so beautiful." Her voice dripped with hunger, and

beneath the delicate skin of her neck, he saw that her pulse had picked up.

"Keep talking like that, and I might let you have your wicked way with me." He eased onto the bed next to her, and though she appeared calm and in control, he could feel the mattress quiver beneath her.

His own hands shook as he drew her against him and just held her. "I won't hurt you," he swore. "Not intentionally. And if you suddenly decide you don't want to do this, tell me. I'll stop. No matter how into it we are."

"We're not stopping." She emphasized her words by sliding her hand down his chest to take his cock in her fist.

Throwing his head back, he groaned. Her palm was soft and hot and a welcome change from months of using his own. God, she could get him off in half a dozen strokes, and he had to seize her wrist to keep exactly that from happening.

When he came, it was going to be inside of her.

"Not yet," he murmured, and began kissing his way down her neck. The skin of her shoulder was like silk against his lips, and he spent a long time making sure it was properly worshipped.

Using his tongue, he forged a trail to her left breast, loving how her breath came faster the closer to her nipple he got.

"Ryan," she moaned, shoving her fingers through his hair and caressing his scalp as he took one hardened peak between his teeth and flicked the tip with his tongue.

His cock throbbed with the fierce need to get inside her, but he did his best to ignore it. Easier said than done, especially when he cupped Meg between the legs and she writhed, bringing her thigh up against his shaft. Damn, he nearly lost it right then and there.

"Easy," he breathed against her navel. "We'll get there."

"Want there now. Make me come." Her raw demand made him smile.

"Your wish is my command." Slowly, reverently, he spread her thighs. There was a brief moment of resistance, when her muscles tensed, but when their gazes locked, she relaxed, her expression softening into a mix of trust and desire.

She opened up to him, and his breath hitched at the sight of her plump lips parting. Her pink flesh glistened, framed by velvety down he knew would tickle his face when he tasted her.

"I'm going to lick you," he said, as he drew one finger from her clit to her tight opening and back up, spreading her moisture through her slit. "Do you want that?"

She shuddered under his touch. "Oh, yes."

He made another pass with his finger, this time dipping it inside her, and she cried out, "I'm going to lick you until you're at the very edge, and then I'm going to suck that pretty little pearl."

The words brought her hips off the bed. Oh, yeah, he was going to get her so worked up, so wet with her cream that he'd slide in with as little resistance as possible. He couldn't help the pain she'd feel when her barrier broke, but he could make it easier—and making it easier would be a hell of a lot of fun.

Mouth watering, he captured her sex with his lips and kissed her hard and deep. Her gasp of pleasure was accompanied by another surge of her hips, and then her fingernails dug into his scalp.

She tasted like sunshine and citrus, and he lapped at her like this was a tropical paradise and he was never leaving.

"Look at me," he said, surprised she understood him because he was drunk with her, and his voice was thick and slurred. But she did look at him as he dragged the flat of his tongue from her core to the top of her slit and then latched onto her clit with his lips.

Gently, he sucked on it, letting his tongue flick back and forth over the tip, and as he watched, she came apart, silently but violently. So violently he had to hold her hips with his hands and lay his torso over her legs to keep her from bucking him off as he kept her coming with long pulls and a vibrating hum.

"Ryan," she panted, after her fourth orgasm. "Oh, my God, Ryan..."

She bucked in release once more, and then he was mounting her, poised at her entrance.

"Are you ready, baby?" He'd stop if she asked him to, but call him selfish, he wanted her to say yes. His cock was like steel and his balls were in a vise grip of need.

But mostly, he was ready to claim her body.

And her heart.

MEG'S LEGS were trembling by the time Ryan moved his body onto hers. She was poised and open—so ready for him—and God, she'd never been more nervous in her life.

"You okay, baby?" he asked. "If you're not ready—"

"I'm ready, Ryan. So ready. It's just..." She drew a deep breath. "I've waited so long for the right guy. And you're here. Really here."

"Always."

She bit her bottom lip at the first entry of his cock inside of her. She was wet and relaxed from the many orgasms he'd given her but nothing could prepare her for the sharp, sudden pain of his entrance.

He'd stopped when she'd gone still, was murmuring, "Try to relax...it gets better. I promise, so much better."

She believed him. And as he pushed in farther, she felt herself open for him, her sex rippling with his girth.

His hands were on her hips, his face set in a mask of intense concentration, as if he was on the most important mission of his life.

She loved that, loved that he could take this much time with her. This much care and concern. "I didn't know...didn't know it could be this good."

"I told you that I couldn't wait to do this to you," he murmured. "Knew you'd be all wet and hot for me."

He remembered everything—that's what he always told her during their online chats...using language that had her blushing on the other side of the computer screen and grateful they never used video software. She wouldn't have been able to hide how embarrassed she was...or how intensely turned on.

She used to play with herself, unable to stop her hands from traveling between her legs, rubbing herself to satisfaction while reading and rereading Ryan's words, late at night, long after they'd logged off with each other.

Ryan's words were something, but Ryan in the flesh was beyond what she could've imagined.

"I can't believe this is really happening...that you're here," she told him, her breath coming fast, even as he leaned down and mouthed a nipple, causing her to arch up and making him slide into her unexpectedly. A long moan escaped her lips even as he continued to tug on the taut nub with his teeth, and her womb gradually relaxed for him.

From the second she'd seen him naked, she'd wondered how he would fit—it seemed impossible, yet he kept telling her he was almost there . . . almost ready to show her how amazing it was.

She felt so full, and then, one last rock of his hips, and she felt the pinch—it made her gasp, and Ryan went still for a long minute. And then he began to move, back and forth—gently at first, so gently, and at the same time it was urgent. Primal.

It was so good. "Ryan—don't stop."

"No worries on that."

She clung to him so tightly, felt her nails digging in his skin and the slick sweat from his body and from hers making traction nearly impossible. But Ryan was tugging one of her legs up and she caught her ankle around his lower back.

"Oh . . . oh . . ." was all she could say as Ryan went deeper and the feeling shot straight through to her womb. And she was moving her hips to meet his as though it was the most natural thing in the world, her body responding to him totally.

He shifted then, angling himself so his cock brushed her clit as he pumped in and out of her, and sooner, much quicker than she wanted, she was flying, over the edge, her sex contracting around his cock.

"Meg, I'm coming," he rasped, and she felt him pulsing, throbbing inside of her, nothing between them at all—it was primal and right, no barriers.

"I love you," she whispered against his neck. "Love you ... love you, Ryan."

He responded by moaning her name, over and over, like a chant, until he stilled against her and her eyes closed in perfect contentment.

She wasn't sure if it was minutes later or hours, but Ryan moved his body off hers and cradled her against his chest. "You okay?"

"Better than okay." She shifted to look into his eyes. "So what happens now?"

"What do you want to do next?" Ryan asked, his hand already reaching between her legs. "Because it's only going to get better from here."

"Well, yes, that. But I mean ... I don't know if I want to work for ACRO."

"You don't have to work there. But I'd love it if you went back with me. Because that's my home. I'd like it to be yours too."

Home. That sounded so nice. Normal. "I can leave the old life behind."

"And there's a new life waiting for you, if you want it."

"Yes, Ryan ... I want," she whispered as he moved to claim her again, the way she'd always imagined it to be.

CHAPTER
thirty

Trance found himself staring up at the ACRO memorial. He'd been here before, several times, stopping on his way through the woods to pay his respects to the men and women who'd come before him.

His eyes shifted past Oz's picture—Devlin had been dealing with that heavy loss for close to a year now, and Trance had finally seen some light around the man's eyes when Trance had first returned to ACRO with Rik.

When he'd last spoken to Dev, it looked as though his boss had the weight of the world—and ACRO—on him. And fuck, Trance hated blaming him for what had been kept from him, and hated it more that the choice to keep Rik in America or ship her off to England was in his hands.

Finally, he let his eyes stray to the picture of Arthur Scott. His hand automatically went to the plaque and touched the nameplate as he searched the man's eyes and thought about the first time he'd met the agent he never knew as father.

"I'm Arthur. Welcome to ACRO." He'd shaken Trance's hand across the meeting table. Trance remembered not wanting to

touch anyone, not wishing to be friendly. No, he'd nearly escaped twice by that point, only to be brought to his senses by the Convincers, who'd been damned good at their jobs, and so he'd grunted in Arthur's direction.

It hadn't deterred the man, who, Trance would learn later, had come to ACRO voluntarily. He'd slid a Coke across the table to Trance and then actually moved to sit next to him during the long-ass boring meeting. Trance had been up all night with a team of doctors, getting checked out and up and down before getting a clean bill of health and the now familiar ACRO BDUs.

"It gets easier."

"Sure," Trance had said disinterestedly. "What's your thing?"

"Same as you. Strength."

Their supervisor, who'd overheard the conversation, had shaken his head. "Trance is a hell of a lot stronger than you, Arthur."

"He can try to prove it, then," Arthur had said innocently. Of course, the afternoon ended in wrestling matches right in the middle of the first Quad outside the Excedo training area—and saw Trance the winner.

There had been a strange look in Arthur's eyes that afternoon—a pride, almost, and Trance remembered thinking he'd never be proud if someone kicked his ass.

He and his father hadn't looked anything alike—the only thing they'd had in common was their size . . . and their eyes. But Arthur had known, and still he'd gone on a mission, fully aware that he might not come back to speak with his son.

He wondered what his father could've possibly said to him that would make up for twenty-something years of abandonment, and realized that the answer was: nothing.

And yet somehow, Rik had made his life feel complete in the space of mere days. The irony nearly made him choke out a sob, but he kept it together. He didn't know all that much about forgiveness, hadn't had to give it or receive it much in his life because he'd remained on the outside in all of his relationships.

Neema hurried by—she was talking into her handheld

walkie-talkie. "Ulrika's going to let the wolf out—we're going to see if she can control it on her own."

Trance's gut clenched and his hand dropped from his father's photo as he wondered why it was that, as Rik gained more control over herself, he in turn was losing any semblance he'd once had.

FOLLOWING THE DISASTER at Trance's house, Rik spent several days working with Neema on her control issues. Yesterday, Kira had come in for a couple of hours to try to convince Rik to shift, but Rik had refused. Though she'd mastered keeping the beast in, she didn't trust the beast once it came out.

She wasn't entirely sure why it was so important that the beast be tested, but as she, Kira, Neema, and Sela Kahne, a researcher from the cryptozoology department, walked toward the forest where she and Trance had shared a picnic, Kira explained.

"Your wolf needs to feel comfortable and in control. For you to both coexist in one body, you need to trust each other."

"But if I don't let her out, there's no need to worry about trust."

"Is that fair to her?" Kira asked quietly. "She's as much a victim as you are. Keeping her happy before this meant doing things you sometimes didn't like. But now, if keeping her happy means letting her out now and then to run, well, isn't that worth it?"

"And I need to be able to trust her to let her out." Rik sighed, slowing as they approached a small clearing, split down the center by a narrow stream running from the lake. "So where is your overprotective mate?"

Kira gave a sly, secret smile. "Oh, he's around."

Rik stopped and sniffed the air, and though she smelled nothing, she sensed multiple presences nearby. No doubt, one of them was Ender. The rest would probably be ACRO security personnel loaded down with tranqs in the event that something went horribly wrong.

The one thing she was grateful for was that Trance wasn't here to watch this.

To watch her turn into the ugly monster that had killed his father.

Except, *she* was the ugly monster. The beast had simply finished the job Rik had started.

"Rik?" Sela lay a hand on Rik's forearm and adjusted the camera slung around her neck. "Are you okay?" She was tall, nearly as tall as Rik, but with her emerald-green eyes and black hair, she was much more exotic.

"Yeah," Rik whispered. "I can do this." She glanced at each of the three women. "But if Cujo hurts anyone, do what you have to do."

"It won't come down to that," Kira said. "It really won't. I have faith in both of you."

God, where did the woman get her calm, trusting nature? Not that Rik was complaining. She was so high-strung that she appreciated Kira's tranquil aura, which seemed to encompass everything around her.

"Let's do this." Neema's no-nonsense voice cut through the Lassie-sweet moment, reminding Rik that there were no gentle do-gooder dogs here.

Squaring her shoulders, she strode away from the three women until she was at the edge of the stream. As if the wolf knew what was going on, it began to stir, growing more excited by the second. Her skin tingled and her muscles tightened.

Quickly, Rik stripped, because although she could shift with clothes on, the clothes would be destroyed, and they could sometimes cause Cujo unnecessary agony. She breathed through the growing panic created by the knowledge that she was letting the beast out.

As the panic receded, the pain began. Muscles stretched, bones popped, and her skin split. With a silent scream, Rik faded into the background, until she was aware only that the wolf was standing on all fours in the meadow, watching the three ACRO women with something Rik swore might be hunger.

KIRA WATCHED Rik's transformation with her mouth hanging open. She'd been around animals all her life, but had never seen a human turn into one. Neema and Sela appeared to be as stunned as Kira, but the cryptozoologist recovered quickly and began snapping pictures.

The Rik-beast—Cujo, as she called it—reared up on two legs and sniffed the air, baring its teeth as it caught the scent of something it didn't like. Probably the half-dozen armed ACRO sharpshooters perched in the trees and hidden in bushes nearby. Though Kira couldn't see him, she knew Tommy was to the right, and she had no doubt he had Rik in his rifle's sights.

Her overprotective mate had better be loaded with tranquilizers and not bullets, or he was in big trouble.

After a long moment, Cujo dropped to all fours and turned her gaze in Kira's direction. She seemed torn between wanting to run off into the forest and wanting to charge at Kira and the other two women.

Before she could do either, Kira moved slowly toward her. "Hey, girl," she murmured, though she didn't need to speak out loud. She could communicate with the beast through a form of mental telepathy, mainly through images, body language and scents, but she knew that deep inside the wolf, the human could understand English, and it would be best for the humans all around her to hear Kira's side of the conversation.

Cujo stared at Kira as she approached, though she didn't show any aggression. Her ears twitched as she listened for sounds of danger, and when one of the sharpshooters in the forest did something to make a twig snap, she let out a low growl, but didn't move.

"We're here to help," Kira said, coming to a stop about five feet away. She knew that Tommy had stepped into the meadow because Cujo tensed, her reddish fur undulating in nervous ripples. "Hey. No one is going to hurt you. We just need to know what you want. What you need to feel comfortable."

Broken images slammed into Kira's brain. Wide-open spaces, forests, deer leaping over fallen logs, Trance.

Damn him. This creature did not trust easily, if it ever had, but it had formed a bond with Trance, and he'd broken it. Like a dog that had been abandoned on the side of the road or at a pound, she didn't understand why the only family she'd ever known had rejected her.

"We're your family now," Kira said. "We won't hurt you, and we won't use you. We want you to be happy here."

They will hurt me.

Kira glanced toward the snipers' hiding places. "No, they won't."

Watch.

Suddenly, Cujo raced toward Tommy, her attack posture so frightening that Kira nearly screamed a warning. Instead, she yelled at him to stand still and for the snipers to hold their fire. For a moment, she didn't think Tom would comply, but after shooting her a you-had-better-be-right look, he lowered his weapon and stood his ground.

Cujo tore across the meadow. Gathered her feet beneath her and leaped straight at Tom. Kira held her breath.

Gracefully, the beast sailed through the air, twisted and came down next to Tom. Kira let out an explosive breath of relief, and she imagined Tom did the same. Sela had taken pictures of the whole thing, and Neema was holding her hand over her heart, as though trying to keep it in.

Cujo whirled around so she was only inches from Tommy, who watched her warily. She snarled. He stared. She rose up on her hind legs, which made her tower over him. Still, he remained where he was, even when she placed her huge, claw-tipped paws on his shoulders and shoved him to his knees.

Tom's gaze shifted to Kira, the look in his eyes telling her how hard this was for him. Boy, she was going to owe him.

Finally, the wolf seemed satisfied that he wasn't going to hurt her, even though she'd threatened him and forced him to submit.

"Do you see?" Kira asked. "He didn't hurt you. None of the men in the forest will hurt you. We want to earn your trust. And we want to be able to trust you too."

I want to run.

"Then run."

Cujo cocked her massive head at Kira, as though not sure she had heard right. This was most definitely a test of trust. The wolf could easily take off, and it would be hard, if not impossible, to locate her again.

She pawed the ground, probably trying to decide if this was a trick, and then she was off like a shot. She leaped over the brook and disappeared into the trees.

"Want me to follow?" Tom asked, coming smoothly to his feet.

"No. Leave her. This has to be her choice."

Neema shook her head. "Dev is going to have your ass if Rik gets away."

"She'll come back," Kira said, even as a distant, joyful howl shattered the tense silence.

They waited. Waited for so long that two hours later, Kira was getting antsy as her need for sex began to overtake her. Neema drew a radio from her pocket to report the situation and call out trackers.

"Don't." Kira wrapped her arms around herself and stared into the forest. "She'll come back. I know it."

"We cannot wait any longer," Neema said.

Crap. "Come on, come on," she muttered, and as if Cujo had heard, she burst from the brush, tail wagging, tongue lolling, and looking like she'd had the time of her life. Kira didn't scent blood, so Cujo hadn't killed, but she'd probably given a few deer a run for their lives.

She came toward Kira at a trot, and when she got to her, she sat.

You waited. You didn't hunt for me.

"You needed to choose to return on your own."

Can I run more? On other days?

"Rik will let you out often, as long as you agree to not harm humans or kill animals for sport. You can't kill domestic animals at all."

Cujo gave a disgusted little huff, but then she stood, pressed her head against Kira's thigh, and with that small gesture, she agreed.

Crouching, Kira wrapped her arms around the wolf's furry neck and hugged her. "Welcome to our family."

Cautiously, Neema and Sela stroked Cujo's long, muscular back. Kira gestured to the men in the trees to come out and do the same. Though the wolf tensed as the men touched her, she allowed it. When each had petted her and stepped back, Kira drew away as well.

"Can we have Rik back now?"

The wolf cast one last glance back at the forest, and the transformation began.

RIK PANTED as she stood in the small circle of ACRO agents, her body aching from the shift. But a sense of joy made her smile through the pain. Cujo had behaved, and she'd done it without any interference from Rik. It had been one of the hardest things she'd ever done, but Rik had kept quiet, had kept her consciousness as boxed up as possible.

The beast had needed to be herself and make her own decisions, and she'd done well.

The male agents had turned away to give her privacy as she dressed, but she'd long ago had the modesty tortured out of her. Still, their gesture was appreciated.

"We're both free," she said, to no one in particular as she buttoned her BDU shirt. "We did it. We're in control. Both of us."

Kira gave her a big hug. "I'm so happy for you."

"Me too." She could now live her life without fear that the beast would break loose, and she could let it out with the knowledge that it would not only behave, but would give back Rik's body willingly.

She could almost call herself normal now. Almost. But it didn't really matter, because no one here was normal. Even those who didn't have special abilities had skills that made them special, and they lived lives that were far outside the boundaries of what most considered normal. So yeah, Rik fit right in.

Now she just had to decide what to do with her life. Living it was one thing; living it happily was another. She'd had enough of misery and death. She wanted to learn. To explore. To put her nose in books and read just to absorb the contents.

Sela had offered her a place in the cryptozoology department, which was fitting, since Rik was what they called a *cryptid*. As far as ACRO knew, she was the only one of her kind, but Sela repeated what Dev had said, that she could help them find other cryptids. Rik would have a job that gave her a purpose, and she wouldn't have to kill anyone.

Sounded like heaven.

Still, as bright as the future looked, nothing could lift the dark shroud around her heart. She missed Trance so much it hurt, though she couldn't blame him for how he felt. And if she was honest with herself, she could see that things wouldn't have worked out for them. Not until both she and Cujo gained control and formed a tether of trust between them.

They'd found both the control and the trust now, but did it matter? Trance still hated her, and that was something she couldn't change.

"There's someone here who wants to see you," Kira said, as she pulled back. Rik's heart skipped a beat. Trance? But then it skipped a beat because it wasn't Trance.

It was Faith. The woman she'd nearly killed.

Panic wrapped around Rik's chest like a vise. God, she'd come so far ... Surely ACRO wouldn't let this woman take revenge ...

Faith, fat with what had to be her ninth month of pregnancy, waddled over to her from the souped-up golf cart that must have arrived at some point while Rik had been transforming.

"Hi, Ulrika," Faith said, holding out her hand.

Tentatively, Rik took it, marveling at the strong, firm shake Faith gave her. "I-I'm not sure what to say. Sorry doesn't seem like enough."

Faith smiled. "I hated you for a long time," she admitted in a smart British accent. "But I know you weren't to blame. We both need to heal, and you need a fresh start. You won't have that if you're constantly worried that I'm going to take revenge."

"But—"

"No buts." Faith gave Rik's hand a squeeze. "I forgive you. And Wyatt will come around. I give you my word. You have nothing to fear from either of us."

"Thank you." The words came out rough and scratchy, and they were meant for everyone around her. For the first time since she was a little girl, she felt like she had a home.

Faith winced and lay a hand on her belly. "I'd better go. I'm due any second now, so being in the middle of a forest probably isn't wise."

Ender snorted and drew Kira up against him in a loving embrace. "You think?"

"Hit him for me, will you, Kira?" Faith rolled her eyes and started toward the golf cart with a little wave.

"Ready to head back?" Neema asked, and Rik nodded. The security guys dispersed, and after telling Rik she'd see her in a couple of weeks, Kira gave Ender a seductive smile and dragged him toward the trees—not that she truly had to drag him. Obviously, they'd been here long enough for her needs to kick in.

Rik watched them disappear. A spike of jealousy speared her, because she wanted that same kind of relationship with Trance. But it wasn't to be, and for now she'd just have to deal with it.

Even if, deep down, she knew that she'd only be pretending.

CHAPTER
thirty-one

Rik spent the next few days pretending not to miss Trance. Her ACRO training kept her busy, which helped, but the downtime was torture. The fact that the full moon was only days away wasn't doing much to keep her thoughts off Trance either.

The wolf missed Trance too, and with the pull of the moon making her antsy, Rik knew she had to let Cujo out tonight.

Neema agreed, so they walked together to the lake, and in the darkness, Rik transformed. She let the wolf take over, let herself relax as Cujo tore off into the night. Together, they ran hard, chased deer and rabbits, and then headed back to the ACRO compound.

As she approached the lake, the sound of someone coming up the trail drew the beast to a stop. Instinctively, she sniffed the air, and when she caught a familiar scent, she froze.

Trance rounded the bend and spotted her in the middle of the trail. He froze as solidly as she had. The wolf wagged her tail wildly, but inside, Rik screamed at her to not get excited. Cujo didn't understand that Trance still didn't want them. She was just happy to see a pack mate again—like a dog who waited at home for its people to return.

She thought Trance had come home.

Rik knew better. But she couldn't stop the wolf from making a mad dash toward Trance, who stood there like he thought he might be torn apart by the creature who had done the same to his father.

Cujo skidded to a halt in front of him, and Rik breathed a sigh of relief. Had the beast leaped for him, he very likely could have mistaken her intent and hurt her. Instead, he watched warily as she went up on two legs and put her paws on his shoulders. Her tail still whipped back and forth in excitement, and then she was all over him, licking his face and using her front legs to drag him close against her.

Down, girl, Rik pleaded, her heart breaking for the wolf, because she knew Trance was going to reject them once again.

So when he gently pushed her off him with a curse, she braced herself. But Cujo circled him excitedly, nosing his leg and pawing at him.

Rik couldn't watch, couldn't protect the wolf from this.

Reluctantly, Rik closed her eyes and let herself drift into the darkest depths of Cujo's consciousness, and just waited until it was time to pick up the pieces of the beast's broken heart.

TRANCE STOOD stock-still as the wolf hung by his side, pacing around him like a happy dog. It was bigger than he'd remembered—maybe because it was dark and he could only see the outline of the fur in the moonlight, or maybe because the eyes glittered. Or maybe because he still wasn't sure that Rik's wolf would ever know friend from foe.

He hadn't believed that a few days earlier—now everything had changed so fast he still couldn't get a footing on solid ground. And he'd never expected to meet her out here, in the woods, alone.

You told her yourself she wouldn't be a prisoner.

The wolf bucked its head up at Trance's hand as if forcing him to pet its head. For the moment he'd stood face-to-face with the beast that had killed his father in cold blood—killed simply because it could—he realized that the fear he felt had been generated by his own torn alliances, not fear for his life. The wolf could easily overpower him now, take him to the ground and rip out his throat, even though he knew deep in his heart that it wouldn't.

For the past few days, he'd wanted that, wanted some sweet relief from the pain of this entire situation.

He could let it go on so many levels—understood what the wolf had done. But it would've been a hell of a lot easier if he wasn't in love with Rik.

You have to separate them, separate her from who she was, Kira kept urging him.

But Rik was in there—*this is who Rik is,* the part of her she could now supposedly control but never shake completely.

And then he sank to his own knees and the wolf watched him curiously, not sure if he was playing or surrendering—or if he was hurt. "Jesus, I can't sleep because I keep hearing your cries—your cries and Rik's cries. I can't eat. I can't fucking do anything."

The wolf whined, pawed his back, his neck, wanted him to rise. But he couldn't, buried his face in his hands so he was curled in the fetal position on the ground. "Why did you do it? Why him, of all fucking people?" he whispered, more to himself than to the wolf, and still, the animal let out a mournful howl as if trying to tell him why.

But there was no reason—never was, never would be—it was simply that Arthur had been there and the animal that lived inside Rik had been tortured to the point of irrationality.

"I lost him, Rik," he said fiercely. "I lose everyone I love. And I told myself I wouldn't give a shit about anyone anymore—not like that. Keep it all business. And then you came along and you fucked that up for me."

The wolf lay down next to him, hitting the earth heavily and pressing its warm body against Trance's own as if comforting him. As if it was in need of comfort itself. And then there was total silence and Trance lifted his head for a second and wondered if the wolf had spotted something and was in hunting mode.

But no, it was lying on its back, belly exposed to the open air. Neck exposed as well . . . and all for him.

The wolf didn't want to die—Rik didn't either, Trance knew that—but it seemed that somehow, the wolf offered him an eye for an eye.

"I can't do that, Rik. Jesus, I can't—I couldn't. It wasn't your fault."

The wolf was up in a second, sitting next to him, nearly knocking him off his knees in the process. And, in that next second, he buried his face in the fur at the scruff of the wolf's neck, did that until he felt a pair of strong hands wind around his shoulders, and his nose breathed in the scent of Rik's smooth skin.

"You saved my life, Trance. I'll never be able to repay that debt."

He pulled back from her so he could look into her eyes. "I don't want you to owe me anything. I don't work like that."

"Why did you come here?"

"This is what I do now at night instead of sleeping," he said irritably. "I never thought you'd be out roaming the woods."

"Well, I am." Her tone was almost defiant. The old Rik—the confidence he remembered from the clubs—was back. And she remained naked, bathed in the soft light, and she looked even more beautiful than his memory had kept reminding him over the past days. "I'm different since I met you. The wolf is different. I know they say that people don't change, that animal instincts are just that, but I don't believe that anymore. Not from what I've seen. A lot can happen from simple kindness. I'm hoping the same can come from forgiveness."

He didn't stop her from kissing him, from wrapping her nude body around his, from pushing him back on the soft bed of leaves that lined the forest floor, leaving him helpless. He let her take him then, strip his clothes off while he watched her, lying prone with the smell of pine needles rising up as sharply as the scent of lust.

And when he was naked, he propped himself on his elbows as she climbed him, sheathed herself around him and rocked, surrounding him with a wet heat that made him cry out with a hungered need that came from deep within his soul.

RIK AND TRANCE walked back to the training quarters after stopping at the place where she'd left her clothes, to get dressed. They hadn't spoken a word since they'd made love, but now Trance pulled her down on a bench outside the dorm building.

"Once your training is done, I want you to move in with me," he said.

"It's a big step . . ."

"Do you have doubts?"

"Me?" She squeezed his hand. "Not at all. I'm worried about you. Are you sure you can deal with what I am?" She looked down at her lap. "With what I did?"

"Look at me." When she didn't—couldn't—he tipped her face up with a finger under her chin. "You've been beating yourself up for so long about what happened that day, and you didn't deserve how I beat you up about it too. I know you want me to forgive you for killing my father, but the truth is, I need your forgiveness for how I abandoned you after finding out." He traced her lips with his thumb. "Will you forgive me?"

"Yes," she whispered. "And yes, I'll move in with you. I love you, Trance." Inside, the wolf yipped, and she smiled. "We both love you." Trance laughed, which wasn't exactly the reaction she was expecting. She punched him in the shoulder. "I'm not running a comedy act here."

"I'm sorry," he said, but he was still smiling. "It's just that I see and do some weird shit on a daily basis in this job, but I never in a million years would have thought I'd tell a woman that I love her and her, ah, beast."

She slid him a sly look. "You still haven't told a woman that."

"You're right," he said, drawing her into his arms. "I love you. I love you both."

"Wolves mate for life, you know."

"Good." Trance kissed her with such possessiveness that she melted in contentment. "Because I'm never letting you go."

She smiled, because not long ago, only chains would have held them. Now they were both free of all restraints save one.

Love.

Which was the most flexible chain of all.

About the Author

SYDNEY CROFT is a pseudonym for two authors who each write under their own names. This is their fifth novel together. Visit their website at www.sydneycroft.com.

IF YOU WERE TEMPTED BY SYDNEY'S SEXY STORY,
LOOK FOR THE AUTHOR'S

steamy new novel

Tempting the Fire

by

SYDNEY CROFT

TO BE PUBLISHED BY
BANTAM

ACRO is back with their most ferocious mission yet: to track and hunt down the mythical chupacabra. When Marlena, a Seducer new to the team, and Sela, a cryptozoologist, travel to the depths of the Brazilian jungle to tangle with the deadly animal, they get caught up with creatures even more dangerous: a Navy Seal turned part beast, and an agent who is literally half man, half machine.